DIVISIBLE MAN™
NINE LIVES LOST

by

Howard Seaborne

ALSO BY HOWARD SEABORNE

DIVISIBLE MAN
A Novel – September 2017
DIVISIBLE MAN: THE SIXTH PAWN
A Novel – June 2018
DIVISIBLE MAN: THE SECOND GHOST
A Novel – September 2018
ANGEL FLIGHT
A Story – September 2018
DIVISIBLE MAN: THE SEVENTH STAR
A Novel – June 2019
ENGINE OUT
A Story – September 2019
WHEN IT MATTERS
A Story – October 2019
A SNOWBALL'S CHANCE
A Story – November 2019
DIVISIBLE MAN: TEN MAN CREW
A Novel – November 2019
DIVISIBLE MAN: THE THIRD LIE
A Novel – May 2020
DIVISIBLE MAN: THREE NINES FINE
A Novel – November 2020
DIVISIBLE MAN: EIGHT BALL
A Novel – September 2021
DIVISIBLE MAN: ENGINE OUT
AND OTHER SHORT FLIGHTS
A Story Collection – June 2022
DIVISIBLE MAN: NINE LIVES LOST
A Novel – Nine 2022

PRAISE FOR HOWARD SEABORNE

"This book is a strong start to a series...Well-written and engaging, with memorable characters and an intriguing hero."
    —*Kirkus Reviews*
    DIVISIBLE MAN [DM1]

"Seaborne's crisp prose, playful dialogue, and mastery of technical details of flight distinguish the story...this is a striking and original start to a series, buoyed by fresh and vivid depictions of extra-human powers and a clutch of memorably drawn characters..."
    —*BookLife*
    DIVISIBLE MAN [DM1]

"Even more than flight, (Will's relationship with Andy)—and that crack prose—powers this thriller to a satisfying climax that sets up more to come."
    —*BookLife*
    DIVISIBLE MAN [DM1]

"Seaborne, a former flight instructor and charter pilot, once again gives readers a crisply written thriller. Self-powered flight is a potent fantasy, and Seaborne explores its joys and difficulties engagingly. Will's narrative voice is amusing, intelligent and humane; he draws readers in with his wit, appreciation for his wife, and his flight-drunk joy...Even more entertaining than its predecessor—a great read."
    —*Kirkus Reviews*
    DIVISIBLE MAN: THE SIXTH PAWN [DM2]

"Seaborne, a former flight instructor and pilot, delivers a solid, well-written tale that taps into the near-universal dream of personal flight. Will's narrative voice is engaging and crisp, clearly explaining technical matters while never losing sight of humane, emotional concerns. The environments he describes...feel absolutely real. Another intelligent and exciting superpowered thriller."
    —*Kirkus Reviews*
    DIVISIBLE MAN: THE SECOND GHOST [DM3]

"As in this series' three previous books, Seaborne...proves he's a natural born storyteller, serving up an exciting, well-written thriller. He makes even minor moments in the story memorable with his sharp, evocative prose... Will's smart, humane and humorous narrative voice is appealing, as is his sincere appreciation for Andy—not just for her considerable beauty, but also for her dedication and intelligence...Seaborne does a fine job making side characters and locales believable. It's deeply gratifying to see Will deliver righteous justice to some very bad people. An intensely satisfying thriller— another winner from Seaborne."

—*Kirkus Reviews*
DIVISIBLE MAN: THE SECOND GHOST [DM4]

"Seaborne...continues his winning streak in this series, offering another page-turner. By having Will's knowledge of and control over his powers continue to expand while the questions over how he should best deploy his abilities grow, Seaborne keeps the concept fresh and readers guessing... Will's enemies are becoming aware of him and perhaps developing techniques to detect him, which makes the question of how he can protect himself while doing the most good a thorny one. The conspiracy is highly dramatic yet not implausible given today's political events, and the action sequences are excitingly cinematic...Another compelling and hugely fun adventure that delivers a thrill ride."

—*Kirkus Reviews*
DIVISIBLE MAN: TEN MAN CREW [DM5]

"Seaborne shows himself to be a reliably splendid storyteller in this latest outing. The plot is intricate and could have been confusing in lesser hands, but the author manages it well, keeping readers oriented amid unexpected developments...His crisp writing about complex scenes and concepts is another strong suit...The fantasy of self-powered flight remains absolutely compelling...As a former charter pilot, Seaborne conveys Will's delight not only in 'the other thing,' but also in airplanes and the world of flight—an engaging subculture that he ably brings to life for the reader. Will is heroic and daring, as one would expect, but he's also funny, compassionate, and affectionate... A gripping, timely, and twisty thriller."

—*Kirkus Reviews*
DIVISIBLE MAN: THE THIRD LIE [DM6]

"Seaborne is never less than a spellbinding storyteller, keeping his complicated but clearly explicated plot moving smoothly from one nail-biting scenario to another. As the tale goes along, seemingly disparate plot lines begin to satisfyingly connect in ways that will keep readers guessing until the explosive (in more ways than one) action-movie denouement. The author's grasp of global politics gives depth to the book's thriller elements, which are nicely balanced by thoughtful characterizations. Even minor characters come across in three dimensions, and Will himself is an endearing narrator. He's lovestruck by his gorgeous, intelligent, and strong-willed wife; has his heart and social conscience in the right place; and is boyishly thrilled by the other thing. A solid series entry that is, as usual, exciting, intricately plotted, and thoroughly entertaining."

—*Kirkus Reviews*
DIVISIBLE MAN: THREE NINES FINE [DM7]

"Any reader of this series knows that they're in good hands with Seaborne, who's a natural storyteller. His descriptions and dialogue are crisp, and his characters deftly sketched...The book keeps readers tied into its complex and exciting thriller plot with lucid and graceful exposition, laying out clues with cleverness and subtlety...Also, although Will's abilities are powerful, they have reasonable limitations, and the protagonist is always a relatable character with plenty of humanity and humor...Another riveting, taut, and timely adventure with engaging characters and a great premise."

— *Kirkus Reviews*
DIVISIBLE MAN: EIGHT BALL [DM8]

"Seaborne's latest series entry packs a good deal of mystery. Everything Will stumbles on, it seems, dredges up more questions...All this shady stuff in Montana and unrest in Wisconsin make for a tense narrative...Will's periodic sarcasm is welcome, as it's good-natured and never overwhelming...A smart, diverting tale of an audacious aviator with an extraordinary ability."

— *Kirkus Reviews*
DIVISIBLE MAN: NINE LIVES LOST [DM9]

"This engaging compendium will surely pique new readers' interest in earlier series installments. A captivating, altruistic hero and appealing cast propel this enjoyable collection..."

— *Kirkus Reviews*
DIVISIBLE MAN: ENGINE OUT & OTHER SHORT FLIGHTS

THE SERIES

While each DIVISIBLE MAN ^{TM} novel tells its own tale, many elements carry forward and the novels are best enjoyed in sequence. The short story "Angel Flight" is a bridge between the third and fourth novels and is included with the third novel, DIVISIBLE MAN - THE SECOND GHOST.

DIVISIBLE MAN ^{TM} is available in print, digital and audio.

DIVISIBLE MAN ^{TM} is available at or can be ordered from your local independent bookseller.

For advance notice of new releases and exclusive material available only to Email Members, join the DIVISIBLE MAN ^{TM} Email List at **HowardSeaborne.com**.

Sign up today and get a FREE DOWNLOAD.

ACKNOWLEDGMENTS

This pilot is blessed with a crew that deserves recognition for their patience, dedication, expertise and collaboration. My wife, for the "read and write" evenings spent in connected silence. My dear friends and family for invaluable help with big events like the EAA AirVenture (thank you, Robin, Rich, Ariana and Chryste!) My incomparable editor, Stephen Parolini, for his unflinching assessment of these characters and their motivations. The team at TWD: David, Carol, April, Claire, Kristie, Rebecca and Steve for operating the machinery that makes this possible. My medical expert, Stacey, for helping me get it right. My dear friend, cheerleader, trivia challenger and beta reader Rich. The indispensable Robin Ann, my incredible beta reader and re-reader and re-re-reader. My Copy Editor, the same Robin Ann, who giveth hyphens and taketh them away. And finally, special thanks to Sue and Rich at J&J Guide service for their hospitality and generous participation in this production. This is the Divisible Man's ninth mission. Like all before it, and the many more to come, it would never have left the ground without such willing and supportive hands. Thank you.

For Steve, Kevin and Rebecca.
Writing requires unconditional love.
Thank you for teaching me.

TWO WEEKS AGO

Although the Corona Andy served lacked a twin, I lifted the bottle anyway.

"Us."

Andy rapped a knuckle against the bottle. "Us."

Looking for reassurance where we always found it.

Just as I touched the lime-tinged bottle to my lips, I spotted a silver car decelerating on our quiet country road. Andy turned her no-longer blonde head.

"Who do we know that drives a Prius?"

Oh, crap.

PART I

1

NOW

"Earl's looking for you."

"Pidge did it."

"What?"

"Whatever has him on the warpath." I checked the coffee station for Styrofoam cups, figuring I could pour the fresh contents of the mug I held into something portable and make a run for it. Plan B: make my getaway with the ECAS mug in hand and return it later.

"Don't fucking throw me under the bus, Stewart!" Pidge's voice hunted me from the flight instructor's office down the hall.

"Sorry! Didn't know you were back there!" I turned to Rosemary II and silently mouthed, *She did it.*

"You two are worse than children." Seated behind the front counter, Rosemary II turned her attention to her computer and the shop orders stacked for billing. She issued commands with her mouse. The computer beeped obedience. I have offered to turn off the audio that annunciates her every action, but the Goddess of the Sacred Schedule insinuated that touching her computer would result in amputation without anesthetic.

I reconnoitered the hallway that runs down the center of the one-story fixed base operation building attached to the Essex County Air Service hangar. The stretch outside Earl's office radiated the aura of Mordor. I edged toward the front door.

Without looking up Rosemary II said, "Do not test me."

Earl Jackson may be the owner of Essex County Air Service, but Rosemary II is the commander-in-chief.

"I don't even work here anymore," I muttered.

"Then why are you here every morning drinking the coffee?" She pulled a fresh invoice from the printer and stapled it to the work order.

"It's your fault for making it so good."

"Go. *After* you wash out that mug."

This was not the way I planned to start my day.

EARL JACKSON WAS NOT in his office. I found him reclining on a creeper on the concrete floor of the maintenance shop. He probed an open inspection cover in the aft empennage of a Beechcraft V-tail Bonanza. Doc, the company's licensed mechanic, bent over him, glasses perched on the tip of his nose.

"This one?" Earl asked.

"Which one?"

"This one, dammit. Wiggle it!"

Doc manipulated the airplane's ruddervator.

"Nope."

"How 'bout this one?"

Doc repeated the wiggle.

"That's the one."

Earl pulled his hand out of the tail cone. "Tell 'im he's got to replace it or he's gonna find himself flying with no pitch control."

"That's what I said."

I'd seen this comedy routine before. In a moment, the two of them would vigorously argue the same point. Instead, Earl spotted me. He rolled off the creeper, heaved himself upright and launched his bowlegged stride in my direction.

"You lookin' for me, Boss?"

A head gesture told me to follow him to his office.

"Close the door," he commanded. "Siddown."

In my early days of working as a flight instructor and air charter pilot for Essex County Air Service, Earl's Attila the Hun management style petrified me. I've since determined that true danger only exists when he stops speaking. I took the only other seat in his tiny office. He dropped onto his Army surplus office chair and fixed a searing squint in my direction.

Ever since Earl watched me leap out of a Piper Navajo without a parachute one thousand feet above the Chowan River and then saw me vanish, his piercing stare carries something extra. Like he expects me to disappear at any moment.

I can count on my fingers the number of people who know about me and my ability to vanish, which I unimaginatively call *the other thing.* One of those fingers represents a deceased FBI agent named Lee Donaldson. Another represents a Washington lobbyist facing multiple life sentences for murder. A third represents a former White House advisor and Special Counsel to the Director of Homeland Security who was apprehended naked on a hotel ledge after threatening to kill the President. He can talk about me all he wants. It only makes him sound crazier.

Closer to home, Earl Jackson and Essex Police Chief Tom Ceeves both know I can disappear at will. They fall in the "boss" category. Andy works for Tom Ceeves. My paycheck comes from the Christine and Paulette Paulesky Education Foundation, but Earl will be my boss for as long as he draws a breath. Maybe even after that.

Pidge told me that after Earl witnessed my airborne departure from the Foundation's Piper Navajo, he slid back into the copilot's seat, snapped his seatbelt, slipped on his headset, and turned his Inquisition Squint on her. She claimed that she seriously considered following me.

Earl asked her one question.

"You knew about this?"

I don't recall Pidge telling me how she answered, but she did tell me that after my leap, even after the explosion at Siddley Plantation nearly tossed Pidge and Earl into Albemarie Sound, Earl initiated no further discussion on the matter. Since then, opportunities for Earl to interrogate me have come and gone. He asked nothing. I said nothing. Now, bathed in his searing squinty-eye, I surmised that the moment had arrived.

I was wrong.

"'Member me telling you about Tommy Day? My backseater?"

"I do." Lieutenant Thomas Day had been Captain Earl Jackson's Weapon Systems Officer in the back seat of a McDonnell Douglas F-4 Phantom II flying out of Udorn Air Force base in Thailand. A lucky shot from the ground hit the jet's ejection seat and blew Earl out of the plane. Day didn't make it and was never found. Earl has no memory of the shoot-down. An itch he told me he cannot scratch. He shared the story after my own aviation accident left a hole in my memory.

So...connect the dots.

My mind jumped to a woman in Minnesota with five married names trailing her maiden name. Last winter, I met Tommy Day's widow, who later married Earl, albeit briefly. Earl and I helped her dispose of some unwanted property.

I now wondered if the caper had come back to haunt her.

"Tommy had a kid sister," Earl said.

"I didn't know."

"'Course you didn't. I never told you. She must'a been twelve years younger than Tommy. I only saw her twice. Once when we were still training at Luke when she was just a little squirt. Then once more when I got out in 'seventy-six. I went up to see her and her parents. They lived in Portland."

The squint shifted from me to somewhere on the Pacific Coast.

"She was older then, a handful of angry hippy teenager who hated the government, hated the Air Force and most vehemently hated me. I had it in my thick skull that I oughta look out for her, or something equally stupid. When she got done laughing at me, she called me names her mommy and daddy never taught her. She kicked my ass off that property right smart."

"Sorry to hear that."

"Yeah, you hear that shit about people calling soldiers baby killers, and some of it is true, but some of it is just fat old farts down at the VFW trying to belong to something that's grown larger with time. I can tell you for dead sure, however, that hippy chick sister of Tommy's had me down as an A-Number-One Murderer of Innocents—starting with her brother. I don't remember leaving anyplace on this earth with my tail between my legs except for that little vegetable patch in Portland."

"Doesn't seem fair."

"Nothing about that shit show was fair. I know they would'a hung me for treason but emptying a couple hardpoints on McNamara's head crossed my mind more than once. That foul-mouthed little sister of Tommy's wasn't entirely wrong."

I glanced up at the portrait of Franklin Roosevelt above Earl's desk. A sworn Democrat, Earl did not let party affiliation put rose-tinted lenses on his view of history or the Kennedy/Johnson policies that strapped his ass to an F-4 Phantom II over Vietnam.

"I need you to look in on her."

"What? Who?"

"Tammy. Tammy Day. The kid sister."

"Uh…" my mouth hung open. "Isn't she…? Wouldn't she be like *old*? I mean…grown up?"

"Well, you ain't gonna find her in bell bottoms shimmying to Janice Joplin. Of course, she's grown up—although she might still wear bell bottoms. She dove into the deep end of the whole anti-war movement, and the feminist thing after that, and then Greenpeace and what-all."

"Sounds like you did look out for her." Earl shrugged off the notion, which told me it was true. "And Joplin had a set of pipes."

"That, she did."

"You want me to go to Portland?" Excuses formed ranks in my head. Arun Dewar, the *de facto* boss of the Christine and Paulette Paulesky Education Foundation that writes my paychecks, had been patient with me over the last few weeks, during which time I'd been AWOL from my pilot duties. Not that he hadn't, on a few occasions, benefitted by my absence when Pidge filled in on one or two overnights. One of the worst kept secrets at Essex County Air Service was that Pidge and Arun were dating.

"Why would you go to Portland?"

"Because you said…"

"She lived in Portland fifty years ago. Nah. She's up in that little hole in the wall Sandy Stone's been pumping money into. What-cha-call-it…Ekalaska?"

"Ekalaka. Montana."

"Ekalaka."

"No, it's Eee-kalaka. Eee. Not Eh."

"Whatever the hell. Tammy Day has a ranch up there, if you can call it that. It ain't exactly the Ponderosa."

I had no idea what a chain steak joint had to do with this but chose to conceal my ignorance.

"She claims twenty or thirty thousand acres, but last I checked, she just had a couple double-wide trailers in the weeds, and she spends her time raising vegetables."

"She's not a rancher?"

"Hell no. She raised and sold homeopathic veggies or some shit, and before that she ran some new age crystal therapy scam. She might'a farmed some weed, but I don't think it grows well there."

"So, you want me to fly to Montana…and what?"

"Look in on her. I told you."

"You mean…?"

The squint tightened.

"Do what you do. Christ, Will, do I gotta spell it out?"

7

"No. I just want to confirm that you're not telling me to drive up to her double-wide, introduce myself and tell her that Earl Jackson says hello."

"Use my name around that woman and you're like as not to get your ass full of buckshot. Hell no." Earl scratched behind his ear. "Look. I got a couple friends up that way."

"I remember. You told me." Earl's tale of hauling a load of marijuana from Tijuana and sliding off Ekalaka's single runway in a snowstorm still tickles me.

"After I heard that Tammy bought that ranch, I checked up on her from time to time through those friends of mine. Everybody in that part of nowhere knows everybody else. There ain't enough population to leave anybody a stranger."

"And?"

"And lately they said she stopped coming into town. Nobody's seen her doing her shopping up in Baker. She had a couple horses, but the vet says they're gone. There's a guide service that used to lease her land for hunting. I hear she cut them off, too. Nobody's seen her for a while. On top of that, there's rumors that she took up with some new folks. Outsiders."

"What outsiders?"

"I dunno. It's all rumors. Could be anything. Animal rights. Eco terrorists. Save the Montana Whales for all I know. Maybe it's nothing. Maybe she's running a nudist camp."

"You think something serious is going on?"

Earl didn't answer. His gaze shifted back to the west, this time not as far as Portland. "I tried calling. Got her number from those friends of mine. She didn't pick up, so I told her if I didn't hear something from her, I'd be at her door. And if she didn't want to see my ugly mug, she should get a message to me to stay away. I didn't hear nothing." He reeled in his distant gaze and focused on me. "So? Are you up for this or what?"

Earl knew I couldn't say no, but it was decent of him to ask.

"Just one question. They named their son Tommy and their daughter Tammy?"

"It was the fifties."

I stood. My Earl Sense told me the meeting was over. "Andy made dinner plans with her sister and her parents for tomorrow night."

"That mean you'll go on Saturday?"

"Hell no. It means I'll leave in the morning."

2

Earl gave me the company's other Beechcraft Baron, a 1971 E-55. I like flying the Education Foundation's Navajo, but I love flying that Baron. The E-model arrived near the end of the 55 series production run and uses the larger engines and larger tail intended for the follow-on 58 series. It's a hotrod, stable and solid, easily trimmed, light on the controls and comfortable to fly. Earl's model has up-to-date avionics, including a lovely digital autopilot. I rolled for takeoff just after dawn, tearing up to cruise altitude at 130 knots with a nineteen hundred foot per minute climb rate. I popped out of a layer of lightly iced clouds at sixty-five hundred feet with nothing but blue above. At my cruise altitude of 8,000 feet, I found smooth air and a negligible headwind. Since Earl was picking up the fuel tab, I set the power for speed instead of economy. Even with the headwind, the GPS groundspeed pegged at 189 knots on the Aspen primary flight display.

Full fuel tanks could have taken me all the way to Ekalaka, but only barely and with no reserve. I stopped in Aberdeen, South Dakota to top off the tanks and empty my own. The Hangar 9 FBO offered good coffee, quick service, and a quiet lounge space for the most challenging portion of the trip.

Andy picked up the call after the third ring.

3

———————

"You're where?"

"Aberdeen. It's in South Dakota."

"I know where Aberdeen is." I grimaced. Andy's tone told me she also knew where this conversation was headed.

"Earl asked me to do this. It's a personal thing. It has to do with Tommy Day. You remember me telling you about him."

"You're going to blame this on Earl?"

"Blame what?"

"You know perfectly well what. Dinner tonight. Unless you're going to tell me that it's a quick turnaround and you'll be home in time to change and have cocktails with Lydia, Mom and Dad."

"Yeah…that's the thing. Aberdeen is the halfway point. I'm on my way to Ekalaka, Montana."

Silence.

After years of family warfare, peace broke out between Andy and her parents for two salient reasons. First, after three years of marriage, she finally introduced me and explained that I may have saved their daughter and her unborn granddaughter. And second, because Andy's father finally saw the passion in Andy's love of law enforcement, a passion she never could have nurtured in the legal career he had crafted for her. It helped that Andy's sister Lydia moved the grandchildren—all four of them, counting the stepchild carried and delivered by Lydia's teenaged nanny—to Leander Lake in Essex County. Lydia's miserable excuse of a dead ex-husband managed to impregnate the nanny within days of doing the same for Lydia. Lydia delivered a beautiful baby girl named Grace. The nanny brought The Infant King Alex into the world—the only male in a household full of women. I admit to a little jealousy of that smiling kid. Giving my nieces a baby brother dislodged me from God-like status in the eyes of Grace's two older sisters, Elise and Harriet, whom I adore. Those little girls cannot get enough of their baby stepbrother.

Each time the family gathers Andy reminds me that her parents, Louis and Eleanor Taylor, have embraced me. I don't argue, but a gremlin voice whispers in my ear that her society-conscious mother and father wish their daughter had done better. As much as I love spending time with my atomic-powered nieces, dinner with Mom and Dad rates on par with getting an FAA Flight Physical.

"Sweetheart, you know I was looking forward to dinner."

"No, you weren't." I detected a hint of a smile at Andy's end of the digital connection, which gave me hope.

I bit my tongue. Half the battle is not overselling.

"When do you think you'll be back?"

"Earl wants me to look in on Tommy Day's sister at some ranch. Discretely. I think I can get that done tonight, rest overnight and be outta there in the morning. I'd say I'll be home for dinner tomorrow night."

"Okay. That works. Because Mom and Dad are staying through the weekend."

Now I knew she was smiling.

4

The Ekalaka Airport ramp was deserted when I taxied in. An agricultural operation hangar dominated the ramp, but it appeared closed for the day, if not the season.

I took my time shutting down the myriad switches on the Baron's panel, double-checking that I didn't neglect something that would drain the battery. I spent a minute with the iPad reviewing the flight path to the Day Ranch, which lay ten nautical miles to the south adjacent the highway that bordered the airport. Ten miles fell within the limits of my battery-powered BLASTER—Basic Linear Aerial System for Transport, Electric Rechargeable—a device that looks like a flashlight with an electric motor driving a model airplane propeller on one end. I carried four on this trip, with extra batteries for each. A charged BLASTER yields roughly forty minutes of use at maximum power, which I rarely use. Half power gives me a speed of nearly thirty knots. Reaching the Day ranch required a flight time of twenty minutes each way. That left power in reserve. I brought along a pair of ski goggles to keep the wind out of my eyes at higher speeds.

Cracking the cabin door open introduced a sharp chill to the heated cabin. I grabbed my flight jacket and gloves from the back seat and shoved them out on the wing. I laid the row of BLASTERS and their companion propellers next to my phone on the seat, then scooted over them and performed the gymnastic move that is climbing out of the Baron's front seat onto the wing.

"Hi! You must be Will."

A woman wearing a goose down vest over a flannel shirt and jeans leaned against a well-worn Chevy Tahoe that she had parked behind the tail of the Baron. She had short brown hair, an attractive face with a confident smile built in. Her chipper presence and friendly recognition of me caught me by surprise. I stood upright on the wing and pulled on my jacket, leaving the power units on the front seat out of sight.

"I'm Sue," she said. "I heard you fly over. I live right over there." She pointed across the runway at several buildings on the other side of the highway, the last structures counted in the town census before empty ranchland took over.

The confused look on my face changed her smile from one of greeting to amusement.

"Deb called me. She would have come, but she doesn't have a car right now. Terry has the rear end taken apart. She had to use a neighbor's car this week to deliver meals to seniors."

"Okay," I said cautiously. "I have no idea who Deb is. Or Terry."

"Oh." Sue laughed. "Deb and Terry are your boss's friends. Your boss is Earl Jackson, right?"

"That's the boss."

"Mr. Jackson called Deb to let her know you were coming. He thought she might be able to give you a car and a place to stay. Unless you planned on staying up at the Midway or the Guest House, but this time of year, during hunting season, they're booked up." I guess I still had a lost look on my face, because she repeated, slowly, "Earl called Deb. Deb called me."

"And you are...?"

"Sue. I'm still Sue." She laughed. "My husband and I own J&J Guide Service. And since Deb doesn't have a car or a place for you to stay, here I am. You can have this SUV, and we have one empty bunk—if you don't mind snoring hunters. We're fully booked, but one fella dropped out sick."

"I don't know what to say. Thank you."

"Well, hop in."

"Uh...okay. Lemme get my bag."

I leaned into the cockpit and stuffed the four power units back into my flight bag.

SUE DROVE out of the airport gate and followed a narrow road toward the cluster of buildings that constituted metropolitan Ekalaka. For the next five minutes she identified town landmarks with pride in her voice. The post office. A church. The new hospital. She explained that the hospital joined the senior living facility, and that she worked as a nurse at both when she wasn't cooking meals for hunting parties. And sometimes when she was if staffing fell short.

The "downtown" area appeared to be a triangle of gravel roads. She identified the fire department, the storefront public library, and the Dawg House Pub. A message board at the Dawg House advertised an all-male dancer review appearing for one night only, about which Sue made no mention.

"That's the new Mexican restaurant." She pointed. Neon signs decorated the windows of a brick building that had the look of a bank. "It's really good. Everything is authentic—although I wouldn't try to get in much after five. It gets pretty busy." She turned from one gravel road onto another. "That's the Carter County Museum." A stone building topped with a cavalry fort blockhouse hugged the sidewalk. An Indian lance crossed with a cavalry sword shared signage with silhouettes of dinosaurs. "It's a great museum, if you have extra time."

"Probably not on this trip."

"Hey, my brother is a pilot."

"I like him already. What does he fly?"

"I think he flies something with two engines, like what you came in. And he flies a helicopter. He built it himself. In his garage."

I thought that was crazy but didn't say so.

"You're here about Tammy Day."

I glanced at her to determine if this friendly reception masqueraded as a warning against poking around where I didn't belong. Her friendly aura remained undimmed.

"My boss, Earl, knew her brother."

"Didn't he die in Vietnam? The brother, I mean."

"Do you know Ms. Day?"

"Yes. Oh, yes. We buy vegetables from her. Or we did. Not so much this past year. We used to buy a lot of her stuff. Fresh raspberries, lots and lots of zucchini."

"People who grow zucchini always have lots and lots of it."

The smile faded a little, replaced by a cooler assessment aimed at me. "I trust Deb. Deb trusts Earl. That means you should be trustworthy. Are you trustworthy?"

"My wife tells me that I blush automatically if I stray from the truth. I guess that means you'll be able to tell."

"And you're not here from ParaTransit? Or Energy Stone?"

"I don't know who either of those are. Is that something you might want to tell me?"

"I wish I could. We've been worried about..." She let the sentence trail off. She assessed the nonexistent traffic and turned onto the widest paved road I'd seen so far. The highway marked Montana 323 headed out of town.

"Worried about?"

"Well...like I told you. My husband and I run a guide service."

"I'm not sure what that is."

"We lease land, government land and private ranch land, and we guide hunters. My husband Rich and our hired guides. All the seasons. Gun and bow. We have three camps in Montana. We're the second-largest service in the state with access to over a million and a half acres."

"Impressive. Is that a good business?"

"We're booked up for the next three years. In fact, I'd go with you, but I start cooking for fourteen hungry hunters in about an hour. I know, it sounds like I'm bragging, but my point is that we depend on leases and Tammy's land was one of them. Until this year. She didn't renew. And she stopped providing produce for us. She never was much for visiting town, but she wasn't unfriendly either. Something changed. I haven't seen her since summer."

"Does she live alone out there?"

"Mostly. I heard that recently she had outsiders with her. People said it was kind of a religious thing. Other people said it was oil speculators. We have no shortage of rumors in our small town. Honestly...I'm not sure."

"So, who is Para...Transfer? Or that other thing?"

"ParaTransit and Energy Stone. We don't know. That was another rumor. People said a real estate agent from Baker went out to the ranch, representing those two names. That's the rumor. I have a feeling Tammy would have run somebody like that off the property."

"Do you think it's about oil or mineral rights?"

"Not much of that around here. You'll see a few wells down by Alzada."

"Anybody been out to the ranch to check on her?"

"I went last month. She had a locked gate on the road up to her place. I called a few times, but she didn't answer."

"Did you report any of this to the local authorities?"

She chuckled and pointed to the left side of the road. A black and white Sheriff's SUV sat nosed up to a small ranch house on a cluttered property.

"That's our deputy. Not a bad guy, but not exactly an investigator. Most of the time, that's where you'll find him. But a locked gate could mean she isn't home, or it could mean she just doesn't want to be bothered."

Just as the highway entered open country, she pulled off the road onto a broad gravel shoulder. To my right, on the other side of a grassy field, I could see the airport and the Baron tied to the ramp. Sue pointed left.

"This is me." A tidy house spread itself beneath shade trees at the end of a mid-length driveway. A small cabin shared the property on one side of the house. A Quonset-style shed hid behind trees on the other side. I had expected a hunting lodge made of logs and adorned with antlers. This residence had the pleasant look of suburbia. Small gardens, now brown for winter, accented the home. "The mail came, so I'll get out here. The truck has gas. When you're done, just drive it in and knock. Don't worry if it's late. I'll set you up in the new cabin. Oh. Do you need a map?"

"I have my iPad." I patted the flight bag between my knees.

Sue's smile and the sparkle in her eyes remained undiminished, but she hesitated for a moment before climbing out.

"If you see Tammy, ask her to call me. I'd be careful about trespassing, though. That's a thing around here."

"Noted. And thanks for the wheels. Much appreciated. It was nice meeting you."

"You, too!"

We both hopped out. She crossed the road. I trotted around the front grille and took the driver's seat. She tossed me a cheerful wave as I pulled away.

This hadn't been my plan. Earl's interference twice removed had derailed my intention to simply fly up to the ranch property for a look around. Now I saw the benefits. Connecting me with this pleasant woman provided information. The owner of the guide service also revealed another vital detail.

The location of a good Mexican restaurant.

I performed a U-turn and drove back into Ekalaka.

THE WARMLY LIT café had the interior dimensions of a railroad car. Tables lined the wall to my right. A bar occupied the first quarter of the room to my left. A narrow kitchen joined the bar and took up the remaining space. At the far end of the room, a glass-fronted cooler offered bottled soft drinks and beer, and a second entrance. None of the tables were occupied at three-fifteen in the afternoon.

I seated myself at a table for two along the wall. A moment later, a dark-haired woman wearing a blue sweater over jeans approached the table bearing a greeting and a menu. I checked for a name tag but found none. Her dress and demeanor suggested owner. Her quick appraisal of me said she knew a stranger when she saw one. I expected small talk, but she opened by asking what I'd like to drink. I ordered an iced tea and she hustled off to the kitchen.

A few minutes later, the iced tea arrived.

"Give it a try. It's a new batch. If it's not right, I can get you something else." She waited. I sipped.

"Mmm. Good tea." Her smile told me I'd been set up.

"Our homemade recipe. Would you like to hear the special?"

"I'm sure it's special, but I'm a sucker for a good enchilada. With beef, hold the onions please."

"You can't go wrong there." She plucked the menu from my hand.

"Can I ask you something?"

"If I don't know the answer, I'll make something up."

"A lady by the name of Tammy Day. Do you know her?"

"I know everybody. And yes. Nice lady. I bought produce from her for a short time, but she stopped selling last summer. Too bad. She had some fine tomatoes. We used to buy a lot of her stuff. Never knew what to do with all the zucchini, though."

"Have you heard from her lately?"

She touched her pen to her temple and squinted. "Not for a while. She started up with some Moonies or Hindus or some such a year or so ago. Wasn't very social after that. We weren't friends or anything, and nobody takes it personal when someone around here wants privacy. I just took it to mean she was busy with visitors. We get that kind up here sometimes."

"What kind?"

"Religious. Cultish. You know. A little...out there. Looking to bond with or worship nature here in the wild west. Most of 'em don't make it past the first winter storm." She chuckled. "I don't judge. One man's Bible is another man's crystals or pyramid or ancient aliens."

"Was she alone on her ranch?"

"Mostly. But like I said, I heard there were some new folks up there with her. You planning to pay a visit?"

"Looking in on her for a friend."

"Well, if you see her, tell her the TSO Cantina would still love some of her tomatoes. I'll take 'em fresh, canned or stewed."

"I will."

CHARTER FLYING TAUGHT me the art of eating alone. Before the age of the personal device, the trick was to carry a paperback. I filled countless hours of pilot wait time in the company of C.S. Forester, Stephen King, Ian Fleming and Craig Johnson. I fed my appetite for history with James Holland, Stephen Ambrose, Edwin Hoyt and a dozen others. For a time, I resisted reading on a screen, but the ease and convenience of carrying an entire library on my iPad eventually overcame my preference for the familiar feel of a book in hand.

The iPad served as my dinner companion while I savored my new number one all-time favorite enchilada. Instead of picking up where I left off in a Holland book on the air battles over Europe during World War Two, I went hunting on the internet for ParaTransit and Energy Stone.

I learned that *paratransit* is a commonplace term meaning a supplement to scheduled public transportation, most often in the form of for-hire transport of disabled individuals. Lift vans and the like. Beyond that, I found nothing.

A Google search for Energy Stone opened a floodgate of links to healing crystals, chakra gems, copper power spheres and dozens of equally inventive ways to part people with their money. I thought Energy Stone might be the name of a corporation—maybe an oil exploration outfit—but nothing floated to the surface of the internet cistern.

The restaurant remained mid-day empty. The owner/server visited the table from time to time. She demonstrated earnest interest in my satisfaction. I have no idea how she imagined I would order a dessert after eating an enchilada the size of a tortoise, but she asked. I countered with a request for the bill and left a generous tip.

A high cloud deck seeped in from the west during my early dinner. An hour of daylight remained, but the world dimmed quickly as the sun lost its battle with the clouds. Once again, Earl's inadvertent interference benefited my planning. Night seemed like a better time to visit the Day Ranch. Not because I wanted the cover of darkness, but because it reduced the chances that the rancher would be out tending to her property or animals, if she had any. Nightfall, I hoped, would find her cooking her supper for her guests, or curling up with a good book and a glass of cabernet.

She's fine Earl. Just playing the hermit.

I had in mind that later that evening I'd leave Sue's Chevy Tahoe in her driveway with the keys and a twenty for gas, then scoot back to the Baron and depart. Sue would assume I hiked across the field to the airport. I took her at her word about the local hotels being booked. A short flight up to Dickenson or even a longer flight back to Aberdeen, and I could easily find a room.

Departing the TSO Cantina, I followed Sue's route out of town

5

Tammy Day not only put a sturdy steel gate across her ranch driveway, she also dumped stones the size of golf carts on either side of the gate posts, eliminating the possibility of bypassing the gate. Both sides of the driveway sloped sharply into a rough gulley that effectively became a moat with the driveway as drawbridge. The Tahoe's headlights showed me a heavy log chain and padlock the size of my fist. Somebody meant business, as if the stern No Trespassing sign hand painted on the gate's steel cross-piece failed to convey the message.

Beyond this impediment, the driveway carved a straight-arrow lane across a grassy field before it ascended into a tree line. Halfway up the slope, gravel gave way to tire tracks on grass. Higher still, the lane curved right and disappeared behind the trees. The view from the road deceptively suggested the ranch proper lay on top of that first rise. I knew from studying the satellite imagery on Google Maps that the driveway snaked through wooded terrain, crossed more open range, then followed a dry creek bed for a mile or so before swinging left where it rose onto a plateau. The southern edge of the plateau gave the impression of a miles-long plate of land that had been shoved two hundred feet upward, creating a flat, rocky cliff. The road ran parallel to the cliff line for several miles until finally coming to open land on which, from Google's sky view, I had seen rectangles representing structures.

It was into this cluster of civilization that I eventually descended behind my handheld power unit and propeller after following the dirt track from the gate. My concept of a ranch springs entirely from the silver screen; Hollywood cowboys living in bunkhouses and rich ranchers playing lord of the land in broad-shouldered log or timber homes. Those notions bore no resemblance to the sagging double-wide trailers and random fencing I found.

Tammy Day's little piece of Montana heaven consisted of the two double-wide trailers, a leaning garage I hadn't noticed on Google, and a fenced patch too large to be called a garden, too small to be called a field. Rows of wire towers identified the source of the TSP Café's favored tomatoes. Missing from this scene was any kind farm implement. The only vehicle in sight was a Saab parked beside one of the trailer units. In a land of pickup trucks and SUVs, the yuppie chariot from Sweden stood out enough that I made it my first stop. I navigated close to the back of the vehicle to check the license plate and lost a bet with myself. Colorado, not California.

The second thing I checked was the windshield. Clean. If the vehicle had been sitting for any amount of time, there would have been dust. The wind hissing through the trees guaranteed it.

The windows of both trailers were black and lightless. A pole at the corner of the nearest edge of the tilled garden mounted a light. Unlit.

The word that came to mind was *deserted*.

This ranch wasn't deserted in the sense of having been abandoned to the elements. The buildings were closed and looked secure. Nothing littered the yard. I began to wonder if Earl's secret ward had simply headed off to sun herself at an Airbnb on the Gulf Coast.

I cruised around the trailer beside the Saab and found no sign of life. Starlight sharpened detail but that didn't help with the windows on the trailer. I could not tell if the glass covered closed curtains, pulled shades, plywood panels, or simply dark rooms. Pulling up nose-close to the panes didn't help. I saw nothing.

The garage gave away no secrets either. It had seen better days. A slight lean testified to the relentless Montana wind, but the wood siding had been maintained. A window frame on the side of the building had been covered over by plywood. Recently. The wood was new and smooth.

A power line connected to a glass insulator near the garage peak. I followed the line to the garden area where I found an upright fuel tank and a generator. The generator motor smelled of oil and grease and recent exhaust. I wondered how long a full tank of fuel lasted in the winter.

From the garage, I rose over the wire fence bordering the tilled land. Gaining height, I saw sections of varying vegetation. Stakes and tomato towers had been driven into the soil. Rows corrugated the ground. Mounds of discarded plant matter and mulch punctuated the rows and lent an odor of rot to the air. On a fence post, a weathervane with a prop not much larger than the one in my hand charged into the wind, spinning furiously. The weathervane snapped left and right with each gust. In the same way, I maintained steady application of power to my handheld unit, fighting the wind to hold my position.

The gardens were done for the year. A few rotting vegetables lay in the dirt, but the harvest had ended some time ago. Any day now the entire area could be blanketed in snow. It might bury the garden for the rest of a long winter, or it might come and go on the whim of a warm front carrying heat from the American southwest. Either way, the plot below me was as lifeless as the rest of the ranch.

My theory about the ranch owner dipping her toes in warm Gulf waters gained weight. I turned the BLASTER in the direction of the remaining trailer. One more circuit and then I'd fly a tailwind-enhanced route back to the parked Tahoe where I would rehearse my report to Earl. Make the call. Return the vehicle to its owner. Zip across the field to where the Baron lay waiting. Make a quick hop to Dickenson, SD and check into a nice hotel. Maybe grab a late dinner if the enchilada allowed it. A call to Andy would top off the day.

I lined up on a path for the second trailer.

The door burst open.

A figure filled the frame, backlit by soft yellow light that threw the occupant's shadow halfway across the yard toward me. His appearance startled me. I cut the BLASTER and glided silently, rapidly losing speed against the wind.

I expected a woman. The figure in the door was male, young, thin, and wiry. He held the door open with one hand and posed with his head turned. Listening. Light escaped the trailer via the doorway. None of the black windows hinted that the unit had been occupied. Tammy Day owned some serious curtains.

I lost headway. The wind brought me to a standstill, then started to push. I needed to think fast about using power to hold my position—thereby creating noise that threatened to let this guy know he wasn't alone.

I decided to accept the drift when I heard what he heard.

Motors.

I don't know how I missed it before. Perhaps the wind flow carried the sound away from me, or my power unit drowned it out. Somehow the guy in the trailer heard the sound before I did. Motorcycle engines. Probably not motorcycles, given the terrain. ATVs. More than one. The sound carried from the direction of the dirt track.

The guy in the doorway jumped back into the lighted room, briefly solving the problem of drift. I gave the power unit a shot and re-established forward movement.

I cut the power again when light spilling from the door extinguished. A moment later, the shadow figure leaped through the frame. He stopped long enough to spin around, close the door, and snap a padlock in a hasp and loop. He carried a backpack slung over one shoulder and a collection of what looked like clothing, a wadded sleeping bag and some other gear clutched against his chest.

With the lock secure, he bolted across the yard for the Saab. He pounded the ground at a dead run. Reaching the side of the Saab, he jerked open the back door and tossed his goods inside. He slammed the door, opened the driver's door, and jumped behind the wheel. Brake lights flashed. The car started. Tires ground dirt and threw pebbles. He launched the Saab across the yard.

Instead of taking to the driveway, he drove in the opposite direction, parallel to the garden plot fence. At the end of the fence, he angled onto open terrain. The car exited the smooth yard and heaved over uneven ground. He ran without lights.

His pursuers did not.

Beams of light bounced through the trees, sweeping the grasses and junipers with each turn and jog. Headlights emerged from the trees. Four off-road all-terrain vehicles—the kind with motorcycle grip steering and controls—raced into the ranch yard. Light splashed the trailers and terrain, making shadows dart away. Two of the ATVs were driven solo; two mounted riders behind the driver. The vehicles charged across the ranch yard and into the field, chasing the Saab, catching air from bumps in their path.

The Saab lurched across the landscape. One unseen gulley or lurking boulder and that passenger car would be finished. The driver's wild attempt to escape these visitors suggested he felt greater threat from them than from a broken axle or smashed radiator.

All five vehicles kicked up dust that hurried away on the rising wind. The pursuers fanned out behind the Saab. Two of the ATVs broke to the right, racing to flank the Saab. The move made sense. To the Saab's left, closing in quickly, the plateau's cliff eliminated any avenue of escape for miles.

I pushed my ski goggles down over my eyes and aimed the BLASTER in the direction of the high-speed pursuit. The jury was still out on who was who in this drama, but rifles slung across the backs of two of the four-wheeler riders pushed my allegiance in the direction of the outnumbered

Saab driver. From the feel of the wind against me as I accelerated, this chase closed in on sixty miles per hour. I played catchup behind a BLASTER whining at full power. The wind eddying across the treetops bumped and jarred me.

The flankers achieved their goal, herding the Saab toward scattered trees that lined the top of the cliff. I hoped the poor sod behind the wheel knew about the precipice, or that Saab was going to imitate its namesake Swedish fighter jets. Briefly.

I raced to catch up. Relative wind streaked against my skin. My clothing flapped.

Crump!

The Saab's end came quickly. I don't know what he hit, but the vehicle nose-dived to a hard stop in a cloud of dust. The hood flew up over the windshield. The jolt blew the airbags, which covered the side windows. Dust billowed up around the vehicle. The pursuers circled and closed in, hemming the crash scene against the cliff line two dozen yards away.

As I caught up, a black figure burst out of the dust cloud at a dead run. He sprinted on a line paralleling the cliff. One of the four-wheelers launched to cut him off. Another zoomed in from the side. For a moment, it looked like the driver of the second ATV intended to scoop him up. Instead, an arm and fist shot out. The Saab driver took a blow to the side of his head and tumbled, arms and legs flying.

The ATVs skidded to a halt. A semi-circle of headlights braced the victim lying in the dry grass. The wind cleared dust from the air and six men dismounted. I counted on the idling ATV engines to cover the noise from my power unit. Twenty feet overhead, I reached the scene.

One of the men, broad-shouldered with tattooed and muscled arms hanging from a puffy down vest, strolled to the figure on the ground and delivered a rib-cracking kick. I heard the Saab driver grunt sharply, then gasp to fight for the air ejected from his lungs.

The muscled man reached down and scooped up the Saab driver's collar. He lifted the convulsing victim out of the grass like a child. The Saab driver's thin arms and legs flailed and kicked but posed no threat to his attacker. I dropped into hover upwind and used a light application of BLASTER power to maintain my position.

"You don't seem to take a hint, asshole."

Saab Driver didn't answer.

"Maybe I need to make a stronger impression."

"I think *he* needs to make a strong impression." One of the riflemen gestured at the drop-off.

"Teach this fucker to fly, Danzig," another man said.

Danzig glanced at the cliff, then dragged the Saab driver onto a rock platform jutting into empty air. Saab Driver alternately clawed at the grip on his collar and clutched his torso in agony. Lack of air prevented him from speaking, or even screaming. Harsh wheezing and weak kicking summed up his protest. He tried in vain to dig his heels into the ground. He failed.

Danzig dragged him across rough stone then stopped at the edge. He lifted Saab driver high enough to mutter something in his ear that I could not hear.

Then he threw him over the cliff.

6

I saw it coming.

The moment Danzig marched to the edge I thumbed the BLASTER slide control. I descended over the heads of the men who paraded behind Danzig and the kid. I dove for grass that became rock. I skimmed the rock and shot out over the top of a gnarled tree clinging impossibly to the side of the cliff. A tight turn took me into position within arm's reach of a rock face that dropped straight down for at least two hundred feet before a slope of rocks, gravel, trees, and ancient debris descended to flatland below.

I pulsed the BLASTER and stopped low and in front of the outcropping onto which Danzig dragged his helpless victim. I watched Danzig speak into Saab Driver's ear, then heave him over the edge.

Gravity snatched Saab Driver.

I dropped the BLASTER and spread my arms. Saab Driver dropped and hit me hard. His head glanced off the side of my skull. The impact tore away my goggles and left sparks in my vision. Flailing arms and legs kicked and punched me.

I threw my arms around him. We accelerated toward hard earth.

FWOOOMP!

The black form writhing on top of me vanished. I clasped my hands behind his back and pulled him tight to deny his limbs room to do me damage. He flailed and struggled. Rocks swept past us. In seconds, we dropped a hundred feet with barely half that much remaining. The earth raced to meet us. Starlight brought every rugged feature of the harsh surface below into stark relief.

There was no time to reach for a fresh BLASTER to arrest our fall.

Boulders grew larger and charged at us.

STOP!

The visceral impulse flashed in my head faster than my mind could form the word. The core muscle that runs down my center when I vanish tightened like a steel cable.

We stopped.

Silence.

Saab Driver froze, as if moving or struggling might renew the fall.

I freed one hand, reached down, and touched the rough stones that carpeted the steep slope. We had come to within an arm's length of smashing into the rugged surface.

I rotated and released Saab Driver. He dropped onto the stone surface and cried out in pain. He skidded then stopped.

I reached down and clamped a fistful of his shirt in one hand. I jerked myself close against his ear. "Quiet!" I whispered harshly. "Play dead. Do it!"

He grabbed the rocks and splayed his legs. I didn't think his would-be killers could see his features at this distance, but he closed his eyes tightly just the same.

I searched the cliff face. Two hundred feet overhead, the rock platform that facilitated Saab Driver's execution dominated the sky above me. Black space populated with stars formed a backdrop. I could not tell if anyone looked over the edge or not. If they did, their silhouettes made no impression against the night sky.

Saab Driver struggled to suppress a rattling wheeze pumped out with each breath. I prayed the sound would not rise to the top of the cliff.

I waited.

ATV noise spilled over the cliff, modulated by revving throttles and gear shifts before being carried away by the wind. The noise faded quickly at first, then lingered at a low level until it was hard to tell if I was still hearing it or imagining it. Eventually the steady wind swallowed the manmade motor noise.

I realized I'd been holding my breath. I let it go along with the Saab driver's shirt and one of Pidge's favorite expressions. I tried to steady my hands, which had begun to tremble. I took in, held, and blew air using a four-count to help slow my racing pulse. Wind rising against the cliff face caused me to ascend. After some fumbling, I produced a new BLASTER, attached a prop, and maneuvered back down to where the Saab driver lay.

His eyes flashed open. Dark irises ringed by panicked white probed the air. He stared at the cliff above and patted the earth below in disbelief.

Between ragged breaths he whispered.

"Double-U — (huff) — Tee — (huff) — Eff!"

7

I maneuvered into position beside the sprawled figure, grabbed a rock edge and lodged one foot against the slope.

Fwooomp!

I reappeared and dropped a few inches to the surface. My appearance startled him. Wide-eyed, he tried to speak, but either his ragged breathing or utter disbelief cut him off.

"Don't talk." I clawed my way closer. The slope—at least sixty degrees —invited gravity to take another bite. Had he fallen as planned, I think he would have kept on bouncing well into a stand of trees several hundred feet below us. "Just breathe."

"*How—?*" The word came out as a squeak.

I held up a hand between us. "Lemme check you out first. Okay?"

I gingerly laid my hands on his torso and probed his ribs through a thin black t-shirt. He gritted his teeth and bit down on a scream.

"Pretty sure you've got one or more broken ribs."

"*You—(wheeze)—doctor?*"

"No. But I got kicked in the ribs by a cow once. Hurt like a sonofabitch."

He tried to speak but broke into a cough which ignited pain and prompted another muted scream.

"Relax. Don't talk. Nod yes or no. Does it hurt to breathe?"

Yes.

"Left side?"

Yes.

"Right side?"

He lifted one hand and tipped it back and forth. No-*ish*.

"Can you sit up?"

He tried. Sharp pain prompted a deep groan. He shook his head. No.

"Then don't."

"*How—?*" Another squeak. He pointed at the cliff above us. His eyes flared, emphasizing the question.

"How are you alive? Yeah, good question. That's one hell of a fall. You're a lucky guy. I just happened to be doing some rock climbing, heard the commotion, and the next thing I knew you came flying over the edge. Lucky I was there. I grabbed you and we rappelled down. My safety ropes saved us. And here we are. You should buy a lottery ticket today."

He looked up at the cliff, then at me.

"*Bull—(wheeze)—shit.*"

"Pure, unadulterated. But let me ask you a question. Are you really going to look this gift horse in the mouth?"

He didn't seem too sure.

"You'd better not. Because that's the story we're both going to tell if anybody ever asks. And by my count, there are only six people who would ask, and not very politely. I wouldn't run into them again if I were you. They didn't like finding you at Tammy Day's ranch."

He coughed and grimaced.

"Yeah, we'll discuss that, but right now we've got to get you down off this mountain and to a hospital."

He shook his head sharply and waved his hands in the air. A definite No.

"Really? I'm not sure a rib bone didn't puncture your lung. It won't kill you right now, but if it did poke a hole, you're probably leaking air into the sack around the lungs. I forget what that's called but if you keep it up your lung will collapse. If you think you're having trouble breathing now, brother…"

He lifted his head and surveyed the slope below us. I did the same. Fit and in daylight, the hike to flat ground half a mile away would have been a challenge. In the dark, even if I found a way to carry him without causing more damage, chances were good we'd both wind up in a heap.

He looked at me and shook his head. He wasn't wrong.

I picked up a stone and tossed it into the starlit grass and rocks. The tap and rattle ricocheting down the slope affirmed the hazard facing us.

"You're probably right. Even if I get you down to the flat, we're looking at a five-mile hike to my car. And that's if we don't run into your friends."

He gasped and grimaced against the pain, and maybe against the hopelessness of the situation.

Our options narrowed down to one. I leaned closer. "Here's the deal. I need you to name your most cherished possession. Something you're willing to die for. Something that means more to you than life itself."

I got the blank look I expected.

"No," I said. "I don't want it. I want to know—what is the most sacred person or thing in your life that you'd be willing to swear an oath on? A blood oath. Bible? Michael Jorden rookie card? Old sock worn by Brett Favre? Your mother?"

Bewilderment morphed into suspicion.

"Dude. I need you to swear to keep a secret."

He lay silent for a moment. I mistook contemplation for confusion and was about to try another tactic when he spoke.

"*Metallica,*" he whispered, pushing it with just a hint of vocal tone. "*I have the entire ...(wheeze)... catalog in vinyl including the ...(wheeze)... Metal Massacre I ...(wheeze)... pressing with the misspelled name.*"

"Misspelled name?"

The kid nodded. He broke into a coughing fit, clutched his ribs, and groaned.

"No shit. Okay." I waited for the coughing to subside, and for his breathing to even out. "Works for me. Raise your right hand and swear on your vinyl Metallica collection that you will never speak of what's about to happen."

8

_____

"*This is ...(wheeze)... fucked up.*"

We cruised above the descending tree line. I applied a strong crab angle into the wind to hold a steady course. The high cloud deck had dissipated. Montana starlight nearly approximated the intensity I expected from moonlight. The landscape glowed in black and white. The BLASTER in my hand hummed. I kept the speed low, having lost my ski goggles. Even with low power, we moved quickly over the ground, energized by a tailwind.

"*This is ...(wheeze)... so fucked up.*"

"Language, kid. My ears are delicate."

His breathing had steadied, but he continued gasping for air. Shedding gravity's pull on his body by making him vanish, the pressure on his lungs and ribs had diminished. It seemed to help. We traveled upright, my left hand clasping his right, which I'd taken after he swore on his thrash metal treasures that he would never speak about this night or what he was about to see. Or not see.

"What's your name?"

"*Uh...Wally.*"

"What? You're not sure?"

"*Wally. Look ...(wheeze)... I know I swore, but ...(wheeze)... WTF!*" The string of words and the emphasis made him gasp again.

"Gift horse, Wally. Who were those guys?"

He tried to say something but broke into a cough, which made him bite down on a scream. I felt him clench against the pain.

31

"Okay, okay, okay. I'll stop asking questions. You stop talking."

He regained control, but now I felt him shivering. I eased more power into the BLASTER.

We cruised parallel to the cliff face. To my right, the land flattened out in the direction of Wyoming. Devil's Tower couldn't be far from here. I'd always wanted to visit the lava monolith associated with Indian lore and more recently as a terminal for Hollywood space aliens. Several miles ahead, the highway crossed the T of our path.

I didn't park the borrowed Chevy Tahoe at the ranch gate. I parked it half a mile away using the back side of a small hill to hide and disassociate it from the ranch. I wondered if the marauders who threw Wally over the cliff spotted the vehicle, and if they did, did they think anything of it? On the other hand, they traveled by ATV, which might mean they didn't use the highway.

We'd know soon.

9

I pressed the doorbell, but hearing nothing, added an urgent knock. Almost immediately, I detected movement against the warm light inside. Footsteps approached.

Sue opened the front door to her sedate home and launched her friendly smile in my direction. She noted the Tahoe in the driveway.

"I'm so sorry to interrupt your dinner—"

"Oh, don't be silly! We're just cleaning up. Come in! Come in! I'll fix you a plate."

"Thank you, but no, I need your help. You said you were a nurse." Her expression darkened quickly. "I've got somebody out here. He's hurt."

"Rich!" she called into the house behind her. "Rich, come out here!"

She pushed past me and hurried down the steps to where I'd parked her SUV. She opened the passenger door and leaned in over Wally whose breathing had grown shallow on the ten-mile drive back to Ekalaka.

"What's all this noise?" A large man filled the door behind me. He had short dark hair and a friendly face that harbored quick, inquisitive eyes. He took in the entire scene in a split second.

"Fetch me a blanket," Sue ordered. The big man reversed into the house. "And my phone!"

I joined Sue at the vehicle.

"What happened?"

"No idea. I found the kid lying on the side of the road. He said he got jumped by some guys on ATVs. One of them kicked him in the ribs. Might have broken one or two."

Rich reappeared, nudged me aside, and handed Sue a blanket. Several men assembled in the house and watched us through a big window.

"You the pilot?" Rich asked me.

"I am."

"Did you get up to the Day ranch?"

I shook my head. "The gate was locked and blocked."

"I could'a told you that." The comment might have landed as judgmental, but he delivered it as simple fact. "Where did this happen?"

"About a mile from the Day ranch gate."

Sue probed Wally, touching his torso, checking his breathing. She unfolded the blanket and spread it over him. Rich handed her a phone.

"He said it was guys on ATVs?" Rich asked. "What was he doing out there?"

"I don't know."

"Did you see anything?"

"I didn't see anybody by the road. Are you calling an ambulance?" I asked Sue, partly to evade Rich's rapid interrogation.

"Got one right here," Sue said. "Rich, I'm taking him to the hospital. I'll call Maryanne on my way in. Can you finish up inside?"

"Go. Just go."

"You should come with me," Sue said in my direction as she hurried around the front of the SUV. The sweet tone remained, but it wasn't a request. Rich opened the Chevy's back door for me to emphasize the point. I had hoped to deliver the injured kid and simply slip away.

"Okay." I climbed in. "Maybe after we drop him off you could take me back to the airport."

10

S ue drove the SUV directly to a sally port bordered with blazing red corrugated steel marked with a sign that said EMERGENCY. She tapped the horn and the garage-like door rattled open. She pulled inside.

"I'll give you a hand," I offered, climbing out.

"They're coming out." She no sooner spoke than an electric entry door opened and a man and woman in scrubs pushed a gurney to the side of the Tahoe. Wally bit down hard to fight cries of pain when they lifted him from the front of the SUV and seated him on the gurney. Sue took his shoulders. The woman in scrubs took his feet. The man held the gurney. They rotated Wally and laid him down, then flipped blankets over him. The duo in scrubs pushed the gurney toward the doors. I tapped Sue on the shoulder.

"I can walk to the airport from here. I just want to thank you." I pressed a folded twenty I'd been holding into her hand. "This is for the gas."

"Oh, no! You should stay. I can fix supper for you, and you should probably talk to the sheriff about this."

"I don't have anything worthwhile to say. I didn't see anything. That kid can tell the sheriff whatever he knows. All I did was give him a ride."

"I really think you should stay."

"If the sheriff has questions for me, Deb has Earl's number and Earl can get a message to me. But I need to get going."

The gurney disappeared inside, tugging Sue's attention with it.

"It was good meeting you," I said, freeing her.

"You, too." She hurried inside.

11

I grabbed my flight bag and slipped out the open sally port door looking for a place to vanish. The gravel street in both directions was broad and open. Homes lined both sides, right up to the hospital. Houses were set back, fronted by small lawns or gravel lots hosting multiple vehicles, some on blocks and skirted by weeds. There were no alleys to duck into. None of the buildings hugged their neighbor or the street. The hospital had a tall light above the emergency entrance, but the street I faced had no lights. Illumination from random yard-, garage- and house-mounted bulbs spilled all around me.

I walked in the direction of the road leading to the airport. I felt exposed on the edge of the gravel road. My boots sounded absurdly loud on the gritty surface.

From the hospital I walked to the first intersection and turned right on a street called Putnam Avenue. I hiked one block then crossed a gravel lane called School Street. I searched both directions but spotted nothing resembling a school. Ahead, the road curved left, looking more like someone's driveway than a town avenue. A scattering of sheds occupied an otherwise empty lot. Beyond that, the town abruptly ended. Unpopulated land stretched into the dark distance. Long grass undulated with the steady night wind.

I performed a quick three-sixty scan, saw no one watching and gambled that I had sufficiently merged with the starlit landscape to confuse anyone watching. I pulled my flight bag against my chest.

Fwooomp!

I vanished, checked for wires above, and gently kicked the ground. The wind swept me back the way I had come. I drew a BLASTER from a zippered pants pocket. The unit had burned up most of its battery power on the run from the cliff to the parked SUV, but I didn't need much for the return to the hospital. The wind did most of the work.

At the hospital I returned to the Emergency Entrance. The sally port joined a brick doorway into the building. I maneuvered to the flat roof where the doorway's brick wall joined the corrugated steel of the sally port. I located an exhaust pipe and grabbed it, then released my grip on the flight bag. It dropped into sight on the tarred flat roof. I stuffed the used BLASTER in a pocket and extracted a fresh one, my third of the evening. Satisfied that the bag could not be seen from the street, I maneuvered into position so that the steady wind pushed me against the rectangular exhaust pipe, holding me reliably anchored.

There, I waited.

SUE DIDN'T STAY LONG. Unable to see my watch, I could only guess that around twenty minutes passed before I heard the sally port exit open. A moment later, Sue's SUV appeared and turned onto the gravel street. She hurried away to resume her duties as hostess to a dozen hunters.

I remained stationary for what felt like another half hour, then launched from my perch. Beneath the overhang protecting the street entrance, a set of powered doors made entry to the ER easy. Inside, I found a layout similar to Essex County Memorial, albeit proportionally smaller. Recessed fluorescent lights illuminated sterile tile floors and white walls. A central desk with multiple workstations faced two examination beds. A curtain had been drawn around one of the beds. The other lay empty beside a wall of cabinets finished in warm brown and filled with medical supplies behind glass cabinet doors.

I checked to affirm that no one was in sight. Using a handrail to steer myself toward the split in the curtains, I disturbed the gray cloth briefly as I passed through.

Wally occupied the bed within. The protective rails on each side had been pulled up. His street clothing had been removed. A pale blue hospital gown draped his shoulders. The gown disappeared under white blankets. The head of the bed had been raised and he rested upright against stacked pillows.

My first real look at Wally in the light reinforced my initial impression of someone in his early twenties. He mustered about five feet and seven or eight inches, but I would have been surprised if he topped one-thirty on a scale. No wonder Danzig had been able to drag him across the ground with one hand and effortlessly throw him into the air. The kid had a narrow face with handsome proportional features under thick, long-ish black hair. In the stock teen movie, he would play the rogue outsider who hangs in until the last reel for a shot at getting the girl.

I watch way too many movies.

Wally rested alone in his cubicle. No one occupied the nurses' station or any other part of the ER that I could see.

I grabbed the side rail and edged to the head of the bed. An IV stand dispensed clear liquid down a line into Wally's right forearm. The young man's breathing remained labored, but he no longer gritted his teeth or pressed his eyes shut. The deep pain saturating his expression on the long drive into town had drained, leaving him pale but serene, probably thanks to a painkiller administered through the IV line.

I leaned over and spoke softly.

"Wally, keep your eyes closed."

He alerted to the sound of my voice. His eyelids quivered but remained lowered.

"Keep your shit together."

His brow furrowed.

"It's me. From the cliff."

His eyes popped open. He scanned the room. Seeing nothing made his eyes grow wider.

"Goddammit, kid. I told you to keep your eyes closed. I'm starting to see why you got thrown off a cliff. You don't listen very well."

"*Where are you?*" He grimaced. Talking hurt. "*How do you—?*"

"Shut up. Just listen. Got it? Nod if you got it."

He nodded.

"Close your eyes again. If anybody walks by, I want them to see you resting."

He squeezed his eyes.

"Relax, kid. Just relax. You look constipated. That's better. Now tell me, what were you doing up at that ranch? Whisper."

"*Looking for my Aunt Stephanie. Stephanie Cullen.*"

"What about the ranch owner? Tammy Day? Did you see her there?"

He shook his head, a tight minimal movement.

"How did you get past the gate?"

"*Bolt cutter—replaced all the padlocks with my own.*"

Smart kid.

"Was anybody else there—aside from those goons w. the cliff?"

Another headshake. Sweat beaded on his brow. He a(*gone.*"

"Who's all gone? Where?"

He tipped his head at the side of the room. A sink and countertop lined the wall beneath a row of cabinets.

"*Pants pocket.*"

The kid's clothing had been folded and placed on the countertop. I reached for the sink and gained a grip. The first pocket I probed yielded a wrinkled photograph. Who prints photos anymore? This one had been rendered on plain paper by an inkjet printer, which significantly lowered the quality. Folded several times, torn in one place, and taped back together, the image had some miles on it.

The photo had been taken on the open range beyond the tilled vegetable patch. I recognized the trailers in the distance, the garden a bit closer. A group of people stood closer still in a rough semi-circle. One of them held the remote control typical of a small consumer drone. A few of them looked up at the camera, which explained the location of the drone. The rest stared at the foreground.

Between the drone's eye and the ten people, a flat expanse of grass filled the lower half of the photo. On that grass, a series of black singed-grass circles dominated the image—a large central double circle with four smaller single circles at cardinal points. The graphic spanned at least forty feet.

I'd seen similar pictures. All of them struck me as absolute nonsense. Jokes, even. I lifted the photo back across to Wally who opened his eyes in time to see it levitate into view.

"Is your aunt in this photo?"

He slid his non-IV hand out from under the blanket and pointed at a woman with blonde-gone-gray hair, third from the right. Middle-aged. Fit. Decked out in bib overalls and wearing work gloves.

"Which one is Tammy Day?"

He shrugged.

"Do you know any of the other people?"

He shook his head. I pointed at the circles.

"Any idea what this is?"

He nodded.

"What?"

"*Proof.*"

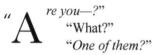

12

"Are you—?"
    "What?"
    "One of them?"

I chuckled. I knew exactly what he was asking. "Forget it, kid. I have a birth certificate from Waukesha County Wisconsin. Straight up natural human live birth."

"*Those can be—(wheeze)—faked.*"

"People who want you to believe bullshit conspiracy theories tell you that things like that can be faked. It's a lot harder in the real world. But no, I'm not from outer space."

"*Could'a fooled me.*"

"Well, I'm not. Neither are these circles. Any halfwit with a plumb line and a propane flame thrower can create these."

He nodded. At what, I wasn't sure, although I sensed that, like me, he wasn't buying the alien artwork.

"*Then how are you—this—?*" He waved his free hand at where I floated beside the bed.

"Bad accident in a government lab."

"*Bullshit.*"

"Dude. We had a deal. Don't make me come for your Metallica collection. Who are these people with your Aunt Stephanie?"

He huffed a sigh. "*I can't believe I'm sitting here talking—(wheeze)—to an inv—*"

A voice approaching the door cut him off.

"Wally, how are you doing?"

I slapped the photo against my chest and covered it with my hands to make it vanish. The woman in scrubs who assisted with Wally's emergency admission breezed through the curtains. Thankfully, she had been absorbed in her phone screen and missed the magic floating photo act. I quickly assessed my space options. I prepared to launch for the ceiling to avoid a collision, however the physician's assistant—according to the title embroidered on her scrubs above the name Maryanne—stopped at the foot of the bed.

"Breathing a little better?" He nodded. "Good. I'm going to let that fentanyl drip do its business, then we'll take you to Imaging and get some pictures of those ribs, okay?" Wally nodded again. "Can I get you anything? Ice water? Another blanket?" He shook his head. "Okay. Don't move. Don't talk. Be back in a jiff."

She hurried away.

"*Some people pronounce it gif,*" Wally muttered, cracking a loopy smile. Evidently the drip was working.

I gave it a moment, then said, "You were up at that ranch looking for something. Did you find anything?"

Head shake.

"How long were you there?"

"*Two days.*"

"Any idea who those goons were that tossed you off the cliff?"

This time he shrugged emphatically. A hard shake of the head ignited a gasp and grimace in pain.

"Kid, you're lying to me. Goon Leader said you don't listen. You had a run in with him before. Plus, when you heard them coming, you knew what to expect. Don't lie to me."

"*Not lying. That guy—Danzig—he saw me at the gate when—(wheeze)— I tried to get up there the first time—(wheeze)—he got up in my face—made me leave—(wheeze)—*"

"Okay, okay. Relax. You're gonna hurt yourself."

A figure moved past the curtain outside the examination bay. The sheriff's deputy stole a glance at Wally through the curtain slit before moving on. I made a guess that the deputy wanted to speak to the medical staff first, and that he would soon be in the room to chat with Wally.

"Cops are here. What are you going to tell him?"

Wally giggled. "*I'm gonna tell him I'm on drugs.*"

"Yeah. That'll go over well. Where did you get this photo?"

"*Martian Mike posted it.*" A goofy smile undermined my confidence in an already absurd answer, then Wally added, "*Podcaster. Abductee. He knows about—(wheeze)—ParaTransit.*"

"What do you know about ParaTransit?"

"*I know Aunt Steffie—(wheeze)—thought it was her ticket.*"

"Ticket for what?"

"*Off the planet.*"

13

I kept the photo. Wally protested but I asked him if he wanted the cops to confiscate the picture. I had no idea if they would, but it prompted Wally to place the photo in my care. I didn't mention that I planned to show it to the cop I married.

I told Wally I was leaving. He asked me to wait, but I didn't answer. I also didn't leave. I pushed off the floor, rotated, and grabbed the articulating fixture over his bed. Adopting a horizontal position, I lifted my legs clear of any visitor's path. Wally called after me several times, but the effort either hurt or interfered with the buzz seeping into his veins. He gave up.

The deputy returned with the physician's assistant, who was not enthusiastic about her patient being interrogated. The deputy ceded to the PA's wishes and kept it brief. He got Wally's full name, Walter Hadley Vandenlock, which I memorized, and his address, of which I was only able to retain Sterling, Colorado. I figured Andy could find his address if need be. When the deputy asked about the attack, the PA interrupted and argued that Wally, who did in fact tell the deputy he was on drugs, was in no condition to answer questions, especially questions with a bearing on a crime. The deputy said something about coming back in the morning and let himself out. The PA was joined by the man I'd seen earlier. They made a few practiced moves around the bed, disconnecting things, then wheeled Wally away to take pictures of his insides.

No one remained in the ER when the power doors to the outside opened and closed as if by themselves.

14

When I reappeared beside the parked Beechcraft Baron at Ekalaka Airport, I was mildly surprised to see that it was not quite midnight. It had been a long day. Hitting a mattress, even a motel mattress, would have been heavenly, but I had painted myself into a corner. I had no reservation at either of Ekalaka's motels, and given the late hour, I ruled out showing up for the bunk bed Sue had offered at her hunting camp. My plan to hop in the Baron and make the half hour flight into Dickenson, South Dakota remained viable, but the brief conversation with Wally tossed a wrench in the works.

New plan.

On the empty, windswept airport ramp, I dropped my flight bag into the Baron's cockpit. I swapped out the drained batteries in my second power unit for a fresh set and pocketed the third unit. I spent a few minutes studying my iPad, scanning the map and satellite images for the route back to Tammy Day's ranch. A direct overland route saved both time and battery power, but flight over unfamiliar terrain at night offered no guarantee I would find the ranch. The miles-long cliff face that marked the edge of the table-like land on which the ranch sat offered a landmark, but I might intersect it on either side of the ranch, and then I'd have to fly back and forth until I found the ranch trailers.

Less efficient, but more certain for navigation was a trip back down the highway to the locked gate, then up the dirt track. The trip would take longer and would be slowed even further by the fact that I'd lost my ski goggles.

I stashed the iPad and locked the flight bag in the plane. BLASTER in

44

hand, I prepared to lift off. One final problem nagged at me, and for this I had no easy solution.

In all the activity, I had not found time to call Andy. Midnight in Montana meant one a.m. in Essex. I deliberated over which was worse, a jarring phone call in the middle of the night or belated and potentially chilly conversation in the morning. Both put me in the doghouse.

I decided morning had the benefit of sunshine which stood a chance of warming her disposition, if only by degrees.

I vanished and kicked off into the night sky.

15

The night flight down highway 323 returned me to the locked gate, then up the rough track to the twin double-wide trailers of Tammy Day's ranch. Approaching above the treetops and fighting the relentless wind, I searched for parked ATVs, or lights, or some other hint of human presence.

I saw no one.

I cruised west and let the ranch yard sweep under me. Along the perimeter of the tilled garden plot, Wally's Saab tracks indented the grass. Multiple sets of lighter ATV impressions paralleled and eventually converged on his tire tracks.

Wally's escape route shot away from the ranch, then went through a series of shallow curves to the left where the ATV posse drove him toward the cliff. Where the tracks ended my next question was answered.

The Saab was gone.

Near the Saab crash scene, many tracks converged, among them heavy dual wheel impressions.

Danzig and his friends had returned and removed Wally's car. The dual wheels probably belonged to a tilt-bed tow truck. The Saab's nosedive had been caused by a small gulley. The damage must have been substantial. I doubted the vehicle would roll, much less run. I considered the implications of its removal, one of which was that the men who thought they killed Wally now knew, at the very least, his name and possibly his address, assuming Wally like most drivers kept proof of insurance in his glove compartment. If nothing else, a credit card and a few minutes on the internet would identify him via his license plate. For now, at least, they presumed him dead.

What happens when they find out he isn't?

And why the fast cleanup?

What was so important about making the Saab—and evidence of Wally's presence—disappear? And less important about leaving a dead body at the bottom of the cliff? Unless they also tried to find and dispose of Wally's body...

I doubted that. If his body posed a problem, they would have killed him topside and saved themselves the trouble. Throwing him over the edge offered the dual benefits of hiding his boot-induced injuries and suggesting that some dumb tourist had simply fallen to his death in the dark.

I circled back to the ranch and eased to a landing near the door to the trailer that Wally had abruptly abandoned.

No lock.

The padlock Wally had taken time to replace when he evacuated the trailer was gone. I glanced at the other trailer. In the starlight, there was no mistaking that both locks had been removed.

Both trailers were dark, but I made no assumptions about them being unoccupied. The steady wind tried to carry me, but I pulsed the BLASTER and eased up to the door. Not only the padlock had been removed; the hasp and staple latch were also gone.

A simple turn of the knob unlatched the solid wooden door.

I grabbed a rusted and bulbless light fixture beside the frame for stability, then eased the door open, keeping to one side in case someone with a shotgun had notions of castle doctrine and a shoot-first ask-later attitude.

The rich aroma of cooked chili wafted through the open door.

Chili?

The blend smelled good, aroused my stomach, and reminded me that my enchilada dinner had burned off hours ago.

I pushed the door fully open and waited. I waited a long time, then waited longer. People in hiding get impatient. They call out. They come to investigate. I was in no hurry and wanted anyone inside the trailer to make the first move.

Nothing happened.

I leaned into the doorway and found a kitchen shrouded in darkness. A long table dominated the space. Glints of reflected light complicated the table's surface, yet the blocked windows hoarded darkness and I could not make out what lay on the table.

Decision time.

Fwooomp!

I reappeared and dropped onto the trailer doorstep. No one shot me or cried out in surprise. I pulled my phone from my shirt pocket, lit up the flashlight app, and followed the light inside.

The kitchen table had been set for dinner. Not just dishes and utensils, but food as well. A bowl of fresh salad greens. A dish of washed and cut carrots. Fresh bread. Butter. Several bottles of wine stood at intervals, all of them open and partially decanted. Wine at various levels remained in wine glasses at each setting. One or two had been emptied, leaving a dime-sized disk of red at the bottom of the glass.

The scene induced the Goldilocks feeling that three bears would stomp into the trailer for dinner at any moment. But that wasn't quite right. This was a meal interrupted, not a dinner bell about to ring. On the stove at the back of the room, a large stainless-steel pot accounted for the chili scent. I moved around the table and waved my hand over the pot. The stove, an electric, was off. The burner beneath the pot was cold. Yet, the pot felt warm to the touch. Not hot. I placed my palm against the outside of the pot. Warm.

A small sitting room, crammed with a sofa, love seat, a fat recliner, and a coffee table, adjoined the kitchen. Two partially emptied wine glasses sat on the coffee table beside a book that had been placed face down. A Sudoku book rested on the arm of the recliner with a pen tucked in the spine's crease.

Opposite the sitting room, at the other end of the trailer, a narrow hallway led to several small bedrooms. I walked down the hall for a closer look. One of the beds had been made. Two were mussed as if recently occupied. I remembered that Wally had come flying out of the trailer with a wadded sleeping bag. These beds did not lack for blankets and quilts, so why the sleeping bag?

The bedroom at the end of the trailer had a doorless cardboard closet in one corner. Clothing jammed the narrow box, some of it feminine. A small chest of drawers shared the space. On it, I saw a well-used canvas bag designed for duty as a woman's purse. I opened the latch and found a cell phone, wallet, keys, and sundry items. I cracked open the wallet and found a Montana driver's license in a plastic sleeve. The woman in the photo had ponytail hair streaked with gray and intense, dark eyes. Despite a perturbed expression, she owned a genial, attractive face.

Tammy Lisette Day. Born December 27, 1959.

I pulled Wally's photo from my pocket and unfolded it.

There she was. Fourth from the left, standing beside the man who operated the drone. I used my shirttail to wipe down the wallet and returned it to the handbag, thinking that its presence poked a big hole in the *she's sunning herself in Clearwater* theory.

"What the hell...?" I said it aloud because the silence inside the trailer had become creepy beneath the steady, moaning wind outside.

On my way back to the front door, I stopped and wiped the side of the chili pot that I had touched. Clutter on the kitchen countertop caught my eye. I lifted my phone flashlight and scanned a man's wallet, two watches, several sets of keys, two more handbags and four cell phones lined up beside a toaster and a paper towel dispenser. Glittering at the center of this collection, I saw a small pile of rings, including obvious wedding rings, some of them expensive. I decided not to touch anything, but I made a guess that if I looked at the identification in each of the wallets, I'd see faces from the photo.

The scene slowly lost the feel of something interrupted and took on the aura of something abruptly abandoned. The problem was Wally. He said he'd been living here for two days, searching the place. I doubted that Wally had left this table set for a large group. The lettuce in the bowl was green and crisp. The chili, warm. The bread—I pressed the crust to see for myself —was soft and fresh. The table touches suggested that everyone in the photo —I counted three chairs on one side, four on the other, and two on each end —was about to break bread in fellowship. Except that didn't account for the temperature in the trailer, which was near or equal to the cold November outside air.

None of this had been here when Wally bailed out. The genial dinner had to have been staged in the last couple hours.

"Jesus, Earl, what have you gotten me into?"

I made one more pass on the kitchen and sitting room with my phone set to record video, then I killed the light. I headed for the door and started to pull it shut behind me when a realization hit me nearly as hard as Wally tumbling out of control over the cliff's edge. I fumbled my phone from my pocket and closed the trailer door, now keenly aware that the light from the phone could probably be seen for miles.

I relit my phone flashlight and turned it on the table.

Three plus four plus two.

Nine chairs.

I tugged the photo from my pocket and stepped inside to the kitchen table wjere I laid it out flat and held my phone over it. The group standing at the edge of the burned circles stared at the circles or up at me. The faces were not perfectly clear. I leaned close and looked at each face. Tammy Day was easy to spot. I searched down the line until I came to the woman at the end. The tenth figure. Even without crisp focus, there was no mistaking the face, the hair, the athletic body. The slightly haughty expression.

I refolded the photo and stuffed it in my shirt, then returned to the kitchen counter. Three of the four cell phones required passwords. The fourth swiped open. I touched the Gallery icon and stroked through a dozen photos before I found what I was looking for.

"Son of a bitch!"

I doused the phone light. Back on my standard screen, I punched the phone app and hit a recently called number.

Andy answered on the third ring.

"It's a little late, don't you think?"

I ignored the ambush.

"You're not going to believe this. I found her."

"Who?"

"Lillian."

16

TWO WEEKS AGO

"Who do we know that drives a Prius?"

Oh, crap.

I was about to answer, and not kindly, when something about the little silver slug rolling down our country road held my tongue. I placed the beer bottle on the side table and stood up. Andy saw it, too.

"Is she...?" Andy asked.

"I don't know." The car wandered across the centerline. "She doesn't look like she's going to—"

She didn't. The Prius, despite steadily diminishing forward speed, crunched over the end of our driveway and plowed into our mailbox without stopping. The aluminum box slammed down on the silver hood, bounced up the windshield and disappeared over the back of the car, which rolled at a ridiculously slow pace off the edge of the driveway and dropped into a shallow ditch lining the road. The car bumped once, then ran out of steam. The ponderous accident reminded me of the way lava consumes a house when the gods let Kilauea run amok in Hawai'i.

"Did she just take out our mailbox?"

"I believe she did," Andy replied. She pressed past me and exited the porch door. Dammit, I had replaced that mailbox after Andy's sister flattened it last winter.

The Prius rested in the ditch. A big crack scarred the front fascia. Loose pieces of plastic grille littered the lawn. The accident had been so sloth-like that none of the airbags triggered. The driver stopped the motor and peered ahead at the steering wheel.

Andy reached the car first. She pulled open the door. I caught up and looked over her shoulder.

"Who's this?"

Andy knelt and carefully touched the arm of the driver. The response was instant and violent. A sharp, high-pitched cry telegraphed the wild swing of an arm, which caught Andy near her face and sent her staggering backward into me.

"Hey!" I shouted, kicking into gear a violent impulse that had more to do with someone striking the woman I love than the actual weight of the blow or threat potential of the attacker.

"Will, no." Andy clutched my arm. "Stay back."

When the red in my vision cleared, I saw why. The child driver wasn't more than eight or nine years old. He tucked skinny arms and legs into jeans, bright yellow sneakers, and an eye-searing Day-Glo green Seattle Seahawks jersey. He had short, light brown hair, a high forehead with a prominent widow's peak, and a rash of freckles across the bridge of his button nose. Everything about the boy appeared ordinary except for the way he glared at the center of the steering wheel and maintained an ear-piercing shriek.

Aside from the woefully underaged driver, the car was empty. I spotted a red backpack on the right front seat, a water bottle embossed with some sort of cartoon character in the cupholder, and a litter of scores of tiny squares of paper, no more than an inch by an inch, all over the floor on the passenger side.

Looking closer, I saw that the driver wasn't staring at the steering wheel. He stared instead at his busy hands, which shuffled a short stack of the paper squares. As he arranged and rearranged the squares, the shriek died to a howl, then faded into a high-pitched hum.

"Will, I think he may be on the spectrum."

"On drugs?"

"No." Andy pressed me to take a step back. She correctly sensed my anger over the mailbox destruction and the blow to her face. She placed her palm on my chest and spoke softly. "Autism spectrum disorder."

"Autistic?"

She touched her finger to her lips and gestured for me to take additional steps back. Moving carefully, she turned and knelt beside the open door.

"Honey," she said sweetly, "my name is Andy. What's yours?"

"My name is Andy."

The response came without eye contact.

"My name is Mrs. Stewart. What's your name?"

"My name is Mrs. Stewart." The boy shuffled his papers, turning them, squaring them up, moving one from the top to the bottom and another from the center to the top. His deft touch did not falter or fumble. From the scores of similar squares littering the passenger-side footwell, I assumed he had practice.

Andy rose and backed away. She pulled her phone from the back pocket of her jeans.

"I don't have training for this. I'm calling Sandy."

"Dee, if this is Lillian's car, then where's Lillian?"

"Lillian." The child driver echoed the name. Andy and I looked at each other with the same unasked questions on our lips. Did he just repeat? Or did the name mean something to him?

17

Andy's call to Sandy Stone's mobile phone failed to connect. She then dialed the administrative office at James Madison Elementary School. Twenty minutes remained in the school day before the bell would release the children to their buses. Andy explained the situation, and after a series of relayed messages, Sandy arranged for someone to take the last minutes of her afternoon kindergarten class. She arrived soon thereafter and parked in our driveway. Nearly half an hour had passed since the accident and the boy at the wheel had neither budged, nor looked sideways, nor ceased shuffling the paper squares.

"Hi Will," Sandy tossed me a friendly but clipped greeting, walking while tugging her blonde hair into a scrunchie-secured bun at the back of her head, all business. Beloved by her students, and no doubt the crush of every boy in the elementary school, Sandra Stone is a woman who can turn heads as effortlessly as my wife and who thinks about as much of that talent as my wife. There was no mistaking her professional focus, which she riveted to the boy behind the wheel. Without a second glance in my direction, she said, "I think you should wait in the house."

I backed away while Andy conferred with Sandy. Both women fixed their attention on the child still strapped in the driver's seat of the Prius. During the wait, Andy had informed me that in addition to Sandy's certification in early childhood education, she neared completion of her master's degree in special needs education.

I could not argue my summary dismissal. I did not have a clue. Not about autism. Not about what it means to see the world from within autism's boundaries. Not about reaching across those boundaries.

A cold beer waited for me on the porch. Well, a cool beer, by the time I retreated and took up a ringside seat. On my front lawn, Sandy kneeled on the cut grass and leaf litter beside the open car door. She stayed there for a long time while Andy watched. Talking, I presume. Trying to get the child to speak, perhaps, although from where I sat, the boy never lifted his eyes from his busy paper shuffling. Twice I saw his mouth move in short bursts, but I couldn't be sure he wasn't simply repeating Sandy's words.

Just about the time I wondered if there may be no alternative to physical removal of the kid from the car, he abruptly unbuckled his seatbelt, swung his legs out and dropped onto the grass. He stood for a moment until Sandy rose and walked toward the house. Without a word, without a gesture, without offering a hand, Sandy led the boy across the lawn. Andy remained behind and watched them from beside the car.

I prepared to make myself scarce as Sandy and the boy approached, but the two-person parade bypassed the porch in favor of the back door. I heard them enter, then I heard the downstairs bathroom door close. A moment later the toilet flushed.

Ah...that's how you lure a kid out of a car.

Sandy pulled back a chair at our dining room table. The boy seated himself and quickly went to work on his paper squares. His back obstructed my view, so I could not see if he continued shuffling them, or if he now used the tabletop to arrange them.

I slipped out the porch door, careful not to let it slam. When I reached Andy, still at the scene of the accident, she concluded a phone call and tucked her mobile into the back pocket of her jeans.

"The car is registered to Dr. Lillian Farris." Lillian Farris was on the fingers on the hand that counted people who knew about *the other thing.* I thought of her as the middle finger.

I strolled around the rear fender. My relatively new mailbox lay on the ground, torn from its mounting, but amazingly undamaged. The post, however, was toast. I moved it onto the lawn to await repairs. "These are New Mexico plates."

"That's where it's registered. Her address is in a town called Wagon Mound."

"Sounds about right."

Andy moved to the right side of the car and opened the passenger door. She pulled the red backpack off the front seat and unzipped it. She rummaged inside.

"Anything good?"

"Energy bars. An orange. Um…a lot of…stuff."

"What kind of stuff?" I joined her for a look.

"I would have said toys, but more like random objects. Some Legos. Bottle caps. Pencils. A snow globe. A foam stress ball." She held up a green plastic Army man that might have come from a set I had as a kid. This relentless soldier carried a flame thrower on his back and hunched ready to spray fire from its nozzle. "He doesn't have a phone in here. This looks like —I'm not sure if this is the word—a *comfort* collection?"

"Is that a Barbie doll?"

"Malibu Barbie." Andy held up the small plastic woman, then glanced at me. "What? I had one during my 'I want to be a blonde' phase."

A few weeks ago, Andy looked good as a blonde, but I knew better than to say so more than once. "I guess he brought his girlfriend. Do you see a note?"

She checked the backpack pockets and shook her head. She leaned into the car. When she stood up again, she handed me one of the paper squares.

"What the hell? This looks like—"

"Pieces of a map," she said. "These are pieces of a road map—cut into squares. Must be a hundred of them."

I held up the piece of paper she'd given me. A red line angled across a white background. The number 26 had been printed beside the red line. I recognized it as the mileage for a single segment of road. Near one edge, three letters remained of the name of a town that had been cut off.

"Why have a paper map at all? The car has a navigation system."

"You're assuming he can relate to an electronic navigation system."

"I don't see how he could relate to a bunch of sliced up squares."

"That's because you don't think in pictures, dear."

I wasn't sure that was true. More and more frequently, in the heat of a moment, *the other thing* that makes me vanish also made me move. Not because of a verbal command forming in my head, but because an instant impulse generated in my mind imprinted meaning without words. I suddenly wondered if I had experienced an alternate thought process in the same way an infant speaks its first word—and if by contrast the boy who had driven this car was fluent in the same language.

"Are you telling me this kid drove here from New Mexico following a puzzle-piece map?"

"No," Andy said. "Not New Mexico."

"Why not?"

"Because the range of a car like this is probably only six hundred miles, and I don't think he stopped for gas. He doesn't have a wallet. And I didn't find cash or a credit card in the backpack."

"Jesus, even so—do you think an autistic child who can barely reach the pedals drove this car six hundred miles? How is that possible?"

Andy pondered for a moment, then said, "I'm not saying he drove that far. Or anywhere near that far. But driving is pictures, Will. Sight pictures. Mirror pictures. Traffic flow pictures. I don't know. Maybe."

"Dee, you've got adults in this county who barely know the traffic laws. You can't suggest that the kid knows how to read signs, lane markings, and God knows what."

"Why not? If he rides in a car at all, he has seen the sight pictures, possibly over and over. There are people, not just children, but adults with autism who remember every image they've ever seen. If that boy has been riding around in cars for a few years, he's seen more than enough to recognize the patterns. I'm not saying he did, or he didn't. I'm saying we need to open our minds to the possibility. He could have driven a few miles to get here, or a few hundred miles."

"I don't know much about Lillian, but one thing I'm sure of is that I never heard her say she had a child."

"Lillian's old enough that he might be a grandchild."

"So, where is she? And why does this child have her car?"

Andy gazed at the house.

"I need to ask Sandy to take care of him and then I need to get to the station. There might be an Amber Alert out on this boy." She took back the slip of paper and laid it on the floorboards, then closed the passenger-side door. "I'll get a tow out here for the vehicle. We better not touch anything else."

18

"He was hungry," Sandy said.

We found the boy seated at our kitchen table. An open sleeve of graham crackers, a jar of peanut butter and a bear-shaped plastic bottle of honey had been arranged in an assembly line in front of the boy. He slid a cracker from the sleeve, snapped off a perfect rectangular segment, applied a layer of peanut butter, then drew a careful spiral of honey on the slab before devouring it. Eat. Repeat.

"How did you know what he'd eat?" Andy asked.

"He helped himself. You must be very predictable people because he went straight to the correct cabinets."

Thinking in pictures.

Andy drew Sandy into the dining room for a quiet conversation about taking charge of the child, at least until Andy could investigate the matter. Sandy declined. I expected her to cite her obligation to teach kindergarten in the morning, but she gave Andy the name of a social worker for Essex County, a woman who, Sandy said, had experience with autism and who would be far better equipped to see to the boy's care. She activated her phone to make the call.

Andy abruptly hurried into the kitchen. She handed me a large Ziploc bag. "Do me a favor and gather up all those paper map squares."

"I thought you didn't want to disturb the evidence."

"I didn't. But you're right, I think it *is* evidence. I also think it's more important that it stays with the boy. And the backpack. Bring that, too."

I did as commanded.

Following consumption of a full sleeve of crackers and a quarter of a jar of peanut butter, the boy returned to shuffling his short deck of paper squares. I gathered up the map pieces from the car, finding them not just on the passenger floorboards, but under the seat, behind the seat, and even in the back seat. I had the feeling these pieces had been discarded. The child seemed obsessed with the organization of the squares he had in hand but appeared to give little or no consideration to the pieces he left strewn in the car.

Back in the house again, I laid the backpack on the dining room table near the boy. He paid it no attention. I handed Andy the Ziploc bag. She stuffed it into the backpack.

"I half expected you to take that to the station and spread out a puzzle for the night shift to work on."

"I don't think I have to. I think the answer is right there." She pointed at the back of the boy's head. "We just have to find a way in."

19

NOW

"Are you saying Lillian is in Montana?"
"I don't know about now. Definitely was. And she had the child with her. Our mailbox warrior."

"When?"

"I don't know." I told Andy about the photo, which meant telling her about the kid and the cliff, which meant describing the trip to the hospital and the decision to return to the ranch. I told her about the find in the trailers, culminating with a look at the cell phone Gallery where I found a picture of Lillian with the eight-year-old boy standing at the picturesque cliff's edge. Andy listened without asking questions, which wasn't to say she didn't have them.

"The group photo has no date stamp," I said. "The landscape looks about the same in the picture as it does now, but that doesn't mean much. It's been dry in these parts all summer. Could be a few days ago. Could be a few months ago."

"And this picture has the young man they tried to kill?"

"No, it's a picture of the people from the ranch and...I'm going to say circles. Like, you know...crop circles."

"Alien crop circles?"

"I think they're meant to look that way, yes."

"Great. Explains why Lillian was there." Andy's low opinion of Dr. Lillian Farris's predisposition to UFO lore oozed from her reply. My wife is not prone to prejudice, but where Lillian is concerned, she cuts no slack. Even after Lillian helped recruit the billionaire, Spiro Lewko, as an ally in exposing a mass murderer, Andy nurtured a cold shoulder for Lillian Farris.

"I need to understand this, Will. Lillian is in a crop circle photo? With Earl's friend and the child who drove her car?"

"No, the kid's not in the crop circle photo. I found him in a different photo. But, yes, our crazy Lillian is in a photo with Earl's—I don't know what to call her—in Montana, Tammy Day—which strikes me as one hell of a coincidence—"

"You might want to chat with Earl about that." Andy considers coincidence about as likely as polar bears on Miami Beach.

"—our Lillian who gave her car to an autistic eight-year-old boy and told him to drive from God-knows-where to our house in Essex."

"Stop calling her 'Our Lillian.' Sweetheart, what's that sound?"

"The wind. It's crazy up here on this plateau. I think it's getting stronger." I paused for a moment. We both listened to the steady howl racing unseen through the night sky above me. "Hey, listen. I'm sorry about this late call. It's been a long day...and night."

"Is that young man okay? I can't believe you caught him like that."

"His luck, not mine. He hit me like a ton of bricks."

"Any idea who those men were?"

"No clue."

"Have you spoken to Earl?"

"Not yet. What do I tell him? That his friend and a bunch of her friends got picked up by aliens?"

"Don't be silly."

"That's what it looks like."

"No. That's what someone is trying to make it look like. The question is why? And where are they?"

"And what does Lillian know about it? And does that have anything to do with her dumping an autistic child—"

"Will!"

"Sorry. *Sending* an autistic child to us with no explanation, no information, no clue what's going on."

We ping-ponged questions back and forth. Neither of us had answers. Eventually we ran out of questions and let the wind sing on the line.

After a moment Andy said, "Miss you."

"You, too. Again…sorry. How was dinner?"

Andy released a sigh. "I go into those things thinking it will be the same as ever. It's hard to wrap my head around how much has changed. Daddy asked me about work—do you believe that? Like he was interested. He's up in arms about the FBI Academy. He wants to start calling Senators."

"Maybe you should let him…"

"Oh, God, no!" I waited for her to say more, but she let the topic slide.

"Peace with your parents. Wow. Maybe there's hope for the Middle East."

"You'll see for yourself. We're on for dinner again tomorrow—er, tonight."

"Don't take this the wrong way, but I'm surprised your parents even notice you."

Andy chuckled. "Oh, true that. I am *not* the star of the show. That would be Grace and Alex. That little boy never stops smiling."

"Why would he? He has five women doting over him."

"Grandma and Grandpa cannot get enough of him. I don't remember my dad being such a big teddy bear…ever. Not with us, anyway. And I am shocked out of my socks at how he's treating Melanie. Like a long-lost daughter."

"Who is this guy? Did you check for a pod version of him in the basement?"

"I should."

I wanted to ask how Andy felt about being around infants. We had recently leaped the decision threshold about having children of our own. Just as abruptly, the decision had been put on hold when Andy abruptly joined the FBI Academy. With that opportunity up in smoke—a wound still bleeding and a disappointment my wife was still processing—the question became a question again. The only problem was that we were so busy not discussing her feelings about the lost FBI career path it was hard to find time to not discuss children.

"I should be home in plenty of time for dinner. Hell, I'm thinking about going back to the airport right now and just heading east. I could be home by dawn."

"Don't you dare. How many times have you warned me about flying with fatigue? Besides, you can't."

"Can't what?"

"Can't come home."

"Why not?"

Andy sent a patient sigh down the line to my ear. "Will, you can't leave.

62

We need to know what Lillian was doing with Earl's friend—and if possible, why she sent that poor child to us in her car. And you have to go back to that hospital and get that young man out of there."

"What? Why?"

"Don't you see? Someone he can identify killed him once. What's going to happen when they find out he's sitting in a hospital room mending broken ribs?"

20

_____

I cut across open country. Finding the smalltown lights of Ekalaka in the dark posed far less challenge than finding Tammy Day's ranch in the dark. On top of that, the route to town benefitted from a twenty- to thirty-knot tailwind. Except for minor course adjustments, I could almost let the wind carry me.

I intended to go high. Added altitude would reveal the town from farther away, and therefore the most direct route. I had just cleared treetop height when lines embossed in the grass below caught my eye. The lines came from the lane that connected the ranch to the road. I recognized the pattern, brought into relief by starlight and shadows.

Tracks from the tow truck with a spread of ATVs escorting it.

They didn't return to the highway.

It made sense and I should have thought of it sooner. The gate remained locked when I arrived the second time. Unless the ATV riders duplicated Wally's trick of using bolt cutters on the lock and replacing it with one of their own, that lock still belonged to Wally. The ATVs might have managed rough passage through the gulley on either side of the gate, but not the tow truck.

Danzig and his gang chose an overland route, the same as me. Their wheels crushed the grass creating indentations that were clearly visible in the silver starlight. Following their trail proved surprisingly easy.

I leveled off at roughly two hundred feet. The tire impressions guided me. The tailwind carried me. A mile slipped by, then two. Somewhere in the third mile, a small herd of something large and fast bounded across the wheel marks. Deer? Antelope? I wasn't sure what kind of wildlife wandered into the sights of the hunters lodging with Sue and Rich, but it seemed abundant. Near a smudge of trees, I heard wild yipping, the call and cry of coyotes either at play or on the hunt.

The tire-track trail occasionally disappeared. In spots where the grass was sparse and short, or where the trail cut through stands of pine or dipped through shallow gravel gullies, the lines faded. When that happened, I angled the BLASTER upward and gained height for a longer view which revealed the trail again. The course remained consistent. Like me, the vehicles followed a route toward town, reinforcing Andy's worry. I had no idea how Danzig might discover Wally's admission to the ER, but I wasn't willing to bank on him not finding out. Andy's suggestion that I make the kid disappear from his hospital bed—literally—suddenly resembled a mission. I had no idea whether his condition would allow it, nor did I have a clue what I would do with him after making him vanish.

About seven miles into the journey, rising to cross a wide hill, a cluster of ranch lights appeared. For a moment, I revised the idea that Danzig and his crew were returning to town and jumped to the new conclusion that they had operated from another ranch. But the wheel marks deviated, using the hill to shield their passage from the small ranch. The path made a wide arc that resumed its heading toward town after skirting the ranch line of sight.

I wondered if I might catch up to this caravan. I increased the power until the air through which I passed began to sting my eyes. Combined with the tailwind, I estimated my speed at close to forty knots.

Another set of rolling hills approached. The tracks followed a serpentine path through the hills, weaving between the heights rather than cresting them. I assumed they had driven without headlights, since the winding path suggested an effort to avoid detection. Night vision equipment isn't hard to obtain. And the sky had not only cleared, giving the starlight full strength, but a quarter moon climbed the eastern horizon, adding definition and shadow to the landscape.

Twice the trail encountered narrow gravel roads. Both times I feared the ATVs would turn onto the roads and terminate the trail. In one sense it did. The dual-wheel indentations from the tow truck ceased at the second road. The tow truck had been dispatched. The ATVs, however, continued their overland route.

My luck ran out at the third road crossing. Rough and rugged land sprawled to the east. To the west, open grassland gave way to tilled fields with fences that blocked overland passage. Where the gravel road intersected the trail the tire tracks ended. The gravel road cut a line directly north, putting the town's glow, still five or six miles away, about forty-five degrees to my right. I followed the road for a mile or two, thinking I might have to resume navigation overland if this road did not veer toward town. Then the road curved right. Rugged hills dotted with lodgepole pines closed in.

The town glow rose from behind high terrain ahead. On the other side of that higher elevation, the Baron remained chained to the ramp at the Ekalaka Airport and the town spread out to the north of the airport.

Just as I angled the power unit upward for more altitude and a better look, I heard the distinctive sound of turboprop engines. A set of navigation lights broke the black ridgeline and ascended into the night sky.

I cut the power unit and let myself glide and listen. The throb of twin props pulling hard reached me. A red navigation light mounted on the right wing of the departing aircraft traced the steep climb, accompanied by the red rotating beacon on top of the aircraft and white strobe lights on the belly. The combination told me they were turning southeast.

Rising from the runway several miles away, it was impossible to determine the aircraft type or size. Given the late hour and the near total absence of traffic in and out of Ekalaka, I could think of no reason to believe it was anybody but Danzig and his ATV cavalry.

I aimed the BLASTER directly up and pulled the slide control into full reverse thrust, inducing a sharp descent. The empty road below raced to meet me. Too fast. I switched to a sharp blast of power to arrest the descent, then pulsed back and forth between thrust and reverse thrust to get my feet near the ground again. A gust of wind shoved me forward across the gravel.

Fwooomp!

I reappeared, dropped into the full grip of gravity, and staggered foolishly for another ten feet before coming to a halt.

I jammed the silent BLASTER into a pocket and pulled out my phone.

"Pick up pick up pick up…" I muttered as the call contemplated whether to connect or not. "C'mon!"

"Will?"

"Dee! Listen, I need you to do something as fast as you can possibly do it."

"Wha—?"

"Go get your laptop. Keep me on the line. Go."

I heard a sharp intake of breath, then jostling of the phone.

"I'm going. What's happening?"

"I need you to get online. Tell me when you're ready."

She didn't speak for a moment. I pictured her hustling out of bed with the phone to her ear, finding the bedroom light, then hurrying down the hall. I heard her on the stairs. Her bare feet drummed the wooden steps. I gave my wife credit for not peppering me with questions or pointing out the time. A moment later, she spoke. "Opening it now…okay…ready."

"Go to ForeFlight.com."

"I'm putting you on speaker." I heard the phone bump the dining room table. A moment passed. "Got it."

"Click on login. Upper right." I gave her my login and password. "All lower case."

"That's your password?"

"Don't judge. Let me know when you're in."

"I'm in." Andy types fast.

"Okay, click on my name in the upper right and choose the first item in the pulldown. I forget what it is."

"ForeFlight Web."

"Yeah, that's it."

"Okay. I'm in a new screen."

"Left side, choose Maps."

"Done."

"There's a search box in the upper right corner. See it?"

"Yes."

"Type in 97M. Nine seven mike. Then hit search."

She took a few seconds, then said, "Okay, I see it. Ekalaka, right?"

"Right. Zoom in so you're looking at a span of about fifty miles across the screen. Do you see any little blue triangles? They should be moving. Or will be as the data streams. It might take a minute."

"I don't see any."

"Anywhere on the screen? Little blue triangles?"

"Will, I don't see any little blue—"

"Wait! I forgot. Go to the menu on the left, and near the top, to the right of the menu, there's a little icon for opening a preferences menu. See it?"

"Hang on…yes. Okay. It's open. It's got Aeronautical, Street Map, Aerial Map—"

"That's it, that's it. Look down the right column. Do you see an item listed as 'Traffic?'"

"Hang on…yes. Traffic."

"Click to activate it."

"Done."

"Okay, now go back to the map. See any of those triangles?"

"No."

"Just give it a minute."

We waited. I felt mild pain in my right ear and realized I was pressing the phone hard against my head.

"I see one!"

"Good. Hover the mouse over it and click on it. A data box will appear."

"Yes."

"What does the first line say?"

"DAL2953 then 27,975. Is that what you're looking for?"

"No. Which way is that going?"

"Looks like west."

"No, that's Delta Airlines flight 2953. Is there another one? Should be going southeast, away from the town."

I waited. The wind moaned across the sky overhead. I felt an irrational fear that it might carry away my connection to Andy.

"Yes. Got one. N881CG and 11, 250...now 12,000."

I closed my eyes to picture the data box. The second line gives heading and speed. "Read the third line."

"97M to KSUX."

"Gotcha!" I lifted the phone away from my head and threw a triumphant shout to the wind.

"Will, what is this?"

"This is the reason I'll miss dinner again. I'm going to Sioux City, Iowa."

21

I hit a wall.

    After my conversation with Andy ended, I launched in the direction of the airport, due east of my landing spot on the road into town. I fought the strong southerly wind, essentially flying on an angle through the air so that the resulting path would take me where I wanted to go. Cresting the high ground bordering the airport, I dipped as low as possible to let the ridge shield me from the wind. I swept down onto the airport ramp where Earl Jackson's Beechcraft Baron sat alone. The ag operation hangars remained sealed. The ramp lay empty. I looked for the ATVs but saw no sign of them or the tow truck, not that I expected to find the latter. I looked for parked vehicles of any kind. There were none. The airport had hangars plus the big crop-dusting operation. Any one of the buildings could have housed the ATVs, but two things told me that was unlikely. First, I had a hunch that the ATV cavalry was as much a visitor to this small Montana town as I was. Second, hangar space on this airport was at a premium. I didn't think it likely that a local owner would have room to spare.

    I circled the airport hangars and saw no sign of activity. I returned to the ramp, landed beside the Baron and reappeared. I climbed the wing and ducked into the pilot's seat, sealing the door against the cold night air. I pulled my iPad from my flight bag and opened the same ForeFlight application that I had roused Andy out of bed to view. On the map page, I tapped in a route from Ekalaka Airport, designated 97M, to Sioux City Gateway Airport. Traffic in the form of small blue triangles appeared on the map. I searched the magenta line connecting my two map points and found my target. The little blue triangle traveled steadily across the screen. Touching the triangle activated a data box with the same N-number Andy had given me.

N881CG 19,075'
Hdg: 106° Speed 187kts
97M to KSUX, ETA 04:28 CST
ECG C-23B

"Okay…what's a C-23B?" I closed ForeFlight and opened Google. A moment later a Wikipedia entry for a twin turboprop cargo plane built by Short Brothers answered my question. It answered another question as well. The stubby flying box looked fully capable of hauling four small All-Terrain Vehicles.

"Dummies." I sat back and thought about the fact that these operators, who were up to no good if murder falls in that category, had failed to list their aircraft as 'Private' which would have prevented their flight data from being made public and appearing on the ForeFlight screen. Stupidity or arrogance. Maybe they thought their activities were sufficiently cloaked and considered the added step of concealing their aircraft identity superfluous.

A chill dug into my bones. I realized a minute or two had passed and I had been sitting and staring at nothing. The cockpit was the same temperature as the night air outside. I had been in the vanished state for the better part of the past hour and hadn't noticed the cold.

Fwooomp! I disappeared again. The familiar sound in my head signaled gravity's release. A cool sensation flowed over my entire body, a sensation that was warm in comparison to the chill burrowing into my skin. I lost contact with the seat, so I tugged my seatbelt over my lap and cinched myself down.

I slipped the iPad out of its case and popped it into the mount on the control yoke. By the light of the iPad screen, I found the checklist for engine startup, thinking I would launch in the direction of Sioux City and tap a flight route into the Garmin 750 as I climbed.

I made it three items down the checklist before I remembered that I had not unchained the aircraft from the ramp. Nor had I refueled.

Stupid.

Exactly the breed of insidious errors that sprout from deep fatigue.

The momentary blank stare. The chill. The screw ups. And the fact that in a couple hours the sun I'd already seen rise once today would rise again all added up to one inescapable conclusion.

I shut down the iPad, tilted my seat back, and closed my eyes. I had never tried sleeping in the fully vanished state out of fear that I might float off the bed to the ceiling and then unconsciously cause myself to reappear, dropping with bad results. Being strapped in the pilot's seat of the Baron solved that problem while the cool sensation offered sufficient insulation against the cold. Relaxing without the influence of gravity was new. I consciously released tension in my arms and legs. I wasn't sure what to do with my limbs, so I tucked my hands in the front pockets of my pants and pushed my toes under the rudder pedals. Around the time I convinced myself that this experiment was idiotic, and I would never fall sleep in this manner, pre-dawn light broke through the cockpit window and my watch reported four hours had passed.

22

TWO WEEKS AGO

"What the hell was all that?"

Andy looked up at me with a mix of innocence, tolerance, and a hint of knowing something I didn't.

I found her at her desk in her assigned police department cubicle. This was my first visit with Andy at work since our return to Essex. My first impression jarred me. The cubicle seemed small and pedestrian, diminished by the fact that she had left it behind to join a training class at the FBI Academy in Quantico, Virginia. Returning to her job as a detective in a smalltown police department felt like a step backward.

"You mean the *Recallistas*?"

"The what?" I slid into the only chair that space allowed in her tiny office.

"*Recallistas.* That's what we're calling them."

I popped my head above the divider and looked out the police department's front windows. A line of half a dozen citizens strolled up and down the sidewalk in front of the building. They held up signs, waving them at the few cars that glided past the cop shop at precisely twenty-five miles per hour, the posted limit.

RESTORE INTEGRITY.

REBUILD TRUST.

RECALL DUNN WITTEN & STROPP.

I might have paid no attention to this tiny demonstration if not for another sign that caught my eye when I drove past. The group had set up a table between the sidewalk and the street. Two people sat at the table which displayed a banner that said, "Sign Recall Petition HERE." Below that, another sign had been taped to the table.

REMOVE DET. STEWART.

"When were you going to tell me?"

Andy dropped her eyes to the paperwork on her desk and needlessly squared up the corners of a short stack.

"That? It's nothing."

"That doesn't look like nothing. How long has it been going on?"

"It just started a few days ago. After that thing on Fox."

We didn't see the interview ourselves, but Tom Ceeves called late in the evening when it happened. The President of the United States did a tele-phone interview with one of his favorite evening "entertainment" hosts on Fox News. Tom learned of it from a burst of urgent calls he received. During the interview, the leader of the free world was prompted to comment on the recent assassination attempt against him. The sniper attack on the President had not quite sunk to the level of Old News, as much as Andy and I wished it would. Nor would it, apparently, because the President told his commen-tator friend that there were "many, many unanswered questions, many bad actors involved..." The commentator specifically asked if the President referred to the police officer suspected in the shooting attempt. What should have been a clear and resounding no came out instead as "...you know who I mean, everybody knows, bad, bad actors, terrible people, with the election coming everybody knows..." Despite the incoherence the implication rang clear as a bell. The suggestion that the President's political opponents tried to have him killed blew up in the media. Worse, he once again gave his ardent supporters cause to believe the shooter was my wife.

"He's probably not talking about me," Andy told her boss on the phone that night.

Tom and I cried *Bullshit!* at the same instant.

Our point was proven when, for the next two days, the department fielded relentless calls from reporters and journalists. Someone found Andy's work phone number and the mobile phone she carried on the job had to be decommissioned.

"And now this?" I asked, pointing in the direction of the group patrolling the sidewalk outside. "Dee, that's your name on their sign out front!"

"These things blow over."

"That sign isn't hand-painted. It's professionally printed."

"Meaning?"

"Someone is spending money to see you gone."

"Well, they'll have to go through the chief."

"Technically, that's not correct," a voice on the other side of the cubicle divider chimed in. Mae Earnhardt, the department's senior dispatcher stepped up and folded her arms on the divider wall. She propped her button chin on her wrist. "Their tactic is to force a recall election of Dunn, Witten and Stropp."

I made a blank face and shrugged, which earned a disapproving look from Mae. "City Council, Will. Where's your civic pride? In fact, I think Stropp represents your district."

"They can't just recall people like that, can they?"

"They're not supposed to. A recall is meant to remove someone from office for cause. Corruption. Malfeasance. That sort of thing. This is a political recall. This same baloney is being tried with school boards all over. They're using recall elections as a means of bypassing elections to gain political leverage in local governing. I also think it's meant to mobilize political support for the President's reelection. In any case, this isn't new. It was a tactic used during the Civil Rights Movement."

"Why those three?"

"Because they're the Council representatives on the Fire and Police Commission. And on that commission, they constitute a majority. Which means they can remove someone." She cast a pointed look at Andy.

"Don't be ridiculous, Mae. No one's going to fire me because some idiots think I tried to assassinate the President."

I looked to see if certainty in Andy's eyes matched her declaration. It was iffy.

"I don't know if they can get away with it, but they're using you as a rallying cry, Andy. And they're getting a wink and nod from The White House. It's wrong. It's a lie. But they don't care. They think they can knock three people off the City Council in one stroke and replace them with their own. Essex has been surprisingly apolitical. If they pull this off, it will polarize the council." Mae shook her head. "I'd take this seriously. I really would."

On that dark note, Mae departed. Andy's eyes met mine. "Mae worries too much."

"If that's true, then I do, too. You and I both know there's a fringe element that believes you tried to kill the President. Leslie warned us to be aware."

"No, she said we didn't have cause to worry."

"She lied to make us feel better." Andy started to speak, but I cut her off. "Stop. I know what you're going to say. I know you will try to downplay this. I know that the more I worry about it, the more you will pretend it's nothing. Therefore, I will make you a promise. I won't go off the deep end if you will promise to be realistic. Promise?"

"Promise." She squeezed my hand. "Now let me show you something." She lifted a sheet of paper from her desk and passed it to me.

The photocopied image of a newspaper article displayed the face of a young woman. Despite being a stranger to me, the woman's features looked familiar. The headline reported a highway fatality. The victim's name was Delta Marianne Freemont, aged twenty-seven. The accident took place in Santa Barbara, California. A drunk driver ran a stoplight and struck the woman's car, killing her instantly.

The face teased me. I felt like I should know her. "Who is this?"

"Keep reading."

I skimmed the paragraph describing the drunk driver, his many previous offenses, and the tragic—at least to me—fact that he was not injured in the collision. The next paragraph mentioned that a three-year-old child was also injured in the fatal crash—the woman's son, who was not named in the article. The story described the woman as divorced, with sole custody of the child, and went on to say that authorities were attempting to locate the boy's father.

"Why does she look familiar to me?"

Andy didn't answer. She lifted a second document from her desk and handed it to me. This wasn't a newspaper story, but rather a printed screen capture of an internet story. The byline named a Santa Barbara television station. The headline salaciously announced, "Deadbeat Dad Refuses Custody of Autistic Son." The lead paragraph explained that police located Nathan Reed Freemont in Nevada after conducting a search following the death of his divorced wife. The story repeated the details of the woman's fatal car crash, reiterated the guilt of the drunk driver who faced manslaughter charges, and declared that the fate of the surviving child was in doubt because the biological father refused to assume responsibility for the boy.

I glanced at the mother's photo in the first story. The resemblance to the underaged driver of Lillian's Prius clicked as if I'd thrown a switch.

"Is this the child? The same one?"

Andy lifted her eyebrows. "We're working on verifying it. Did I tell you that his name is Boyd?"

"Boyd? Seriously? One consonant away from Boy?"

"Ellen Brooking, Sandy's social worker colleague, found the name inscribed on the tag inside that Seattle Seahawks t-shirt he's been wearing day and night. She succeeded in coaxing him out of it only after she located and purchased an identical shirt online."

"That child must love Russell Wilson. You think it's this kid?"

"We're working on it. I'm waiting for a call from Social Services in Santa Barbara."

"And then you will look for a connection between this woman and Lillian, I presume."

Andy tapped her nose.

"I'm impressed," I said. "Nice work, Detective. You free for lunch?"

The invitation elicited a frown. Not the reaction I was expecting. Andy's lower lip gained prominence, an effect generated by a slight underbite that I find deeply attractive, but which can also signal intense thought, warn of imminent danger, or in extreme cases prompt prudent evacuation of the immediate vicinity.

"The department just received a pile of Open Records requests." Andy gestured in the direction of the sidewalk marchers. "From them."

"What kind of requests?"

"They're digging into duty schedules, duty assignments, staffing attendance records. My records."

"What are you saying?"

"I'm saying that some of what you and I have been through—you know—with a certain *other thing* and where it has led—has caused me to take time away from the job."

I felt heat rising in my face. I spoke evenly, coldly. "Yes. It has. Putting serious shitheads behind bars. And saving some goddamned important asses. Dee, it's not like you were sloughing off on a beach somewhere."

"I'm aware. But taken out of context, my absences don't look good. And that's all compounded by my departure for the Academy."

"A leave approved by the department."

"Under protest by the city manager. Yes, Will, I found out about that."

"Jesus, Dee! They can't—!"

"Easy there, cowboy. Tom has it in hand. I'm just saying, maybe right now, me being seen out to lunch with my husband on a workday might not be the best optics."

I thought of a word to put in front of optics. Pidge would have used it without taking a breath. I held it on my tongue.

"This is messed up."

"I don't disagree. But I meant what I said. This will blow over. Those clowns won't get the signatures they need, there won't be a recall, and all of this will pass." She dished out a warm smile. A little forced, but it melted a tiny portion of my anger.

"Fine, but I'm taking you out to dinner. And I'm pulling out the stops. There could be pizza in your future. Maybe even cloth napkins. Screw the *Recallistas*."

23

NOW

The two-hour flight from Ekalaka to Sioux City Gateway Airport took an extra sixteen minutes, thanks to the strength of the winds I had been brawling with all night. After a smooth landing on Runway 18, the tower gave me a left turn onto Taxiway Alpha. Ground instructed me to take Alpha to Charlie to Hawthorne Aviation where a young woman in a yellow reflective vest guided me to a stop using orange wands. She waited for me to shut down the engines and crack the door, then asked if I needed services. I requested the fuel truck. She gave me a thumbs-up and placed a set of chocks at the nose wheel before trotting off to the FBO office.

My four-hour nap refreshed me, but I recognized that my energy would not last. My watch read close to one p.m., accounting for the time change. Two hours of flying would get me back to Essex County, but I had no estimate of how long I would be in Sioux City. I told Andy my return for the family dinner was unlikely. She asked me to promise to check into a hotel in Sioux City for rest before flying again. It wasn't a bad idea.

When the fuel truck arrived in front of the Baron, I strolled around the wing, removing the fuel caps on the right, then on the left wing.

"Top 'em off?" the fuel truck driver—the same girl that chocked my nose wheel—asked. I guessed her to be in her late teens, smitten by aviation, and working the flight line to pay for lessons. The caramel color of her skin reminded me of Andy, but her jet-black hair, almond eyes and high cheekbones advertised Indigenous American genes.

"All four, please," I replied. I stepped out of the way as she connected the ground wire to the nose gear, then unreeled the hose and nozzle. I watched to verify that she intended to dispense Avgas. Pumping jet fuel into piston engine tanks is not unheard of. She started with the right outboard auxiliary tank. I leaned on the wingtip as she worked.

"This yours?" she asked.

"Essex County Air Service. Charter."

"Nice." She looked the Baron over appreciatively. I remembered what it was like to dream of getting my hands on the controls of something fast and powerful, something with more than one engine. "E model?"

"You know your Barons."

"What's it like to fly?"

"She flies like a dream. Solid, but light on the controls. Almost never need to trim it. Cruises close to two hundred knots if you don't mind the fuel burn. High one-eighties if you like economy."

She smiled. "I'd throttle back and log the time."

I laughed. "Working on your license?"

"Working on the instrument and commercial."

"Excellent. Looking for a life with the airlines?"

"If they'll have me." She carefully topped the tank, then twisted the nozzle skyward to prevent straggler drops from falling on the wing. The mark of a pro.

"I'll cap it. I like to be sure." I walked around the wing while she moved to the inboard main tank. "What about that thing? Over there?" I pointed at the boxy cargo plane sitting beyond a line of parked business jets at the other end of the ramp. It had a white finish with a pair of blue stripes down the side. There were no windows for passengers. Strictly cargo. I spotted it as soon as I landed and confirmed the N-number when I taxied to parking. "Who does that belong to?"

"Enterprise Cargo Global. C-23 Sherpa. Used to be a military cargo plane."

"Think you'd like to fly one of those?"

"I already talked to them about flying copilot after I get my multi-engine. To build some time."

"Sweet. Enterprise, you say? Sounds familiar. They have offices here?"

She pointed at a hangar between Hawthorne Aviation and the commercial terminal.

"Where do they fly?"

"Same routes every night. Mason City. Springfield. Jonesboro. A couple other places. A to B to C to D and back again, every night. I think they subcontract for UPS. Not sure about that. 'Cept that one today. I'm pretty sure they leased that one out because it just came in and I totally didn't know any of the crew. And I know all the ECG guys." She finished filling the right main and left the cap for me to seal.

"A lease?"

"I guess you'd call it a lease. Or a rental. I heard it was a one-off. Some outfit that has a C-23 of their own, but it had some maintenance issues, so they called up ECG to borrow that one. There aren't that many around. Like I said, I didn't know the pilots."

I capped the right main tank and followed her to the left side.

"I should have asked. Do you want the outboard filled first?"

"Doesn't matter. Any idea who was leasing it?" I felt it instantly. *One question too many?*

She glanced at me.

"I ask because I have a buddy who hired on with an outfit in Milwaukee that flies those Short Brothers boxcars."

She shrugged and returned her focus to the task at hand.

"Bet they can get a lot into one of those," I said.

"And how. They rolled a bunch of four-wheelers out of that one this morning right after I got here at five."

She finished filling the left main. I sealed the tank.

"Bet you have to use a ladder to get fuel into those wings."

"Oh, yeah. But they don't have wing tanks. The fuel tanks are overhead in the fuselage. Weird, right?"

"I did not know that."

"Yeah. That wing is a skinny little thing for such a big box fuselage. I don't know how they fuel the fuselage tanks. ECG has their own truck."

She carefully finished topping off the last tank. I replaced the cap while she ran the power reel to retract the hose.

"Sixty-eight point six," she reported. She unhooked the ground wire and reeled it in. "I'll have the slip in the office straightaway."

"Thanks very much. Good luck with the flying."

I PAID the fuel bill with an Essex County Air Service credit card, then walked back out to the Baron. Access to the ramp at an air carrier airport can be tricky, but the commercial terminal and its sterile ramp areas was several hundred yards away. I climbed into the Baron's cockpit and dug around in my flight bag until I found an envelope for fuel receipts. I dropped in the Hawthorne slip, then took the envelope with me after closing and locking the cabin door.

I strolled across the ramp toward the C-23 Sherpa. The aircraft looked like a shoebox with a wing glued on the top and a twin-fin tail attached to the rear. The wide cockpit placed the pilot and copilot far enough apart to play catch. Slung from each wing were a pair of turbine engines, deceptively small for the power they put out. I hadn't seen many of these aircraft and wasn't certain that the Short Brothers name still existed in aerospace. If the Irish company wasn't out of business, it had probably been swallowed up by a bigger fish. The Wikipedia entry I glanced at suggested that these slab-sided transports were reliable and cheap to operate, which accounted for their continued service long after production ended.

As much as I would have liked a much closer look at the airplane, I angled away from it toward the hangar that the girl pointed out. A small sign beside a solid-looking door said Enterprise Cargo Global. I thought the Global part of that was a little pretentious for a company hauling freight around the Mississippi Valley.

I rapped on the door, then opened it and stepped into a small office. Hauling freight means not having to impress the passengers. The ECG office reminded me of Earl Jackson's office. No frills. An old desk. Shelves stuffed with maintenance manuals and other debris. A mismatched pair of filing cabinets nudged a back wall. A small hallway disappeared into darkness, perhaps leading to a restroom or to additional offices. A door to my right opened into the attached hangar. Through a small window, I could see another C-23 painted in the same white and blue scheme.

A woman with a round face and a cap of tightly curled brown hair looked up at me from behind an old CRT monitor that dominated her desk.

"Help you?"

I waved the envelope in the air. "I'm supposed to give this to a guy named Danzig. He's coming in from Montana. Do you know when he might be here?"

"Scott Danzig?"

"I guess."

"Come and gone, friend. They got in before dawn this morning."

"Does he work here? Maybe still here?"

"Nope," she said. "He's not with us. Him and his crew leased one of ours, but they're long gone."

"Shoot." I worked up a frown and tucked the envelope in the breast pocket of my flight jacket. "I ran late getting out of Minneapolis this morning."

"That your Baron that came in?"

I wasn't keen on giving the woman that information.

"I wish." I pulled out my phone. "I don't have his number. You wouldn't happen to know how I could get hold of him…?"

"No idea." She leaned to one side and lifted a folder from a stack of folders. She flipped it open and scanned through several pages that looked like a contract or lease agreement. "I can give you the contact info for his company. Well, not a company. A law firm. They're the ones signed the lease. But I would guess they could put you in touch with him."

"That sounds about right," I said. I patted the breast of my jacket. "They told me this was some kind of legal document."

She read off a number, which I tapped into my phone. When she finished, I repeated it for confirmation. She affirmed my readback. She answered my next question before I could ask. "Baker McCallen is the name of the firm."

"Thanks!" I retreated to the door. "Have a great day."

"You, too."

I walked away with my phone in hand, assigning the name of the law firm to the phone number and adding it to my Contacts list.

"Lawyers," I said to no one. "Huh."

24

Back at the FBO counter, the flight line gas truck commercial instrument student pilot girl offered me a crew car, one of several parked in a lot outside the airport security fence.

"I'm supposed to tell you there's a two-hour limit but take as much time as you need. We don't have anything booked out today."

"Much appreciated."

I DROVE the route suggested by Google to reach the law firm of Baker McCallen. The drive took me into a grid of residential streets with old growth hardwood trees and tidy homes built before FDR became president. Where the residential neighborhood ended, a wide avenue named Morningstar hosted brick commercial properties. Some of the buildings had stone accents I recognized as Masonic. I wondered if the fraternal organization remained alive and well in western Iowa. I also wondered where in hell the legal offices of Baker McCallen were located, because nothing on the brick building at the address I found listed the name or suggested law offices. The building had seen better days. A single exterior sign advertised Personalized Counseling Services. A rusting Century 21 sign offered commercial office space available, an offer repeated by a small handwritten FOR RENT sign— the kind you can buy at a hardware store—taped to one of the doors. Second floor windows above built-in air conditioning units were blocked by curtains or vertical blinds. A few windows had large cartons stacked against the glass.

I parked on the opposite side of the street and crossed to a door with the address number tacked into the frame above it. Inside, I found a narrow lobby with a set of ornate mailboxes. The building smelled of onions and curry spice.

The second mailbox from the top on the left came as close as I was going to get to the name I'd been given.

EZRA BAKER LAW

Box 207.

I climbed a narrow uncarpeted stairway. The steps creaked all the way up. The stairs opened on a hallway running the full length of the building, lit by fluorescent bulbs in the ceiling and by windows at both ends.

A door marked 207 shortened the name further. BAKER LAW was laser printed in bold type on a piece of paper that had been taped to the door, diminishing my expectations further still. This hardly looked like a thriving firm in the business of leasing cargo planes. Maybe that was the point.

"In for a penny…" I muttered.

I didn't knock. I opened the door and stepped into a small reception area containing four plastic chairs and a dusty fake Ficus tree. A half wall separated the reception area from an inner office. Frosted glass topped the half wall and extended to the ceiling. A set of Christmas jingle bells hanging on the door announced my entrance to a figure that moved behind the frosted glass.

A man appeared. He was as short as Pidge, balding, and dressed in a white shirt with suspenders holding up pinstriped wool suit pants. He wore a tie that hung slack around his neck. His face consisted of spheres. A round nose, round reddish cheeks, a round chin and a dome of hairless skull. He wore glasses with heavy black frames, the kind I'm told are ironic on fashionable young people but considered dumpy on everyone else.

"Hep you?"

"Is this Baker McCallen?"

"Baker. Just Baker. If you're here for a traffic case, you can fill out all the forms online."

"No. Not traffic."

"I see. And you are?" The face may have been disarming, but the eyes and tone were sharp.

"Special Agent Leslie Carson-Pelham, FBI." The lie sent an electric charge up my spine.

"Mind showing me some ID?"

"I do. This is personal, not official."

"Then why mention it?"

"To avoid giving the impression that I was hiding something."

"Okay. Personal business. What sort of personal business brings you to my door, Agent Pelham?"

I fished Wally's photo from my pocket and held it up. Baker tipped his head back to bring the lower half of his glasses to bear on the image.

"I'm looking for this woman." I pointed at Wally's aunt. "Stephanie Cullen."

Baker stepped through the doorframe and came closer. He reached for the paper, but I pulled it back. "Sorry. This is my only copy. I'm nervous about losing it."

"What kind of photo is that supposed to be?"

"Alien landing site, I'm told."

My imagination may have been feeding me what I expected to see, but I swear recognition flashed in Baker's eyes. Just a flash. The kind that leaves you wondering if you saw it at all.

"Sounds like nonsense to me. May I ask how you happened to come to me about this woman?"

"Do you know her?"

Baker smiled. "The FBI is accustomed to asking the questions. Let me repeat mine. How is it that you think I know her?"

"Your name came up in conversation."

"Conversation with whom?"

"Scott Danzig. I just talked to him out at Gateway."

Baker held a poker face. He also didn't ask who Scott Danzig was. I folded the photo back into my pocket.

"And what is this woman to you?"

"She's my aunt."

"Well, I am sorry you made the trip here, Agent Pelham, but I cannot disclose information about a client, not even to confirm or deny that I ever met or had contact with this person, which would itself be revealing. You must understand my position."

"Do you know Tammy Day?"

He shrugged. "I don't recognize that name either."

"Then you're saying you don't recognize the name Stephanie Cullen?"

He smiled, and not in a friendly way. "I misspoke. I think, Agent Cullen—"

"Carson-Pelham."

"Yes. Certainly. I think this is when I should inform you that my hourly consultation rate is one hundred and seventy-five dollars. You are welcome to my time at that rate. Otherwise, I'm sorry." He gestured at the door.

"No problem. I'll see myself out. Have a good day."

I grabbed the door, opened it as wide as possible, hooked my hand on the doorframe and strolled out. I hoped it didn't look as awkward as it felt.

Fwooomp!

In the hall, beyond Baker's line of sight, I vanished. My grip on the doorframe jerked me to a stop. I turned around and pulled myself back into the office. The door, driven by a hydraulic piston at the top, had already begun to swing shut. Baker stood at the door to his office and watched it close. Using both hands on the frame, I levered myself laterally, toward the side wall. I yanked my hands free of the frame just as the door latched and gave out a cheerful jingle.

Baker stepped across the reception area and twisted a deadbolt lock on the door, then hurried back to his inner office.

My palm landed on striped tan and blue wallpaper, which stopped my glide. I held my breath and floated in silence.

An office chair creaked. I heard Baker lift a phone receiver and tap the touchpad. After a moment, he spoke politely.

"This is Ezra Baker. May I speak to Peter Giles, please? It's urgent."

Baker waited. The better part of a minute passed before he spoke again.

"Mr. Giles, a gentleman was just here looking for Stephanie Cullen. He said he was an FBI agent, but that his was a personal inquiry. He claims Mr. Danzig directed him to me, and that Cullen is his aunt."

Baker listened, then spoke.

"Tall. Six feet. Dark hair. Thirty-ish. Fit. No. No, not at all like that. This man easily topped one-ninety, maybe two hundred. He said his name was Leslie Carter Pelham. Could be hyphenated."

One eighty-three, thank you very much.

"No, he refused to show me."

"No."

"Yes, I understand, but he had a photo…a group of people including Cullen."

"Yes. I'm certain."

"He said the photo was taken at an alien landing site. His words."

I grabbed a chair back and pushed gently sideways. A short glide took me to Baker's office door. He sat behind a heavy, dark wooden desk with almost nothing on the surface except a phone far too capable for the size of this office. The phone bristled with buttons and lines.

I ventured closer and fixed a grip on the edge of his desk. Less than four feet away, Baker stared straight ahead and listened attentively.

"Right."

"Right."

"I understand. Sir, he also asked about Tammy Day."

He squeezed his eyes shut. He did not speak again. The call ended without Baker speaking another word. He looked blankly at the receiver, then replaced it in the cradle.

Baker sat back in his chair and gripped the armrests. He didn't seem likely to leap out of his chair. If anything, he looked like a man in a trance.

I studied the phone. The unit belonged in a much larger office. The phones at Essex County Air Service were similar, but they were part of a multiline, multi-phone system.

I took a chance. I leaned over and carefully pressed the button for the first line. A dial tone jumped from the phone's small speaker, causing Baker to jolt. Before he could react, I found and pressed REDIAL.

The phone beeped ten times.

Baker clutched the chair and stared, bewildered. I focused on the small gray LCD screen on the face of the phone. Ten digits appeared.

323 area code. Los Angeles.

The next three numbers matched one of Boeing's most popular airliners. Easy to remember.

The last four digits read 7600. The aircraft transponder code for lost communications.

I repeated all three cues in my head and prepared to shove off for the outer office. Just as I pushed, I heard a woman's voice answer the call.

"ParaTransit. Your journey begins with trust. How may I direct your call?"

25

ONE WEEK AGO

November is my second least favorite month for flying. April is the worst. April doesn't know if it's winter or spring, throws crusading lines of thunderstorms across the Midwest and seeds all altitudes with ice. Funnel cloud tantrums are common in April. November's crime is the introduction of cold air, carried on the shoulders of high-pressure systems out of Canada, a jarring contrast to the often beautiful and benign months of September and October. November air masses contain steep pressure gradients and howling winds, along with messy mixtures of rain, sleet, and the first fat flakes of snow.

Which is why, for the bulk of a return flight from a Foundation trip to Nashville, I found myself entranced by the high color and smooth air filling the sky. The day trip carried Arun Dewar to Education Foundation meetings and school tours. Our return flight promised landing in Essex less than half an hour after the annoyingly early sunset. Skirting Chicago at ten thousand feet, my view from the cockpit grew more spectacular by the nautical mile. The sun kissed the rim of the earth and sprayed gaudy pinks and purples on the underbellies of the high clouds above us. Color spanned the sky from horizon to horizon. I wondered why the streets nearly two miles below us were not filled with crowds of people watching the show.

Around the time Chicago Center handed me off to Rockford Approach, I could not contain myself. I reached back and waved to snag Arun's attention. He lifted his face from the folders and documents spread across the fold-out table hugging his seat. I tapped my headset. Catching my drift, he slipped on his headphones. I switched on the intercom.

"Are you seeing this?"

"What?"

"Look out the left windows, man."

Arun is a nervous flyer. Anything outside the bounds of boring brings him to high alert. He shot a worried look at the left-side windows, searching.

"What?"

"The color. Holy crap, it's amazing." How had he not seen the pastels flooding the cabin? "You gotta come up for air once in a while, pal."

"Uh-huh." He gave the spectacular sunset a cursory look. "Nice."

"Nice? That's it?"

"Quite lovely."

"Now you're talking. There's that British understatement."

"Indeed. Victoria Falls; we named it after our frumpiest queen. The Atlantic Ocean; we're the ones who called it 'the pond.' Remember, understatement is a British art. We have Yeats. You have Yankovich."

"Weird Al sold more records."

I like when Arun joins in conversation over the intercom. He tends to bury himself in his work. There are times when the demands of flying call for a sterile cockpit, but on long stretches between departure and arrival, a little conversation can be nice. Arun has a sharp mind and equally sharp wit.

I expected more, but he went silent, which made me turn around. I found him gazing at the sunset. He caught me looking his way and shook off the hypnotic effect of the sky.

"Will, if I may ask, how is Andy?"

"Fine. Why?"

"I mean, how is she dealing with the controversy?"

"The *Recallistas*? She's ignoring them. She's doing her job. And I like to point out that there is no 'controversy.' There's reality here on earth, and there's the looney tunes world of the conspiracy nutballs dispensing disinformation and making insane accusations."

"Yes…I daresay. I hope she's avoiding the noise on social media. That is, what I mean to say is, I hope she's able to filter it out. Some of it, the postings, some of it is quite disturbing."

"She doesn't do social media unless it's work-related. Her sister practically lives on the Face thing. I had to have a frank discussion with Lydia about it. She kept calling Andy and ranting about the latest outrage."

"I monitor a bit of it. Disgusting, unfounded bollocks. They're like dogs that have been let loose and those responsible, those in power, are choosing not to reel them in, but rather are letting them spread filth to reap a political benefit while they pretend to keep their hands clean. Please let Mrs. Stewart know that I wish her well."

I glanced back and read sincerity in Arun's face that solidified his words over the intercom.

"I will. Thank you."

"And I wish those spreading the filth an eternity in a lake of fire."

I SENSED something was up when I rolled the Navajo to a halt in front of the Education Foundation Hangar. Pidge slouched on the Essex County Air Service tug with her feet up on the fender and her hands buried in the pockets of her flight jacket. Ordinarily, I roll the big twin in and out of the hangar by hand with a battery-powered tow bar. A free pushback from the tug was welcome, a nice way to end the day, yet her presence waved a red flag. Had she simply intended to end her duty day by meeting Arun, she would have waited in the hangar.

I killed the engines, secured the cockpit, packed my flight gear, and followed Arun out the airstair door. By the time I reached the nose, Pidge had already positioned the tug. She sat behind the wheel.

"What, you're too lazy to get down off that seat and hook this up? I gotta do it?" I lifted the tow bar off the rack at the front of the tug and locked it on the Navajo's nose wheel. Pidge inched forward until the loop snapped into the hitch.

"That's fucking gratitude. Here I am doing you a favor."

Arun, who has the good sense to stay clear of repositioning operations, stood inside the hangar clutching himself against the cold. He lifted a hand and waved at Pidge, who waved back.

I hopped up on the tug and sat on the fender. Pidge pulled the aircraft away from the hangar to straighten the wheels. The big hangar door finished its ponderous rise. Pidge shifted gears and slowly pushed the airplane into the hangar.

She turned her head and spoke softly. "You need to get your ass home."

"Why? Is Andy okay?"

"She's fine. But it's a fucking shitstorm at your house. She told me to tell you not to drive home. She wants you to arrive discretely."

"You mean...?"

"Yeah, *I mean*...shove some pixie dust down your pants and do your thing. I'll distract Arun."

"I bet you will," I slid off the fender and hopped clear.

"I'll take that brown bonbon right here on the cold ass concrete floor," Pidge laughed.

"Please let me get out of here before you do that." I scooped up my flight bag. "And thanks."

"Go."

26

Arun remained under Pidge's spell as she deftly parked the big cabin class twin. I dropped my flight bag in the office. I extracted my ski goggles and two power units from a zippered pocket. Arun might notice that I departed without my car, but that was easily explained with a fib about stopping over at the ECAS office.

I ducked out the door, checked to be sure the road running between facing lines of hangars was empty, and shoved the levers I picture in my head hard against the stops.

Fwooomp!

The sound only I can hear had hardly ended before I flexed my ankles and broke contact with the asphalt. I thumbed the slide control on the BLASTER unit to maximum power and aimed the device skyward. My weightless, inertia-less body, encased in the familiar cool sensation, extended behind the whining prop.

Pidge's words rang in my head.

"... it's a fucking shitstorm at your house..."

At my house? My home?

Over the past week, the lame little demonstration in front of the police department spread like chicken pox. Yard signs popped up all over Essex. The group spending their days on the police department sidewalk grew larger, especially in recent days when southerly air flow brought uncharacteristic warmth to mid-November air. Andy did precisely what I expected. She brushed off the growing political storm as irrelevant to her work, which she dove into with mounting intensity. Tom Ceeves gave her a solid case load, but she heaped more on herself by bringing home old files. Tom regarded her singular focus as a positive—keeps her busy, he told me privately. I saw her intensity for what it was—a meter for just how much the political sideshow needled her.

Arun's question during the flight touched on something Andy and I ignored. Social media. We didn't need to dive into the cesspool of unfounded opinion, disinformation, outright lies and anonymous rage to know it existed. I worried about the consequences for Andy. What happens when she follows up with a witness or suspect whose endless hours on the internet has them convinced that she was the intended assassin of their beloved leader? What happens when someone answers the door thinking that *only they* can dispense the justice that the President's most ardent followers demanded?

Initially, the recall effort couched itself in vague political phrases about "integrity" and "restoring the police" and similar verbal placebos. Gradually, outliers heaped the bandwagon with attacks on political movements for racial equality and police reform. Tuning it out became harder and harder.

The yard signs irritated me the most in rural areas where huge political signs marred the landscape, especially as a new political season loomed. Incomprehensibly, signs denouncing Detective Stewart shared lawn space with signs trumpeting "We Back The Badge." I fell into a routine of saluting such properties with one finger—at least when Andy was not in the car.

And now this.

"... it's a fucking shitstorm at your house ..."

A MILE FROM HOME, I spotted emergency lights winking against the silhouette landscape. My anxiety heightened. I pushed the power unit to the max and skimmed just above treetop and power line height, angling *as the Will flies* directly across yards, meadows, and recently harvested cornfields. The simple two-lane blacktop that runs east-west in front of our rented farmhouse had been bracketed by first-responder vehicles. Blue and red police lights dominated both ends of the road.

I climbed higher to gain a better look.

White lights clustered directly in front of our yard. A flatbed truck carrying a rack of spotlights, the kind usually mounted on poles at high school football fields, lit up the house. Three blazing rows of illumination turned night into day and sent black shadows fleeing, bracketing the otherwise warm and friendly two-story farmhouse with ominous, skeletal maple trees. Two mobile television vans contributed spotlights of their own to the scene. Microwave masts extended to a height that threatened my flight path.

The scene had motion. People carried and waved signs as they paraded in a long loop in front of the lights. More people lined the row of parked vehicles. Many held up devices to record the event, competing with the professional camera operators attached to the media vans. I spotted three separate remote setups where pro photographers lined up their lenses and lights to frame on-camera talent against the marching protesters and the illuminated house.

I intersected the road at the west end of the organized confusion. Essex PD deployed patrol units to close the road. Parked beyond the blue-red lights of the roadblock units, two county snowplows added their yellow rotating lights to the scene.

Andy's patrol colleagues had been deployed in a sparse line across our lawn, separating the mob on the road from our house. I knew every one of the officers, either from Andy's work or as my wife's teammates on the police department softball team. None of them looked happy.

I crossed the road and eased off the BLASTER. Any concerns about prop noise being detected quickly dissipated. The chanting crowd marching in front of my house masked the whine of the power unit. The centipede line of protesters marched back and forth, pumping up their chants and energizing their sign waving in front of the cameras and live telecasts.

"RESTORE THE POLICE. RECALL AND DISMISS."

"RESTORE THE POLICE. RECALL AND DISMISS."

Men, women, a few teens and at least two children took up the cry and waved their signs. I fought off an urge to swoop through the line and kick the signs out of their hands.

Just as my anger approached a boil, the chaos shifted. Organizers hustled up and down the line shouting instructions. The line stopped, broke, then began to form ranks beside my recently replaced mailbox. Recall organizers arranged the protesters the way a wedding photographer maneuvers bridesmaids and groomsmen. Select signs were brought to the front, some of which were emblazoned with my last name. Someone produced a low wooden platform.

I recognized people. I'm not good with names, and I am often forced to fake familiarity when I meet people who seem to know me. But I knew some of the faces of people chanting and carrying signs. A cashier from the hardware store who always asks for my Ace Rewards card. The guy that rents shoes at the other bowling alley in Essex. People I see at the grocery store. Neighbors. Citizens Andy protects every day.

One young woman hurried back and forth, smiling and calling for people to look her way as she shot photos with her phone. She looked the image of the activist, full of energy, hurrying from one person to the next. Despite a knit cap pulled down over her long brown hair, and a plaid scarf wrapped around her neck, I recognized her. I could not think of her name, but I knew her face and easily imagined her voice.

Andy knew her too. The department's dispatch trainee.

Not for much longer, I ventured to guess.

I had been about to turn for the house, thinking it might reduce my blood pressure if I put my back to this scene. Instead, I hooked right and circled back above the vehicles, sweeping past the broadcast masts.

The news crews jockeyed for position directly in front of the wooden platform that had been laid in the road. The crowd on the road constricted. The vanguard of officers on my lawn tightened.

Minor confusion broke out around the raised platform. The organizers pushed and maneuvered several individuals until three of them stood on the platform. I recognized one of the actors being herded. Armand Collingsworth. A former member of the school board, a minor local politician and major ass. The three on the platform watched a fourth man in a suit and tie stroll through milling onlookers and amateur video artists. He clapped one of the on-camera reporters on the back. They shared lips-to-ears comments and a laugh, then the man took center stage on the platform. He vigorously shook hands with Collingsworth and his two companions, then turned and faced the cameras.

I had no idea who this was. His handsome features and tidy haircut were made for a camera. He wore a tailored suit, the bright red tie favored by conservative politicians, and no overcoat, despite dropping nighttime temperatures. Absorbing light from multiple angles, he fit the cookie-cutter image of the political types I had seen too much of lately.

I steadied myself above and behind the news crews that dominated the center of this makeshift stage.

Someone rushed forward with a small speaker box and dropped it in front of the platform before handing the man in the suit a microphone.

"Testing, testing," he said. "Is this on?" His baritone voice boomed from the box. He laughed. "How 'bout that? It's on alright!"

He glanced back at his backdrop audience. Applause and cheers broke out.

"Alright! So happy to be here with you all tonight. Thank you. Thank you so much." He faced the cameras, but skillfully spread his focus, giving the impression of speaking to a large crowd instead of the darkness and empty cornfield beyond the camera lenses. "My name is Charles White. Some of you know me. I am honored to serve the people of this great state as a Republican member of the Assembly and—" the crowd took their cue and broke into a loud cheer, which White pretended was humbling and unexpected. "Thank you. Wow. Thank you, so much." He let the applause go on for a moment, then waved to tamp down the enthusiasm. "I appreciate that so much. I do. But tonight is not about me. Tonight, I'm here to bring focus to a grave issue and to make an important announcement."

The prop crowd behind him settled.

"We all saw what happened in Detroit."

Boos and growls swelled from the studio audience.

"We were all shocked by the recent assassination attempt on our great President. We all know that serious questions remain unanswered." The crowd rumbled. White amped it up. *"We all know that something stinks and I'm here tonight to join you in a commitment to get to the bottom of it!"*

Stationed behind and beside the news cameras, the group's organizers lifted their arms and signaled for a rousing cheer. The crowd let loose. White glanced back and dished out emphatic nods of approval.

"That's right! That's right! We want answers. We want reform, and not the defund and disarm and dissolve and disband the police reform that BLM and Antifa and the woke left mob is talking about. We want to *restore integrity* and hand real power back to true police."

Cheers.

"We want to know how a suspect can be taken into custody at the scene of a heinous assassination attempt and then simply let go! Somebody is hiding something. Am I right?"

"Damn right!"

"Fuckin'-A!"

"We're not letting Detroit go unpunished, not on my watch! Not in my America! *Not in this President's America!*"

Wild cheers.

White took an exaggerated pause for breath. Someone handed him a water bottle. He sipped and waited.

"People! You are the power behind a mighty crusade for truth. Look around. Look at the power here tonight. This is *real* power. This is the *real America.* This is how we deliver a message. That's why, tonight I'm pleased to tell you that your heroic drive to secure the signatures necessary to recall corrupt elements in your local government—elements that are satisfied with what sure feels like a coverup to me—*is damned close to success!*"

The crowd broke out the biggest cheer yet. White shot a fist in the air and pumped it. Organizers moved up and down and waved for the wild enthusiasm to sustain. White shouted over the roar.

"That's right! This is happening! This is happening!" He waited. Pumped his fist. Waited again. The crowd eventually settled. "Tonight, I've been given the honor to announce to the public, right here, in front of the home of someone you all know needs to answer for her actions—*you know who I'm talking about*—"

Huge cheer.

"—I've been given the honor of announcing the slate of candidates for the coming recall election! Candidates committed to restoring integrity, empowering police, and demanding that there be consequences for those who would use assassination to end the noble destiny our Greatest President has carved out for himself in history! And let me tell you something right now—let me tell you that if they want to resort to assassination—if they want get out the guns—I say bring it! *Because we've got the guns!*"

He pointed left and right. Heads turned. Cameras tracked.

On the fringes of the compacted crowd, men emerged from darkness in camo hats, camo jackets, web belts and thick vests with military badges. They held semi-automatic rifles at port arms and posed for the cameras. The young woman with the camera danced around them, eliciting stoic, menacing poses, snapping photos.

"Second amendment! Second amendment!" White chanted. The crowd took up the chant.

Backdropping this increasingly insane scene stood my home, drained of color by the intense floodlights, protected by a thin line of police whose faces reflected deep unease with the introduction of high-powered weapons to the equation.

My home. Sheltering my wife.

Enough.

I turned my wrist and fired up the BLASTER. Resisting temptation to swoop low and kick White in the face, I cruised over his head, across my front lawn, and angled toward my back door. The crowd loudly chanted its undying support for a well-regulated militia. I failed to see anything well-regulated about the men brandishing weapons in front of my house. My thoughts shifted to grabbing my wife, making her vanish, and reappearing on a beach in Belize.

Andy's current ride, an unmarked police department Chevy Tahoe, occupied a space in front of the garage. Police Chief Tom Ceeves' big Essex PD SUV sat on the barn hill, parked out of sight of the occupation force on the road and hidden from the spotlights. His presence eased the tension knotting my guts.

I dropped onto the high concrete stoop at my back door and found the door locked which instantly reminded me that my car and house keys remained safe in my flight bag at the hangar. Getting inside meant breaking in. I wasn't in the mood to create a new fix-it project or get shot by my wife and her boss. Instead, I rapped on the door.

Beyond the dark mudroom, the kitchen light was on. No one hurried to answer my knock.

I pushed sideways and drifted past the dining room windows. Lights on. No one home. The dining room and what I could see of the living room at the front of the house were empty. Curtains and window shades facing the road had been drawn.

I tapped on the dining room window in case Andy and the Chief were hunkered down beneath the line of sight.

No one responded.

Second floor?

None of the windows on the second floor showed light. Looking into dark rooms, especially with near daylight being thrown at the house, wasn't likely to reveal anything to me. Nor did I think Andy and the Chief would choose a defensive position on a second floor with only one exit.

I hung in the air beside the dining room window and asked myself, *How would the chief, who obviously came here to protect his subordinate, handle this situation?* Tom Ceeves is a giant of a man whose first impression suggests a bit of clumsiness and a disdain for the trappings of his office. He wears flannel shirts and is rarely armed or badged. Anyone interpreting his casual appearance as unprofessional or intellectually dim does so at their peril.

So, as a tactical solution, where did he put Andy?

The answer came in a flash.

I rotated, extended my arm, and goosed the power switch on the BLASTER.

Lights painting the house spilled onto the big red barn. Tom's decision to park his SUV on the barn hill at the back crystalized as an exit plan if things got ugly. An old cow lane led to the back of the property. Even without that lane, the SUV was more than capable of bouncing across the cornfields. Tom would not have parked the vehicle behind the barn as an escape valve if it meant having to cross the farmyard from the house.

I did not aim for the barn hill or the vehicle. The Chief and Andy needed a lookout. The hay loft offered a view of the road, but walls were made of thin boards. Rifle rounds, even handgun rounds, could easily penetrate the old wood. Neither Tom nor Andy would have considered the hay loft accept-able cover.

Not when eighteen-inch-thick fieldstone walls were an option.

The whitewashed barn foundation had been made of mortar and stones clawed from the surrounding fields over a hundred years ago. Twelve to eighteen inches thick, the foundation walls offered ample protection from small arms fire. Windows, the frames beginning to rot and the glass broken in a few places, offered a clear line of sight to the road. The ground floor of the barn contained rows of stanchions into which a long-gone dairy herd stuck their heads for the twice-daily feeding and milking. A stairway led to the hay loft above—the escape route to the parked SUV in back.

I navigated a direct line to the wide barn door facing the house—a flat wooden panel hung on a steel rail. Ordinarily I had no cause to enter the lower level of the barn except to poke around and make sure it hadn't been invaded by raccoons. I knew the rusted door rollers screamed at the slightest movement. I decided not to scare my wife or the chief. I called through the door.

"Andy? Are you in there?"

"We're here! Go around and come in through the loft."

I veered right and cut around the corner of the barn. A moment later I entered the empty hay loft through barn hill doors that had been left open—more evidence that my guesses about an escape plan were correct.

Spotlights from the road lit the entire south wall of the empty loft. Shafts of light seeped through pinholes in the old walls. The effect was eerie and at the same time majestic. I would have loved setting up this kind of lighting, opening a bottle of wine, and then taking Andy in my arms for a joyride among the old beams and rafters.

Another time.

Fwooomp!

I reappeared in stride and jogged across the uneven wooden floor to where an old wooden stairway—more of a ladder—joined the loft to the lower level.

Andy lifted her head through the opening in the floor.

"Hi. Pidge texted that you were coming."

I followed her down the stairs. Our landlord, James Rankin, had long ago removed all electrical wiring and connections in the barn as a precaution against fire. After sunset, without lights, the inky interior can be haunting. Tonight, light streaming through the windows painted the old lanes and gutters, stanchions, pipes and pens. Weird shadows marred the whitewashed walls.

Andy wore her winter coat, calf-length boots and her hair ponied out the back of a ball cap. At the bottom of the worn wooden steps, she paused for a kiss and hurried embrace. I felt her ballistic vest beneath her coat. The scent of her hair mingled with dry old wood and hay scent. I held her for a moment.

"You okay?"

"Fine. This is overkill."

"No, it's not," Tom Ceeves growled. He moved out of shadow near one of the windows. "Hi, Will."

"Chief."

"I would have been fine in the house," Andy insisted.

"Not," the hulking shadow declared.

"I don't appreciate being driven out of my home," Andy protested.

"It's a rental," Tom countered. "Who wants to die for a rental?"

Andy let her skeptical posture substitute for insubordination.

"Can I ask a question?" I asked.

"Sure," replied the darkness.

"What the fu—?"

A crackling radio interrupted the tirade I had been rehearsing in my head. The radio voice asked, "Chief, you there?"

"Go ahead."

"We're ready."

"Do it."

Andy took my hand and pulled me to one of the windows facing the road. She planted me on one side of the window, then dropped and duck-walked to the other side, avoiding the light streaming through dusty glass and aged spider webs.

"Keep your face out of the light," she instructed me.

I leaned forward to spy on the unfolding action.

At the western end of the road, the two police cruisers serving as a road-block parted. Beneath cycling yellow caution lights on top of the county snowplows, big headlights and auxiliary plow lights blazed to life, igniting the road and its occupiers. A police loudspeaker drowned out the small speaker through which Assemblyman White continued his cheerleading.

"THIS IS AN ORDER FROM THE CITY OF ESSEX POLICE DEPARTMENT. YOU ARE BLOCKING THIS ROAD. MOVE IMMEDI-ATELY OR FACE ARREST."

The announcement did not wait for a response. Diesel engines growled to life, then revved and roared. The big orange trucks surged forward, skirting the repositioned squad cars. Clear of the police units, one of the two big trucks pulled alongside the other. The plow drivers dropped their blades onto the dry asphalt road. Steel clanged loud enough to be felt in my chest. A steel barrier stretched from one side of the road to the other.

"We have a right to—" Assemblyman White shouted, only to be cut off when both truck drivers laid on their air horns. A continuous one-note blast that drowned all other sound. Anyone in front of those trucks would be lucky to hear themselves think, let alone speak.

The trucks jumped and jolted forward. Car-sized blades scraped the pavement, side by side. Sparks danced where metal ground against stone. The wall of steel and sound advanced.

"Holy shit," I muttered, unable to hear my own words. I glanced at the hulking shadow by the next window. Tom had stepped back for a better view. Invading light betrayed a grin on his face. I felt my face crack its own smile.

The crowd responded with defiance. Fists and fingers shook at the advancing trucks, but resistance was short-lived. Individually at first, then in clusters, the protesters hurried to their parked vehicles. The media crew lights winked out. The flatbed blasting light at my house remained illuminated, but the lights jerked forward a few feet before the truck found itself stalled by a van with America First Network stenciled on the side panels. The crew belonging to the van scrambled to load their equipment. The plows bore down on them at an implacable and ominous crawl.

The handheld signs disappeared, tossed into cars that started their engines and lit up their headlights. Brake lights flashed. The police units blocking the eastern end of the road pulled away and formed the head of a parade, leading with their still-flashing emergency lights. One by one, loaded cars and SUVs followed, adding their own horns to the cacophony when drivers cut each other off.

In their haste, the organizers of White's staged speech left their wooden platform and portable speaker in the road. As the media vans pulled away, the plows reached my new mailbox and snagged the platform and speaker, shoving both forward. They bumped and scraped the road, then broke apart. As the plow cleared my lawn, the driver adjusted the angle, which shoved the crushed debris into the ditch.

The plows never exceeded a brisk walking pace, yet in a matter of minutes, the entire event dissolved into taillights disappearing into the eastern distance. Clear of the farm property, the plow drivers let go of their horns and lifted their blades. Their growling diesel engines were low and passive in contrast, fading away with their taillights.

The chief's radio chattered. Officers monitoring the dissipation of the mob reported the road clear. The chief directed units at both ends to close the road.

Andy lit her phone flashlight and led us out of the barn. We crossed the now pleasantly dark yard and were met at the house by a handful of Andy's colleagues, the officers who formed the picket line across my lawn.

"Dude, where did you come from?" Officer Del Sims asked. In the dark, in the heavy gear he wore, he looked imposing despite his diminutive size.

"Back way," I said, hiking my thumb in the direction of the back of the farm.

"What a shit show," another officer, Ray Garland, the star pitcher on the department softball team, declared. He tore open the Velcro on his heavy vest.

"Snowplows! Who knew?" Sims said. "Nice one, Chief!"

"Did you see those fucking ARs?" Garland asked. I caught a trace of quivering anger in his voice. He tugged at his vest. "This goddamned thing won't stop a round from one of those."

The gathered cops muttered general agreement.

"Thanks, guys. All of you. I really appreciate you being here," Andy said. "I'm so sorry for all of this."

"Shut the fuck up, Sarge."

"Pay it back in shots."

"We thought you called us here to rake your lawn."

"Next time you throw a party, at least bring a keg."

The comments gathered momentum and absurdity, draining the tension, and leaving Andy wordless.

Tom eventually broke up the chatter. "Let's wrap this up."

The uniformed cops bid Andy a goodnight and parted company.

Tom lingered a moment, then said, "This shit is not over. Not by a long shot."

27

A ndy hurried through the house, turning off lights. I waited for her in the kitchen. When she returned, she found me in the dark and wrapped her arms around my waist. I pulled her close. We stood without speaking. I stroked her hair. She rested her head on my shoulder.

"I am so angry," she said quietly, evenly and without venom, which made the declaration more deadly.

"Can I join the club?"

"Count yourself in."

"Do I get a membership card? Please tell me there's a decoder ring."

She shook in my arms. An involuntary laugh. She pushed back and looked up at me in the dark, then found my lips for a long, hungry kiss. I started thinking that the energy her anger generated might be put to good use. My hands slipped down her back. Lower.

Lights swung through the front windows, flashing in the kitchen, briefly painting the sublime surfaces of her face.

"Now what?" I muttered. She released me and hurried to the mudroom. The vehicle in our driveway rolled to a stop below the back porch steps. A moment later the door opened. Andy returned to the kitchen where she turned on the light over the sink. Not full illumination, but enough.

"I think I got everyone." The voice belonged to the young woman I had seen shooting photos and encouraging the crowd—the department's dispatch trainee. The young woman I had planned to report to Andy as a traitor to the department for having joined the *Recallistas*.

"Will, you know Alicia, don't you?"

"Hi, Mr. Stewart," the girl said, making me feel old.

"You're training for dispatch," I said, hiding the hesitation in my voice. We traded a handshake. "Nice to meet you."

Alicia unwrapped her scarf, pulled off her hat and shook out a cascade of long brown hair. She dug in the pocket of her peacoat for an iPhone.

"This thing takes pretty good shots in the dark, but lighting was no problem out there. It was like daylight." She handed the phone to Andy who led us into the dining room. Andy pulled her laptop from her utility bag and opened it on the dining room table. She dug out a cord and joined the phone to her computer as it booted up.

"You were taking pictures for the department?" I asked.

Alicia beamed at me. "My first undercover assignment."

"And last for a while," Andy warned. "I was not happy with some of the attendees there tonight."

"Tell me about it," Alicia said. "Wait 'till you see."

Andy worked her way through a few screens and prompts, then sat back as the computer downloaded the phone's photo gallery. Alicia and I gathered behind Andy. The download bar finished its casual crawl across the screen prompt. The first image popped up. Andy tapped the trackpad and clicked through image after image while Alicia narrated.

"Okay…these are the usual suspects from the petition table…these guys are regulars on the sidewalk in front of the department…okay, go back, go back one…yeah, he was doing a lot of the organizing at the park this afternoon where they assembled. I think he's big in the group…"

Andy nodded. "Lester Connelly. He and his wife formed The Committee Organizing Police Support. He's listed as treasurer."

"Cute acronym," I said. "They have a treasurer?"

"There's a lot of outside money being pumped into this recall. Did I tell you I ran into him?"

"I hope you were doing at least sixty."

"At the grocery store. I introduced myself and he acted like he barely heard of me. Then he tried being all friendly and neighborly, until I asked him to explain to me his basis for the recall. The wheels came off fast, oh my God. Liberal media bias hiding undocumented aliens who are driving high crime rates, uh, something about how defunding the police will turn our cities into war zones, and—you name it, he went there. Ended up with him telling me that the political battle lines have been drawn and we are all headed toward a revolution. I asked him what that looked like."

"And?"

DIVISIBLE MAN - NINE LIVES LOST

"All he said was, 'Second Amendment' and 'You'll see,' and then he walked off."

I didn't like the sound of that and doubted very much that this clown had ever read the amendments to the Constitution.

"I'm sorry, Alicia. Go ahead."

Alicia pointed. "I shot this as they lined up...mostly the same people we see on the street in front of the department...keep going...keep going... okay, him! That's Assemblyman White. He introduced the candidates they plan to run in the recall election. I've got pictures of them—"

"We know who they are," Andy said.

"White plans on running for the open Senate seat." Alicia drew an impressed glance from Andy. "He hit on me. Told me he's headed for big things. He asked me to work on his campaign. Said he expects to get *a very important endorsement* in the next couple days. From the top. Wink, wink."

"Right," I said, "so now we know why he was front and center for this goddamned circus. He's kissing royal ass to get a White House endorsement. Explains why he's singing the assassination song. Son of a bitch."

Andy scrolled. Alicia narrated.

"...that's White...here he is with the recall candidates...okay, stop, stop! This guy...he's the one in charge of all these guys dressed up for LARP Call of Duty...I didn't think he'd let me take his picture, but then he kinda posed for it when I asked him for his number...to send him a copy."

Alicia was cute. And she knew it.

The photo showed someone who might have been mistaken for a soldier, or the type referred to as an *Operator*. The man cultivated a scruff of beard and despite the darkness, wore yellow-tinted plastic sunglasses. He covered his shaved head with an olive drab knit hat. He wore a camo vest over camo shirt. Web belts crisscrossed his chest, stuffed with supplies. Pouches and a canteen dangled from his belt. He gripped a tan military-style rifle with his index finger extended outside the trigger guard. The rifle was slung across his chest with a substantial magazine attached.

Andy zoomed in.

"See this?" She pointed at a patch sewn into this faux soldier's uniform.

Alicia and I both leaned closer.

The round black patch had circular text surrounding a death's head skull with a W etched into its forehead.

COMPANY W and WHITE AMERICA'S MINUTE MEN.

"Shit," I said. "Toto, I don't think we're in Kansas anymore."

Andy sat back without taking her eyes from the screen.

"That's not the line."

28

Andy's new phone rang in the dark. She jolted on the mattress beside me. She had remained tense after Alicia departed. I deployed my best effort to numb the aftereffects of the night's very public personal attack. A glass of iced Bailey's. A gentle backrub. A John Wayne DVD western guaranteed to weigh down her eyelids. A little after eleven, the effort paid off. Tucked under my arm on the sofa, her breathing sank to a slow and steady rhythm. She slept while Wayne searched the west for Natalie Wood. I stopped the movie before the climactic reunion. The absence of sound and action woke Andy. We climbed the stairs for bed and found sleep quickly.

Until this.

Andy grabbed her phone. The clock radio showed 3:38 in satanic red digits. Whoever called at whatever hour this was, they were off my Christmas list for at least the next five years.

"Stewart," she said, reminding me that only a handful of people had this phone's number. "When?...Did anyone see him?...Any idea what direction?...Okay. No, you did the right thing. I'll call my office."

I felt her weight leave the mattress, signaling that this night's abbreviated sleep had ended.

"You can turn the light on," I said, letting her know I was awake.

"I'm sorry." She hurried across the bedroom and flicked the wall switch.

"Who was that?"

"Ellen Brooking. It's Boyd. He's gone."

. . .

106

I CAUGHT up to her in the kitchen.

"I'm going with you," I said.

"Don't be silly. Go back to bed." She slipped into her winter coat and tucked her hair under a knit cap.

"Right." I grabbed my flight jacket and my gloves. On our way through the mudroom, I pocketed a charged power unit from a cabinet. "You hear anything back from the social services people in California?"

"Best we can tell, the system lost track of him after a couple years. They had him placed with a family. The family moved without notifying anyone. The people we talked to say they're still looking, but I get the feeling they're not trying too hard. Finding him only gives them more to be embarrassed about."

"I take it you didn't admit to knowing his whereabouts."

"A little embarrassment will be good for their souls."

I followed Andy outside. We climbed into her unmarked unit. The seat felt like an ice tray.

"Does this thing have seat warmers?"

She ignored me. "Ellen said she checked on him at nine. She got up to use the bathroom and felt cold air on her feet. She found his bedroom window open. That gives him as much as six hours."

"Where's an autistic child going to go at three in the morning?"

"Wherever the pictures in his mind tell him to go, I imagine."

I snapped my seatbelt while Andy performed a reverse Y-turn in our yard. She launched down our driveway in a hurry, turned a gravel-grinding hard right onto our now-silent little road.

She slammed on the brakes. The anti-lock system chattered. The SUV shuddered to a halt.

Boyd stood pale in the headlights, his head cocked slightly to one side, no more inclined to make eye contact with the vehicle lights than he had been with anyone he'd met so far in Essex. He wore a light gray fleece hoodie over the blinding light green Seahawks jersey. His busy hands met at his waist, flexing and shuffling his prized collection of paper squares. I marveled that his bare fingers could move at all, given that the temperature had dipped toward freezing.

"Jesus," I muttered. "What are we…a homing beacon?"

Andy shot me a glance that credited the offhand comment with more than I intended. I opened my door to hop out.

"Wait," she grabbed my arm.

She put the SUV in reverse and backed up past our driveway, angling until the headlights painted our lawn with light for the second time that night.

Boyd, showing no concern for having nearly been run down, resumed his stroll down the center of the road. When he reached our driveway, he turned in. Andy eased the unmarked unit onto the gravel after him.

He walked up the driveway to our back steps, climbed the steps, then halted on the concrete stoop. He did not knock. He paid no attention to the SUV when Andy parked it in front of the garage.

"Let me."

I watched her walk across the yard without urgency. She climbed the steps. Boyd sensed her coming and shuffled aside. Without a word to him, Andy opened the back door and held it. He tucked his chin and stepped inside. I followed.

Andy led the way to our living room. The child gave no sign of connecting with Andy except to trace her footsteps until he stood on our living room carpet. Andy paused for a moment. I thought she might try to speak to Boyd, but instead she hurried to a linen closet in the dining room, pulled out a thick, fuzzy blanket and a spare pillow, and laid them out on our sofa.

The boy's eyes never left the floor, but as soon as Andy stepped aside, he shuffled to the sofa and sat down. Andy fluffed the pillow at one end. He tipped sideways and landed his head on the pillow. Andy billowed the blanket over him and then let it settle over his small arms and legs. He closed his eyes.

"Get the lights," Andy whispered to me. I killed the kitchen, then dining room, then living room lights until we were two shadows in a room illuminated only by light spilling down the stairs from the upstairs hall.

Andy caught my arm and pulled me toward the stairs. I looked back at the sofa.

"You think he'll be okay if we're not down here in the morning?"

She looked over the child-sized lump under the blanket and the small head indenting the pillow. Something warm radiated from her expression. She nodded. Just as we were about to climb the stairs full of faith, the boy's small hand slipped from beneath the blanket. He reached out and carefully placed his stack of paper squares on the coffee table, then retracted his hand.

29

NOW

"You need to go back up to Ekalaka."

"What? No. I'm coming home."

"Will, you have to go back and get that young man," Andy said.

I pinched my eyes closed and bit my tongue against the argument forming there. The kid would be fine. Sore as hell but fine. The people who threw him off a cliff had left town. Even if he opened his mouth about how he survived the fall and how he traveled from the cliff to the road, no one would believe him. It would be his story against mine. His truth was batshit crazy. My lie was rock solid.

"I can't think of a single reason he won't be fine without me."

"Do you have your iPad?" Andy asked. "Can you open it?"

"Hang on. I'm putting you on speaker." I laid my phone on the dash of the Hawthorne Aviation crew car. After leaving Ezra Baker's office, I drove the car around the block and parked fifty yards down the street, playing detective, thinking he might rush off somewhere interesting. So far nothing. "Got it."

"Do a search on KSVI-TV. Billings."

It took a minute to fumble through a Google search that took me to a screen displaying *YourBigSky.com* on a blue banner. Billings' CBS affiliate.

"Okay. What am I looking for?"

"Scroll down past the headline."

"The double semi- rollover? Canned beets? That looks like a mess." I stroked the screen until two columns of headlines appeared. "Oh, shit."

"You see it?"

"Uh-huh."

Halfway down the page, a headline read *Ranch Disappearances Eerily Unworldly*. I tapped the text to read the article and was rewarded with a spinning screen ball.

"I think the screen locked. What's the deal?"

"It's just breaking. Authorities are investigating the disappearance of—they say—up to a dozen people from a ranch outside the small town of Ekalaka in eastern Montana. Whoever is editing the story is going full UFO. They mention that unusual markings have been found on land near the ranch. The group was reported to have gathered in the belief that they were to be transported off Earth by aliens. Authorities found signs of an unfinished meal, personal possessions left behind, cell phones, wallets, that sort of thing."

"Which we know is a setup," I said.

"Of course. But Will…have you asked yourself how whoever did this got their hands on all those personal possessions?"

"I'm not sure I want to."

"We need to find a way to report what you know to the investigating authorities."

"Maybe the kid can do it. Maybe he can explain that he was up there and saw the goon squad making this whole thing look like E.T. came home, or went home, or whatever."

"He can't lie to the police, Will."

Like I can tell them my side? My head was starting to hurt.

"More importantly, if what you told me is correct, that young man isn't aware that someone went back and staged the place."

"I guess he wouldn't be. That would have happened after he got tossed." The spinning ball on my screen showed no sign of going away. "How did they find out?"

"Not sure. The article only said that local authorities were involved."

"I bet it was the deputy. Not such a schlub after all. He must have gone up there to look around after talking to the kid."

The line fell silent.

"Dee? You still there?"

"Will, this is not good."

"No one is going to believe the kid if he says—"

"No. That's not what I mean. If the deputy looked into it after talking to the kid, it's possible the kid told the deputy about his aunt and his interest in the ranch, and if that's the case, then it's only a matter of time before someone from the TV station or local press tracks down the kid and starts asking him questions. And then he disputes the whole—God, I can't believe I'm saying this—alien abduction setup."

"So? This is starting to sound a lot like it's not my problem."

"Will, think. If the press starts asking him questions, then…"

"Then the people who think they killed him start feeling awful damned vulnerable."

"And identifiable."

"Shit."

"You need to go back up there."

30

I returned the car to Hawthorne Aviation, used the restroom, spent a few minutes in the pilot's lounge at the weather briefing console, then filed a flight plan for the return trip to Montana. My watch gained weight. Time now mattered. A lot of hours traversed the clock since the kid checked into the Ekalaka ER. More since the deputy made his discovery. Another two-and-a-half would pass before I reached the small eastern Montana town again, and then I'd chew up more time getting to the hospital. Every ticking second on my watch put that kid closer to a TV camera spotlight. He might even think that making an appeal to the press about his aunt would help him find her. Not a good idea.

I hate flying in a hurry. That's when mistakes are made. I left the FBO office fighting the urge to trot to the plane, fire it up and get moving. Concentrating on the piloting tasks at hand, I loaded my flight bag, mounted the iPad on the control yoke, and secured the bag behind the seat. I hopped off the wing and was halfway through a disciplined preflight walkaround when I broke a cardinal ramp rule by pulling out my phone.

Sue answered the number provided by Google on the fourth ring. Her cheerful voice conjured her smiling face in my mind.

"Hi. It's Will Stewart. The pilot."

"Oh, hi! How are you?"

"I'm good. Listen, um, I really have no business asking this, but I was wondering if I could beg a favor. A rather gigantic favor."

"I'll help if I can."

"That kid. The one we took to the hospital. Um, this is going to be a bit outside the painted lines, but I think he might be in some trouble. Not with the law or anything, but with the people that hurt him. I think they might be able to find out he's at the hospital, and that would be bad. I'm on my way back there now to help him, but it's going to take me a few hours…and I was wondering…would it be—"

"You want me to go and get him?"

"If it's not too much trouble. I mean, you have an obvious in with the staff there, so you might be able to get him discharged without much fuss. And then if you could just keep him at your place until I get there, I'd be very grateful."

I closed my eyes and crossed my fingers.

"Don't worry about a thing. I don't start cooking for another hour. He can join us here for supper."

Yes!

"Wow. That's fantastic. Thank you so much. Honestly, you hardly know me, but you've done so much. You're so kind to help out like this."

She laughed. "You remind me of my brother."

"Well, he's lucky to have a sister like you."

"He sure as hell is." She laughed again.

"Like I said, I hope to be there in a couple hours. One more thing, Sue," I said. "It might be best if you keep this under the radar. Full disclosure, there's a news story busting out about Tammy Day's ranch, and it would be good if you can keep that kid out of everyone's sights for the time being. Reporters…and that deputy…and anybody asking questions. I hope that doesn't change things."

"We already know about the news story," she said sourly. I waited for comment, but she simply added, "I'll fix a plate to warm up for you."

31

The warm southerly flow that dominated the central states of the U.S. blessed me with a fast flight from Sioux City to Ekalaka. My ground speeds topped 235 miles per hour. The air remained largely clear. By the time I set up for landing, the earth and the night sky had gone black, with thin remnants of twilight defining the western horizon. A blanket of stars announced another clear night. I touched down a few minutes after five p.m. local time, landing once again to the south and back taxiing to the ramp.

Two new aircraft occupied tiedowns. It didn't require imagination to assign them to the breaking news story. The question was whether they belonged to legitimate news sources or if they represented the first wave of UFO devotees looking for signs from above.

My question about legitimate news sources was answered moments after I shut down the Baron. Steady throbbing broke over the hills to the west of the field. Sparkling navigation lights, strobes and a beacon arrived in sight. A helicopter swung into the traffic pattern on a crosswind leg, then turned downwind and made its approach to the runway, wisely using the runway lights to orient itself rather than make a direct approach to the dark ramp. After swooping down onto the runway numbers, the pilot heaved the Bell helicopter toward the ramp. He hover-taxied to the north end and settled the ship onto its skids near a fuel station that offered both 100LL Avgas and Jet A. The pilot silenced the whistling jet engine and the blades coasted.

I locked my flight bag in the plane after pocketing the last BLASTER that still contained healthy batteries. Except for the new chopper, the ramp lay empty and silent. All I had to do was duck down on the wing, shielded by the fuselage, and vanish.

Another idea popped into my head.

"HOW'RE YOU DOING TONIGHT?" I strolled up to the helicopter just as the pilot hopped off the skid. He opened the rear door for a young, overdressed woman with stiffly coiffed blonde hair. She angled her bare legs carefully out of the cabin, working hard to manage the short skirt she wore.

"Looking to top off," the pilot answered. He had me pegged for the ramp rat.

"It's self-serve but I'd be glad to give you a hand."

"Is there a restroom?" the woman asked.

"Not that I know of. I just came in. There's no FBO here."

"One too many coffees," she confessed, looking distressed.

"It's a big empty airport and we're the only ones here. If the situation is urgent, I'd suggest out behind those hangars."

She huffed her opinion of that idea, then shrugged. "That's what makes this job glamorous, I guess. Can I rely on you both to stay here?"

"No worries," I said.

The pilot ignored her, instead studying the fuel pumps and the credit card instructions printed on a metal sign. She hurried off into darkness.

"What brings Fox 4 to this little piece of nowhere?" I asked, picking up a step ladder that lay in the grass beside the pumps.

The pilot pulled the hose off its reel. He dragged it to the side of the helicopter.

"Got a ranch up here that looks like they went all Heaven's Gate."

"The movie?"

"The cult."

"No shit." I stood up the ladder, but courtesy called for me to let him position it beside his aircraft. "Suicide?"

"That would be my guess. They haven't found the bodies yet, but I suspect they will. Bunch of people waiting for the mothership, supposedly. Makes you wonder what causes a mind to think in those terms."

"Some kind of cult, you said?"

"That's the way it's shaping up." He climbed the ladder and opened the fuel tank. I handed him the hose. "Becca knows more about it than me. I just haul her around. She shot some crop circles from the air, though. Either they really did board the mothership, or somebody is good with a string and a blowtorch."

"Wow."

"Local cops are up there now, searching. They asked us to come back tomorrow if they can't find anyone. Help 'em look. That's not gonna happen unless we're back here for another remote. Which we will be if the bodies turn up. If not, we got enough A roll on this trip."

"So…if they can't find the bodies, you won't be back to help search, but if they find them, you'll be back to get 'em on video?"

The pilot might have taken offense, but instead he grinned down at me. "This thing clocks out at close to two grand an hour, so management isn't likely to lend it to a search party. Not unless we can get a shot of Becca lifting a lost toddler out of quicksand and onto the skid. Great business, huh?"

"Yeah."

He topped off his tank, careful not to overfill it in the dark. He handed the nozzle back to me.

"I'll tell you this much," he said. "No matter how this story pans out, this place is going to be crawling with UFO nuts. This close to Devil's Tower? Gonna be a fucking bonanza for the tinfoil hat crowd."

32

F *wooomp!*

After confirming an absence of traffic in both directions, I reappeared beside the highway that ran past J and J Guide Service. If anyone happened to look out the window, I preferred that they see me walk up the driveway. I crossed the road and passed a wrought iron sign that identified the hunting guide service.

Sue answered the door smiling.

"Come in! Come in!" she waved me into her home. A fire warmed a tidy living room lined with a sectional leather sofa and several chairs. Trophies of various animals decorated the walls. Sue's husband Rich, the big man I met last night, lounged in a recliner. Two men occupied the sofa. Four more played cards at a table in the adjoining dining room. Sue led me through to her kitchen. "We got your boy. We put him up in one of the bedrooms. John was kind enough to turn it over to him and take the spare bunk outside."

"He's gonna regret that," Rich chimed in from the living room. "Those guys snore like a lumber crew. Nice to see you again, Will." He waved, then returned his focus to the widescreen in the corner. A cowboy with a white moustache engaged in a deep discussion with a young woman. Something about a horse.

"He's resting," Sue said. "He's in a lot of pain but he ate a good supper. I've got a plate for you in the 'fridge. Why don't you wash up while I heat it up for you?"

The warm room, the smell of food and the hypnotic flames licking logs in the fireplace suddenly tallied up my lack of meals and sleep. My stomach gave notice that I'd been ignoring it.

"I guess there's no rush to see the kid. Has anyone asked about him?"

Sue gave me a sideward look loaded with a twinkle in her eye. "I don't think anyone in the ER will remember that I picked him up. Provided he's not in any legal trouble, that is."

"He's not."

"Is he involved with what's going on up at Tammy Day's ranch?" Rich asked.

"You know about that?"

"It's all over the TV news. Bunch of idiots." I waited for more, but the debate about the horse on television took a dramatic turn when a young hunk of a cowboy arrived to challenge the old cowboy. Rich returned his attention to the drama unfolding on a ranch that bore no resemblance to anything I'd seen yet in Eastern Montana.

"You can wash up in there," Sue pointed down a hall.

THE MEAL DAMN near put me to sleep. Venison stew, twice-baked potatoes, a side of green bean casserole generously topped with crisp onions, and warm corn bread. Strawberry rhubarb pie finished what easily ranked in the top ten meals I've ever had. Being ravenously hungry loaded the ballot box, but Sue's cooking knocked the dinner out of the park. I marveled that she did this sort of thing daily for a dozen or so hunters.

I politely declined a glass of wine as well as an invitation to join the card game. I offered to help clean up, but Sue brushed me off. She cleared away my empty plate, then escorted me to a bedroom at the side of the small house. She knocked politely. Wally called out to let her know he was awake.

His eyes widened in recognition when I slipped in the door.

"We're out of beds," Sue said, "but I have an air mattress if you don't mind sleeping on the floor in here. Or you can have the couch in the living room."

"Let me get back to you on that. We might not be staying."

Adopting an expression of disapproval, Sue slipped out and closed the door.

The room had twin beds. Wally propped himself against a pile of pillows on the bed under a set of windows. Assorted clothing and hunting gear lay on the other bed, which hugged the interior wall. I assumed the gear belonged to one of the men playing cards or sitting with Rich.

"You," Wally said.

"Yeah. Me." I dropped on the edge of the second bed. "How are you feeling?"

"I got three broken ribs and a pneumothorax. Fancy word for a hole in my lung. They tell me there's nothing to be done for any of it, that it needs to heal on its own. They said I don't need surgery, but I shouldn't play rugby for a couple months."

"Good advice. I also recommend you not get your ass thrown off a cliff again."

"The lady said you told her the guys that beat me up might figure out where I was. That you asked her to get me outta the hospital. This is nice, and all, but I gotta get out of here. Somebody's got to take me back to my car. And are you ever going to fucking tell me—? Sorry. That was rude. I mean, I'm grateful and all. It's just—"

"Yeah, I get it. It's a lot to take in."

"I've decided. You can have it. The whole Metallica collection. Just tell me."

"Keep the heavy metal. I prefer female vocalists."

"Dude, you're really not from outer space or anything weird like that, are you?"

"Because of the abduction thing at the ranch?"

"Yeah. I mean—wait. What?"

"Oh. I guess you wouldn't know." I explained the day's developments, starting with my return trip to the ranch. I told him it was unlikely he would ever see his car again.

"That's bullshit," he declared, then winced at the pain his anger caused. "That's such bullshit."

"The car?"

"Well, yeah—but, no. That crap about the dinner and the wine glasses and all the stuff. *Dude, I was there.* There was nothing like that. And there were no wallets. No purses. No keys. No cell phones. Everyone and every-thing was gone."

"Well, somebody brought it all back and set it up to look like dinner got interrupted by the arrival of the mothership. You know anything about that?"

He frowned. "I told you. I came up here to find my Aunt Stephanie."

"She was into all that stuff?"

"That's why she came here. That's why she's in that photo. She was really deep into all that UFO shit."

"Like…tinfoil hat deep?"

"She's not a crazy lady." He winced again.

"Okay, okay. I meant no offense."

"I just mean, okay, she's like…all in. Lock, stock and ready to board. But she's not a looney tune. I think she just—she found a bunch of people on the same page. Gathering here. That's why I came looking for her before somebody else did."

"Who else? Those guys?"

"I don't know who those guys were. Seriously. No, I'm talking about my family. They're kinda having a shit fit."

"I suppose it's hard to see someone get sucked into all that."

He lowered his eyes and shook his head. "That's not it. Aunt Stephanie has a lot of money."

"How much is a lot?"

"Like Power Ball money. Fucking hedge fund money. But that is totally *not* my thing. I came because I like her. I'm worried about her. She was always a little kooky, but she cared about me. She was fun to be around. I just…I just don't want to see her taken advantage of. She has a big heart. The UFO thing, I always figured it was harmless. Money or not, I just don't want to see somebody stomp all over what she believes in."

"Money does bad things. When's the last time you heard from her?"

"Couple weeks ago. She was in California for a while, at some commune or church thing up north of San Francisco. Talk about people trying to get into her bank accounts. She bailed on them. Then she was in Arizona. Then New Mexico. That's when I lost contact with her."

"You ever hear of a lawyer by the name of Ezra Baker?"

"Sure. He's one of the reasons the rest of my family is having a cow. They think my aunt has him handling her affairs now. Whatdya callit?"

"Power of attorney?"

"Nah…some sort of trust. Aunt Stephanie is my mom's sister. My mom and my uncle Al are the ones making a big stink. They say they want to protect her but—and I hate to talk about my mom like this—but all they really care about is my aunt giving away her money. I heard them talk about that Baker guy weaseling his way into the picture—like he's competition. Why? Did you talk to him? Does he know where she is?"

"I did talk to him. If he knows anything, he's not saying. Not to me, anyway." I pulled out the photo and spread it on the bed, then took a picture of it with my phone. I handed the original back to Wally.

"Thanks."

"The woman on the end. Ever see her before?"

He shook his head.

"Ever hear the name Farris?"

"Lillian Farris?"

"You know her?"

"I heard of her. Some sort of authority on all this weird shit. I don't know if that means she's as gullible as my aunt, or she's in on the con."

"I can tell you she's not gullible. How did you hear about Lillian?"

"I told you, man. Same way I heard that Aunt Stephanie might be up here. Martian Mike."

33

I needed sleep and accepted Sue's offer of an air mattress, a pillow, and a blanket. I crashed on the floor at the foot of Wally's bed with my phone alarm set for 3:30 and placed next to my pillow. The alarm proved unnecessary when the third man in the room hit a crescendo of symphonic snoring around 2:45. I thought the framed prints of wildlife in the small bedroom might rattle off the walls. When I heard Wally giggle after one especially thunderous coda, I asked him if he was ready to go. He said yes.

We both slept in our clothes—me because I had nothing else and Wally because he couldn't have taken his off if he wanted to. We had nothing to carry except our shoes. I lit up my phone screen for guidance. Wally's pain was obvious, but he forced himself upright and moved off the bed. He followed me out the bedroom door, down a short hall and out the unlocked front door into starlight so bright it cast shadows.

I sat on a lawn chair and put my boots on. Then I kneeled at Wally's feet and helped him into his shoes. Just as I finished lacing them up, the front door opened behind us. Sue stepped onto the wooden porch wrapped in a fuzzy robe. I expected scolding, but she held out a plastic bag.

"I thought you might sneak out. Here," she said. "I packed this for you. Apples and some molasses cookies. They're my grandmother's recipe. Do you need a ride?"

"I've made arrangements," I lied. Wally accepted the plastic Care package and offered his thanks.

Sue lingered. "I wanted to ask you something. I got a couple calls from neighbors tonight. The smalltown rumor mill is operating at capacity. They're saying the thing at Tammy's ranch might be one of those suicide cult things. Is that what you think?"

"No." I shook my head. "I don't have a clue what happened up there, and I can't tell you those folks are all safe, but I can tell you one thing. My wife is a cop with the sharpest mind I know. I may be a little slow sometimes, but I've picked up a skill or two from her. She knows when something feels... off. She would say this feels off."

"Well," Sue said, "if those fellas that did this to you come around asking, Wally, you were never here."

"I appreciate that. That'll be our story, too."

"I think from meeting your husband, that those fellas would be wise not to come around here," I said.

She smiled in the dark. "Rich? He's a teddy bear...until he isn't."

I turned to Wally. "You ready?"

"Ready to run a marathon."

"Right. Let's just try to get to the end of the driveway. Our ride is picking us up by the road. Thanks again for everything, Sue. Tell your friends Deb and Terry that Earl Jackson said Hi."

"I'll do that. You take care."

WE WALKED to the end of the driveway. Wally marched stiffly beside me. I didn't need to ask to know that every step induced pain. His breathing grew sharp and shallow. Perspiration broke out on his face despite a breeze that, although warm for November, carried a chilly warning of coming winter.

I knew without looking that Sue watched us from the house. The woman projected a powerful mothering instinct. When we reached the road, I turned us toward town. We walked on empty starlit pavement until the Quonset-style shed beside the house blocked us from her sight.

"You ready?" I asked Wally.

"Are we doing that crazy shit again?"

"Well, you sure as hell aren't hiking to the airport. Gimme your hand."

We closed a grip. His right, my left, side by side, elbow to elbow.

"Abracadabra," I said.

Fwooomp!

"Mother Mary, Joseph and Jesus!"

34

Martian Mike, according to Wally, manifested himself as an expert in the field of Unidentified Flying Objects. His credentials extended to having a website and a string of podcasts devoted to the belief that humans are not alone in the universe. Dr. Lillian Farris argues the same point citing mathematical probability with numbers so large that when she talks, my eyes glaze over. Martian Mike differs from Lillian in that he promotes the idea that we have long ago ceased to occupy our planet in privacy.

Despite Lillian's insistence that something unworldly caused my accident and the inexplicable consequences that followed, I didn't have an opinion one way or another—a position that earned me the title of *Dumbass* from Lillian.

What I cared about was that the human posing as Martian Mike produced his web pages and podcasts in Greeley, Colorado not twenty minutes flying time from Sterling, where Wally lived. I planned to drop the kid off and then find Martian Mike and ask what he knew about Wally's aunt and the group that had disappeared from Tammy Day's ranch.

Wally detected my plan to ditch him when I tapped Sterling into the flight plan feature on the Garmin 750 shortly after takeoff.

"Hold on," he pointed at the screen. "What are you doing? I thought we were going to meet Martian Mike?"

"I thought you already met him."

"No, man. I never met him. I read his blogs and posts about ParaTransit and a ranch up in Ekalaka. We texted. Seriously, I never met the guy."

"You just went up to Montana based on what you read on the internet?"

"No. Aunt Stephanie's text to me praised the guy and mentioned Big Sky. At first I thought she was being literal." Wally looked sideways at me like I was supposed to catch his meaning. I didn't. "Big Sky," he repeated. "As in big enough for visitors…? Space…?"

I said nothing.

"Whatever, man. Then I saw Martian Mike's blogs describing a leading edge, select group setting up a landing site at a ranch in Ekalaka, Montana."

"You make my point for me."

"I came up and poked around town—there's an amazing Mexican place there—"

"The enchiladas, right?"

"Yes! OMG. Killer. Anyway, the owner and I chatted. I put the pieces together and found the ranch. It's not as far-fetched as it sounds. Aunt Stephanie was a fan of Martian Mike."

Big surprise. I didn't say it out loud.

"She called him a celestial guide—pointing her to the right people, the right place, the right moment. Dude, we have to go talk to him."

"Dude, you have to stop calling me dude."

"I want to talk to him. In person."

I tapped Activate on the G750 flight plan page. A magenta line connecting Sterling popped onto the map screen. I banked to intercept.

"You're not in any shape to travel, Wally." Boarding a Baron requires a degree of fitness. I had to load us both into the plane while still vanished, floating Wally into the passenger seat after me, since I had to board first to get in the pilot's seat. It was awkward and stupid, and I thanked God no one could see us.

"Don't drop me off, du—er, Will. I'm begging you. I'm the only one looking out for my aunt."

Crap.

"Please."

I reprogrammed the navigation system and turned ten degrees left.

35

THREE DAYS AGO

A ndy padded into the kitchen on bare feet. She slid her hands around my waist and tugged herself against me.

"Morning."

"It is. But just wait a while and it will turn into afternoon."

"Coffee."

I filled her mug and handed it to her. She cupped her hands around it, appreciating the warmth. The first sip brought no complaints. I made the pot solely for her since I planned to bolt for the airport and reserved my first cup for Rosemary II's exquisite blend.

"You were up late last night."

"Mmmph," she replied. She slipped onto one of the kitchen chairs and delivered another dose of caffeine to her system. "Still digging through the facial recognition on the rogue's gallery from Company W."

I joined her, although the coffee aroma teased me. "Anything interesting?"

"Plenty. Ashley captured twelve of their mugs. Their records would fill a binder. Not one of them is from Essex or even Wisconsin. They're imported from Missouri, Nevada, Utah and a few other states of the wild west. Big contingent from Idaho. Old pals of yours."

"Congregating here for a little city council election. Now that's a sense of civic duty."

"No. There is no recall election. Not yet. They have to get 4,000 signatures before there will be an election."

"Sounded like they're close," I said. "At least that's what Senator Wannabe sold to the mob."

"Impossible. It's been less than two weeks since it started. I'll believe it when I see it. Anyway, we identified four of the visitors as having outstanding warrants. Tom is working with the county DA who is working with the issuing jurisdictions."

"To make arrests?"

She shrugged. I sensed there were complications.

"I got a reply from New Mexico."

"Nice change of subject, Dee."

She smiled, unleashing dimples to mock me. "I thought so. We reached out to the sheriff's office in Mora County last week. They poked around Wagon Mound for us."

"And found Wild Bill Hickok's grave?"

"Wild Bill is buried in Deadwood, South Dakota. This is New Mexico. Your pal Lillian was living in a trailer park under the name Lila Ford. And she had a child with her. A boy."

"Our mailbox assassin?"

"We sent photos. The neighbors weren't sure about the photo because they didn't see much of the boy, but they confirmed that the child was 'special.' So, yes, we're fairly certain."

"Huh."

"We still don't know how that boy wound up with Dr. Farris after social services in California lost track of him."

Andy sipped her coffee and let her gaze drift out the kitchen windows. Her rich auburn hair showed a hint of morning rebellion. I wanted to touch it. To touch her. That happens a lot. She caught me staring and flashed a quick smile that I recognized.

"Okay. What's going on?" I asked. "What aren't you telling me?"

She shook her head and slid her hand across to cover mine. I said nothing, leaving the question open. She dropped her eyes to the fascinating surface of the coffee in her mug.

"Tom heard from the District Attorney last night. They're pushing back my deposition in the Johns case."

Andy's pivotal role in the arrest of former NFL star Clayton Johns for the rape of an underaged girl last summer made her a key witness in a case that was beginning to look like it might never reach a courtroom. Johns had money, the kind that buys the best of the best in criminal defense; money that buys every possible delay and diversion in the delivery of justice. Johns' attorneys had already deployed a barrage of evasive tactics, so much so that I had commented that they planned to outlive the victim, a teenaged girl.

"What is it this time?"

"Me." She looked up and for a rare moment, I could not read the emotion in her face or eyes. Hurt? Anger?

"You? What are you talking about?"

"Tom said that the word is they want to delay past this recall election and my summary dismissal, which they then can then use to impeach me as a witness."

I uttered an expression more often spoken by Pidge.

"It gets better. This recall group is spending a lot of money. Rumor is that some of it is coming from the state party, but Tom thinks a big chunk is coming from Clayton Johns, well laundered, of course."

I saw it now. It was both. Hurt and anger.

I repeated my first comment. Andy said nothing more on the subject. She squeezed my hand, threw a kiss at my cheek, and said she was getting dressed. Having nothing but useless simmering anger to offer her, I set off for the airport. I planned to spend the morning in the Foundation hangar catching up on logbook entries and updating navigation databases. First, I needed a stop at the Essex County Air Service office to steal a mug of Rosemary II's coffee.

I had just pulled off the heist when she called out from behind the front counter.

"Earl's looking for you."

36

NOW

"This is not what I expected."

I docked the heaving Buick Roadmaster wagon at the curb. Even after locking it in Park, the big boat wallowed and settled. Airport crew cars come as is. I once drove a retired ambulance.

The flight from Ekalaka to Greeley had taken an hour and forty minutes, bucking a fourteen-knot headwind, my constant companion of late. Dawn broke on the eastern horizon during the flight, treating us to a spectacular sky that even the kid couldn't stop commenting on. High strands of red and pink blazed across the flatlands of eastern Colorado. I mentioned the old sailor claim that a "red sky in morning" means "sailor take warning." Like many such expressions, the rhyme had a basis in fact. Unlike the sailors burning their hands on ropes and their skin in relentless sun, I had access to digital Prog Charts forecasting the future of gigantic air masses in six-hour increments. A huge low-pressure system developing over the Pacific Northwest signaled an end to good weather. Rain for Seattle. Snow for the Rockies and plains. In another thirty-six to forty-eight hours Wisconsin would see the first snow of the season.

I planned to be at home and in the arms of a beautiful woman long before flakes carpeted our lawn. That meant doing business in Colorado quickly, whether it answered questions about Tammy Day, Aunt Stephanie, and Crazy Lillian or not.

The Buick engine chugged a few revolutions before rattling to a halt. Wally stared out the side window.

"What a freaking sellout. There's a gift shop. Do you see that? There's a damned gift shop. And look." Wally pointed. "Is that a food court?"

"Looks like a courtyard with food trucks."

Wally gingerly detached his seat belt. Gritting his teeth, he reached for the door handle.

"Hold on. Why don't you let me scope this out before you break another rib trying to get out of this car? I can't zap you and lift you out. Not out in public like this. Let me see if the guy is here."

He answered by releasing a breath he'd been holding against fresh pain.

I climbed out of the driver's seat. Morning sun warmed my face. I paused and pulled off my flight jacket and tossed it on the seat.

"Be right back."

RIGHT BACK TOOK ALMOST AN HOUR, and when I returned to the car, I had nothing to show for my efforts.

The unlikely headquarters of Martian Mike Enterprises occupied a glass and brick corporate center, sharing leased space with a brewery supply company, an architectural design firm and a gymnastics studio in one of several matching single-story office buildings built around a central court-yard stocked with benches and picnic tables. High occupancy and the expan-sive size of the courtyard attracted a row of food trucks to the nearest curb. The midday business looked brisk, aided by warm sunshine.

The old Buick sat less than two hundred feet from the courtyard, well within view of at least two dozen people. As I approached, it became clear that Wally was gone. An irrational thought flared up. I checked the street for ATVs.

How did they find us?

"Idiot." I said it to myself. They couldn't possibly have.

I turned and scanned, and quickly spotted Wally at a picnic table. He sat across from a young woman who appeared both fascinated and charmed by him. Wally smiled and chatted. Except for his stiff posture, he showed no sign of his injury.

I crossed a span of well-manicured lawn and wove through the scattered tables hoping my Ray Ban Aviators emphasized the scowl on my face. I hadn't really slept in two days, wore the same clothes I left Wisconsin in, and was being tortured by the scent of something fabulous coming from those food trucks.

"Oh, hey, Uncle Will," Wally waved cheerfully. "Did you find a t-shirt?"

"They didn't have my size."

"I might be able to check stock for you," the girl chimed in, flashing a bright smile clearly meant for Wally. "What size are you?"

"It's okay," I said, "I found something better." I threw Wally a glance meant to land the ball in his court.

The girl lifted him off the hook by standing up and gathering the paper debris from her lunch.

"Brenda, thank you so much for the help and the information. Super helpful!" Wally said.

"Really nice meeting you." She gave him a look that lingered, and then wiggled her phone. "Call me."

She performed a turn meant to let him watch her walk off, which he did. Taking his gaze with her, she disappeared through a set of glass doors without glancing back.

I sat down.

"Seriously? I'm inside wasting my time trying to find your favorite Martian while you're out here lining up dates?"

"Nice girl," Wally said, letting pain chase the smile off his face. "What did you find?"

"Not a damned thing. Complete bust. I couldn't get into half the offices. The rest are nothing but a mid-tier small business selling crap to UFO believers. I didn't see anything that looked like a podcast production studio and there's nobody in there named Martian Mike, at least according to a couple of desk signs, door names and one fire exit plan map I found. I think this whole thing is a scam."

"Did you like…do that thing? Flying around?"

"It's a lot harder than you think. For one thing, I couldn't use my—why am I explaining this to you? You get one whiff of perfume and you're out here picking up girls."

"That girl is a temp. She works in the shipping department. Yes, they have a shipping department. And she had a lot to say about this operation— not much of it good."

"Any of it useful?"

"Yes. She told me where we can find Frederick Michael Dowd."

"Lemme guess. Martian Mike."

Wally lowered his voice. "I think we shouldn't discuss it here. Let's talk in the car. We have time. It's about an hour and a half drive."

"Huh. If that's the case, I'm going to make a stop at those trucks. You want anything?"

Wally gritted his teeth. "Probably make me throw up. I have no idea how I'm going to get back to or get in that car."

"I can't fly you out of here. Not with all these people around."

"Just leave me here to die, man."

"I'm getting tacos." I stood up. "You've got five minutes to choose life or death. Oh—and before you choose death, do me a favor. Pull out your phone and find us the nearest hardware store."

"MARTIAN MIKE SOLD out six months ago. Brenda said she used to listen to his radio show. She said it was a big thing when she was in middle school. Kids doing sleepovers would stay up all night to hear him come on the air at two or three in the morning with wild tales about alien abductions. Blue Book, Roswell, Betty and Barney Hill. All the golden oldies, of course, but new stuff, too. The new Congressional report. The Navy videos. She went to work for a temp agency, and a couple weeks ago they set her up in the shipping department of Martian Mike Enterprises. She said it was a huge letdown, like believing in Disney princesses, and then winding up working the gift shop counter in Cinderella's castle."

"Who did he sell out to?" I asked. I drove west on a wide four-lane avenue through flat suburban Greeley. I felt self-conscious in the quarter-century-old Buick, cruising through a tidy upscale community dotted with expensive homes, and sharing the roads with an armada of small SUVs that looked barely broken in and wouldn't be caught dead off of pavement. I checked the rearview mirror for a cloud of blue oil smoke, but the durable GM V-8 remained strong and steady. After a quick stop at an Ace Hardware, I programmed Ashley's directions into my iPad. Close to an hour would get us through Greeley, then Loveland, then another half hour of travel would take us into the foothills west of civilization.

"She didn't know. But she said it was a total sellout. Word is he cashed in for serious bucks. The new owners turned it into a booming merchandising operation. She thinks he's still doing the podcasts, but he doesn't seem to have anything to do with the business. She's never seen him. The lease on those offices is less than two months old."

"What about ParaTransit?"

"I asked. Didn't ring a bell."

"And how does she know where to find him?"

"Ashley said they had her deliver a package to him about a week ago.

She thought she might get to meet him but only got as close as a locked gate. They told her to leave it."

"What are we talking here? A Ted Kaczynski shack in the woods?"

"No idea. She couldn't see the place, but it's no shack. The rumor is he got millions out of the deal."

"For a website?"

"For a brand. There's talk of a Netflix series. Convention tie-ins. Heck, I wouldn't be surprised if they launched a theme park. Or sold the whole works to Disney. The mouse owns everything else."

"Maybe Disney bought him in the first place. That's a lot of money."

Wally didn't comment. He stared straight ahead, looking pale. The walk back to the car had taken a lot out of him.

"You okay? Did they give you anything for the pain?"

"Tylenol. Can I ask you something?"

"If it's the same question, you're getting the same answer."

"It's not. What were you doing up at that ranch?"

I explained Earl and his story about Tammy Day.

"And now you're looking for the other lady, too? Dr. Farris?"

"Two birds. One stone."

I doubted the short answer satisfied him, but he must have recognized it was all he would get because he asked nothing more.

WEST OF LOVELAND, the scenery changed dramatically. Flatland gave way to foothills. Open fields morphed into dry grass and low green scrub. The terrain rose and was soon dotted with pines. To my Wisconsin eye, a glance in almost any direction composed a picture post card or a scene from any of a dozen Hollywood westerns I've seen. U.S. Highway 34 climbed into what looked and felt to me like mountains. In countless places the road had been cut between walls of solid rock.

"Are you sure about these directions?" I asked Wally. The two-lane road wound back and forth, its path a product of the terrain and engineers choosing a path of least resistance. I fought the urge to hurry. Double yellow lines prohibited passing for miles at a time. No one appeared to live in this area. There were no crossroads, no driveways joining the highway. For a long stretch, a creek ran beside the road, separated from the highway by a thirty-foot drop and a guard rail. Steep slopes bordered both sides of the highway.

Eventually the scenery became less rocky, more hilly. The constant curving of the road and wallowing of the car didn't bother me, but I worried about Wally. He said nothing. He stared through the windshield. I recognized the signs, having had more than one airsick passenger in the sky with me.

"Crack your window," I told him. "Get some fresh air."

He found the power window control without looking and dropped the glass a couple inches. The higher elevation air felt significantly cooler than the near-summer temperatures in Greeley.

Sunset came early. I knew we would not get back to Greeley before dark, but I now began to wonder if we'd find Martian Mike's lair in the light. The iPad told me we had another half hour to drive but the sun had already dropped beneath the hilltops. Granted, that wasn't the actual horizon, but it threw us in shadow that prompted me to turn on the vehicle headlights.

We drove closer to the map point Brenda the Temp had given Wally. I looked for driveways joining the highway. Few and far between, they were universally narrow gravel lanes that dropped away from the road or vanished behind low hills and into stands of pine.

Brenda's instructions directed us to a bend in the road near a handful of houses that went by the name of Big Thompson River, which was also the name of the creek whose ancient path guided the engineers building the road. Two miles past that curve, she said to look for a turnoff onto the grandly named Washington Canyon Highway. I nearly missed the sign because it had slipped one of its bolts and hung at a forty-five-degree angle from its post. The so-called highway was a single lane of gravel that swung down off Highway 34, cut across a culvert laid in the Big Thompson River, then began a winding climb on a slope of pine that grew thicker with each cutback.

The Buick heaved on its suspension. Wally threw a hand up to the dash. I fished around at my feet until I found the empty bag that had contained my taco lunch. I shoved the bag at Wally who took it without moving his eyes from the windshield. No explanation was needed. A moment later, like the old station wagon, Wally heaved.

"God! That hurts," he cried through clenched teeth. Then he heaved again. Cried out again. Coughed and dry heaved, moaning against the pain.

"Big mistake bringing you," I muttered.

He didn't argue. The convulsions tore at his ribcage. He squeezed his eyes shut and held the bag open at the ready but tried rapid breathing to thwart the urge to vomit again.

I slowed the Buick to a crawl, then braked and halted.

"Don't stop for me," he whispered through gritted teeth.

"I'm not. We're here."

37

N O TRESSPASSING.
KEEP OUT.
VICIOUS DOGS.

"He should have added ones that say, 'Radiation Hazard' or 'Ebola Quar-
antine Zone.' Like in that movie about the two old guys."

Wally said nothing. He closed his eyes tightly.

"Alright, you stay here. I'll go find our guy."

"No."

"Suit yourself. Hop out. Climb that gate. Hike up however much
driveway still lies between us and his shack. I'll meet you there."

Wally started to protest, but the effort triggered another convulsion. He
shoved the bag against his mouth, which probably wasn't the best idea,
considering its contents. My stomach raised its own warning flag. I opened
the door and hopped out for fresh air.

Between the higher elevation and the missing sunlight, the temperature
had dropped sharply. I opened the back door and pulled on my flight jacket.
From my flight bag, I extracted two power units and their companion
propellers. I scooped up the plastic bag from the hardware store but decided
not to dig into its contents.

"I'll be back," I told Wally. I moved my flight bag to the floor. "Get
some air. Maybe lie down on the back seat."

He weakly waved me to stop but could not speak. After fumbling to find
the window switch, he dropped the glass all the way and tossed the bag into

the brush beside the car. I resolved to keep the plastic hardware store bag, since it was the only barf bag we had left, although I doubted Wally had anything left to barf.

I closed the rear door and wrapped my arms around my cargo.

Fwooomp!

I pushed my toes against the gravel and launched. The faded roof of the Roadmaster with its pitted and rusted cargo rack dropped away. Tall pines in every direction sank, paying their respects to the miracle of flight. Above the treetops, the landscape expanded. A rim of fire, sunset's finale, touched the high terrain to my right. The valley containing Highway 34 wore a cloak of shadow, made darker by its contrast with the last light of the day.

I pulled a power unit from my pocket, snapped the prop in place, and held it out. The batteries were weak, but the unit produced enough power to pull me forward.

Martian Mike's threat laden gate slid beneath me. The gravel road continued through the pines, winding in ever-tightening switchbacks that would have put Wally's head back in the bag. I cut directly across the tan zig-zag line.

Three quarters of a mile ahead, near the crest of the hill, a peaked roof broke through the treetops. Halfway there I slowed and lowered myself through the pines. My boots touched down in the center of the gravel road.

Fwooomp! I reappeared well out of view of the house and crouched, laying the hardware store bag at my feet. Darkness closed in around me.

I replaced the batteries for both power units. I wasn't happy to do it, but I tossed the old batteries into the weeds. Next, I extracted a long silver flashlight from the bag. I had loaded it with batteries and tested the light in the hardware store. I elected not to test it again. I rolled and folded the plastic bag and stuffed it in my pocket for Wally's future use. Then I practiced finding the control button for the LED flashlight by feel. Certain of its position and function, I shoved the big flashlight, nearly ten inches long, into my shirt, enduring a jolt of cold against my skin.

Fwooomp!

Freshly powered and armed, I kicked off the gravel and rapidly shot up through the trees. I thumbed the slide control on the BLASTER in hand. The prop whined and converted my ascent to forward speed. I aimed for the rooftop.

MARTIAN MIKE'S shack probably pulled a cool million out of whatever check he'd been written for his fringe franchise. Built with log walls, a full-façade rustic porch, and a bank of glass overlooking a canyon on one side, it might have been a ski lodge or boutique hotel. The building wasn't new, but it appeared well-kept. The immediate grounds remained naturally wooded. The gravel driveway ended at a three-car garage connected to the cabin by a glass breezeway. A hundred-thousand-dollars-worth of Land Rover sat beside the house.

I flew counterclockwise around the house to determine if Martian Mike lived alone. Warm light glowed from lamps in a large sitting room with the canyon view. None of the second-story windows showed light.

I had no illusions about the man simply welcoming an uninvited guest and answering questions about his business. He had reasons to hide things. Embarrassment for selling out. A Non-Disclosure Agreement enforced by his buyer. Or worse.

On the second orbit, I slowed and dropped to window level for the Peeping Tom portion of the exercise. Floor-to-ceiling glass made up an entire wall that stuck out several feet over a sharp drop. The rock wall below the building foundation reminded me of the cliff where Wally had taken up involuntary skydiving. Straight down for at least one hundred feet, the wall then sloped into a rugged skirt of boulders and gravel, eventually giving way to a creek bed. The view was spectacular. Beyond the creek, rolling pine-covered hills stretched east into the distance. A thin span of lights marked the horizon. Loveland, or Greeley. On a good day, a sharp eye might see the flatlands of Nebraska. My estimate of the real estate price hiked itself.

Two lamps illuminated the sitting room. Recessed lighting lit up an open concept kitchen. Both spaces were empty.

I cruised the length of the glass wall, then hooked around the back of the house, which had a full span porch matching the front. The glass of the main room extended to the first one third of the porch and included sliding doors. Next came a back door, then an unlit utility room, an empty bedroom, and then a small office lit by the screensaver of a desktop PC. Colored lightning bolts crawled around on the screen, making it possible for me to see piles of papers, magazine, newspapers and folders on the desk, and walls full of pinned maps. Martian Mike may have sold out, but he did not appear to have retired.

My surveillance produced nothing. Most of the rooms were dark and empty. I saw no movement, no one planted in front of a widescreen television. By the time I finished checking the windows, I began to doubt that anyone was home—until I finished back at the big picture windows.

A man stood at a countertop in the kitchen musing over the instructions on a cardboard package of frozen food. I recognized the face from a brief glance at his website and from a poster hanging in the Martian Mike Enterprises offices. Somewhere between a healthy sixty and a worn out forty, he had longish hair of an indeterminate light color that hung limp against his pencil-thin neck. He had a narrow jawline on a face carrying bags of excess flesh beneath the eyes. I guessed him to be my height, but thirty pounds lighter, a little on the bony side. He wore the aura of a university professor past his prime.

He pulled a set of readers from his pocket and planted them on the end of a narrow nose, studying the instructions on the cardboard box. It looked like a single serving packet. Only one plate had been placed on the countertop. I took both as confirmation that he was alone.

Showtime.

I aimed the BLASTER straight up and rose. Clear of the roofline, I angled toward the smaller second story of the house. Where the upper roof sloped down to within six feet of the lower roof, I grabbed a corner. I shut down the power unit and pocketed it.

Using both hands to grip the edge of the upper roof, I planted my feet on the shingles of the lower roof. This would have been easier with the help of gravity, but I could not afford to be seen.

I stomped both feet against the shingles.

Boom.

Not house-shaking, but I felt certain the sound and vibration reached the kitchen directly below. Again.

Boom.

I gave it a casual pause, then began a rapid march in place. The effect I wanted was a steady rumbling—a vibration. I kept it up, increased the impact and the volume, then let it fade to a stop. I paused. Repeated. The second time I increased the duration.

After the second round, I pushed off and circled back to the big windows. Martian Mike startled me. He stood inches from the center pane of glass, pale blue eyes squinting, his face a question mark. He cocked his head to listen.

I took advantage of the moment and shoved the BLASTER to full power. The prop buzzed and whined. I held it out so that I accelerated less than a foot past his face, unseen. He jumped back, startled by the passing sound.

I picked up speed and shot past the edge of the house, cutting a hard right to circle back in front of the windows. No question about it, I had the man's attention. His head tipped back and forth, searching the falling darkness, aiming his oversized ears for better hearing.

I used full reverse thrust to stop at the next window panel over from where he stood. He alerted to the sound. I drifted closer to the glass, turned the BLASTER around, and gently placed the heel of the power unit against the glass. I slid the control into reverse, causing it to thrust against the glass. The effect was immediate and dramatic. The entire panel drummed. The glass amplified the BLASTER vibration. Martian Mike hopped away from the windows, crouched, and searched for the cause. I increased the thrust. His moonlike eyes hunted the alien sound. I pounded the power unit against the glass twice, then cut it off sharply.

Martian Mike stood frozen, debating fight or flight. I half expected him to dive behind a fat brown leather sofa.

I initiated a quiet climb out of his sight and pulled the LED flashlight from my shirt. I found the switch and clicked through the settings. Steady white. High-powered steady white. Flashing white. Flashing red. I settled on flashing red.

Although unseen like me, the flashlight still emitted light. Flashing red LEDs painted the rooftop and the trees surrounding the house. I felt a grin slip across my face.

This is going to look really cool.

With the flashlight in one hand and my BLASTER in the other, I took off. I climbed, curved, and then swooped past the house, dipping into the canyon. Martian Mike gaped at the strobing light that scribed an impossible path through the air beyond his windows. I accelerated and cut left around the back of the house, soared above the garage, then dove for another pass. This time I came in fast from his right, diving deeper into the canyon. The red light flashed against the rock wall.

Climbing back up, I centered on the windows and hit full reverse thrust to stop. I hung there holding the flashlight toward the house where the UFO evangelist plastered himself against his windows, aghast.

Time for a classic move. I remained still for a long minute, then hit full power and shot straight up. I could not help it. I found myself laughing, wondering if he had acquired the presence of mind to grab his phone to capture fresh new video for his UFO archives. With the red light aimed at the house, I rose to at least five hundred feet above the rooftop. Then I clicked the light off.

Put that in your X Files, Mikey.

I stopped the climb and started a slow descent back toward the house. A door slammed. Hard footsteps pounded the wooden porch boards at the front of the house. Martian Mike leaped down a set of wooden steps and raced onto the gravel driveway near his British luxury four-wheel drive. A hint of twilight remained in the western sky. It ignited a glow in his pale, upturned face.

Perfect.

I reduced power and quietly moved into position directly above the man. Descending, I aimed the flashlight straight down and hit the button. A circle of white light surrounded Martian Mike. He crouched but did not run. He stared straight up. The white LED light—or maybe the meaning of it in his mind—drained his skin of color.

I dropped. Twenty feet over his head, I hit the light a second time. It flashed to the high-bright setting. Mike threw one hand over his eyes to shield himself from the powerful LED.

This part got tricky. For what I had planned, I wanted as much thrust as possible. I needed my feet on the ground.

I pulsed the power unit several times, keeping the flashlight aimed at his face, but maneuvering a few feet away. I lowered myself until the soles of my boots contacted the gravel. The entire time, Martian Mike faced the light, holding one hand up, peeking past his fingers and squinting, awestruck.

Arm extended, I flicked my wrist and tossed the flashlight over his head. An electric snap bit into my fingers when the flashlight left my grip and reappeared. As I hoped, Martian Mike ducked and spun, following the trajectory of the light the way a cat follows a laser pointer. The instant he had his back to me, I powered forward and closed a grip on the back of his skinny neck. He jolted. Just as fast—

FWOOOMP!

—I slammed the levers in my mind against the stops. The flashlight spun through the air. In the dizzying strobe effect, Martian Mike vanished. He tried to crouch and spin away from whatever terror grabbed him from behind, but I was too fast. I lifted him. His feet detached from the surface. He lost his power to pivot. I bent my knees and kicked hard. We both shot up. The flashlight hit the ground and spun in circles, a mad beacon illuminating the yard below us.

Martian Mike screamed. He reached for the grip on his neck. His hands found mine.

"HUMAN!" I shouted in an atonal voice. "IF YOU FIGHT, I WILL RELEASE YOU."

Either the outcry or the threat froze him. His screaming and pinwheeling stopped. The roof dropped away. The treetops. In seconds we were fifty feet up. Then a hundred.

"DO NOT RESIST!" I tightened my grip to make the point.

He gasped.

"What—? What is this?!"

"SILENCE!"

"Oh God oh God oh God—!"

We coasted higher and higher.

Martian Mike gulped. I felt it in his throat. His voice cracked when he spoke.

"Who are you? Where are you taking me?"

"Human! Do not speak unless spoken to. Do not resist." My flat, robotic voice sounded laughable.

"Is this real? It is. This is real. Oh God, this is real."

"That is a poor imitation of silence, human. I will now release you and you will return to the surface at high speed."

"NO! NO! Please! Please don't!"

"Then speak only when spoken to. Do you understand?"

"Yes."

I raised the BLASTER and initiated quiet reverse thrust. Our ascent slowed.

"Where are you taking me?"

"I will ask the questions, human. What are you called?"

"Uh—it's Dowd. Mike—er—Frederick Michael Dowd."

"Are you the human called Martian Mike?"

"Yes. Yes—that's a name I use."

"Why do you use the name of a dead planet?"

He swallowed again. "Uh...I dunno. Jesus, I don't know—it's a thing here. On Earth. Because Mars is...you know...close?"

"You are incoherent, human."

The climb stopped. I shut down the BLASTER. We hung in the silent night sky three hundred feet above his mountain mansion. A light wind pushed us over the house toward the black that denoted the canyon.

"Puh-puh-please! Please, may I ask a question?"

"State your interrogatory." *Interrogatory? Jesus.*

"Are you...are you not from this world?"

"We are from many worlds. We are determining whether we shall become of this world."

"Are you taking me to your ship?"

"Ship?"

"Up. Up there—Christ! I can't see myself!" He must have pointed. I felt him wiggle, probably throwing his arms up in front of his face and waving them back and forth. *"How is this possible?"*

"Silence! You have been acquired for interrogation. You will divulge all. You will be probed. You will be disassembled."

He began to shake. Maybe that was too much.

"Please! Please don't hurt me. I've always believed. I can help you!" His voice broke and squeaked.

"Chillax, human. That is a human term, is it not? Chillax now and reduce your heart rate and consumption of atmosphere. You will answer my questions."

"I will. I will. Please don't disassemble me!"

"Explain to me your knowledge of the gathering of humans in the place called Ekalaka."

"What? Wha—is that you? *That's real?* Are you saying that's real?"

"Explain."

"I swear I didn't know that was you. Honest. I had no idea. If I had known you were *real* and that was you, I promise you I never would have said a word. You have to believe me."

"How did you come to speak of this event?"

"I...uh...I just, you know, picked up chatter...I don't know..."

I flexed my grip on the back of his neck.

"My sensors detect fabrication. You will be released now."

"WAIT! *Please!*"

"Further fabrication detected will trigger your release. You will return to the surface of the planet at high speed."

"No, please, wait. Please, I was told, okay? I was told to talk about it."

"Who commanded you?"

"Just—people I work with—er, for."

"Who commanded you?"

"Giles! Peter Giles at ParaTransit told me to promote it."

"Promote?"

"Uh, talk about it. Play it up. Sell it—to certain—followers. It was—it was part of the deal. I had no idea you would actually pick them all up. I knew nothing about your plans. Honest. I was just, you know, doing a *thing.*"

"A thing?"

"A thing. A deal. A—*schtick.* The stories—they're just stories. For a bunch of people waiting around for something that would never happen. They told me to talk it up."

"You received instructions?"

"Yes. They approached me. They wanted my, uh, backing. My endorsement. People listen to me. If I had known it was real, I would have said no. You have to believe me."

"It was a…fabrication?"

"They offered me a lot of money. Too much money."

"You were paid for a fabrication?"

"Yes! I took it. Okay? They made demands. Threats. I had to go along with it. Part of the deal."

"The human called Stephanie Cullen. Did you speak of this with her?"

"She was one of them, yes."

"Many times?"

"Sure. Many times. She wanted to go, you know, *to meet you*. Hell, I wanted to meet you, but not like this. I told her what she wanted to hear. I told her to go there. And the others. The ones they told me to tell."

"The others?"

"The people on the list. They had a list. I…uh, consulted with the ones on the list. Advised them. Told them what I thought. Showed them photos."

"Photos?"

"Pictures. Representations. Images."

"I am aware of the meaning." *Idiot.* "Photos of what?"

"Landing sites. Honest, I didn't mean to give anything away. You have to believe me."

"We have seen your landing site photos and your crop circles. They are stupid."

"I get it. We all get it. Look, I want to believe, but most of it is BS."

"Then why do you do…BS?"

"People want to believe. They want to hear stories. You know, you could have helped us understand. You could have been more open."

"The human named Farris. Did you speak promotion to her as well?"

"Farris? You mean Dr. Farris?"

"Affirmative."

"Hell, no. She didn't want anything to do with me or Ekalaka. She was all on about some other thing."

"What other thing?"

"Old news. A rumor out of Michigan—no, Wisconsin. Some BS about a gash."

"A 'gash'…?"

"I don't know. A story that got passed around last year. People send me that stuff all the time. She had me dig up the file. She hammered me on it. But she—she was government, you know. Probably still is. Is she on to you? Is the government after you?"

"What did you tell her?"

"A couple of weird stories from some farmers or hunters or I dunno what. Nothing substantiated. No photos or anything. No firsthand stories. I gave her an NTSB report—and she took my goddamned map. She stole that."

NTSB report?

"Explain this 'report' to me."

"What? I don't know. Some airplane crash. The guy survived. Nobody knows why."

My NTSB report?

Unless I hadn't been notified, as far as I knew the National Transportation Safety Board report on my accident remained Pending.

"We will now return to the surface. You will surrender your documents and files to me. Do you understand? If you do not comply you will be disassembled."

"No! Hey, no, take it. You can have it all. Are we...? Are you going to...?"

"State your interrogatory, human."

"Are we still going to your ship and...and are you planning to do all that other stuff?"

"If you comply, you will not be probed. You will not be disassembled."

He blew out a loud sigh of relief. Part of me could hardly believe that he was falling for all this. Maybe I'd become too familiar, too comfortable with the effect of *the other thing.* On the other hand, how could he not? Vanishing and floating hundreds of feet in the air certainly sold it.

Frederick Michael Dowd would never have believed this conversation if both his feet were on solid ground. To my ear, I sounded like a skit on *Saturday Night Live.*

"We will return to your planet. You will provide me with everything I require. If you cooperate, you will not be disassembled."

"Thank you! Thank you! I will! I promise."

POSSIBLY TO MAKE A POINT, but mainly because my sweaty hand was close to cramping, I let go of him while still five or six feet off the ground. He dropped hard and sprawled on the gravel near his back door, which I chose as a landing spot to avoid letting him see that the alien light laying in his driveway was this week's special at Ace Hardware.

He staggered to his feet and spun around, searching the empty air.

"Take me to your data," I commanded.

"It's inside."

"I will follow you. Do not deceive me. I am, as you humans would say, armed."

"I get it—I get it. You can have it all."

Martian Mike staggered to his feet. After a moment's hesitation, he climbed a set of steps onto the porch. Following Martian Mike required BLASTER finesse. I chose instead to bypass him. I pulsed the BLASTER and passed Martian Mike on a straight shot to the porch rail.

Just as I closed my hand around the porch rail and heaved myself over, the back door opened. A dull black metal pipe emerged ahead of a dark figure. Martian Mike stopped in his tracks. Too late, I recognized the black tube.

A figure stepped through the door.

"Hi, Mike, you asshole."

BANG!

The shotgun flashed. The report punched my right ear. The pressure wave slapped my face.

My entire body jolted. Halfway over the rail, I lost control.

Fwooomp!

I reappeared and dropped hard onto the wooden porch boards.

"What the—?" The startled voice sounded dangerously familiar.

Danzig turned toward me. The weapon followed. I scrambled to my feet and grabbed for the steel barrel. My hand closed over his hand. I felt muscle and power—more than enough power to bring the barrel to bear on me.

I slammed the levers in my head forward.

FWOOOMP! I vanished us both. Shock gave me the edge. I levered my grip upward, lifting his feet from the boards while my boots remained planted. I drew him toward me, then heaved.

BANG!

Blazing white light.

Black.

38

F ire.
Searing pain lit up my body. I irrationally thought that I was in a cockpit, consumed in flame. A pilot's worst fear. Early combat pilots carried a pistol, not for the enemy, but to put a bullet in their brain and deny death by fire. They weren't wrong. Simultaneously, I felt the cool sensation generated by *the other thing*. Soothing. And yet—fire.

The shotgun.

This wasn't the first time, but it was the worst. Compounding the agony, I was blind. I hung in a black void. My jaw muscles clenched, or I would have screamed. I feared breaking my teeth under the pressure.

Twice before, I made the mistake of discharging a firearm while vanished. Something went wrong. A blast of feedback energy. I don't know what, but I learned my lesson both times. Yet here I was again.

My breathing lifted and compressed my chest. Every muscle in my body sang out. A cramp bit the back of my leg. I tried to stretch it out but moving felt worse.

By degrees, the agony faded.

I regained enough cognition to question the darkness, then realized my eyes were clamped as tightly shut as my jaw. I focused and forced the muscles of both to relax. My eyes opened but my vision flooded with tears that would not leave my eye sockets.

Because there was no gravity to pull them free.

Because you're still vanished.

This was new. The last two times this happened, I had been blown out of the vanished state. The first time, I landed in a road. The second time, I nearly went over the edge of a forty-story building.

I floated. That demanded attention, but first I needed to move my limbs.

Legs. Feet. Toes. The muscles were rigid. Breaking through was like flexing a frozen garden hose. Each sore muscle protested.

Arms, elbows, hands, fingers. The same. Each responded slowly, reluctant to give back control as if they feared I would allow this to happen again.

I pressed my thumb into my eye socket and pushed away the accumulation of tears. My vision improved, but blackness still dominated. I blinked both eyes, over and over.

Shapes emerged from the black. Fissures and cracks. Crenelated surfaces. Twisted branches growing out of star-lit rock.

The canyon. I was somewhere in the canyon, not far from the rock face. I wasn't sure which way was up. Twisting my head, I found pinprick stars in a black sky over my left shoulder. I tried the other muscle I have, the one that only makes itself known when I vanish, the one that runs down my center.

To my surprise, it worked without pain. I rolled my body until the stars hung over my head. I floated horizontally in the air like someone lounging on a beach.

At the edge of the star field above me, I saw glass. The wall of Martian Mike's cabin where it overlooked the canyon. Above that, his roofline. I had gone over the railing of the back porch. Was I thrown? Was I propelled by the shotgun blast? Or was it self-propelled? With increasing frequency, I have been able to command *the other thing* to move me without using a power unit. It stopped the fall when Wally flopped onto me from the cliff near Tammy Day's ranch. The response is always pre-conscious, a thought executed before the words can form in my mind. Autopilot.

Did autopilot sail me into this black canyon?

I needed to get to the top. Martian Mike had been about to show his alien abductor his files.

Martian Mike is dead.

Someone shot him in the face.

The voice.

Danzig killed Martian Mike.

The voice was familiar. The same voice warned Wally about not listening. Danzig. Danzig killed Martian Mike after calling him an asshole.

How did Danzig get here?

Oh shit.

Wally.

39

The BLASTER I used during my thousand-miles-off-Broadway performance as an alien was gone. My backup remained in my pocket, but I didn't trust my hands to extract it. Tremors wracked my fingers, crawled up my palms, shook my wrists and weakened my arms. I feared dropping it into the canyon, which at present was as black as a barrel of old oil. There would be no finding it.

I felt a desperate urge to get back to Wally. If Danzig arrived at Martian Mike's the same way we did, he had already found the miraculously alive kid. I took inventory of my body and my surroundings. The rocks that had been near me when I first opened my eyes had sunk. Other rocks shifted into position. They were close. The canyon wall was less than ten feet away from my feet. I used the undamaged core muscle to pivot. Placing my head near the wall left less than six or seven feet of gap.

I felt for the BLASTER in my pocket, then stopped. A breeze blowing through this canyon lifted me, taking me closer to the wall.

A twisted trunk of pine stuck out of a fissure. My hands shook when the tip of a pine branch brushed my fingertips. I closed two fingers on the twig and pulled, gained ground, pinched the skinny branch, and pulled again. In seconds, I had a grip on a gnarled trunk.

I stopped to breathe. The effort had been costly. I needed air.

What about Danzig?

When I vanished, I took us both. I had my hand on his hand. I lifted and threw him. He fired. Had he been caught in the same energy feedback? Was he still up there? Paralyzed on the porch? Maybe he didn't discover Wally. Maybe he came to the cabin another way. Maybe Wally heard someone coming and hid.

Any chance that Wally remained undiscovered renewed my determination. I rotated to an upright position. Using the branch for leverage, I gained a grip on a rock. The rock provided an anchor point. I located the next good grip point and pushed. My hands and arms remained unsteady, but my grip held.

The climb took time and care. Rock climbing is not a sport I would try without vanishing and removing gravity from the game. Even with that advantage, I found it difficult, sometimes grabbing where no handhold existed, sometimes knocking loose stones that clattered into darkness. By the time I reached the top, I regained a degree of steadiness in my arms, but not enough to trust pulling my only BLASTER from my pocket while still over the canyon.

I fixed a final grip on the porch rail and pulled myself over. The table and chairs had been knocked off their legs.

Martian Mike sat on the porch steps. His head was bowed. His knees were spread. One hand dangled at his side. The other hooked a limp thumb in the shotgun's trigger guard. The shotgun rested against his crotch with the barrel below what would have been his chin. Most of his face was gone. I thanked the darkness for hiding the details. The weapon's position suggested suicide. Someone positioned the weapon and fired it again because dark spatter painted the porch, the walls, and the sliding glass door.

Danzig was gone. It irritated me to think he had recovered. I hoped instead that he had to be carried off by his goon squad.

The house lay quiet. The patio door had been left open, perhaps to suggest a last careless gesture by an owner about to end his life.

Safely over the porch, I pulled out my remaining BLASTER. Attaching the prop took several frustrating minutes and exposed just how far from normal my motor skills remained. Eventually, a satisfying snap transmitted through my fingers. I gripped the device to be certain of not losing it. I slid the control to full power.

I shot off the porch, into the air, and flew a wide arc around the house, looking for movement, finding none. I recovered the flashlight, still spraying its beam on the driveway.

Ten minutes later I arrived over the old Buick. The gate remained closed. I used the flashlight to search the car interior. My flight bag lay hidden in shadows behind the driver's seat.

Wally was gone.

PART II

40

NOW

W hen I reached the car, I checked my watch. Eight-ten.
Jesus. I lost three hours.

Figuring that I abducted Martian Mike shortly after the end of twilight, and calculating sunset at around four-thirty, I estimated that the shotgun blast that sent me over the canyon edge took place around five p.m.

I wasn't ready to pilot that Buick back down the mountain in the dark. My limbs felt weak and uncoordinated. I dismissed the idea of pursuit. Danzig was long gone. At best, Danzig took Wally with him. At worst, Wally lay at the bottom of the canyon, completing the fall Danzig intended for him from the start. Even through lingering brain fog caused by the shotgun blast, I saw no logic or reason to chase after Danzig. I had another idea.

I cruised back up to Martian Mike's house. Outside the back door, I slowed to a near crawl and bypassed the corpse on the back steps—

— *wondering how I can possibly report this*

—*wondering if animals will get to the body before the authorities*

—floating over the porch rail and through the open patio door into the expansive overlook room. I had the good sense to remain vanished and weightless. By slow maneuvering with the BLASTER, I avoided touching anything.

I slipped past the kitchen where the package of General Tso's Chicken lay thawing on the countertop beside a single empty plate. A short hallway took me to the office, which was now dark. Inside the open door, I found the wall switch with my elbow and flicked on a desk lamp.

Empty.

The desk that had been cluttered with piles of paper, magazines, and files looked pristine, like something from a furniture store showroom. The monitor with the PC screensaver I'd seen before was gone, along with the PC and its power cords. The empty outlet on the wall near the floor molding suggested that even the surge protector, if there had been one, had been taken.

The walls were bare. No maps. No bulletin boards. No pinned clippings.

Cleaned out.

Danzig and his crew had several hours. They made the most of it. Martian Mike would be found dead of an apparent suicide and his house stripped of any sign of his past passion.

Poor guy. He sold out and slipped into a depression.

He gained a bank account and lost his purpose in life.

The conclusions would be easily reached. Meanwhile, I not only failed to find what led Lillian Farris to Martian Mike, I now had to wonder what Danzig had taken—and more importantly, why?

I made a cursory search of the rest of the house but had no illusions about finding a secret stash of vital clues. Danzig had much more time to search than I, and possibly better control of his motor function, although I took a measure of pleasure in the fact that he'd been inside *the other thing* the same as me when he pulled the trigger of his shotgun. With any luck, he felt as shitty as I did.

I gave up and returned to what was left of Martian Mike on the back porch. My stomach lurched at the sight of his head. Gore leaked down the front of his shirt and pooled on the steps. His khaki trousers were black across his abdomen and crotch, but dry along his left thigh where I found what I had hoped to find.

I pinched his phone and slid it from his pocket, said a prayer that the device was not locked, and swiped the screen. A selection of icons appeared over the bulbous head of an alien with eyes the size of tennis balls and the color of coal.

I dialed.

"9-1-1, what is your emergency."

"Frederick Michael Dowd, the owner of this phone, was murdered tonight by a man named Scott Danzig. The murderer also kidnapped and may have killed a young man named Walter Hadley Vandenlock of Sterling, Colorado."

"Sir, what is—"

I wiped down the phone and laid it beside Martian Mike with the connection open and the operator urgently asking for a response.

REAPPEARING at the driver's door of the Buick nearly brought me to my knees. Weight on my legs caused them to quiver so badly that I quickly vanished again. For the first half hour of driving back down the mountain and onto Highway 34, I stayed that way, tightly strapped to the seat and holding onto the wheel. There wasn't much traffic. If anyone saw the driverless car rolling down the highway, they didn't see it long enough to let their eyes convince their skeptical brain.

I watched for emergency vehicles. Nothing raced in the opposite direction, but that didn't mean that someone hadn't been dispatched via a different route. At the very least, the emergency services dispatcher would pinpoint the call location and investigate.

Around the time I transitioned from the foothills to the flatland, I tried reappearing again. There was no question that being vanished numbed the pain and reduced the demands that weight puts on the body, but the shakiness diminished. My motor control improved. I stayed visible.

By the time I parked the S.S. Buick outside the FBO, I estimated that I might be able to walk without looking drunk. As for flying? That remained to be seen.

First things first. I needed to deal with what I'd been putting off.

"IT'S ME, BOSS."

"Then I'm gonna guess it's not good news." Earl's rapid assessment of the hour and the caller cut straight to business. "What's the story with Tammy Day?"

"I'll explain in a minute, but I need to ask you a question first. When were you going to tell me that Lillian Farris reached out to you?"

"You mean that Dr. Farris woman?"

"The same."

I almost heard Earl scratching his leathery scalp over the cell connection.

"Christ, I dunno. She called me a couple weeks ago. I thought she was just some busybody. Told me she knew Tammy, spent time with her in Montana, and hadn't heard from her. Wanted to know if I heard from her. I didn't think it was any business of some goddamned stranger and I told her so. 'Course, it got me to thinking. I tried calling myself. Then I asked you to take a look-see—three goddamned days ago, fer chrissakes! Didja lose your phone?"

"Did my name come up?"

"You? Why the hell would your name come up?"

"Because I know the woman. And I'm starting to think the reason she called you was to point me in this direction. How would she know to call you about Tammy anyway?"

"'S what I asked her. She told me that she got my name from Tammy herself, who told her the story about her brother, in which context my cursed name came up."

Earl Jackson. Of Essex County Air Service. The connection back to me was obvious but convoluted. Why wouldn't Lillian reach out directly to me?

"Did she mention an outfit called ParaTransit? Or a guy named Peter Giles?"

"Nope."

"Or Scott Danzig?"

"Never heard of 'em. Are you gonna tell me what's going on?"

I spent the next ten minutes explaining what I'd seen and learned. Earl, about as far from being a patient person as any man I've ever met, said nothing until the end.

"So, this Danzig fella killed the Martian guy and probably killed this kid whose aunt and eight other people are most likely with Tammy, wherever she got herself…is that how you see it?"

"Pretty much."

"And you think this Para-whatever outfit is pulling the strings?"

"That would be my guess."

"And you can't report any of this to anyone because you can't answer the first goddamned question a cop would ask."

"Nail on the head, Boss."

"Christ!" Earl huffed loudly into the phone. "I'm starting to see why this thing you do ain't exactly a blessing."

"You heard about that autistic boy that showed up at our house?"

"Rosemary II mentioned him. Her girl has taken an interest in the child."

"Lane?"

"Yup."

DIVISIBLE MAN - NINE LIVES LOST

That part, I did not know. It didn't surprise me. Lane Franklin has a huge heart. I wondered if Lane had become involved via Andy.

"That boy was in Lillian Farris's custody. It was her car he was driving. I think that whatever happened to Tammy Day and her fellow UFO congregants may have happened to Lillian, but not before she set that child on a path in my direction."

"And what, exactly, would that be?"

"You mean Tammy and the people at the ranch? They freaking disappeared."

"Whaddya mean, 'disappeared'?"

I explained as best I could, trying hard not to sound completely nuts.

"That's completely nuts," Earl barked.

"You might want to check the news. It's a local story in Montana."

"Din't see nothing here."

"Which might be a good thing. The last time a big cult story hit the national news it was because of a mass suicide—"

"Heaven's Gate?"

"Right, so if you haven't seen a story that tells me they haven't found bodies yet."

"Jumpin' Jesus. Are you coming back? 'Cuz if you are, you best get moving. Have you seen the Prog charts?"

"Yeah. I figure I have about twelve hours before the shit hits the fan across the Great Lakes."

"Might be less."

Not what I wanted to hear. "I'd really like to try and find that kid Wally. I feel like it's my fault he was grabbed. I should have dropped him off like I planned to do."

"Sounds to me like they would have found him anyway."

"I'm not sure they knew he was alive. I'm guessing that came as a shock to them."

"Where're you gonna start?"

"Beats the hell out of me. Around this time in the movies, a perfect clue pops up outta nowhere. All I have is a snowstorm coming."

"Then I suggest you get your ass home. Your wife is a lot smarter than you, anyway. She's more likely to figure this out than you are."

"I'd be insulted if that weren't absolutely true."

At that point, I think Earl hung up. He never says goodbye. A moment later the screen reported that the call ended.

41

The trip from Greeley to my home base flight planned at over four hours, which was too much to undertake in one shot for a pilot as fatigued and bodily beaten up as me. After returning the crew car, I camped in the FBO pilot lounge for a couple hours, dozing fitfully. Then I strapped in the pilot's seat of the Baron for another attempt at a nap in the vanished state. It didn't work as well the second time. After an hour and a half of fitful dozing, I gave up and went back inside the FBO for coffee and a bathroom break. I texted Andy my plans. Fifteen minutes later, I went wheels up.

I broke the flight into two legs. I had a good reason for stopping and refueling at the halfway point. I wanted to talk to someone at the Sioux City Airport and I got lucky. The person I had in mind started her shift at five a.m. She waved me into a parking spot a little after five-thirty and waited for me as I shut down first the left, then the right engine of the Baron.

"Welcome back," the dark-haired girl called out when I cracked open the door. "Nice to see you again. Need services?"

I didn't try to climb out, at least not with her watching. Hopping from the front seat of a Beechcraft Baron onto the wing requires a degree of flexibility, and at that moment I felt about as flexible as frozen roadkill.

"Can we top off all four, please?"

"Sure thing. Lemme get the truck. I'll be right back."

I watched her trot in the direction of the FBO office, then hooked my headset on the control yoke, double-checked to make sure all the appropriate switches were off, and slid over to the right seat. There was no easy way to do it. I swung my legs out the door and onto the wing, then pulled myself out. I prayed no one was watching as I slid myself down the wing on my sore butt until one foot extended past the flap and reached the step. I sounded and looked old and feeble for the next few seconds, heaving myself off the wing and upright with a loud grunt. I gripped the handhold long enough to confirm that my knees wouldn't betray me.

"Son of a bitch," I muttered, hating the way the effects of the blast on Martian Mike's wooden porch plagued me. My muscles, bones and joints were not on fire, but they smoldered.

By the time the girl returned with the fuel truck, I managed a reasonable facsimile of walking. I strolled the length of the wing's leading edge, opening all four fuel caps for her.

She hooked up the static line and unreeled the hose.

"Mains first?" she asked.

"Doesn't matter."

"Got some weather coming," she said. She fueled the right auxiliary tank. I walked to the end of the wing and propped my elbows on the tip.

"What's your name?"

"Delilah."

"I'm Will."

"They call me Del around here. Nice to meet you, Will." She said it without taking her eyes off the task of filling a fuel tank without splashing overflow down the wing. I also detected her guard lifting. I understood why. An attractive young woman working the flight line meets a lot of men with oversized egos. Some with poor manners.

"Del, I need to ask you something."

"Fire away."

"When I was here, we talked about that C-23 Sherpa. You mentioned that the crew wasn't from Enterprise. Do you recall our conversation?"

"I do." I gave her points for not being evasive.

"Can you tell me anything about them? The crew?"

She squeezed the last of the fuel into the aux tank, turned the nozzle upright, and then capped the tank. All without looking in my direction. She moved to her left and began filling the main tank.

"I really…I hope you understand…I shouldn't discuss other customers with anyone. Kinda policy here. Besides, ECG fuels their own equipment."

"I do understand. Here's the thing. My wife," I held up my left hand to show her the ring, "is a police detective with the City of Essex in Wisconsin. My question relates to an investigation she is conducting. More importantly, the life of a young man—a kid about your age—may depend on any information you can give me."

"How so?"

"If he's alive, they may have him. If not, it may be because of them."

She lifted her eyes and looked me over.

"Del, I'm asking pilot to pilot. I need to know where those guys came from. If you have any idea, it could help lot."

The mains were not as depleted as the auxiliary tanks. She finished up quickly and capped the tank. I followed her to the left side, keeping a courteous distance.

"Maybe you should talk to Carrie over at Enterprise."

"I already did. She's in a worse position than you are. For her it's a legal issue involving contracts and liability. You and me...we're just chatting."

"I know, but I probably shouldn't say, either. I mean—no offense—I have no way of knowing what you're saying is true." She finished the main tank and moved to the aux tank.

"Okay. I understand. I don't want to put you in an awkward position. I appreciate you talking to me, Del. I'm going to hit the restroom. I'll meet you inside to pay the bill."

I pushed off the Baron's nose to take the long way around the right wing.

"I'm sorry, sir."

"Will. Call me 'sir' and you make me feel like an old fart."

She laughed, just a little bit forced.

I DID MY RESTROOM BUSINESS, then spent a few minutes bending, stretching, and flexing, hoping no one would come in and catch me. I felt better when I emerged. At least someone watching me wouldn't think I'd had too much to drink.

At the front counter, Del's friendly demeanor returned. She handed my credit card back with a warm smile.

"Coming back anytime soon?"

"I hope so. Excellent service."

"Well, thank you. You have a good flight."

I paid her a nod and left the office. On the walk to the Baron, I switched my concentration back to piloting. A quick session on the iPad would give me a weather update. My flight plan for the final leg home was already filed. If nothing got in the way, I expected to land in Essex County just before sunset and ahead of the first snowflake. At the end of this long road, I envisioned a shower that would use up all the hot water in the house.

"Lemme get the chocks for you!" Del caught up to me on the ramp.

"Thanks."

We walked without talking. I split off to climb the wing. Del hurried around to the nose and pulled the chocks from the wheel. She stood up and approached the leading edge between the right engine and the nose. She looked up at me with dark, serious eyes.

"They came from Frankfurt."

"Germany?"

She smiled. "That's what I asked. No. Michigan. Some cargo operation out of there. They fly a C-23 but it was down for maintenance, and they had an emergency they had to deal with. Really bad timing, the guy said, but lucky because they know somebody here in Sioux City."

"Did you get a name?"

"Nah. Just ramp chatter. I didn't really feel like hanging out with them." She made a face that landed her opinion of Danzig in line with mine.

"How did they get here? Commercial?"

"Business jet. A Citation."

"Thanks."

"You have a good flight." She flicked the chock rope over the back of her head and let the blocks rest against her neon reflective vest. She turned to step clear.

"Hang on. Did you say you don't have your multi-engine rating?"

"I'm hoping next summer. It's really expensive."

I leaned into the cockpit and unzipped one of the small pockets on my flight bag. I pulled out a card, jotted a word on the back, and handed it to her. She read my scribble.

"Pidge?"

"You bring that card up to Wisconsin, to Essex County Air Service. Ask for Pidge. She's a multi-engine instructor. Best there is. If you pay for the gas, I'll see that you get her time and time in this Baron at no charge. Check-ride, too."

"Are you serious?" The smile broke out, startled and genuine.

"My name is on the flip side. I don't work there anymore but look me up. My wife and I will toss in a place to stay, if you want. Okay?"

"Holy shit, sir—uh—Will. Do you really mean it?"

"Swear on my pilot's license. And don't worry. We never had the other part of this conversation."

I had to promise her I was serious four more times before she cleared the wing. Strapping in, I noticed I wasn't as sore as before, or as tired.

42

I raced the leading edge of the winter storm back to Essex County at maximum cruise speed. Layers of clouds, an advance guard forming along a juggernaut cold front, played hide and seek with me across Iowa and western Wisconsin. Things got a bit icy. I requested and was granted a block altitude clearance from five to eleven thousand feet. For the last hundred and fifty miles I climbed and dipped half a dozen times as the Baron's wings and tail formed and shed ice. Forty miles from home, I broke into clear air for a visual approach to familiar ground.

I will always love to fly, but there are days when nothing feels better than climbing out of an airplane and planting my boots on solid ground. One of the young instructors appeared on the tug. I helped him hook up to the Baron, then asked if he would see that it got topped off as well as tucked in.

Earl Jackson's office was empty when I dragged my sore body through the Essex County Air Service building. I found Rosemary II at the front desk and was surprised to see her fixing a scarf around her neck and sliding on gloves.

"Quitting early?"

"My goodness, where on earth have you been?" She hustled around the end of the counter and threw me a hug. She does that from time to time, and I know why, but it always surprises me. Her embrace squeezed sore bones. I bit my tongue. "And since when are you a clock watcher? I am leaving five whole minutes early."

She pointed at the office clock. Four-fifty-five.

"Shit, I'm still on Mountain Time. In that case, take the rest of the day off." I leaned over the counter and dropped the Baron's clipboard on her desk. "Where's the boss?"

"He's over in the engine shop arguing with Doc." She dangled her keys.

"That's not an argument. It's a ballet."

"Put some pepper in your step and let's go. You can follow me home."

"Home? Your house?"

"Your house. I'm picking up Lane. She's visiting your wife."

I liked that idea. I liked that Andy has company when I'm away, and I hoped that in Lane she might find an outlet for some of what she's been bottling up lately.

Rosemary II waited for me at the door. "You coming?"

"I need to talk to the boss, first. Then I'll be right behind you."

THE HALLWAY RUNNING past Earl's office ended at a door to the tool shop where drill presses, grinders and specialized metal working devices were mounted on heavy steel benches. Always tidy, never completely clean, I spent many hours in this workshop attending to whatever tasks Doc assigned me.

From there, I wove a path through the attached hangar where several of Earl's aircraft were carefully parked wing to tail. At the back corner of the hangar, a door opened to an annex on the west side of the building where Doc handled engine repairs. In my years of working for Earl, I can probably count on one hand the minutes I spent in Doc's engine shop. He guards the space jealously. The work performed there is part mechanics, part black magic. Parts and pieces extracted from aircraft engines mounted on heavy stands are placed in precise order and touched by no one except Doc, who does not wear coveralls, but prefers what looks like a heavy white lab coat, smeared and stained with grease that never really washes out. Every time I see Doc in that coat, I expect to see a stethoscope hanging around his neck.

I found Doc and Earl leaning over an open crank case as if meditating. Neither spoke. I rapped on the door as I entered to avoid the appearance of sneaking up on them.

"So, you do know how to navigate," Earl muttered after glancing at me.

"I just pointed the airplane in this direction. It found its own way home."

"Hi, Will," Doc said cheerily, the inverse of Earl's deep scowl, which meant whatever they were arguing, Doc was winning.

"Hey, Doc." I pulled up to the bench and joined the staring contest. "Somebody break a crankshaft?"

"Spun the main bearing." Doc pointed. "Got melted brass here…and here. Dollars to donuts those rollers will come up distorted."

"Alright," Earl announced glumly. "Go ahead."

Doc smiled. Victory. I decided not to ask, and Doc had the good sense not to gloat. Earl left the battlefield without another word. I followed him into the main hangar. We pulled up alongside his Piper Mojave. Despite being the only two people in the hangar, he spoke in a low voice.

"You look like something the cat dragged in."

"I'm beat. Anything new on the news?"

"Oh, hell yes. It made the national news. Bunch of suicidal space heads catching the mothership to another galaxy."

I feared the worst. "Did they find bodies?"

Earl shook his head. "Nope. That just makes the media crazier."

"That guy Danzig that I mentioned—he might be connected to a freight operation out of Frankfurt, Michigan that flies those boxy Short Brothers turboprops. You know anybody over that way?"

"Knew a guy in Traverse City operated a D-18, but nobody in Frankfurt."

"I was thinking of running over that way."

Earl shot a look at the ceiling. "What? Tonight?"

"The Baron's gassed up."

He huffed a low opinion of the idea. "You ain't. You look like shit. And we're gonna get socked here."

"I know, but Danzig grabbed that kid I was with. It is not going to end well for the kid, if it hasn't already. I feel like I need to try."

"Which likely won't end well for you, either. What does your wife have to say?"

Earl holds a high opinion of Andy and will sell me out to her if necessary. Lying to him wouldn't do me much good.

"Haven't discussed it with her."

"Yeah, well, I doubt that will be much of a discussion, but if she doesn't cuff you to a bedpost and you decide to go, I won't stop you." He dropped his gaze to his shoes. "It don't sound good for Tammy. Girl always had more money than sense."

"Tammy had money?"

"A lot. That's how she got to piss away her life chasing whatever hippy idea popped into her head."

"How? I mean—how did she make her money?"

"I don't think that girl worked a day in her life. Her old man made a fortune manufacturing high-pressure steam lines they use in Navy ships. When her folks died, what with Tommy gone, she got it all. Why?"

"I don't know...that kid's aunt was loaded, too."

Earl worked his squint on me. "Well now that's interesting. On the radio news everybody's fixated on the little green men side of the story, but the AP wire said one of Tammy's fellow passengers on the mothership is some tech whiz-kid famous for a dumbass video game—forgot his name—and again, unconfirmed."

"Rich?"

"I guess. The news doesn't get excited about people who ain't."

I WALKED across the ramp and let myself in the side door of the Christine and Paulette Paulesky Education Foundation hangar. The Foundation's cabin class Piper Navajo posed on the polished concrete floor, waiting for someone with Michelangelo's skill to render her in marble, the ultimate vision of flight. I skirted the wing and gave the fuselage a loving pat on my way to the glass wall at the back of the hangar. The offices were dark, including Arun's lair. I checked to see if he hunched over his laptop so absorbed in his work that he forgot to turn on the lights. He wasn't.

I pulled the iPad from my flight bag and dropped into Arun's office chair. For the next five minutes, I studied the current and forecast weather for the Great Lakes. The picture looked ugly, but I saw a chance. If I left before midnight, I could make it to Frankfurt, Michigan ahead of the storm. The Baron had full fuel tanks.

I closed the screen and stared at nothing for an entire minute, thinking about the forecasts, AIRMETs for icing over the lake, fatigue, the lingering effects of the shotgun blast, and the excellent chance that the airplane would wind up buried on an open ramp by a foot of lake effect snow. A high-speed run ahead of the storm carried multiple risks with no guarantee that Wally would be found there, or alive.

Everything about the idea was terrible.

I locked up and drove home to convince Andy it wasn't.

43

A ndy met me at the back door. The kitchen lights backlit her loose auburn hair, lending the fringes a starlight effect. She wore a deep red cashmere sweater. I got my hands on it and her before my flight bag hit the floor. She pulled me into a sweet and lingering kiss.

"Missed you," she said when we came up for air.

"Missed you." I held on, pulled her close, and buried my face in her hair. "I lost the kid."

She waited a moment, then leaned back to read my face. Her serious expression mirrored what she saw on mine. She glanced over her shoulder.

"We have guests."

"I know. But we need to talk. I don't have much time."

"Did you—?"

"Yes. I reported it. For all the good it will do."

I had anticipated Andy's first question. She needed to know that law enforcement, her world, had been informed—that someone doing her job had been alerted. I didn't share her faith. The chances that my anonymous murder tip landed in the lap of someone with Andy's skill and determination were slim.

"What do you mean, 'I don't have much time'?"

I explained about Frankfurt. She asked about the weather. I hedged, poorly. She shook her head.

"Absolutely not. We're under a Winter Storm Warning." I started to protest, but she put two fingers on my lips. "There's nothing you can do right this minute, but there are things I can do. First…come." She squeezed me again and led me into the house.

"Hi Will!" Lane Franklin's bright voice and smile met us in the kitchen.

"That's *Mister* Stewart, young lady," her mother admonished.

"*Mom!*"

"Hi, Lane!" I greeted the once shy and awkward young girl who had taken a magic potion sometime in the last year and transformed into a striking young woman. She shared her clear milk chocolate skin with her mother, along with blazing near-black eyes and locks of wavy long black hair. I swear she had grown another inch since I last saw her. She stood nearly as tall as Rosemary II. "Who are you going to fly for?"

"Federal Express! Work all night, sleep all day!"

Lane's reply drew a pursed-lipped frown from her mother who was less than enthusiastic about her daughter becoming a pilot.

"I hear they have dental." I tried to notch a point in favor of Lane's career hopes.

"Come and see what we did." Lane scooped up my hand and pulled me to the dining room table.

"What's all this?" The Ziploc sack of paper squares from Lillian's Prius lay on the table next to Lane's iMac monitor, keyboard, and mouse. "You brought your computer over? Jeez, kiddo, we need to get you a laptop for Christmas."

I caught a glimpse of Andy whose eyes flared, telling me I may have just stepped on Santa's toes.

"Lane did some work for the department," Andy said quickly. "Show him, honey."

Lane slid onto the dining room chair and set her fingers to dancing on the keyboard and guiding the mouse. The screen flashed through several different windows until an image of a road map filled the left half. She opened a second window on the right half. Rows upon rows of small icons lined up, descending out of sight. We clustered behind her chair. I wrapped an arm around Andy's shoulder. She intertwined her fingers with mine.

"Okay. These," she pointed at the right side, "are scans of all those paper squares you collected from Boyd's car. The ones in that bag, that is. He has a handful that he won't let anyone touch. Believe me, I've tried. That boy can throw a tantrum. Anyway, I scanned each one and added the images to this folder here. You were right, Will. Andy said you guessed that they're pieces of a road map."

I felt Lane's mother cringe at her daughter's familiar use of our first names. A losing battle. Andy was the big sister and best friend Lane needed to navigate between childhood and womanhood. I was the crush she was starting to outgrow, which broke a tiny little piece of my heart.

"Okay, and on this side, I scanned like four or five state highway maps, you know because they're printed front and back, and I wasn't sure how far out I needed to go, how many states. Andy said that about six hundred miles was the limit for the car, but I added fifty percent as a margin for error."

"We ran what credit cards we could find for Lillian," Andy added. "No recent charges for gas or for a charging station, so the six-hundred-mile radius is probably a good starting point. She may have used cash, but I don't see Boyd getting away with that."

Made sense to me. An eight-year-old, even a fully communicative one, strolling into a Kwik Stop with a wad of cash for a tank of gas would have drawn attention. Especially when he tried to drive off.

"I probably could have downloaded maps, but I wanted to use the actual paper originals. I synchronized the map scale and merged the scans. Then I used an image recognition software program with a super cool matching algorithm, which can not only do shape recognition, but you can set the color tolerance—"

"Lane, honey, why not just show them?" her mother asked.

"Right. Okay, here, watch this." Lane clicked open a control window, made a few selections, assigned a source folder, and clicked on a button that said Match.

The screen came alive. One by one, the images in the window on the right graphically leaped across to the image on the left, shrank and landed on its match on the map.

"Remind me never to play 'Where's Waldo' with you," I muttered.

The tiny squares flew across the screen at a rate of two or three per second. As it worked, Lane zoomed closer. The tiles paved a broken line of individual disconnected squares. Soon the line solidified as sections began to fill and tiles joined. The line snaked across the map.

Son of a bitch.

Without needing to wait for the big reveal, I saw the answer. "That was his map. That's how he got here. Holy crap."

Andy nodded.

Lane said, "It was a jigsaw puzzle. We probably could have done this on a tabletop, but that could have taken forever. And some of the squares are just a line, which could fit anywhere, plus you have the orientation to deal with. Like is it up, down, sideways? You know? This way it's so much faster. Look at how he did this!"

The line filled in. The path wound across the map like a stream on a prairie. Hooks and turns formed where the line avoided towns and cities. The boy kept Lillian's Prius on the backroads.

"Thinking in pictures…" I said with no small degree of awe.

Lane beamed up at me. I grinned back at her, which added fuel to her smile. "I know! Boyd is incredibly bright. I've been spending time with him after school."

The process continued. Square after square jumped to the map. When it stopped, Lane zoomed the image out and sat back.

The line of square tiles ended at our driveway in Essex.

It started in Sioux City, Iowa.

44

I waited until Lane and Rosemary II departed before telling Andy about the cargo plane that carried ATVs to and from Ekalaka, about the lawyer in Sioux City, and about Martian Mike and how I lost Wally. I wanted to leave out the shotgun blast because I knew she would worry about damage done to me, but I couldn't find a way around it. She felt an urgent need to hug me, but then worried that I was still in pain. She asked if I had taken anything, and I said no, so she ran for ibuprofen and a glass of water.

"I need a shower and a shave. And then we have to find that kid." I explained my stop in Sioux City and the conversation with Delilah. "I can make it over to Michigan before it gets too shitty."

I expected an argument. Instead, Andy rubbed my chin. "Yes." She exaggerated taking a whiff of me. "And yes. You need both."

"What?"

"A shave and shower."

"C'mon, Dee. I'm serious."

"Serious about going to Michigan? Tonight? After what you just told me? No."

"It's the only idea we have."

"No. It's not. Not if you let me do my job. Go get cleaned up."

I stood my ground.

"Go. I mean it. And when's the last time you ate?"

"I had three tacos from a truck in Greeley, Colorado. That and a Snickers bar from the FBO in Sioux City."

"Well, I just happen to have what you need. After you are clean and presentable, we're going up to Lydia's for dinner with—"

"No." I said it a little too harshly and it gave Andy pause. I backtracked quickly. "*Please...* no. I need to—"

"To what? Tell me. What do you plan to do? You're dead on your feet, Will Stewart. You were hurt in God only knows what ways. You haven't slept. Do you think I don't see that?"

"And what if that's where they took the kid?"

"I hate saying it, but from what you said, the chances are that he's already dead. But I pray he isn't. What if you go running off tonight and there's nothing there? And you end up stuck in Frankfurt for three days until they plow the runway? When you might be needed somewhere else?"

My wife stepped up to me and rapped her knuckles on my chest.

"Ouch!"

"Go. Upstairs. Shower. Shave. Get dressed. There's nothing you can do for that young man tonight, but there may be some things I can do. You're no good to him or me in a pile of wreckage, God forbid."

"Then we're skipping dinner with Lydia? And I assume your parents?"

"Don't be silly. I can make some calls while you clean up. You need a good dinner and a stiff drink. Now move it."

"Fine. If I fall asleep in my soup, turn my head so I don't drown."

45

Sleet tickled the bathroom window just before I turned the shower nozzle all the way to hot. The sound pronounced my last shred of hope for flying to Michigan dead. Recognizing the obvious took some of the starch out of my body. Ten minutes under the hot shower washed away the dirt that had been holding me up. Andy was dreaming if she thought she could keep me upright through an entire family dinner.

Clean clothes felt heavenly and brought back a small spark of energy. The heat on my sore muscles worked away the pain I carried for the last twenty-four hours. I dressed quickly and studiously avoided looking at the mattress and pillow on my bed. I swear, just as I killed the bedroom light to go downstairs, both called my name.

Andy dressed while I showered. She looked fresh and ready in a dark skirt, calf-length boots and a white sweater that beckoned my touch even more than the red sweater had. I found her at our dining room table, deep in thought at her laptop.

"What time do we have to be there?"

No answer. I've seen her like this before. Half of the police work she does is in the two-dimensional world of her laptop screen. The film noir version of that popped into my head.

She prowls the dark alleys and sinister side streets of social media...

"Spiro Lewko called. He's giving us a billion dollars."

No answer.

I was tempted to grab a Corona and flop on the sofa while she worked

172

but knew I'd end up drowsing into oblivion quickly. Instead, I went to the mudroom and opened the cabinet beside the door to the kitchen. A row of battery chargers winked green lights at me, telling me that the cells were powered up. I spent a few minutes changing out batteries in my two remaining power units and pairing the units with props. I lost too many of the hand-made devices lately. Time to have Amazon restock me. I also had some ideas for reducing the size of the units and making the slide control a better fit for my hand. My garage workbench was littered with pieces, parts, and early-generation units. With cold weather coming, working in the unheated garage had no appeal. I'd been thinking for a while about packing everything and taking it to a side office at the Foundation hangar. The issue stopping me was Arun. He still had no knowledge of *the other thing.* Hiding such a project from him would be impossible, given his relentless curiosity.

A phantom conversation with Arun was playing out in my head when Andy tapped me on the shoulder. I involuntarily jumped.

"Jeez! Don't do that!"

She smiled. "Lydia says we can come anytime for cocktails, and I placed an order for a new dishwasher."

"What?"

"We can afford one now that we have a billion dollars. Let's go." She swished her skirt at me when she turned to get her coat. "I *was* listening."

WE MOUNTED up in the police SUV that had become her daily driver. Andy drove but kept the speed within ten of the limit. Conservative for her.

"I talked to the authorities in Greeley and Sterling. They know about the young man, Wally."

"Did you tell them about me?"

"No. I framed it as part of an on-going. It wasn't easy."

"Thanks."

"The police in Greeley wanted to know why Wally was at the scene of a murder under investigation by the Weld County Sheriff's Department. That means—"

"My anonymous tip made it to the right ears."

"Sterling PD is on their way to Wally's home in case he simply returned there. I had to give them a connection to his aunt at Earl's friend's ranch. I hope that's okay."

"It's in the news. No reason not to," I said. "I don't know how Wally would have gone home, though."

"It's protocol, love. Oh, and I called the office and asked the night supervisor to spend some time on the computer running Scott Danzig's name through the databases. I went online and did some digging. There's not much about an air cargo operator flying from Frankfurt, Michigan. I mean, not in a public sense, like if you wanted to hire them. But I did find some information with the State of Michigan. Scott Danzig Air Cargo is a registered LLC, but wholly owned by—I forget the names—a stack of companies who own companies who own companies. Russian nesting dolls. I suppose that's not unusual in the aviation business."

"'Fraid not."

"A few names did come up listed as members of the holding company LLCs. I made a list and will check them out. I recognized Alton Cain, Coastal Investments, Green Hill Gamers, and a few others."

"Who the hell are they?"

"You don't know Alton Cain? Big time director. Your pal Lonnie Penn would know him. I think she did a picture with him. Coastal is a hedge fund, so they're probably just in it for the portfolio—although hedge funds don't usually play with small stuff. Green Hill Gamers is a sports book operation."

"Gambling? As in, the mob?"

"If by 'the mob' you mean political donors and U.S. senators, then yes."

"Then I was right. Criminals."

"There are a lot of legal changes that have gone through, or are coming through, that make sports book betting mainstream. Green Hill is owned by a bunch of former NBA and NFL players."

"Wow. Didn't know you were a fan."

"Right. Evidenced by the amount of sleep I get while you watch Packer games. No, silly. I know about Green Hill because one of their shareholders is—guess who."

"Clayton Johns." Andy tapped her nose for me. "Are you telling me that Clayton Johns, who you are currently hoping to put away for a very long timeout, owns this cargo outfit?"

"I doubt he knows it exists. I told you. Holding companies. Pieces of a portfolio. Coastal is just another hedge fund managed by that guy—whatzisname—Dodge. Matthew—no, Myron. Myron Dodge. You know. The guy that famously called Steve Jobs 'a hack, not a hacker.' Do you read anything besides *Sport Aviation*?"

"Advisory circulars."

"The point is, it's a giant game of smoke and mirrors. Hedge funds are all about financial instruments. They also don't waste their time with small investors. Generally institutional money. They probably don't even know they have a piece of a little cargo company in Frankfurt, Michigan."

"My money's on the mob connection."

She flicked on the wipers as specs of precipitation began to dot the windshield. "Oh, and I initiated an inquiry with the Division of Criminal Investigation at the Montana Department of Justice, asking for information on that news story about nine people disappearing from a ranch near Ekalaka. I didn't mention that you were there."

"How did you pull that off?"

"Richardson. We have friends there, remember?"

"I seem to recall the Montana AG trying to have you fired."

"No, silly. *Richardson*. The prosecutor on the Parks case. He likes me. That AG wasn't re-elected."

She seemed finished. It was a lot. I didn't realize I'd been in the shower that long.

I told her what Earl said about Tammy Day and filled in what Wally told me about his aunt's money. I mentioned the rich game maker but added that I had no specifics to preempt her from asking. Altogether I wasn't sure it had relevance, but Andy sees things differently. She didn't have her note pad out, but I knew she'd jotted the item in her memory.

Andy steered the car onto Sunset Circle Road. Leander Lake, not yet frozen, lay dark to our left. The sleet I had heard on the bathroom window became tiny flakes that made the road wet.

I didn't realize I'd drifted into recriminating thoughts about leaving the kid alone in that Buick, playing out *what ifs* that might have changed things until Andy reached across the police unit's console and squeezed my hand.

"Honey, I know you. I know you want to fix this thing with Wally. But this is the part where you have to let the official wheels turn."

"Easier said than done."

46

L ydia's daughters, Elise and Harriet, tumbled into me at the door before I could unzip my flight jacket. The greeting was not unusual, but the jolt to my arms and shoulders surprised me. Andy caught me taking a sharp breath and uttering a clipped cry of pain, which I then exaggerated to make it look like part of the act.

I scooped up both girls and lifted them.

"Good heavens! What have you been eating? You guys weigh a ton. A ton and a half."

"We do not!" Elise, the three-and-a-half-year-old protested. "I weigh twenty-eight and Harriet weighs thirty-eight."

"Ellie, stop! You're telling my part!"

"Hmmm," I hefted the two of them. "Now that I think about it, Harriet, I think you're light as a feather. It's this beautiful baby sister of yours that weighs a ton."

Harriet laughed.

"Do not!" Elise cried. I jiggled her in my arm so that her protest sounded funny. She broke into a giggle.

"Two tons."

More jiggling, more giggling. And on it went.

Lydia, Andy's sister, appeared.

"What no handcuffs? He came of his own accord?" Lydia swept in and planted a kiss on my cheek. "I was beginning to think you were avoiding us."

"Work." Lydia bears a remarkable resemblance to her younger sister, Andy. The similarities make the differences stand out. Tonight, she upped the discordance with deep red hair. "Something's different…"

"Like it? There's some Irish in the family. Somewhere. Come in, come in. Girls, let your Uncle Will have a few minutes with the grown-ups, please."

"Come and see my room!" Harriet begged. "I changed it."

"Again? What day of the week is it?"

"Mine, too!" Elise chirped.

"Mommy, she's copying me," Harriet complained.

"Scoot," Lydia ordered. I watched them trot off. "Let me take your coats. We're in the big room." She leaned a little closer and whispered, "And we have a guest. I invited one of our neighbors. Actually, Mom did," Lydia threw her sister an encrypted glance.

I looked for a chance to register a protest with my wife, but she must have seen it coming. She avoided eye contact with me.

Lydia led us into the largest room in the house. A wall of windows overlooked Leander Lake. Scattered contemporary furniture, much of it leather, anchored a broad oriental rug that I had not seen before. Low recessed lighting added warmth to paneled wood walls. Opposite the windows, a well-stocked bar became Lydia's first stop.

"What can I get you?"

"Got any coffee?" I asked. "That is, if you don't want me to nod off during dinner."

"Nothing for me," Andy added. Lydia shot her a loaded look. "And no. I'm not pregnant."

Lydia's loaded look turned into reproach and sailed in my direction, but my attention shifted to the people at the far end of the room. Seated at the big bank of windows were Lydia's parents and the surprise guest.

"Oh, you've got to be kidding me."

Andy hooked my arm and pulled me toward the cluster of conversation.

"Senator Keller, how nice to see you again," Andy said, smiling.

An attractive, sharply dressed blonde-haired woman whose age hid behind every trick in the cosmetic book looked up from an animated conversation with Andy's mother. Lorna Keller had been chief of staff to Sandy Stone's father when he served in the Wisconsin State Senate. After his murder, Keller used what she knew of the governor's tangential involvement with the murderer to land an appointment to the late senator's seat. I can't say I like the woman, but she proved fiercely loyal to Sandy Stone at a very dark hour. For that, I gave her a pass.

Andy's mother and father anchored the conversation in separate seats, with Andy's mother on a sofa adjacent to the Senator. Andy's near perfect genetics spring from her mother, but Eleanor Taylor lacks her daughter's spark of warmth and humor, a difference that defines true beauty, at least in my eyes. Sharing a room with a state senator, Eleanor was clearly in what I dubbed her *social mode*. The way she sat. The way she smiled. The way she rose and pecked each of her daughter's cheeks as a show of affection aimed more at Keller than Andy.

"The children of the hour," Keller said, rising and exchanging a hug with Andy. She dished me a curt handshake.

"Senator," I said. "How are you?"

"Well," she replied fixing her attention on Andy. "The question is, how are you, dear. I saw that debacle at your house."

Andy shrugged. "Wasted energy. Hi, Daddy."

Andy's father gave his daughter a hug, then sent a handshake my way.

"Evening, sir," I said.

"I don't think I can handle you calling me 'Dad,' but I'd be fine with you calling me Louis."

I almost choked. My dominant memory of the man was having him accuse me of nearly killing his daughter. Granted, things had warmed since, but this was a line we had not crossed before. I noted that he had his favorite Highlands scotch in hand and wondered how many he'd had.

"I think I can handle Mr. Taylor, sir."

A shockingly warm smile crossed his face. "That will do for now, Will. Good to see you." He patted my shoulder. The man had gained some gray since I last saw him. That and a few extra lines at the eyes. Both added to his Captain of Industry aura. Still, something about him seemed less terrifying.

"Andrea, darling, you must tell the Senator about that awful night," Andy's mother pulled Andy to be seated beside her.

"It was nothing. People got a little out of hand is all."

"Nonsense, they attacked your home."

"Nobody attacked our home, Mother." Andy shifted her attention to Keller. "It's good to see you, Senator. How's everything in Madison?"

"My dear if I told you, you would run screaming from the room and apply for citizenship in Canada. I side with your mother tonight." Eleanor Taylor shifted her pose, letting the glow of Keller's endorsement wash over her. "I'd like to hear more about this recall."

"Local politics," Andy brushed it off.

"All politics are local," Keller replied.

"The Cliff's Notes, then. There's a recall petition. They need four thousand signatures. If they get them, they're doing a block recall of three city council members. The idea is to put up their own candidates who, if they win, replace these three on the Council, and then on the Fire and Police Commission, and if they're successful, agenda item number one is to fire me."

"For?"

Andy shrugged. "Being in the wrong place at the wrong time."

"That's absurd!" Andy's mother said.

"Mom, that's local politics."

I watched Keller listening to Andy as if this was breaking news, thinking there was no way this woman didn't already have all these details and more. At the very least, if she was staying on Leander Lake, she was staying with Sandy Stone, just a few doors away. Sandy would have explained everything.

Louis leaned forward in his chair. "Andrea and I have discussed this matter. This is about that assassination attempt in Detroit. The person behind that was identified."

"The FBI issued a statement," Andy told Keller.

"And Andrea's involvement—"

"She wasn't involved, Louis," his wife interrupted.

"I wasn't implying that, Eleanor. I was simply saying that circumstances have given certain people the idea that our daughter had a role—no, a presence—in an attempt on the life of the President. Those circumstances need to be explained. We simply need to find the right people to step up and make that case. What do you think Senator?"

Keller spared a sly glance at Louis, who bounced it back at her. It was fun watching them. Like a couple of NFL coaches managing the last two minutes of a game with a two-point difference.

"I think a fresh drink would be just the thing. I wonder, Louis, would you mind?" Keller lifted her not finished tumbler of something golden at Andy's father.

And there's the winning field goal.

Louis nodded to concede the point. Game over. For the moment. He stood and took Keller's drink. "Will, anything?"

"I've got coffee coming, thank you, sir—er, Mr. Taylor."

Louis shook his head and gave me another of those weird, warm smiles. I wondered what Harriet and Elise had been feeding their grandfather.

"Eleanor, would you kindly excuse Andrea and me for a few minutes of semi-official state business?" Keller placed a hand on Eleanor Taylor's knee. Andy's mother flashed a look that suggested Keller's touch burned.

"Of course, Lorna. It's past time for me to check on Lydia in the kitchen."

Eleanor stood. "Will, shall we see if your coffee is ready?"

"Oh, I'd like Will to stay," Keller said. "He seems to be neck deep in your daughter's affairs—or maybe it's the other way around."

I glanced at Andy and mouthed, *Ouch.*

She pointedly ignored me. Eleanor stalked off toward the kitchen.

"Do you also wrestle alligators, Senator?" Andy asked with an open smile on her face.

"Sometimes. Your mother and I are a lot alike, Andrea. I understand her. I'm not always about politics. I like to think of Sandra as a daughter, which of course, I never had. But I understand the protective instinct. I see that nature in your mother."

Andy didn't comment.

"Sit down, Will. You're like a cell tower someone built in the neighbor's yard."

I dropped into a weirdly low leather chair that had no arms.

"Andrea, I know you well enough to know that you did a thorough assessment of the people in the crowd outside your house. And by now you have identified the nasty outside participants in that well-organized supposedly spontaneous demonstration of community outrage."

"I have."

"Good. Because I don't want you to minimize the danger. Do you understand my meaning?"

"I do."

"I don't," I said. "I'd rather you spell this out in plain English, Senator."

I braced for a shot back from Keller, but she simply looked at me and nodded. "Of course, Will. This isn't the time to be cryptic. Your wife has become the mascot for a very corrupt agenda. The opposition party, at a very high level, has decided to politicize the lie that she was involved in the assassination attempt. Not overtly, mind you. They'll hide behind social media and political operatives and gullible loyalists. But make no mistake, this recall, ostensibly a matter of local politics, is not just being keenly watched by the national party. They're pumping money into the effort. A lot of money. They want to see Andrea fired for her role—"

"Her role was to save that fucker's fat ass!"

Keller flashed me a patronizing smile. "You know that, and I know that, but politics is not about what's real or right. Very powerful people see an opportunity to feed raw meat to their base in a lie that will energize them, anger them, motivate them."

"For what? How does this lie have anything to do with anything?"

"This lie gets the President re-elected, and his party a shot at taking both houses of Congress. Spoon feeding this lie to the public and whipping up the base is pure political gold. Better than an October Surprise."

"But it's a lie."

"Of course, it's a lie. Will, I know you don't live under a rock. You are, I'm sure, familiar with the outcry for police reform since last summer."

"I am. Please don't tell me these clowns plan to jump on the police reform bandwagon after they've been fighting it for months."

"They do not. But they feel the heat. Their weak talking points have been that the issue is not systemic racism or biased police training or outdated traditions. It's the 'bad egg' theory. These unfortunate killings are terrible tragedies brought about by one or two bad eggs."

"They're not entirely wrong," Andrea said. "That's just not the whole story."

"A shred of truth invests all the best lies. The national party has been struggling with that lame talking point in the face of a tidal wave of public support for the Black Lives Matter movement and police reform movement. The 'bad egg' angle works to a point, but they need to make it resonate. They need a poster child—but not one that just killed an unarmed teenager." Keller dipped her face at Andy. "Remember, they're pumping out propaganda about threats to law abiding suburban families, about suburbs being overrun by rioters, about rampant crime on the rise—"

"It's not," Andy protested. "The statistics are irrefutable. Nationwide crime has been down year after year."

"Please, Andrea, don't let facts muddy the political gin and tonic. My point is that they need to build fear, then call for more police power. To do that, they need to dismiss the real issues. Theories and complexities and statistics don't play with their base. They need to make an example and they need to keep it simple. What could be better than a diabolical secret plot to assassinate their savior."

"All this from a recall election in Essex, Wisconsin?"

"The recall case here is pivotal. A lot is being bet on it. Therefore, it demands a certain outcome. With the right outcome, a political tale can be told that will become topic number one at every rally the President holds until election day."

"I'm the 'bad egg.'" Andy said.

"Exactly."

"And you know this how?" I demanded, feeling anger rise along with the color in my cheeks.

Keller looked me in the eye. The patronizing smile flashed again, but then faded into something I was tempted to view as sincerity. "I don't think you like me, Will." She wasn't wrong. "And I can accept that. You have good reason not to like me. I swim in a sewer. And I don't shower after I swim. Do you know why?"

I didn't answer. I don't think she expected me to.

"Because it gives me power to move among my enemies. And because I do that, I understand my opponents. And what they are willing to do."

"Forgive my saying so, Senator, but that's a lousy way to live."

"Perhaps, but that brings me to something else I need to say. You were probably surprised to see me here tonight. Your mother and sister are a delight, Andrea, but I must confess to asking Sandy to introduce us and then maneuvering your mother into extending the invitation. I need to convey something to you both—in person—and seeking you out via my office or your office has no chance of privacy." She focused directly on me. "This is for you, Will, because your wife still believes in truth and justice and due process."

"Me?"

"You're a student of history, I understand."

"I like to read history. Yes."

"Do you know why we were caught flat-footed at Pearl Harbor?"

Her question surprised me, as did the idea that she knew the answer and the history that supported it. I knew, of course, but rather than respond, I wanted to hear what a career politician had to say. I expected something stupid, which I planned to shoot down and feel satisfied for doing so.

"People remember Pearl Harbor as a dastardly sneak attack, but the fact is, everyone who mattered knew we were going to war with Japan. Halsey put his ships on a war footing days before the attack, even told his captains to shoot first at any Japanese ship they encountered. We remember and honor the *Arizona* for being sunk that day, but we don't remember that she and the other battleships had been training for weeks for a battle with the Japanese fleet."

I was amazed that she knew this.

"Halsey was at sea, spoiling for a fight. His subordinates had to talk him down. And yet, even knowing that war was inevitable, we woke up utterly astonished on Sunday, December 7 by the sound of Japanese torpedo bombers over Pearl Harbor. Do you know why? Because in that day, in that age, no one could conceive of an entire fleet crossing six thousand miles of ocean undetected to deliver an attack. It was beyond imagination."

She had it right. "I'm impressed."

"The President's party is footing the bill for a big chunk of this recall. They see a golden opportunity to build momentum on a 'law and order' platform going into the election. Wisconsin is a swing state. The state party sees a chance to buy a seat at the national table, and there is *nothing* they won't do to curry favor and bring in more money. That's why this effort must not fail. The trouble is…there are rumors that the organizers of this recall are falling short of the signatures they need."

"That's not what they told the mob last week," Andy said.

"Of course not. You never tell a mob the truth."

"I hope they fail," I said. "It's a stupid idea."

"Be careful what you wish for, Will. Failure backs the party into a corner after they bet a lot on the outcome."

"Serve them right," I muttered.

"Pearl Harbor, Will. Imagine the unimaginable. There are people with deniability who will have this victory one way or the other. And by 'other' I refer you to the people who showed up in front of your house, armed to the teeth."

"That's insane."

"So was sailing six thousand miles, risking an entire fleet."

Keller paused to affirm that we understood.

"You're talking about those cosplay militia assholes, right?"

"Take them seriously, Will," Keller warned.

"We've ID'd most of them," Andy said. "We know who they are."

"Good. Do not, for one second, leave anything out of your imagination, both of you. Do you understand me? It is dearly important to me that you understand what I am saying." She scooted forward on her chair and grasped both of Andy's hands. "This recall is failing, and it *cannot* fail. Which means they're being backed into a corner. There is *nothing* beyond imagination in their thinking."

"We understand," Andy said.

Keller did not look at Andy. She looked directly at me.

I nodded.

"*Tora. Tora. Tora.*"

47

I didn't fall asleep in my soup. Or flop onto the tenderloin roast that Lydia served. I kept my head up and eyes open for the entire evening, including a rousing game of hide and seek with Elise and Harriet. I let them make me the seeker each time, because if I'd gone off to crawl under a bed, my snoring would have given me away.

Lydia and Melanie made a dual appearance with their infant children. Lydia passed baby Grace to Andy with the clear intention of triggering a biological urge in her sister. I was handed the Infant King Alex, who grinned up at me like an idiot, which I considered him to be given his blind faith that I wouldn't drop him. Andy and I were watched like subjects of a science experiment by Andy's parents. Andy passed the test, but by the time I handed grinning Alex back to his mother, everyone in the room was just happy the child had been returned uninjured.

Earning another notch of my undying love, my wife excused us early, citing the snow that had begun to fall, and the hazardous drive home. Senator Keller used the opportunity to thank her lake neighbor Lydia, and her mother, for the invitation and lovely dinner, and to walk out with us. The move suggested she had more to say. I braced for it. We walked to our respective cars commenting on the snow and the coming storm and the quality of predictions for how many inches we would find on our yards in the morning.

Just when I thought we would escape, Keller hooked Andy's arm.

"I'm sorry about the Academy, Andrea. That was wrong." Andy

DIVISIBLE MAN - NINE LIVES LOST

attempted a dismissive response, but Keller cut her off. "It went a lot higher than you think. You should know that. They wanted you back, but their hands were tied."

"Whose hands—er, who did the tying?" I asked when Andy remained speechless.

"Never ask that question, Will. You would be tempted to act on the answer. Now take your lovely wife home and please keep in mind what I said earlier."

48

"That woman drives me nuts," I said, hanging my flight jacket on a hook by the door to the mudroom. "There's always something going on. Some deep, dark shit that us ordinary rubes could not possibly understand."

"She means well." Andy slipped out of her coat, then unzipped her boots and rendered herself barefoot. "I was pleased to hear that she thinks the recall signature drive will fail."

"Me, too. But she even made that sound like doom."

"You should give her a break."

"Dee, she thrives on crisis. Why does everything have to be a giant conspiracy? She reminds me of people who believe they are reincarnated. They always think they were someone famous. Never just a guy who cleaned stables or a farmer or some worker that scraped barnacles off ship hulls before drinking himself to death. Keller thinks anything she knows or hears is earth-shattering or belongs to some nefarious political agenda."

Andy padded across the kitchen. She extracted her police service weapon from her handbag and left the bag on the counter. She returned to me for a one-handed embrace. She nudged close and cooed in my ear.

"Oh, my. I love it when you talk political agenda, you gorgeous hunk of strategist, you."

My hands found the delightful convex curve at the small of her back. I slipped them under the cashmere sweater and found smooth skin.

"You place a lot of confidence in my stamina, woman."

"Say something legislative," she whispered. She pressed her lips to my neck. I fought a shiver that raced down my neck, into my shoulder and arm. "Talk to me about committee assignments. Redistricting. Render that bill for markup, Senator."

"You do remember you're holding a gun."

"Am I?" Her free hand moved freely. "I might not be the only one."

49

I missed my wife. She missed me. We let each other know it.

I became two people. One remained sore and weak and exhausted. The other made tireless love to the same woman for the fourth year in a row feeling like it had been barely a minute since we met. I did so with untapped energy. Somewhere at the end of this passionate moment, I knew I would crash, but for what Andy gave me, and I pray I gave her, it would be a glorious and utterly satisfying pileup. At the end, falling asleep with her tucked under my left arm, her head on my chest and shoulder, the tension of the last three days evaporated. Exhaustion took me. My last conscious thought was a prayer that I would sleep for a week.

Andy's phone shattered that hope. She rolled away from my grasp, leaving the left side of my body cold and exposed.

"Detective Stewart." I heard her voice in the dark. She shifted on the mattress, swinging her feet to the floor. "Ashley?"

I heard the young dispatcher trainee speak but could not make out the words.

"No, that wasn't us."

"No, it was towed in."

"When?"

"Because it wasn't in impound. I told them to just leave it there in the back lot so the techs could look at it."

"Okay."

"Okay."

"Thank you, Ashley."

The call ended. Andy pulled the phone away from her ear, which automatically lit up the screen. I saw her outline in the dark, her smooth skin, her wild post-sex hair. She turned and reached back to shake me.

"I'm awake," I said. "What's happening?"

"Get dressed. That was Ashley at the office. The Prius is gone."

50

Andy dresses faster than any woman I've ever seen or heard of. She blessedly left the lights off and hurried out of the bedroom. Her bare feet pounded down the stairs.

Still tucking things in, zipping, and buckling, I caught up to her in the kitchen four or five minutes later. She had pulled her boots back on.

"What's happening?"

"The Prius was in the lot behind the station. Ray Garland mentioned to Ashley that it was gone when he came in for a mid-shift. She thought it was odd because the key is still on my desk."

"How does the car get taken without a key?"

"Andy produced her phone. "God, I hate to do this at this hour..." She poked the screen several times, then lifted the phone to her ear. I heard it ringing.

"Who are you calling?" I got a hand signal meant to put me on Pause. Rather than stand there staring, I headed for the coffee maker. The stove clock said 3:47. I hit the coffee maker button to start things warming and leaned close to the window above the kitchen sink. Fat snowflakes dropped just outside the glass.

"Ellen? It's Andrea. I'm so sorry to call you at this hour." Andy looked at the floor and jammed her free hand deep into her hair. I reached behind her and plucked two clean coffee mugs from the cabinet and placed them on the counter. "I hate to ask you to do this, but can you check on Boyd?...No, I'm hoping it's nothing...Thank you." Andy swung the phone away from her mouth. "I shouldn't have woken you for this, sweetheart. It might not be anything."

"Might as well make some coffee. It sounds like you won't be coming back to bed anytime soon."

"I'm sorry—Ellen? No, I was just talking to Will…He's not? Dammit. Okay, just stay there and I'll call it in…No, don't go out. I don't think he's on foot…I know, I know. Let me handle it, okay? Thanks!" Andy ended the call.

"I get one guess. Boyd is gone."

The hand stayed buried in her hair. Andy shook her head. "I should have seen it."

"How? The kid's an inscrutable wild card. He's—"

"No, Will, I should have seen it. You're absolutely right. The car doesn't go without the key. When he hit our mailbox, the key was in the cupholder. Dammit! This is Lillian, being smart. She hid a spare. It's somewhere in that child's backpack, in all that crap that he carries around. It's probably not even the key, but just the chip and battery. It could be hidden in any one of those toys or souvenirs he has in his collection."

"You think he took the car? From the police station parking lot?"

"Yes. Ellen's place is just a few blocks away and she's been taking him out for walks. She brought him over a couple times, thinking we might be able to talk to him, but we didn't get anywhere. He must have seen the car in the back lot. I need to go."

Andy grabbed her satchel, which I presume had been reloaded with her service weapon.

"Hold on," I said. "Don't you think you should stay here? He came here last time. Chances are good he'll come here again. I think there's something about us that Lillian programmed into that kid."

Andy paused.

"Think about it, Dee. Where else would he go?"

We looked at each other and both shifted gears in the same instant.

"What's that sound?" she asked.

I heard it, too. "Is that…?" I looked out the window at the falling snow. "Is that hail? That can't be right."

"Hail? In a snowstorm?" Andy went to look through the mudroom and out the back windows at the farmyard. "Will, the security light is out."

Something peppered the house. Then hammered it. Then we heard breaking glass. A moment later a box of Kleenex on the kitchen table exploded, creating a cloud of tissue fragments. One of the two coffee mugs shattered. Chips flew everywhere. I ducked and shielded my eyes, then looked at my wife wearing a face full of *What the hell?*

"GET DOWN!" She lunged across the kitchen at me and threw her arms around me. We dropped to the floor in an awkward tangle.

The kitchen erupted. Hammer blows struck the cabinets. Chips of wood, glass and ceramic filled the air. The light bulb over the sink exploded. Darkness swallowed the room. We clutched the floor tiles.

I felt Andy move. She crabbed away from me.

"Dee!"

The noise grew louder, no longer hailstones on a rooftop, but smashing, pounding, shattering.

"Will! This way!"

I scrambled toward the sound of her voice. She sank her fingers into my shirt and pulled me forward. We reached the threshold to the basement steps side by side. I lunged forward and grasped the first, then the second step. I pulled myself headfirst down into utter blackness. Andy did the same. We made a bruising side-by-side descent, fighting to keep control. Something happened to Andy. She bumped down the stairs ahead of me. On her way, she kicked me in the shoulder. I dove after her, reaching the bottom in a heap on top of her.

We untangled and found our feet. She pulled me away from the stairs, backward, into darkness. I banged into a table topped with storage boxes. She knocked over a gas grille we kept in the basement during the winter. The sound of clattering junk joined the sound of glass breaking, wood chipping, and walls being hammered above us.

We found each other in the dark. Andy pulled me into a crouch.

"Christ!" I uttered. "What the fuck!"

"Stay down," she ordered. "Are you okay? Are you hit?"

"Hit?" In the dark, her hands flew all over me, patting and feeling for damage. "What the hell? What do you mean hit?"

"Someone's shooting at us!"

Until that moment, the idea that the hailstones were bullets simply did not connect.

The rapping continued, transmitted down to us via the walls and the wooden structure of the house. It came in bursts, fits and starts. Something large toppled over upstairs. More glass broke.

"Stay here," Andy ordered.

Before I could protest, she darted away in the darkness.

The farmhouse basement is black as pitch at night. The few windows at the tops of the stone walls are tiny and below the outside ground. The window wells have plastic covers. By now the covers wore a layer of snow. We keep a battery-powered radio on a shelf along with a box of kitchen matches and several candles. The radio and candles saw service twice during storms when the county sirens sounded a tornado warning.

This was different.

"Where are you going?"

"I'm right here," she said.

I followed the sound of her voice. Andy had moved across the floor to where a set of steps climbed to exterior storm cellar doors.

"You're not going out there!"

"No. But I can hear better over here."

She crouched by the steps. I dropped down beside her.

Scores of bullets penetrated the farmhouse walls and windows above us. The chorus of destruction seemed never ending.

"I don't hear gunshots."

"They're using suppressors. They're not at the back of the house. It's all coming from the front. From the road."

"We can't get out this way," I reminded her. The Bilco doors to the cellar were padlocked from the outside. We talked about changing the lock numerous times. Andy told me that we should be able to get out of the cellar from the inside. I had agreed and now felt guilty for not getting around to the task.

The hammering and shattering stopped briefly, then started up again, but with less enthusiasm. I wondered if they still had a single square inch of the building to shoot at that hadn't already been shot.

When it finally ceased, the silence felt like a trap. We found each other in the dark and held hands, squeezing tightly. I prepared to tackle my wife if she gave any indication of jumping up and running after our attackers. Nothing in her armory matched up to the rifles that had been carried by the Company W warriors parading on our road. To my relief, she remained with me on the stone steps, waiting.

A new sound caught us by surprise. Popping. One. Two. Then six in rapid succession. Then more. Gunshots. They sounded close but muted. I did not detect strikes on the house.

"That was a handgun," she whispered. The popping stopped as quickly as it started.

"What...for good measure?"

We waited. Seconds ticked into a minute. Then two.

"We should look, but not so we can be seen. Can you get us up the stairs?" Andy asked.

"Don't you think we should stay down here, like until next week?"

"C'mon."

She led me by the hand back to the steep wooden steps to the kitchen. At the foot of the stairs, we both stopped. She hooked her right arm into my left and closed her hand in a fist with mine. I flashed on a memory of square dancing in grade school gym class. *Circle left!* or some such call from a cheap speaker on the gymnasium floor.

Fwooomp!

We vanished. Andy tugged us up the stair by grasping the railing. We bumped through the open door. The light over the sink had been blown out. The big security light on a pole over the farmyard had been shot out. Only the ambient city light reflecting on the low clouds dumping snow on Essex gave the kitchen definition.

A layer of chipped glass, wood and plaster covered the floor. Kitchen cabinet doors bore big holes. Two of them dangled from a single remaining hinge. The ceramic kitchen sink was shattered. I felt a flash of relief that none of the pipes had been struck, adding flood waters to the disaster. One of the counter-height chairs at the kitchen table lay on the floor with a leg missing.

Andy heaved us away from the cellar doorway. At least we didn't have to step on the broken glass. We made no sound floating across the kitchen. On the other side, we stopped at Andy's satchel. The flap flew open. Her Glock 26 lifted out. It floated close to us, then disappeared when she slipped it either under her sweater or covered it with her hands.

"Just don't shoot that thing," I warned her, too recently reminded of the effect of gunfire from within *the other thing.*

"Affirmative," she said. "Mudroom."

She pushed off the counter with a creditable move that sent us over the debris to the mudroom doorway. We passed through and bumped up against the back door.

Every window in the mudroom was broken. Wrapped in the cool sensation generated by *the other thing*, I could not feel the cold seeping into the house, but I felt the pressure of a light breeze. Snowflakes drifted through the broken windows and landed on the mudroom floor, quicky melting while the room retained its warmth.

That won't last. These were not the only windows blown out. In short order, the house would fall below freezing while the furnace ran non-stop in a vain battle to keep out the cold. At least the furnace remained undamaged.

Andy flipped the back door deadbolt. I braced us against the wall to give her leverage. She pulled the door open.

"Wait," I said. "I'm not going out there without power."

I pushed us away from the door and rotated.

The cabinet door had been damaged, but the contents inside were intact. My power units with rechargeable batteries sat plugged in at the ready. The green LED on the charger told me the house still had power. Small favors. I pocketed one unit and grabbed the other. Rotating again, I pushed off. Andy opened the latch on the storm door. I fired up the BLASTER. Thrust pulled us from the house into the falling snow which muted sound all around us.

Looking left and right, I saw no running figures or fleeing vehicles in the yard.

"There!" Andy instinctively pointed, which I felt but could not see. I followed her body shift.

Low yellow light on the road painted a curtain of falling snow ahead of a parked vehicle. Crouching near the end of our driveway, a black figure struck a familiar pose, hands joined around a weapon. The figure swung the weapon back and forth.

I didn't wait for Andy's orders. I shoved the BLASTER control to high power. A twist of the wrist aligned us with the driveway. We shot forward and swept down on the crouching attacker.

Hitting someone within *the other thing* is like throwing Styrofoam at a brick wall. Without mass or inertia, it's more likely to do damage to myself than my target.

"Be ready!" I warned Andy. I angled to one side to take the brunt of the collision while she dropped away free.

"Will wai—"

FWOOOMP!

I jammed the levers in my head into full reverse. Andy and I reappeared in stride, inches above the ground. Andy broke away to one side, trotting fast to catch up with her body, slipping wildly in the snow. She threw her arms out to fight for balance.

I hit the figure full-bodied. We went down on the snow-covered pavement and crashed onto the road. The weapon our attacker clutched in both hands clattered to the pavement. I dropped the BLASTER and threw my arms around narrow shoulders. The hard surface bit into my knees. The collision brought a startled outcry from my victim, my first clue that something was not right.

A woman.

I bear-hugged her thin figure and locked her arms against her torso, rolling backward to pull her away from her gun.

"Will! Stop!" Andy's voice froze me. "Stop! Let her go!"

Andy stooped to pick up the weapon that dropped in the snow. I released my grip and rolled away. The dark figure raised a hand, which Andy took. She lifted the figure upright and the two women looked down at me as snowflakes fell in my face and eyes.

"Hi Will."

"Hi Leslie." I flopped flat against the pavement and sucked in air. "Sorry about that."

51

FBI Special Agent Leslie Carson-Pelham maneuvered her car into the driveway. Andy ran to the house and returned with her coat and my flight jacket.

"Goddammit! They shot a hole in my jacket!" I held the garment up and poked my finger into a hole in the leather. Andy stared at me blankly. "What?"

She lifted a finger and pointed at the house which had broken bits of siding hanging from the walls and not one window intact.

"I know," I said, "But this is my flight jacket."

"I dropped my phone somewhere," Andy said. "I'm going back in to find it."

"Grab mine, too."

I slipped on the leather jacket. The damned hole was right above my spleen. Bastards. Leslie joined me. Black jeans. Black turtleneck. Black overcoat over a black jacket. It hadn't been difficult to mistake her for an attacker. We walked across the front lawn and examined the front of the house.

"Assholes even shot up the gutters. See that?" Leslie pointed. One of the roof gutters dangled. Others had holes.

"What are you doing here?"

"What do you think? I told you I was working on domestic extremism groups. Spellman and his pinhead pals in Utah were Company W. I've been keeping tabs on them. They showed up at your little rally here. If I know your wife, she already knows that. And I will bet this whole farm—what's left of it—that they were here tonight."

"You knew they were coming?"

"I wish. After we picked up chatter about Essex, I drove up. I was going to call you, but..." She shrugged. "Guess I was trying to give you two a little space after...you know..."

Leslie's effort to get Andy reinstated at the FBI Academy had gone all the way to the top. I was a little surprised she wasn't reassigned to Anchorage for her efforts.

"Hey, don't worry about it. We know you tried."

"Doesn't make me feel any better."

This was awkward. I changed the subject.

"How did you end up here tonight?"

"Last couple nights, I tagged them hanging out in a sports bar. One of them closed the joint about an hour ago, then drove around in this snow-storm like some amateur trying not to be followed—except he's an idiot and I followed him. I wanted to find out where they're camping. Maybe get a line on who brought them to the party. Anyway, he rendezvoused with a couple other pickups, and they caravanned their way to your front door. The next thing I knew there were muzzle flashes all up and down your road. As soon as I figured out that they were firing, I tried to call to warn you."

"By that time we were on the kitchen floor."

"You saw them coming?"

"No, but we were up. It's—we got a call about something else—I'll explain later. When the fireworks started, Andy and I crawled down into the basement."

"Thank God for that," Leslie said. "I wasn't much use to you. I had to hang about a half mile back or they would have seen me following them, and once the action started, I gotta be honest, charging in against automatic weapons would not have been too bright. When they finished and loaded up, I let them get rolling before I popped off a magazine in their direction. Maybe put a bullet hole in a tailgate for ID. I didn't have a prayer of hitting anyone, but I figured it would goose them a little bit. Make sure they kept going. Guys like that are brave as hell when no one is shooting back."

Andy returned. She handed me my phone. A spider's web of cracks filled the screen, radiating out from a hole the size of my pinky finger. A perfect bullseye.

"Nice." I pocketed the wreckage. "First my jacket. Now this."

"I should call this in," Leslie said, lifting her own phone. "I should have called your people when the shooting started. Andrea, you call your team, I'll call mine. We need a task force up here. Yesterday."

"Wait," Andy said. "Just...let me think for a second."

"What's to think about?" I asked.

"Andrea, this was meant to kill you. Both of you. This was raw meat for extremist social media sites. The justified execution of the woman who tried to kill their glorious leader."

"These fools will want credit either way—for the job done or for the brave effort. Let's not give them their day in the limelight. I don't want to turn this into a media circus. I'll call the Chief. Quietly. Let's get him out here and the four of us will sit down and figure out the best next step, okay?"

Leslie spread a devilish look on her face. "Set them up to expose themselves?"

Headlights appeared on the horizon, faint in the heavy snowfall, approaching the turn onto our road.

"We should go inside," I suggested, thinking we might not want to be standing out in the open if one of the shooters came by for a strike assessment or some selfies.

Nobody moved.

The headlights turned onto our road. Beams of light created a curtain of falling snow ahead of the vehicle. Both women produced their weapons, checked the magazines, and snapped the slides to chamber a round.

"That's not a pickup truck," I said. The vehicle drew closer. "That's...oh, shit."

Lillian's Prius slowed as it approached our driveway. The driver turned the wheel, but the snow rendered the steering useless. The anti-lock brakes chattered. The vehicle slewed across the on-coming lane and bumped across the driveway.

"Are you fucking kidding me?"

Even slower than the first time, the Prius bumped into my mailbox. The car stopped. The fresh new post that I recently installed snapped. The mailbox leaned over and dropped into the snow.

Andy hurried past me.

"Not bad," Leslie said. "Good aim. That's the only mailbox on this entire road, right?"

I marched past her.

Andy pulled open the driver's door. Boyd sat behind the wheel contemplating his collection of paper squares. I contemplated murder.

Andy touched the child's shoulder. I expected a repeat of his violent performance, but the boy turned his head. He did not look up or make eye contact with either Andy or me.

He spoke.

"We have to go."

The statement, without tone of any kind, nevertheless carried an unmistakable urgency.

"Boyd, are you okay?" Andy asked. She knelt beside him.

"I'm fine. We have to go. We have to go now."

"Honey, I don't understand," Andy said.

"Get in the car, Will. We have to go. We have to go now."

"Who's this?" Leslie asked, stepping beside me.

"Long story."

"Boyd, why do you need Will to go now?" Andy asked.

"Get in the car, Will. We have to go. We have to go now. Danzig is coming. Get in the car, Will."

52

"This is insane. I'm not getting in that car and letting an eight-year-old drive me through a snowstorm in the middle of the night."

We stood a few yards away from the Prius, which continued to run. Boyd remained behind the wheel. He stared down at his lap, shuffling his precious paper squares.

Andy landed a hand on my chest. "Will, if you try to move him out of that seat, chances are excellent that he will shut down. Right now, whatever he thinks is so urgent has him communicating with us. He sees the world from a place and in a way none of us can fathom, and he's reaching out to us from that place."

"What are you saying?"

"That I don't think you have a choice."

"What? I'm supposed to run off? Look at this place. It's a crime scene. I'd like to hang around and find the people that just shot the shit out of my house and tried to kill us both. We haven't even gone inside to find out what's broken."

Andy shifted her gaze to the house. "Do you really want to know? I'm not sure I do."

"Don't you think *this*, right here, right now, is more important?"

"Yes. It's important—but I just—something triggered that child. A window has opened and it will not stay open for long. Look, Leslie and I will handle this. We have already identified most of them. We'll find them. Nothing more is going to happen here tonight."

"Andrea, I know I'm late to the party, but this is some pretty weird shit. Are you sure about this?" Leslie asked.

Andy answered by lifting an index finger, begging Leslie to hold her thought. "Will, you heard him. He said, 'Danzig is coming.' That's the guy, right? The one you ran into? The guy you think has that young man?"

"Yes."

"So, think about it. How does that child know about Danzig?"

My head spun. I groped for words.

"We have to go," Boyd said flatly from the car.

"I think you have to go," Andy said.

I sent Leslie a look that pleaded for moral support.

"Don't look at me, bud. With you two, it's always nuts."

Andy circled the Prius and opened the door. I followed her. I glanced down at Boyd.

"At the very least, I should drive."

"I don't think so," Andy said. "Your favorite movie, that mummy film, where the map burns up and the guy says, 'I'm the map.' Well, he's the map. If you drag him out of that seat, you might burn up your map."

"You did *not* just quote my favorite movie at me."

"This is what you get for making me watch it ten times." She flexed up on her toes and pulled me into a kiss. I held on for a moment.

"Are you okay?"

"I'm pissed," she said.

"That's because somebody shot the shit out of our house. Just sayin'."

"I know."

"Jesus, Dee, if you hadn't gotten that call—I don't even want to think about it."

"I know. Me neither."

Our eyes traded a flood of feelings that needed no words.

"It's just things. Inside. In the house. Just things. We can replace them." I thought ahead to the pain she would experience picking through our broken possessions.

"Go. I'll be okay. Leslie's here."

"Fine. Go find those bastards." I poked my finger at my left side. "They shot my jacket."

She generated a weak smile and kissed me again. I dropped into the front seat. Andy rejoined Leslie.

Boyd closed his door and dropped the Prius in reverse. He backed up a few feet. The headlights swept across my dead mailbox, already blanketed by fresh snow.

Nice work, kid.

He deftly rotated the steering wheel and cut past the mailbox, accelerating on the snow-covered road. Fat flakes raced at the windshield.

I snapped my seatbelt and tugged it as snug as possible. I marveled that the child could even see over the steering wheel. He drove with his head turned slightly toward the center of the dash, looking askance at the road ahead. He held both hands on the wheel at a perfect 9 and 3 o'clock. In his left he clutched the short stack of map squares.

"I don't suppose you're going to tell me where we're going," I said.

"Danzig is coming."

"How do you know Danzig?"

He said nothing.

"Why is Danzig coming?"

Nothing.

I twisted in the seat to catch a glimpse of Andy. She and Leslie headed for the house, doing that stiff-legged trot that people do when they hurry on a slick surface. The scene of the crime slowly disappeared in the falling snow.

53

It was a one-sided conversation, but I plowed ahead anyway.

"Lillian knows something that Danzig doesn't want known. Just like Danzig didn't want Wally to know something about that ranch."

Boyd let the digital speedometer climb all the way to 30 and then pegged it. Wherever we were going, we weren't going there quickly.

"Lillian figured out that someone was coming for her. Or the information she had. Something about that group at the ranch, or about whatever hoax this Danzig was trying to execute at that ranch."

Boyd stared ahead. Snowflakes rushed the windshield. I have a lot of hours flying as an instructor with students in airplanes. Nothing they ever did to try and kill me came close to letting this eight-year-old drive me in a snowstorm. Every clock spring muscle in my body was wound tight. My hands and feet reached for phantom controls I didn't have on my side of the front seats.

"Your big road trip started in Sioux City, right? That's where I found that lawyer. Lillian found him, too, right? A guy named Baker? Did you meet a lawyer named Baker?"

No answer.

"Sure you did. Baker let you walk out the door, then immediately hopped on the phone, just like he did with me. And Lillian became a target. Did somebody come after you? Was it Danzig? Is that how you know him? He was there a few days ago. Was he there when you were there?"

Yes, Will, I imagined the boy answering, *he came after us.*

"So, Lillian had to hide or run. That's why she gave you the key to the car and this jigsaw puzzle map and said, 'Take her for a spin, kiddo.' Right? She sent you in our direction. My direction. Why me?"

"Lillian says you're interesting. I don't think you're interesting."

My mouth hung open.

"Did you just—*shit*—did you just make conversation with me?"

"That's a bad word. Don't say bad words."

"You should meet a friend of mine."

Boyd didn't answer. He didn't move. The absence of eye contact and renewed silence made the startling verbal exchange seem unreal, like it hadn't happened.

"Look, my wife Andy, the really good looking one back there, she has a certain opinion of Lillian and her beliefs but I keep an open mind." It was a lie. On some level, smart as she was, I considered Lillian Farris crazy. "You really need to try and tell me what this is all about, kiddo."

"My name is Boyd."

"Okay, good. Boyd. Talk to me, Boyd. Tell me about Danzig. Tell me about Lillian."

"My name is not Kiddo."

"Were you at the ranch, too? Tell me why someone wants it to look like a scene from a Spielberg film. Did Lillian have evidence that it was all a setup? Is that why Danzig is coming?"

"My name is not Kiddo."

"Got it. Your name is Boyd. Is he coming for you? Danzig?"

Are you *the evidence?*

Nothing but the whisper of the tires through the snow and the slap of the windshield wipers replied.

"Lillian was looking for something at Martian Mike's place. Is that what this is about? Except Martian Mike was in partnership with Danzig. So...did Mike rat Lillian out to Danzig? Before his partnership with Danzig got ter—"

Boyd abruptly interrupted. "Go straight. Go straight."

He blew through a stop sign.

"Christ!" I said. I grabbed the dash. "Kid, that was a stop sign."

"Stop sign," he repeated.

"Right. Just saying 'Stop Sign' out loud doesn't meet the requirement."

We rolled forward through the blinding snow.

"Seriously, kid—er, Boyd. Talk to me."

He said nothing.

. . .

BOYD OBEYED a stop sign or two, but only when cross traffic would have properly t-boned us had he failed to stop. At every intersection, I frantically checked traffic in both directions while he sat with his head cocked slightly to the right and seemed to pay no attention. Yet, if a vehicle appeared, he waited until it passed before proceeding. Thankfully, between the snowstorm and the insane hour, traffic was almost nil. Most of the stop signs we saw were little more than frosted road decorations.

I know Essex County but eventually lost any idea of where we were and on what roads. Boyd called out "Straight" or "Left" or "Right" at each intersection and junction, but the street signs, even if they had been visible in the snow, were unreadable to me. I caught a county road marker several times. Even those were snow-coated and difficult to read. Was that County C or County O?

He's the map.

I understood nothing about autism. I tried to imagine how his mind processed the connected tiles of a sliced-up road map into the mental GPS image he had of our whereabouts and our path forward.

Despite becoming lost, my sense of direction remained intact. We headed east, then north. I gradually grew less tense, letting go of the dash and the assist grip above the door. My non-conversation with Boyd dwindled and stopped. Eventually I decided that I didn't want to tamper with the child's attention to the road.

We followed our headlights through the snow and the night.

54

I leaned over and checked.

"We need gas." No sooner had I said it, than a light blinked on at the gauge and a message popped up on the dash screen warning us of low fuel and asking if we would like directions to the nearest service station.

"We don't need gas," Boyd replied.

I searched the steering wheel and found a mode button for the driver information display. Boyd paid no attention as I tapped through settings for temperature, mileage, audio settings and more. I stopped when a reading for Distance to Empty appeared.

"Sixteen miles. Then we're out of gas, Boyd."

"We don't need gas."

At least he was confident.

I estimated that we had driven around forty miles in an hour and a half. We rolled across open farm country separated by occasional squares of untouched woodland. Broad hills like slow ocean swells gently lifted and dropped the narrow two-lane county roads we followed. Our only contact with state highways was the mildly terrifying process of crossing them with Boyd looking in neither direction, yet accelerating correctly in traffic gaps, or rolling through without stopping when there was no traffic at all. Civilization diminished to nothing but widely spaced farmhouses. Fields of corn stubble or smooth snow carpets spread on either side of the road. The sun would rise soon, but night would linger thanks to thick clouds delaying the daylight.

I noticed the boy's backpack behind the driver's seat. I lifted it forward and unzipped it, thinking I might solve the mystery of the car key.

"Please don't touch my things," Boyd said.

"I'm sorry, I—"

"Please don't touch my things." The boy's voice rose sharply.

"I'm putting them away. Look. See?" I quickly zipped up the backpack and dropped it behind his seat. "Not touching."

"They're my things," Boyd said, bringing his voice back down and returning his attention to the road.

"They're your things," I agreed.

I wondered how things were going at home with Tom Ceeves. Tom would be pissed. I tried to imagine what that was like but having never been in an earthquake, I could not come up with an image.

Worse than Tom being pissed, I thought about Andy confronting the wreckage in our house. She would reign in her anger and put on her professional face for her boss and for Special Agent Carson-Pelham, but this was our home, and seeing it pumped full of bullet holes would hurt. A mental catalog of our more cherished possessions began to line up in my head. I pushed it aside, feeling anger brew.

The Distance to Empty calculation diminished. When it hit seven miles, I said, "I think we'll be walking soon."

"We will," Boyd said.

"Really? Kid, I think you're a whole lot more able to hold up a conversation than you let on."

"I am."

"Okay. Then why don't you?"

"Nothing interesting to say. No one interesting to say it to."

I felt a twinge of anger rising.

"What about Lillian?" I asked.

"Lillian is smart. Lillian is almost as smart as me."

"Then tell me. What did Lillian instruct you to do?"

"Find Will. Take him to The Gash."

"What do you know about The Gash?"

"I know where it is."

Son of a bitch.

"Why didn't you tell me this sooner?"

Boyd said nothing.

He suddenly slowed and brought the Prius to a stop in the road. I glanced back to make sure we didn't have anyone bearing down on us, but ours remained the only vehicle in sight.

Gentle hills and snow-covered fields spread in all directions, edged by dark spans of woodland. Somewhere beyond the limit of the quarter-mile visibility, either ahead or behind us, stood the farm that owned this land. The Prius hummed beneath us.

"Why are you stopping?"

"We don't need gas." He reached over to the footwell on my side of the car with his left hand. He opened the hand and let the paper squares that he had been clutching since the day we met fall. They fluttered onto the front floormat. I knew without guessing that if we gathered them up and gave them to Lane, she would render the last leg of the child's trip on her maps, and the trail would end where we now idled on an empty road.

I pushed the shift lever into Park, poked the emergency flasher button, and climbed out. I closed the door behind me, leaving Boyd alone in the car.

Silence, the kind deepened by falling snow, compressed the air all around me. Weak light came from the sky, perhaps the clouds filtering moonlight or starlight above it. Flakes falling on my head and shoulders came at the same rate as they had in Essex, but these were smaller, lighter. We had driven north toward the upper edge of the moving storm front. The air was colder here. I jammed my bare hands into my pockets.

I scanned the landscape in all directions.

Empty.

"Jesus, Lillian, is this another alien landing site? Is that what you want him to show me? Because if it is, Danzig's crop circles just got buried by a freakin' snowstorm."

I opened the door and leaned into the Prius cabin. "Boyd? Are you sure we're here?"

"We don't need gas."

"I'm having trouble seeing what you want me to see. Can you come out and show me?"

He shocked me by opening his door and stepping out with his red back-pack. He slipped his arms into the straps and mounted the pack behind his shoulders, closed the door, and walked around the front of the car. Instead of approaching me, he trotted down a shallow embankment, crossed a short span of tall grass, then walked into the field adjacent to the road.

"Where are you going?" I called after him.

He ignored me.

"Shit!" I hustled to the driver's door and climbed in, dropped the shifter into Drive and rolled the still-running Prius ahead. A farm access lane dropped away from the road into the field. I turned in and stopped on a downslope, not feeling all that certain that the little hybrid would be able to get back on the road. I shut it down and hurried after Boyd. The kid set a pace that forced me to trot to catch up. He marched across a field of what was most likely winter wheat, judging by the well-groomed surface and how the snow created a smooth tabletop of white.

We walked several hundred yards without a word. Behind us, the Prius and the road disappeared. Ahead, a fencerow separated the wheat field from undeveloped pasture. Old oaks spotted the landscape. A shallow creek bed snaked back and forth across the pasture. The creek carried a decent flow of water with fringes of ice at the edges. A dirt track crossed the creek over a concrete culvert.

Boyd ducked between strands of barbed wire to transit the fence, then veered right to follow the dirt track across the culvert. I followed in his footsteps. Falling snow dusted our trail behind us. Tall, dried bull thistles, some of them above my head, stood guard all around us, looking like ancient aliens as the snow stuck to the dead thistle blossoms. Thin old men with white hair.

Boyd crossed three quarters of the pasture, then stopped. He pointed.

"There."

The pasture gave way to woods. Hundreds of tall, dead ash trees spread in three directions away from us. Many of the blighted trees had already fallen, victims of the invasive emerald ash borer first found in Michigan and now plaguing dozens of states. Fallen black tree trunks formed random angles in the forest where they tipped against the dead still standing. The weakest or earliest to die had fallen first, but in a matter of years, these acres would look like the slopes of Mount St. Helens after the eruption.

I opened my mouth to tell Boyd I wasn't seeing whatever it was that he pointed at—then I stopped.

Something about the dead trees didn't seem right.

I walked forward a dozen yards, then halted. Boyd did not move.

"Are you coming? Do you want to see?"

He did not look up at me. "Lillian said you were interesting. I don't think you're interesting."

"Well," I said. "Lillian is not wrong. I am quite interesting. You just haven't seen it yet. Come, or don't come."

I resumed walking. I heard his footsteps behind me.

We reached another fence where the pasture ended, and the ash woods began. I waited for Boyd, then lifted the top strand of barbed wire for him to step through. He stopped and held the wire up for me. It was a little thing, but it felt significant. We marched forward side by side.

The ground was rougher here. Grasses were longer. Fallen branches from the dead ash trees littered the forest floor. Leaves and twigs crunched under our feet beneath the snow. We had to duck under or climb over fallen tree trunks. As we went deeper into the trees, the anomaly that caught my eye earlier became more apparent. Fallen ash trees formed a line running from my right to left. There were random trees down throughout the forest, but as we approached, their number increased, and a pattern became clear.

We crossed another fifty yards of forest before reaching the line created by the dropped trees. The perspective gradually changed until we ducked under a fat trunk and emerged in what appeared to be an avenue sliced into the forest. Had there been a wheeled track on the ground, I would have called it a fire lane. This was something different. Ash tree trunks tipped and tumbled to the left and right of the path, leaving a car-width center lane open. Looking up, I saw a straight slice of uninterrupted sky stretching on a near perfect line.

A gash.

"Son of a bitch," I muttered.

"That's not a nice word," Boyd informed me.

"Do you see it? Do you see The Gash?"

Without looking left or right, without raising his chin from that permanent, just slightly off-center position it seemed locked into, Boyd said, "Of course."

The sky became a tiny shade lighter. The trees that remained standing were rendered in India ink against a near-black shade of gray. My watch said that on a day with a clear sky, the horizon would already glimmer with the dawn.

I looked in both directions. To my right, the destruction thinned out. Trunks were sheared off higher up. Less than two hundred yards to my left, the damage stopped entirely. Only stumps remained.

I closed my eyes. The ride in the Prius with Boyd had been an endless zig and zag on backroads, county roads and in-between roads. I lost track of where we were or what we were near, but my innate sense of direction remained intact. I knew, roughly and in compass terms, what heading we had been on when Boyd rolled the Prius to a stop. I factored in walking perpendicular to the road across the winter wheat field, across the pasture, and into the wooded path that led us to this anomaly. I stretched out my mind's eye in the direction of the gash, and then reversed it to point down the reciprocal course.

Is that possible?

I recalculated. Without a map, without satellite imaging, I couldn't be certain. But my inner compass is rarely wrong. I had an idea where a line on a map would lead if the centerline of this gash were extended and why Crazy Lillian thought I fit as a piece of this puzzle.

I opened my eyes. Boyd waited silently beside me.

"Let's go look. Could be interesting."

"Lillian is interesting. I am interesting. You are not interesting. This could be interesting."

Boyd stepped off and had five paces on me before I realized I had no comeback.

55

The going improved. Fewer downed branches tried to trip us. There were no full-length ash trunks across our path. If someone wanted to convert this gash to a fire road, one pass with a bulldozer would do it. Here and there, an ash stump rose out of the forest floor, cleanly broken off, near to looking as if the tree had been felled by a chainsaw. Telephone pole lengths of downed trees that belonged to the stumps lay to either side of our path, neatly tossed aside.

How did this happen?

I imagined Lillian's ready answer to the mystery. I also heard my wife respond to Lillian in my head.

It could be any number of things, Will. A potent wind gust. A powerful dust devil, whipped up to mini-tornado strength and carried on a freakishly straight line. Dead trees, already weak, falling in a line.

Factoring our starting point and how far we traveled after ten minutes, I put the length of this tear in the forest at nearly a quarter mile. It was becoming easy to understand how this had crossed Martian Mike's radar, along with the chat channels in the UFO community.

We trudged forward at a steady pace, opening the snow curtain ahead, letting it close behind us.

I felt a twinge.

A tremor.

A ping on the muscle that I sense down my center when I vanish. The sensation startled me. A lingering symptom of the shotgun blast? I wondered. I remained sore. A few joints muttered discontent when I moved, but the deep agony of that incident was long gone.

Not enough sleep, I rationalized.

Andy and her athletic affections, God bless her.

Boyd skirted another stump. I followed him.

Another tremor.

This time, the vibration ran down my spine. Dr. Doug Stephenson, a neurologist and friend and the original member of my inner circle, performed a scan of my body and found what I think of as car stereo wires running down the center of my brain into my spine. They were not there when Mrs. Stewart brought her son into the world. The best we can figure is that they emerged the night I wound up in the hospital after crashing Earl Jackson's Piper Navajo.

The sudden tremor tickled those wires.

I recognized the sensation.

Spiro Lewko's lab. His secret project. The artifact.

The last time I felt a tremor like this, when those wires began to vibrate, I felt an overwhelming *need.* The wires vibrated when I approached the artifact that allegedly came from the collision that tore apart my airplane and ejected me from disintegrating debris five hundred feet in the air at one hundred and forty miles per hour. The closer I came to the artifact secreted away in Spiro Lewko's lab, the more an irresistible need flooded me.

A need to vanish.

The same impulsive tickle now danced down the back of my skull, down my neck, down the center core muscle that wakes up when I vanish.

"Hold up, Boyd." I stopped. He stopped. He turned around and looked at me without looking at me.

And just like that, the sensation was gone.

I stood in the falling snow and silence examining myself. The need, the sensation, the tremor had ended.

Was it there? Or was this just fatigue? The rational explanation said fatigue with a dash of post-shotgun blast aftereffect. Easily explained away. That worried me, because in my recent experience rational explanations tended to mask something genuinely dangerous.

Why here? Why now?

I peered ahead. The curtain of snow had thinned, or else we had finally come to the terminus of the anomaly. Ahead, made gauzy by the falling snow, I saw the end of the channel. Gray lines on angles. Fallen trees. A wall of them. Not terribly unusual. Apply the rational explanation. A gust of wind. At its end, the detritus of its passage had collected. Deadfall heaped in a silent forest. Not just one tree here and there, but a pile of them. If a wind did this, I knew the answer to the philosophical riddle. No one heard the trees fall in the forest because the freaking wind was roaring.

I took another step. The wires in my head began to sing.

Drug users must feel this, I thought. A hunger. A want so deep it trembles with power.

Just like Lewko's lab. I felt a desperate need to vanish.

Boyd is finally going to think you're interesting if you don't get this under control.

I braced myself against it. I imagined an aircraft cockpit with the power quadrant that has the extra levers I have come to use so readily. I saw again what I'd seen in the lab that day.

The levers in my mind's eye quivered forward on their own.

I reached for them and pulled them back. The trembling stopped. As if nothing had happened, I stood rock solid in front of an autistic boy who stared at me without lifting his eyes in my direction.

Boyd waited. I steadied my breathing.

I took another step.

Need.

The levers in my head lunged forward. I threw my mind's hand over them, felt the firm round shape of their tips in my palm, and pulled hard as the cool sensation that signals vanishing kissed my skin, then ceased.

I felt resistance.

At Lewko's lab, I had come close to vanishing without commanding it. Here, once again, I fought for control.

I took a hard step backward, still firmly grasping the levers, maintaining pressure the same way I hold the prop-throttle-mixture combination full forward on takeoff in an airplane.

"Sorry, kiddo. That's as far as we go."

"My name is Boyd."

I stabilized quickly. I took another step back and the itch dissipated entirely. This would be easy to test. Just take a step forward.

No way. I didn't need to touch a red-hot stove burner twice to know it hurts.

"C'mon, Boyd. We've seen enough." I pointed at the tangle of dead trees several hundred feet away. "Nothing up there but a bunch of dead wood."

I turned around and started walking, listening carefully for his footsteps to join mine.

He did so without a word.

56

The Prius emerged from the snow curtain around the time we approached the middle of the winter wheat field. It had company. A small utility van parked on the side of the road near where I had pulled the Prius onto the farm access lane. My pulse quickened.

Each footstep hammered and shaped an explanation for the visitor. It's the local farmer, stopping to see who's poking around in his field. It's a Good Samaritan driver stopping to assist. It's the Audubon Society doing their annual winter bird count—only that's not until December.

By now the Prius had accumulated a white layer of snow. Wiper blades on the parked van slapped back and forth, keeping its windshield clear. I didn't have an angle to see inside. The side windows were dark.

If someone stopped to help, they might have seen the tracks. They could have assumed anything, including that whoever walked off into the snow knew what they were doing and belonged here. Now they would see us returning.

I ran through excuses—answers to the question that would come.

What are you doing out here?

It was the boy. He couldn't hold it anymore, and he wouldn't relieve himself near the road. We're so sorry. We'll just move on.

Boyd kept up with me. We left the field and approached the embankment. Both the front doors of the van opened.

"Stop there." A solid-looking man climbing out of the front passenger seat held up a big stop-sign hand. He looked familiar. "Don't come any closer."

I froze. Boyd obeyed beside me.

My focus narrowed. I calculated the distance to Boyd and the reaction he might generate if I grabbed him. Vanishing isn't all that effective if one of the people disappearing is screaming his head off.

The man at the van's passenger door hooked his left thumb into his belt and rested his right hand behind his back. The posture screamed concealed weapon.

The driver closed his door and walked around the front grill.

Danzig.

Shit!

A flurry of pieces raced to find connections in my head, like children scrambling to get the best partner for a game. Greeley. Martian Mike. Ekalaka. The shotgun blast. Danzig collecting Martian Mike's maps. Danzig here. Now.

How the hell is he here? *How did he follow us?*

Or did he follow us? Was it possible he was already here, waiting for us? Less than two days ago he had cleaned out Martian Mike's office. Maps. Papers. Files. The computer. Lillian's search took her to Martian Mike where she had asked questions about The Gash. Maybe Martian Mike knew the answers without knowing the questions.

Danzig. Twice I'd seen him kill to further his purposes. Now he sauntered to the edge of the road. He studied me. Bigger than I remembered him, powerful, with close-set, small dark eyes in a chiseled, hard-edged face. He wore his hair military short. A villainous scar stretched above his right eye, cutting a path through one eyebrow.

"Danzig is coming," Boyd said, standing beside me.

"Looks like," I replied softly.

I edged toward Boyd. Danzig called out sharply.

"Move away from the kid. Move. Two steps."

I took two steps sideways. The gap between me and Boyd expanded to six feet.

"Don't fucking move. Not a muscle."

The sliding door to the van opened. A third man emerged and shouldered a shotgun aimed directly at me.

"Aim for the kid," Danzig said. "That guy makes any kind of move, shoot the kid."

The third man, the smallest of the three with a bushy brown beard, swiped the shotgun across me and settled his aim on Boyd. My heart leaped into my throat and hammered at the walls. I sucked in a harsh breath while every nerve I owned fired an angry salvo at tense muscles. Something strong and malevolent stirred in my heart and in the deep recesses of my soul.

Murder.

"Get the picture?" Danzig asked me.

"I get it."

Danzig nodded. "Maybe you do. Maybe you don't. I'll spell it out. Make one fucking move toward me or my friends, we paint his brains all over you. Clear enough for you?"

"I said I get it."

"Okay. So where is it?"

"Where's what?"

I braced for a dangerously stupid game of *you know what I mean* and *no I don't* that could end in frustration and get Boyd and me killed.

"Where is that fucking super Taser you hit me with in Colorado? 'Bout knocked my shit into next week."

I put on my best *Oh, THAT'S what you meant* face. I nodded a couple times and lifted my hands, slowly, carefully. Extending my left arm away from my body, I reached for and unzipped my jacket with my right. The van passenger standing at the right front door pulled his hand from behind his back and aimed a ridiculously oversized revolver in my direction.

"Easy," he warned.

These guys are afraid of me. The shotgun blast that threw me into Martian Mike's canyon must have kicked Danzig's ass. I wondered how long he had been incapacitated. Whatever it was, he did not like or wish to repeat the experience. This also told me that he'd seen me, if only briefly.

I slowly unzipped the jacket, then carefully spread it open and lifted it. I rotated a slow three-hundred and sixty-degree circle.

"Don't have it. It's a prototype. Military grade sub-lethal weapon. I borrowed it from a weapons lab in Colorado Springs. They wanted it back."

"Empty your pockets," Danzig ordered. "Slowly."

The man aiming the shotgun at Boyd's head adjusted himself to make the point that he was ready and willing to pull the trigger.

"Just relax, okay?"

I carefully picked my wallet out of my back pocket with two fingers and dropped it into the snow. I pulled all three BLASTERS from their pockets along with the detached propellers and dropped them, noting that at the sight of these devices, the men tensed. My Ray Ban Aviators in their protective case came out of my flight jacket breast pocket and joined my wallet in the snow. I pulled the hip pockets of my jeans out and tugged to show they were empty.

"Lift the fucking pants legs," Danzig ordered.

One by one, I pulled up the legs of my jeans and then squeezed the tops of my western boots to demonstrate that they concealed nothing.

"What are those?" Danzig pointed at the power units.

"Flashlights converted to electric motors with little propellers. Fans. I'm trying to get the idea patented. I carry them around to show people."

I lifted both hands, palms out, then slowly crouched. I carefully lifted one of the props and one of the power units. I snapped the two together. Making sure not to point it at anyone, I held the unit up and slid the controller far enough forward to make the prop spin.

"Toss it. Over here." Danzig pointed at his feet.

I heaved the power unit in his direction. It dropped into the snow a few feet from where he stood. He studied it but did not pick it up.

"What are you doing out here?" Danzig asked.

"Same thing I was doing at Martian Mike's. Looking for The Gash."

Danzig stared at me.

"Not good enough."

"Do you know who I am?"

"I do."

"Then you read my NTSB report—the one you took from Martian Mike's office. That's why you're here, isn't it? Same as me. Because of that site out there? Because Martian Mike thought I was connected to it? The thing is, I don't remember anything about my accident."

"How did you know to come here?"

"Martian Mike showed me," I lied.

"Izzat so? Who's the kid?"

"Nephew."

"Yeah? Hey, Junior, what's your name?"

Boyd stared and I prayed he would not find Danzig interesting enough to answer.

"My name is not Junior. My name is Boyd Farris."

Shit.

Danzig's brow wrinkled as he did the math. He shot a glance at the Prius. Something dawned. He smiled and shook his head.

"Guys, wanna know why we couldn't find the bitch's car? Because it's sitting in the fucking snow over there. She had a kid with her." Danzig shifted his attention back to me. "Nephew? Want to try that again? Or should we shoot off one of the kid's hands?"

"Fine! Fine. He belongs to a friend who's obsessed with UFOs. She sent him to me. He's the one that brought me here." I made a head gesture in the direction of the forest. "We found what you're looking for. I can show you."

"Your friend…loudmouthed blonde? Farris?"

"Yeah," I said. "A giant pain in my ass."

"That's not a nice word."

Danzig thought it over. He took his time. Made me sweat.

"That was bullshit," he announced. My heart stopped.

"It wasn't bullshit. The woman has been pushing UFO crap my way ever since the accident. She wants to blame my crash on little green men. There's your bullshit. This—here—is nothing but a hoax. A bunch of dead ash trees that tipped over. I can show you."

Danzig chuckled. Bastard.

"No. I meant that crap about a super Taser. That was bullshit. You did it. You grabbed my hand. That's how you shocked me. Christ, I still can't feel my left hand. How did you do that?"

"That's how the weapon works. I had a glove on. Looks and feels like skin, but it can transmit twenty-thousand volts without hurting the wearer. The Army developed it for special ops teams. A silent way to disable enemies."

"Are you wearing it now? Show me."

I pulled back the sleeves on my jacket. "See? No glove. No wires. No battery packs. Nothing." I pulled on the skin on the back of my hand to try and demonstrate that it was just skin.

"How do I know you don't have some kind of fucking superpower?"

"You watch a lot of cartoons, do you?" The insult didn't sit well. "I don't have a superpower. How would that even work?"

"You got something going on. So, if you fucking do anything funny, the kid is gone. Got that?"

"Crystal clear."

"Stay the fuck where you are. Don't move." Danzig held out his hand. His companion gave him the big gun, then stepped down the embankment to me. He produced a set of plastic zip tie handcuffs and waved at me to put my hands behind my back. I complied. He snapped the plastic restraints tight.

"Search him," Danzig ordered.

"I don't want to touch him."

"Do it."

Big Gun obeyed, carefully tapping one hand on my arms, legs, and torso like someone testing an electric fence.

"Fucker's clean," he announced and promptly stepped several paces away. He produced a second set of cuffs and grabbed Boyd by the arm.

Boyd issued a high-pitched wail.

"Leave him alone! Don't touch him. He's autistic."

Big Gun released his grasp. Boyd ceased his outcry and resumed standing without moving, seeing without looking.

Big Gun shot me a mean look. "What the fuck is that supposed to mean?"

"It means he's autistic, dumbass."

"Retarded?"

"No, that would be you. He's probably more intelligent than all of us put together, but he operates on a different level. And he can't stand to be touched. He won't cause you any trouble, but if you touch him, if you force those things on him, you can plan on listening to that shit nonstop until you take them off. Hours. Days. Weeks. He won't stop. Look, he will do whatever I say. Just tell me, and I'll tell him. Okay? Just don't hurt him."

"Check the backpack," Danzig ordered.

Big Gun stepped behind Boyd and gingerly unzipped the backpack. Boyd didn't move. Big Gun parted the opening and peered inside.

"Those are my things," Boyd said. "Don't touch my things."

Big Gun looked without reaching inside. "Just a bunch of kid stuff. Let's shoot the little fucker right here. That'll take care of his goddamned screaming."

Danzig shook his head. "We don't leave bodies near the site. And don't mess up the back of the van. The kid goes with him."

"Why?" I asked. "Why do you want us at all? We came out here and looked at a stupid bunch of trees that tipped over. So what?"

Danzig shrugged. "You're absolutely right. Nothing to see here. No reason to be here. So, get in the goddamned van and we'll drive you wherever you want to go."

"Anywhere?" I asked.

"Sure. Just get in the goddamned van."

Big Gun didn't touch Boyd again, but he had no problem slamming his elbow into my back and knocking me forward.

"Do you want these?" Big Gun pointed at the BLASTER components laying in the snow. Danzig looked down at the one I'd thrown to him but made no move to touch it.

"No. Don't touch. Prob'ly blow up in your hand. Leave 'em. Bring the wallet."

57

We rode on the metal floor of the van, which had three seats, two in front and one on the left side of the second row. The man with the shotgun rode in the rear seat. He sat sideways and rested the weapon across his lap, never taking his finger from the trigger, aiming the barrel at Boyd.

Boyd complied with my request to climb into the van and seat himself on the floor. He rested his hands in his lap and his back, still wearing his red pack, against the van wall. I faced him propped against the opposite side of the vehicle. The van had no windows. A solid barrier behind the front seats prevented us from seeing the road ahead.

I plotted a variety of attacks on Shotgun, the man sitting with Boyd's life on the tip of his trigger finger. None of them ended with the child alive. Boyd kept his eyes on his hands, which he moved relentlessly in his lap, working his fingers in a cryptic patter I could not decode. No one spoke. Danzig, before closing the van door, issued a simple instruction to Shotgun.

"If he twitches, end the kid, then him. No hesitation."

Shotgun simply nodded. Although smaller, he came from the same cookie cutter as the other two. Short hair over a heavy beard. Muscled. Carved facial bones harboring eyes devoid of warmth. The expression stone-cold killer is overused, but I'd seen it firsthand in Danzig. His compatriots shared the trait. I felt certain these men had been on the cliff, cornering Wally, endorsing his execution.

I had no option with the plastic handcuffs. They were tight, strong, and uncomfortable. Worse, they were not metal. Had they been, I could have broken loose easily. Pushing *the other thing* outward over metal causes it to fracture at the line between seen and unseen. It has no effect on plastic. Sitting on the van floor with my hands bound sent searing pain down my back. I spread my knees for greater stability and tried to flex away discomfort that increased with each passing minute, each passing mile.

I had no idea where we were going or in what direction. Or why. The degree to which Danzig was willing to kill for his cause seemed disproportional to the cause. In Montana, he and his crew created a hoax suggesting that nine people were abducted by aliens. In Colorado, he terminated what looked like a collaboration with Martian Mike. He killed Wally once. Did he kill him again? How did any of it require murder?

When I first met her, Lillian Farris tried to sell Andy and me on the idea that my accident had extraterrestrial causes. Andy considered her batshit crazy. At best, I considered her amusing. How was it possible that one of her UFO fantasies had become a life and death situation?

Lillian had glommed onto The Gash. Her interest inconvenienced Danzig and his friends. Why? A strange slice of damage to a dead forest in central Wisconsin could easily be excused as nothing more than a factoid for the weird files.

What about the need?

I rolled out the rational again and tried to tell myself that my imagination ran away with me out there. And that my rough guess that the course line of that quarter mile-long stretch of broken trees pointed in the direction of Essex County qualified as an absurd stretch of uninformed logic and evidence.

Andy likes to point out how UFO fanatics adapt disconnected evidence and unrelated facts to create a narrative that fits their beliefs. I gave Lillian credit for more intelligence than that. Yet here I was, stringing together half-baked assumptions to support an invented truth.

Then why were you starting to feel the other thing *take control?*

Was I? Or was I just exhausted? Reunion sex with Andy topped off a long day and had the promise of much needed sleep in its aftermath. Sleep didn't happen, and its deprivation explained a lot.

Deep fatigue fouls up the way things process. I wouldn't call it hallucinating, but circuits misfire. Memory goes awry. You think you followed the landing checklist and put the gear down, but the next thing you know, you're skidding along the runway with the props bending back. Did you do the checklist? Or did you just carry forward the imprinted memory of doing it hundreds of times before?

Had I been so tired that I imagined a misfire from *the other thing*?

I felt awake now, fueled by adrenaline and an overwhelming desire to gut the man aiming a shotgun at a helpless child and strangle him with his own intestines.

It surprised me, then, that not long into riding in dark droning silence on the vibrating floor of that van, my chin and my eyelids dropped, and I passed out from sheer exhaustion.

58

I dreamed.

A rerun. A dream I've had in variations a dozen times or more since the night of my accident. It always begins the same benign way.

I sat at the controls of Earl's long-gone Piper Navajo. I listened to the clipped conversation of air traffic control in my pilot's headset. The controller asked which approach I planned to use at Essex County.

"RNAV 31, please." Always the same request. I wonder, in my dream, if I were to ask for something different, would the outcome change?

Lake Michigan flowed by beneath me. In some versions of this dream, I reach down beside the pilot's seat and drag my fingers through the smooth surface of the lake at two hundred miles per hour. In this version, I leaned over and looked at my own reflection from ten thousand feet. I saw my face. The controller cleared me for the approach to runway 31 at Essex County Airport.

"You don't want to do that." Boyd sat in the copilot's seat, head turned a few degrees to the right, looking at nothing.

I closed the throttles to descend.

"I have to," I replied. "Got your seatbelt on?"

The black earth of the shoreline passed under me. The airport beacon called out to me in alternating flashes of green and white.

"It's a clear night, but I can't see ahead," I told my eight-year-old copilot.

Something loomed. A void.

"You can't see what can't be seen."

"If you're so smart, then what is it?"

"Dead trees."

He was right. Black dead trees lined up on the nose of the aircraft, dead ahead. I fought to break away. The yoke turned but the airplane held its course. Dead trees hit the left wing and tore it away. Dead trees ripped open the side of the cockpit. Dead trees jerked the pilot's seat from the floor. I tumbled.

Boyd watched me fall.

The cool sensation wrapped itself around me, penetrating my clothes, my skin. A living sheath.

The other thing.

The Navajo cabin disintegrated. Debris rained from the sky. I rotated in my seat and grew angry at the dream because this is always the part where Andy shows up, falling, just out of my grasp. I hate that part more than the part where the airplane is destroyed.

It did not surprise me that my fall took me into a broken window on the thirty-eighth floor of a Chicago high-rise office building. Or that my wife stood beside me, precariously close to the edge, wind lifting her hair around her head.

"This is all Lillian's fault," Andy told me. "Now we'll never have a baby. See?"

I peered over the dizzying edge. Below, Andy had somehow begun her inevitable fall. I dove out the window, straining to go faster, stretching out to catch her. I suddenly had a blaster in my hand. It roared. I recognized the sound of turbine engines. I smelled burned jet fuel. This was a new form of propulsion. The roar of the engines grew both deafening and heartening. With power like this, I had a chance to catch her.

Andy reached out for me. Just as our fingers brushed something slammed into my chest.

I DOUBLED over and hit the cold metal floor of the van, curled up in pain. I gasped for air that tasted of jet exhaust.

Shotgun grinned at me, holding his weapon backward, having just used the butt to ram my diaphragm.

"Wakey, wakey, asshole."

59

S hotgun flipped his weapon around and pointed it at the side of Boyd's head. Boyd remained absorbed in his finger dance.

"Tell this retard to get the fuck out of the van," Shotgun ordered me, almost shouting to be heard over turboprop engines.

I didn't think I could tell anyone anything. The blow to my diaphragm knocked the wind out of me. I sounded like Wally at his wheezing worst when I spoke.

"Boyd, it's time to go." It hurt to speak.

I expected a problem, starting with communication and ending with Boyd screaming when he didn't understand and the Neanderthal with the firearm tried dragging him from the van. I didn't expect Boyd to simply slide over to the rear of the van and step out.

"Go sit over there," Shotgun swung the weapon to point. Boyd did not move.

"Boyd, please do as the man asks," I said. Boyd moved out of my field of view.

The jet fuel scent that invaded my dreams came from inside the van, which I realized now was inside the cargo bay of an aircraft. Not a large aircraft. It had to be the C-23 Sherpa operated by Danzig. Directly behind the open rear doors of the van, a sloped wall made of heavy-grade aluminum blocked my view—the closed rear cargo door of the aircraft.

We were on the move. The engines ran at taxi power. The van floor bobbed and bumped under me. My body shifted and swayed. These sensations uniquely belonged to a taxiing aircraft. I had passed out for a drive of unknown duration that must have ended on a loading ramp at an airport. I made a quick guess of possible suspects. Green Bay. Stevens Point. Wausau. There was no way to know without a look outside.

"Okay, now you. Danzig said to stay the fuck away from you. He also said not to use this in the plane," Shotgun said, slinging the weapon over one shoulder. He extracted a long, ugly knife from a sheath on his belt. "So, here's the deal. I'm going to go over by that kid. You're going to do as I say, or I start poking holes in his skinny little ass. You come near me, I cut him. You speak, I cut him. You look at me sideways, I cut him. Are we clear?"

I nodded, taking him seriously about the speaking bit.

"Get out."

My hands remained bound. My chest felt as if he'd driven that knife into it. My legs were stiff and sore. Lying on the metal van floor, I saw little chance of sitting upright. Instead, I turned onto my belly and slid my legs over the rear bumper and dropped them. When I contacted the floor, I inched backward until I had a decent center of gravity over my feet. Still fighting for air, I levered myself mostly upright. I spread my feet for stability against the motion of the taxiing aircraft.

Shotgun edged away from me like I was toxic. He positioned himself close to Boyd, who had taken a seat on the floor of the cargo bay with his back against the fuselage wall. Shotgun waved the knife in his hand.

"You sit over on that side." He pointed at the opposite side of the fuselage. "On the floor."

I found a spot and let myself slide down the aircraft's aluminum skin until my butt landed on the metal grate that constituted the cargo bay floor.

Big cargo planes make appearances at public air shows and sometimes in movies. Cavernous cargo bays always astonish. Even I wonder how we stuff these monsters with tons of supplies and lift them into the air. The power required is almost incomprehensible.

The C-23 Sherpa is not that aircraft. By comparison, it is small, almost cramped inside. Versions sold to the world's armies were intended to deliver light supply loads to troops via short runways. Carrying a light military vehicle was probably one of the original specifications. The van had been driven up the ramp that doubles as the rear cargo door and pulled as far forward as possible to accommodate the aircraft's center of gravity envelope. Nylon nets with straps secured the front wheels to the cargo floor, ensuring that the vehicle could not roll or slide out of position, disrupting the aircraft weight and balance with potentially fatal consequences. Even positioned as far forward as possible, the van occupied nearly three quarters of the available space.

I sat on the floor near the cargo door, adjacent the rear bumper of the van. Boyd sat across from me, still strapped to his precious backpack, preoccupied within his world. He curled and uncurled his fingers, tapped his palms, and made gestures, touching his chest, his face. Someone else sat on the floor to his left. I could not see past the van, but I caught sight of the sole of a shoe under the van. I scooched down a little, to gain a better look. Athletic shoes. And the cuff of a pair of jeans.

Someone else was aboard.

Wally?

Shotgun stayed in position beside Boyd. He reached up, grabbed a set of headphones, slipped them over his ears. He plugged the lead into a jack in the cargo bay wall, adjusted the boom microphone, and spoke. I assumed the headphones connected him via intercom to the flight crew.

We bumped our way through a long taxi. Swayed through a turn. Stopped. After a few minutes, we rolled forward and swayed through another turn. Before coming out of the turn, the engines spooled up. Power was applied. I knew the drill. We had been cleared onto a runway and cleared for takeoff. The aircraft thudded down the runway, pounding its landing gear against the pavement until it suddenly stopped. The cargo deck tilted. We climbed into the sky.

I blinked the sand and lingering sleep out of my eyes to sharpen their focus. I tested the bindings behind my back. They were tight. My hands and forearms tingled from positional pressure on my circulation, but at least the zip ties were not cutting off blood to my fingers.

The zip tie design left little chance of getting free. Space between the two loops was minimal, and the plastic locking channel between loops stood almost no chance of being sawed open, even if I did manage to find a sharp edge. I could attempt to work a sharp edge against the loops circling my wrists but would more likely saw open my skin before doing any damage to the loop.

The good news was that the loops were around my wrists, and not higher up. It would not be easy, but I felt confident I could work the restraints under my butt, then draw up my legs and wiggle both wrists past my feet to get my hands in front of my body.

All this would require gymnastics and I saw little chance of that. Shotgun maintained his position beside Boyd with one eye on me. The instant I moved he would react. The clear answer to that was to disappear, which provided the added advantage of removing gravity from the obstacles.

Floating free in the air, it would be a lot easier to curl up and get my hands past my feet.

The question was: *How will Shotgun react when he looks over here and sees me gone?*

There are times when I rely on people to not believe their own eyes. It irritates Andy that I sometimes flash in and out of sight where people can see me, but what choice does someone have? Believe that they just saw a man vanish? Or blink it away and adopt a rational excuse? *He must have gone in that door. He probably got in a car when I wasn't looking.*

Coming up with a rationalization in this cargo compartment wouldn't be so easy. Nor would it be easy to avoid Shotgun if he started waving that knife around in the air. The top of the compartment barely cleared the parked van. I didn't have room to maneuver, and no way to avoid a collision with Shotgun or anyone else if they vigorously searched for me—and he would. His first move would be to assume I darted forward beside the van.

The variables piled up as the aircraft climbed. Adding them up, I approached the conclusion that it would be better to wait until we reached our destination to act. I also wanted to find out who belonged to those shoes. I had my fingers crossed that it was Wally, still alive. Danzig said he didn't want to leave bodies near The Gash. Maybe he felt the same way about leaving a body at Martian Mike's place. Finding another body in the canyon below the house would conflict with his suicide tableau.

Fingers crossed, maybe they brought Wally with them.

WE DIDN'T CLIMB HIGH. I detected a change in power settings and the steady chop of low-level turbulence. Being a turboprop, the optimum cruising altitudes are in the twenties. Was this cargo bay pressurized? I couldn't tell. In any case, we had leveled off.

I continued doing the math on my options when movement to my right drew my attention. Danzig squeezed past the van, working his way aft until he stood over me. He issued a nod at Shotgun, then crouched in front of me. He dropped a small canvas bag on the deck. From it, he extracted a set of headphones matching the pair he wore. He slipped the headphones over my ears and adjusted a boom microphone in front of my lips. He straightened the dangling cord and plugged it into a portable intercom box attached to his belt.

"Can you hear me?" His voice entered both ears, rendering the effect of hearing him speak in the center of my head. He touched a button on a control in the cord of my headset, which activated noise canceling that killed nearly all the ambient wind and prop noise.

"Loud and clear." I heard my own voice on the portable intercom.

"Good."

He pulled a length of steel cable from the bag. He looped the cable around the back of my neck, and then like a parent helping a son learn the Windsor knot, he joined the ends at my throat. From the bag he lifted a black ball the size of his fist. The ball had a ring attached. I could not see what he did next, but a moment later, the ball, a lead weight, hung from my neck, thumping against my chest not far from the bruise left by Shotgun's gun butt blow. The weight had to be three or four pounds.

Satisfied with his work, Danzig leaned back on his haunches.

"I'm gonna share a few details with you, then you're going to share some details with me, okay?"

"If you say so."

"Oh, you will. First off, and I love this part, I'm going to tell you where we're going."

He grinned.

"Pray tell."

"We're going to what we like to call Point X. Super dramatic, maybe a little corny, but we didn't make it up." He waited for me to ask.

"What's Point X?"

"It is literally marked as an 'X' on the National Geophysical Data Center bathymetric map of Lake Superior. Forty miles north of Munising, Michigan."

I wanted to punch his smug grin.

"That's nice."

"Did you know that Lake Superior is the world's largest freshwater lake? It contains more water than all the other Great Lakes combined, and then some. It contains ten percent of the world's surface fresh water. And it's motherfucking deep. Thirteen hundred feet deep at its lowest point, which is…"

"Point X."

"Right. And that's where we're going to throw you and the others out of this aircraft. But don't worry, you won't drown. Hitting the surface of the lake will be like hitting concrete. You'll be dead instantly. But here's the thing. You know that song? Gordon Lightfoot's song about the *Edmund Fitzgerald*? Big storm. November, all that shit?"

"I know it."

"I love that song. He quotes a saying about Lake Superior in that song.

The saying goes way back before ol' Gordon wrote his one-hit wonder. They say that Lake Superior doesn't give up her dead. Ever hear that?"

"Gordon Lightfoot had more than one hit."

"Did you hear what I said?"

"I heard you."

"Well, it's not just a saying. It's a biochemical fact. That fucking water is cold. So cold that the bacteria that normally bloats a body and causes it to float can't form. A body goes down in that lake and it stays down."

"Okay. Thanks for the science lesson."

"Not done yet." He reached for the weight at my neck. "After you hit the surface and it kills you, this weight will take you down the full thirteen hundred feet and there you will remain. Ain't nobody gonna come looking for you, either."

I imagined being alive and aware as the lead weight dragged me down into those cold depths. The notion chilled me as much as I anticipated the cold water would.

"Why? Why are you doing this?"

"Fuck you. I'm not telling you that. But I am telling you what's going to happen to you for a reason. See, I'll be throwing you out the back along with that kid over there, and the others."

"Others? What others?"

"Oh, that's right. Allister said you snoozed all the way to the airport."

"Wait. Hold on. Are you telling me that baboon over there is named Allister? For real?"

Danzig smiled. "I'm gonna tell him what you said and let him throw you out. Now listen up. I've got a couple other people to toss out with you. You said that kid belonged to a friend of yours. Farris. She's here. And you remember poking around at that law office in Sioux City? Baker? He's joining the party. And one more, your pal from up at Martian Mike's place. Walter Vandenlock."

"Never heard of him." Danzig studied my face, reading the lie. He smirked.

"Whatever. You're all going into the lake at Point X. And the reason I'm telling you this is because I have a heart of gold. I'm just a softie."

"I'm not getting that vibe from you."

"You will. Because I'll make you a deal. You tell me why the fuck you stuck your nose in our business, every goddamned detail, and I will not toss that child out the back with you. How does that sound?"

"Like you're one sick puppy."

Danzig chuckled. "Suit yourself. I'll throw the kid out first, then you. That way you can watch him screaming all the way down."

"What reason do I have to believe you'd let him live if I agree?"

"I told you." Danzig pounded his chest. "Heart of gold. I'll tell you what, I'll toss in—pun intended—a promise to throw you out first so you don't have to watch anyone else screaming. How's that?"

"You're a prince. Fine. Deal. Let the boy live and I'll answer any questions you have."

"Excellent. One more thing. Lie to me, and the deal's off."

"Standard terms. Sure."

"Damn," Danzig tapped my chest. It hurt. "I hate to say it, but I like you. I mean, a fellow pilot and all. Let's start there." He rummaged in his bag and pulled up a folded sheaf of papers with a government seal on the first leaf. "This was you, right? That Navajo crash?"

"Is that the NTSB report? I thought that was still pending."

"Oh, it is. Probably never see the light of day."

"How did you get it?"

"Let's not get off track here. How the fuck did you wind up surviving that?"

"I have no memory of the accident. None. I woke up in a hospital bed with pain you wouldn't believe."

"Kidney stone pain? 'Cuz, I've had those fuckers."

"Me, too. Worse."

"And no memory of how you fell all the way to the ground sitting in the pilot's seat?"

I shook my head. "What does the report conclude? I never heard."

"Fucking pilot error, of course. Loss of control."

"That's bullshit. There was no engine failure. No structural failure that I know of. Pilot error is bullshit."

"Amen, brother. The Feds always need a scapegoat. Next question. What's the deal with Martian Marvin? How did you end up there? Because it's no coincidence that he had this report among other shit."

"Farris," I lied. "She told me Mike had relevant information about my crash. I told you. No memory. It's an itch I can't scratch. I want to find out what happened. Farris is a looney tune, a UFO nut. I'm only interested in facts."

"Farris, huh." He shrugged. "The lady is obsessed with that shit, I'll grant you. Next question. What the fuck did you hit me with at Mike's cabin?"

"Spectral Defense RD-90210 Anti-Personnel Device. I told you. I have an in with a lab in Colorado Springs. It's slick as shit. A glove you wear that can deliver twenty-thousand volts. No clumsy Taser. Just grab someone and lay them out. Turn this airplane around and let me go, and I'll get you a prototype."

"I appreciate the offer, but...no." Danzig thought it over for a moment. The lie must have sounded real enough, especially with the offer attached. He didn't question. "I gotta say, you came outta nowhere. You had training? Did you serve?"

"That's classified. And you know, if all I have on the way down is my honor, then I'll take it."

"I hear you," he agreed. And now we were brothers in arms. Idiot. "I'm gonna ask you again. What were you doing at that site ol' Martian Mike likes to call The Gash, which I personally hate, if you know what I mean."

I didn't. "I told you, the boy led me there. Farris was hung up on the idea that it had something to do with my accident. Waste of time. I didn't see diddly out there. Wish I hadn't gone. What's that site to you?"

Danzig grinned. "I'm not telling you shit."

"It's murder."

"You? Them? You'll be famous. Alien abduction. The truth is out there, brother. Nobody will ever know for certain, but your name will live on in the hearts and minds of basement web surfers everywhere. There won't be a murder investigation because there won't be a body, right? *Habeas corpus*, right?"

"That's not what *habeas corpus* means."

"Like I give a shit. Who else knows about you going to that site?"

"Nobody."

"See. Now there's where your deal goes south, pal. Because I hear you're married to a cop. Are you telling me you didn't say a word to your wife about your plans?"

"She refuses to talk about my accident. She has no idea. All she knows is that I took off with that child. Hell, I didn't know where we were going."

"Man, ain't no way you'll get me to believe that. Too bad." He stood up. "Looks like the boy goes swimming with you."

"He's autistic. Farris studied that site and showed him where it was located. You grabbed Farris, right? Well, she sent the kid to me. But the kid never told me about her and you. He didn't say anything. He can't."

"Yet you claim he led you to that site."

"Yes. He drove the car."

Danzig chuckled. "This is the part where I'm supposed to believe you because it's too outrageous to be a lie. Lemme clear this up for you. I don't care. You're going out. The kid's going out. Farris, Baker, and that other guy are going out. Nobody will ever know, but you have left us one more loose end, and that's your wife, so sometime in the not-too-distant future she'll be going out, too."

Not if you go out first.

"I thought Baker was your guy. On your team."

"Baker couldn't keep his yap shut."

"What about Peter Giles? We know about him. You should probably throw him out, too."

Danzig laughed. "Giles? Fucking middle-management dweeb."

"Listen," I pleaded. "My wife doesn't have a clue. She hates Farris and doesn't believe a word that woman has to say. Leave her alone. And let the kid go. I kept up my end."

"And you thought I would? Fucking idiot. I'm the bad guy." Danzig glanced at his watch. "We're about twenty minutes out. Enjoy the ride. I'll be up front where it's warm, so... bye-bye." He reached down and pulled the headphones off before I could speak, but it hardly mattered. I had no idea what to say.

However, I knew what to do. And I knew which of us would end up at the bottom of Lake Superior.

My eye caught motion on the other side of the cargo bay. Boyd lifted his busy fingers higher, and it hit me.

ASL! That's what his hands were doing. *American Sign Language!* The kid wasn't wrong about how smart he was. Except for one thing. I had no idea what he was trying to say to me. He sat against the bulkhead, working his fingers, telegraphing a message to me that I had no hope of understanding. He paused, turned his head slightly, waiting for a reply. Then began again. This repeated several times. My frustration grew, knowing that I could not answer.

Hovering over him, Shotgun paid little attention. He had already made the mistake of classifying Boyd as irrelevant, a deep error straight out of society's sad history of classifying autism as being feeble-minded or retarded. Shotgun exchanged a few words through the headset, then checked his watch. I knew what it meant.

Point X approached.

No matter what Boyd discussed with his fingers, I could offer no response. It was time for me to move.

I examined the space above the van to see if I could vanish, then kick myself up there and work on getting the restraints to the front of my body. I prepared to make my move when Boyd ceased signing. He leaned forward and slid his skinny shoulders out of the backpack straps, then lifted the pack around and put it between his knees. He unzipped the main compartment and dug into the bag.

Shotgun reacted. He reached for the bag. I expected him to jerk it away from Boyd, setting off a violent tantrum, but Boyd beat him to his objective.

Boyd pulled out Malibu Barbie. Shotgun drew up short, pasted a stupid grin on his face, and returned to his post. I understood the reasoning. If the doll gave the child comfort, that might not be a bad thing. It might make him more pliable.

I readied myself, rehearsing the move in my head. Vanish. Get upright. Watch Shotgun react. He might race forward, thinking I hid beside the van. With luck I would catch him coming at me. If I could get my back against the bulkhead and bring my legs up, I might get off a kick at his head and—

Boyd stood up. He turned toward Shotgun. He held the doll close to his chest and closed one hand over its head. Shotgun watched him twist off the doll's head and hold it forward as if to make an offering. Fixated on the severed head in the child's palm, Shotgun missed the change in the child's expression. Boyd sucked in a breath, closed his mouth, and puffed out his cheeks, then squeezed his eyes shut. At the same time, he lifted the headless doll and flicked it at Shotgun.

A fine yellow-green powder sailed into Shotgun's face.

Shotgun gasped, exactly the wrong thing to do. He dropped the knife to the deck and sent both hands clawing at his face. He screamed.

The scent reached my nostrils.

Wasabe powder. I instinctively closed my mouth and held my breath. Even so, the potent spice brought water to my eyes.

I scrambled to my feet, positioned myself against the bulkhead, and—

Fwooomp!

—vanished, immediately pushing off and curling my legs, then springing my body to full extension. My neck and shoulders hit the bulkhead for resistance that shot me across the cargo space at Shotgun, now backing away with his hands to his face and eyes. I kicked. Lacking inertia, the blow didn't have as much effect as I would have liked, but it caught him in the side of the head and sent his headset flying free.

I shot backward. Free of gravity, I tucked into a ball and shoved my hands downward. I bent and grunted, pushing the tight restraints past my butt cheeks. The fit was tight. Just as I collided with the fuselage wall, I slipped my wrists forward and under my thighs. I went for my feet. My wrists would not go past both feet, so I squeezed past the right, then the left.

The strain sent a cramp into my shoulder but the instant my wrists broke free I pulled them up past my knees.

Shotgun lost his balance. He tumbled into a writhing, violent ball on the angled cargo door. I had no idea how long the effect of the spice would last. Boyd, holding his breath as if he intended to turn himself blue, smartly twisted Malibu Barbie's head back onto her body.

I took a shaved second to shove the levers in my head hard against the stops. At the same time, I wrapped one hand around the steel cable at my neck and *pushed.* I tugged. The cable snapped. The lead ball abruptly appeared and dropped to the deck.

Fwooomp!

I reappeared without thought to my position or posture. Gravity slammed me to the deck with hard shocks to my right wrist and shoulder. I didn't take time to assess the damage. I clawed my way across the steel and aluminum deck to where Shotgun's vicious-looking knife had dropped. I scooped it up then scrambled away from Shotgun's writhing form in the corner.

I fumbled with the knife, inverting it to attempt to slice the plastic cuffs without slicing myself. Cutting the center joint seemed logical but proved the worst idea. I had no leverage and nowhere near enough pressure to cut the thick locking mechanism. I adjusted the blade in my hands, then poked it between my flesh and the plastic on my left wrist. As careful as I tried to be, I quickly drew blood. Twisting and working the knife under the plastic, I rotated the blade outward against the plastic. I pulled hard. The plastic snapped.

Shotgun pawed away water running from his eyes. He jerked his shotgun off his shoulder and swung it around. I rolled to my knees with the knife still in hand, still reversed, and swept a hard blow into his nose with the knife hilt, then drove it down into his thigh. Once. Again. Again. I hammered the blade into his flesh. He shrieked and tried to drive the shotgun butt into my head, but I ducked. Blood gushed from his face and his leg. He pulled the wooden stock to his shoulder and tried to fire, but I raked the blade across his right hand—the hand fumbling for the trigger guard. Blood spurted. He jerked his hand away.

Wasabi powder in the air stung my eyes, my nose and my throat. It also coated the front of Shotgun's shirt. I slapped my left hand into the pale powder, rubbed it, then smeared his face. He screamed. The shotgun clattered to the deck. He groped for me. I pulled back quickly, then slapped my powder infused hand against his torn thigh.

He screamed again and tumbled to the deck, writhing.

I scooped up the shotgun and tossed it on top of the van. Then I whirled for my first look at the passengers who had been out of my sight on the other side of the cargo bay, hidden by the van.

Lillian Farris kneeled beside Wally, who slouched against the bulkhead, pale and in pain. Her normally handsome and confident features looked worn. There would be time to hear the tale, but I had to wonder how long she had been in Danzig's hands, and to what purpose. Thankfully, she did not appear beaten or bruised.

Beyond Wally, Attorney Baker sat on his butt with his hands bound behind his back and his belly bunched against his thighs. He wore utter terror on his face, fueled by the betrayal of his business partners. I found little sympathy for him.

Lillian looked up at me with something like perturbation. "Took you long enough," she called out above the roaring wind and engine noise.

I hardly noticed her. I found myself staring at Boyd, who looked up at me with his eyes, making direct contact for the first time.

He spoke. I could not hear his voice, but the word was clear.

"Interesting."

60

S hotgun was down but not out. I wanted to cut Lillian and Wally free but had to attend to him first.

He kicked and shoved himself across the cargo deck until he hit the side of the fuselage. He used his legs on the deck and his back against the wall to push himself upright.

I dove for the floor and his feet. He balled his fists to rain them down on me, but before the first blow landed, I hooked the knife behind his ankle and pulled hard. I felt the tendon snap. He screamed again and dropped sideways while I scrabbled out of reach. He howled and grabbed his sliced Achilles tendon. I lunged forward again and drove the knife down as hard as I could against the back of his left hand. The knife powered through bone and tendon and into his leg. I tried to pull the blade free. It resisted. He threw a punch at me with his other hand. It glanced off my shoulder and landed at my left ear, thankfully weakened, but sharply painful. I twisted the knife and jerked it free.

I rolled away. He threw an impotent punch—more of an arm lunge—in my direction. I met it with the knife blade, which drove deep into the webbing at his thumb. He jerked his hand back, screaming.

At any moment, the cockpit door would open and Danzig would appear, probably shooting. I couldn't be sure if Shotgun got off a warning before I kicked off his headset, but the pilots could be trying to speak to the loadmaster. Absent a response, they would come in a hurry.

I crawled back across the deck to Lillian. She sat with her back to the fuselage wall, hands bound, wearing what looked like an old ballistic vest. Wally appeared to have on the same garment. For protection? I wondered, from what? I tipped her forward and found the plastic cuffs at her wrists. Careful not to cut her, I broke open one of the two. Good enough. She quickly unzipped the vest and threw it off. It landed heavy.

Weight. Lillian and Wally didn't get a steel cable and lead weight. They got heavy vests for the ride to the bottom at Point X.

I handed Lillian the knife.

"Cut him loose!"

She closed a firm grip on the weapon and sliced his restraints, then pulled off his heavy vest. I hopped to my feet and moved forward. Baker stared at me through saucer eyes. He also wore a heavy vest.

"You've got to help me!" he cried. "They're going to kill me!"

"They're going to kill us all, dummy." I ignored him and moved to the front of the cargo bay, searching.

The tidy aircraft offered nothing.

I had hoped to find a means to block the cockpit door, which was centered on a bulkhead just ahead of the parked van. Something loose. Something strong. There was nothing except a toolbox, two backpacks, a propane cylinder and a long spear-like device that connected to the propane cylinder through a hose. I'd seen something like it used at the airport to keep weeds down along the fence. A flamethrower. A flamethrower in an aircraft is a terrible idea. Why would they—?

That's how they did it.

The crop circles. The burns. A stupid garden-variety flame thrower. I knew there was never a mothership, but this just seemed absurdly simple.

And utterly useless. I looked for a way to use the long shaft of the flamethrower to bar the cockpit door, but the bulkhead lacked structure to prop the device against or hold the door.

On the other hand...

I dropped to the toolbox and flipped open the lid.

Yes!

Like any good aircraft toolbox, the first and most important tool sat in plain sight. I grabbed the roll of duct tape and hurried to the flamethrower. An igniter dangled from a hook on a small, wheeled frame that held the propane tank. I unwound the hose, then positioned the long shaft so that the business end of the flamethrower pointed at the cockpit door. I leaned over and closed the lid of the toolbox and dragged it against the bulkhead. I pulled free a length of tape and slapped it on my thigh. Then another. Then another. I dropped the tape and positioned the flamethrower shaft against the toolbox, then taped it down. A few more circuits with the tape roll secured the device.

Feeling seconds tick by that would render this entire effort moot, I scrambled for the igniter. I twisted open the valve on the top of the propane tank, then opened the control valve on the side of the flamethrower handle.

I was shocked when my first snap of the igniter produced a foot-long jet of flame.

But not enough.

I grabbed the tape and pulled a section loose, then squeezed the trigger on the handle of the flamethrower.

The device roared. Blue-yellow flame shot from the end, hit the cockpit door, and bloomed for several feet in all directions.

"Holy shit!" I ducked and turned my face away from a blast of heat.

I adjusted the flame to spread over the door latch. With a little luck, it would get hot in a hurry, too hot to touch. Too hot to open.

Fire in an airplane is a bad idea. The jet of flame scorched the aluminum door. The bulkhead was metal. There was no paneling or plastic coating to cause fire to spread. However, electric lines in abundance ran in bundles along the door frame. Flames engulfed the lines, which quickly melted. It would only be a matter of time.

I had known from the start that the only way out of all of this was to leave. It was past time to go.

I hurried back to Lillian, who hugged Boyd. He wore the same blank look and aimed the same distant stare at nothing as always, but surprisingly to me, he returned the hug. Lillian, for her part, wept openly. Tears stained her face. She squeezed her eyes and kissed the boy's head, clutching him tightly.

I pushed past her to check on Shotgun. I had done a lot of damage, but not enough. Where I had been sitting at the start of all this, a blood trail pointed forward. I poked my head around the van and saw him near the van's passenger door, crawling desperately toward the front of the plane. If he made it all the way, he would dismantle my duct taped flamethrower.

Lillian had the knife. I hesitated. The idea of stabbing the man in the back repulsed me.

Instead, I scooted forward between the side of the van and the bulkhead until I caught up with him. He turned his bearded face to me. Wet, wild eyes inflated with terror. He struggled to heave himself forward using his remaining good leg.

I reached down and closed a grip on his ankle. He kicked, but I was too fast for him.

FWOOOMP!

We both vanished. I gripped the side mirror of the van with my left hand. With my right, I heaved Shotgun upward, driving my feet against the cargo deck. He wiggled and kicked, but he was nothing but a wildly flailing Styrofoam piñata in my hand. I swept him over my head and heaved him toward the rear of the plane. When he cleared me, I released. An electric snap bit my hand. He reappeared and dropped instantly. He crashed to the deck and rolled up against the rear cargo door.

Fwooomp! I reappeared and threw a glance at my flamethrower rig. It could have been wishful thinking, but the door latch seemed to have acquired a faint red glow. It would not hold them for long. Danzig was surely armed. He wouldn't have to travel far into the cargo deck to end this.

I jumped to the back of the van and hurried across to Shotgun's crew station. The loadmaster's position at the back of the plane had a control panel. There were numerous buttons, but the main switches I wanted were plainly marked.

"Lillian! Get Wally to his feet!" Lillian acknowledged and released Boyd, who returned Malibu Barbie to his backpack and mounted the bag on his shoulders.

Lillian helped Wally struggle to his feet. Wally was fully conscious, but the pain and shortness of breath debilitated him. He leaned on Lillian. I noticed that Baker had been cut loose by Lillian. He backed away as if we were toxic.

"Come with us!" I shouted at him. "We're leaving!"

Lillian jammed her shoulder under Wally's armpit and moved him aft. Baker stared, bewildered and terrified.

I slammed my palm against the cargo door button. Danzig intended to lower the door and throw us out. Fine. We'd save him the trouble.

Nothing happened.

I hit it again.

Nothing happened.

"Of course," I muttered. I hit it three more times. Nothing happened.

I searched for a failsafe lock, a release, a manual latch that would otherwise prohibit the hydraulic system from lowering the door. Then it occurred to me. Maybe the door cannot be opened in flight. Maybe sensors detected an airspeed above which the door could not be activated. Maybe the squat switches on the landing gear had to be triggered for the door to open. Any number of safeguards might prohibit door activation at the wrong moment.

"Shit!"

I looked forward. The fuselage had a side door, but I saw nothing but problems there. Opening the door in the one hundred and eighty mile per hour slipstream. Mustering all four of us out the door at one time. I imagined Boyd or Lillian torn out of my grasp.

Dammit. How did they plan to do it?

The cargo door had to be restricted by airspeed. That and some sort of locking system I could not find without the aircraft manual. How, then, was I supposed to get the four of us out?

The van.

I spun to face Lillian.

"Hey! Move up against the wall. Hold them against the wall!"

I hurried past her.

The van was not locked. The key dangled from the ignition.

"Of course," I told myself. "Where else would you keep the key?"

I hopped in the driver's seat in time to look up and see the door to the cockpit blow open, driven by a kick from inside. Danzig threw his hands up to shield his face from the heat of the flamethrower.

I didn't wait. I twisted the key. The van started. I threw the van in reverse and floored it. The van jerked backward and stopped.

Shit! The cargo nets!

The cargo nets had to be cut to release the front wheels. Lillian still had the knife, but there was no time. Danzig ducked back into the cockpit, surely pulling out Big Gun's big gun.

I jerked the van into Drive and floored it. The van shot forward and slammed to a stop. I reversed. Floored it again. Wheels spun. The smell of burning rubber joined the wasabi scented propane exhaust in the cargo bay.

Something snapped. One set of the straps parted. The front end slewed to one side.

I threw the shifter in Drive and floored it.

The van shot forward and slammed into the front bulkhead. The bumper crushed my toolbox rig and threw the flamethrower off target. The burner toppled over, clearing the cockpit door for Danzig who had dived back into the copilot's seat when the van hit.

I reversed. Floored it. Tires screamed on the cargo deck grating. The van snapped free of its restraints and lunged backward.

The rear wheels bumped. The van body lifted, then dropped.

So much for Shotgun.

The van accelerated briefly, then smashed into the rear cargo door. The collision jolted the rear of the van sideways. It smashed into the fuselage wall where I had been sitting when this horrifying ride began.

I threw the shifter in Drive and floored it again. The tires squealed.

Rubber burned. The van lunged a few inches then stopped—hooked on something. Metal screamed. I glanced in the mirror to see the geometric patterns of the cargo door, but they were all wrong. The lines were now angles.

Cold wind howled at me through the open driver's door of the van.

I glanced at the left exterior mirror and saw—

Water.

Harsh. Forbidding. Gray with white caps. Water.

We were over Lake Superior. More importantly, the cargo door had torn free and now hung on an angle in the slipstream, a giant rudder creating immense drag on the airplane. The C-23 decelerated and yawed violently. I felt the pilot fighting the controls.

At the cockpit door, the aerodynamic forces pressed Danzig into his seat. He grabbed the doorframe with his left hand. Smoke rose from where his skin made contact. He jerked his hand free and found a new handhold over his head. He produced and raised the big revolver in his right hand.

I had just enough time to stupidly think, *Maybe he'll miss.*

The g-forces on the aircraft abruptly increased. Danzig lost his balance and his aim. He twisted to shout at the pilot, but his words were lost in the roaring sound coming from the rear of the cargo bay.

The C-23 Sherpa pitched up. I saw sky through the cockpit door and the windshield above the instrument panel.

It was the van. The vehicle had been strapped down precisely against this horrifying possibility. Breaking it free and ramming it backward changed the center of gravity on the entire aircraft. Not even full down elevator applied by the pilot could overcome the uncontrolled pitch up. Seconds from now the cargo plane would stall and fall into an uncontrolled and violent descent.

I dove out of the van and slipped on the increasing slope of the floor. I went down.

"Grab them!" I shouted at Lillian. "Hard!"

Baker hooked his arms into a set of cargo straps hanging on the wall.

"Come with us!"

White terror bulged from his face. "Are you insane!?"

I didn't answer.

I found my feet and plowed into Lillian and Wally who hugged Boyd between them. My momentum eliminated the question of a controlled exit. The impact hurled us to the cargo deck floor. Wally cried out. The nose of the aircraft rose higher. The deck grew steeper. The van scraped sideways. The front end slid across the cargo deck and slammed into the side of the fuselage where Baker stood, pinning him.

I pumped my legs, kicked, scraped, and pushed. The lip of the cargo bay where the door had torn from its hinges slid beneath us. Water, vast and wild, spread out. I shoved hard.

We fell.

FWOOOMP!

I pushed as strongly as I've ever pushed and clawed to hold onto Lillian and Wally with Boyd tangled between us. The roaring of the wind ceased. Twin turboprops screamed in vain as the pilots lost an impossible fight against a deadly out-of-balance condition.

The boxy cargo plane reared up and stalled, breaking harshly to the left. The violent turn snapped the van and the cargo bay door loose. I had time to wonder if Danzig might regain control now that the weight and balance of the aircraft had returned to within its limits. The answer came in the form of a deadly flat spin, from which there would be no recovery. Danzig had been descending, preparing to dump us at Point X. He had no altitude to save himself.

The plane spun on its axis twice before smashing into the churned surface of Lake Superior.

A strong wind grabbed us. Because we rode with it, the wind had no sound. With the airplane gone, only one impossible, unworldly, life-affirming sound filled the sky.

Inside our tight group hug, Boyd laughed his ass off.

61

L *ake Superior doesn't give up her dead.*
	Danzig's words rang in my head. Looking down gave me no reason to doubt. The surface of the largest of the Great Lakes roiled and churned. Whitecaps raced across an ugly slate gray seascape. Wind tore away the tops of the waves and sent mist ghosts scurrying ahead. The sky around us carried uneven and ragged clouds. Mist draped the surface as if to stroke and soothe the stormy waters.

	I maintained a tight grip on Lillian with my left arm and on Wally with my right arm. I felt Boyd in the center, held close by Lillian. Wally's arms overlapped mine behind Lillian. The lake spread in all four directions with no sign of land. In our favor, we had good visibility except for low-hanging clouds and random pillars of falling snow. Being this close to the storm center meant high winds. I estimated that the wind carried us at thirty to forty knots. I tested my sense of direction and decided that the waves and wind both marched southwest, which meant we were being driven back toward Michigan, instead of north toward Canada. Danzig said that Point X lay forty miles north of Munising, a town east of Marquette. If that was true, and if we had been close to Point X, then we were less than an hour from the shore at this speed. I tried to recall if Munising had an airport but could not be certain. Not that we needed an airport for landing—or that we would even make landfall there. The northeast wind pushing us might send us to Marquette or into Keweenaw Bay. The jutting peninsula that formed the bay offered some comfort in that sooner or later this wind would put us over land.

The lake swallowed the crashed C-23. Danzig, Shotgun and Big Gun— along with the unfortunate lawyer Baker—were well on their way to a cold, dark bottom in a lake that would never return their bodies.

Serves them right.

I didn't have to reach far for that bitter but satisfying sentiment. The fat grin Danzig wore when he described doing the same thing to us would stain my memory for a long time.

Despite the strong wind and rough waters, we floated in an eerie quiet, broken only by Boyd's laughter, the incongruous sound of pure joy. I felt him jiggle inside our group hug. Lillian hitched and jerked several times. Sobbing? It was hard to tell. Emotion of any kind was hard to comport with someone I considered cold and a little inconsiderate.

"Everybody okay? Anyone hurt?" I asked after catching my breath.

"Okay," Lillian said.

"Where are we?" Wally asked. His rasping voice sounded worse. I didn't think Danzig added to his injuries or he would probably not be speaking at all. But I also didn't think Danzig gave Wally aid or comfort.

"They planned to make us walk the plank around forty miles north of Munising, Michigan. I think we were close."

"Is that Lake Michigan?" Wally asked.

"Lake Superior. Much bigger. Way nastier."

"What do you...mean..." Wally asked, "...walk the plank?"

I gave a brief synopsis of Danzig's plan. "A murder without a body is hard to investigate, let alone prosecute."

"Maybe we can discuss this when there aren't children present?" Lillian snapped. The take-charge tone I recognized was back. "Maybe right now Stewart you need to get us down on solid ground. *My God!* I had no idea you can do this with other people!"

"Apparently. I have no idea how many passengers I can take. It's vital that we stay in contact. Nobody let go." I flexed my grip for emphasis.

"And who are you?" Lillian asked. "Other guy."

"That's Wally," I answered for him. "Don't make him talk. He has three broken ribs and a punctured lung. His aunt was at the Tammy Day ranch. He went looking for her but ran into those guys instead."

"You know about the ranch?" Lillian asked, I presume, me.

"I do. But let's save this discussion. I have a lot of questions."

"He seems to be taking this in stride. Does he know about you?"

"I've already given Wally a ride or two. Long story. Now listen up." I explained my limited control in the vanished state. Lillian had only seen it once, but never in full function and never from the inside.

"What about your power devices? That thing with the propeller."

"BLASTER."

Lillian huffed loudly. "You do understand, Will Stewart, that this *thing* is utterly wasted on a complete dumbass like you."

"Said the woman relying on my grip five hundred feet above Lake Superior."

"Honesty is my curse. Power unit. Yes or no?"

"Negative. Danzig and his crew made me dump everything I had. They thought it was a weapon."

A gust of wind accelerated us. Airborne sleet tickled the side of my head. Boyd let loose a fresh gale of laughter.

"At least... *(huff)* ...someone... *(huff)* ...is enjoying this."

"Stop talking, Wally."

"Stop talking, both of you," Lillian ordered. "Do you understand the physics here? We are not under the influence of gravity. We have surface area, so we are subject to the meteorological forces at work around us. We're temporarily trapped in the atmosphere but let me stress 'temporarily.' We have a bigger problem."

Boyd stopped laughing and recited, "The force of gravity cannot be felt. It is not a contact force. It is an at-a-distance force."

"One to which we are not subject," Lillian added.

"Orbital astronauts are not weightless. They are falling," Boyd said flatly. "We are not falling."

"He's right," Lillian confirmed.

"I knew that," I said. It came out sounding like the opposite. "Don't worry. I've got this. I have some control."

I flexed the core muscle inside *the other thing.* Up until now we had been drifting in roughly the horizontal position we'd taken when we slid off the edge of the cargo ramp. I rotated us upright.

"Whoa!" Lillian exclaimed. "I felt that! How did you do that?"

"I haven't got a clue," I said. "There's something else, though." I explained how subconscious thought sometimes triggered the core muscle and fired me off in a direction I needed to go.

"Are you saying that all you need to do is think of getting us down and we go down, right?"

"That's the theory. Unfortunately, it doesn't work on command."

"When *does* it work?"

I told her about the first time, in a motel in Montana, when my grip on

Andy and this uncontrollable force within *the other thing* launched us against the ceiling seconds before someone shot up our bed. I gave her two other examples. "The problem," I added, "is that every time I try to do it on command, I get nothing."

"Life and death circumstances," Lillian said. "Also known as fight or flight. Involuntary triggering of pre-conscious neural responses. Stewart, it may seem like we're being pushed by the wind, but the fact is that if we are not subject to the earth's gravitational field, then we are on a linear course beside a spherical object that is moving on an orbital path around the sun. The density of the atmosphere has us marginally trapped, but eventually, we will see that object fall away, leaving us behind."

"Behind...as in...space?" Wally asked.

"Unless something changes," Lillian replied. "This technology renders the limits we know of physics obsolete. This is why Lewko wants it so bad. I can't believe this wound up in Dumbass's head."

"Dumbass has a way to get us down."

"Contact with that which is gravitational," Boyd said. "Make contact with that which is subject to gravity."

"Smart kid," I said.

"You have no idea."

"Make one... *(huff)* ...of us... *(huff)* ...reappear."

"Stop talking, Wally. Seriously," I said. "That won't work."

"Thirty-two feet per second per second," Boyd said.

"That's right, Boyd," Lillian said. "If Will releases us, we'll accelerate at thirty-two feet per second per second. Can I assume that if we start going down that fast, you can't stop us?"

"Right, but maybe we can discuss the physics later. Right now, we need to rearrange ourselves because I need both hands."

I told Lillian to hang on to Boyd. I hooked my left arm inside her right elbow and positioned her at my side. I did the reciprocal with Wally, setting him up on my right. This freed my hands in front of me.

Three abreast, with Lillian hugging Boyd, I rotated us to place the wind at our backs. We sailed forward heading roughly southwest.

"Okay, who's got money?" I asked.

"Not me."

"Me either... *(huff)* ...they took...everything."

"No bills? No coins?

"Nothing."

"Lillian, are you wearing a blouse with buttons?"

"Yes."

"Can you pull one off and put it in my hand?"

She moved. I felt a tug. She found my forearm and followed it to my open palm. She pressed a tiny button against my skin, and I closed my fist around it.

"Okay, here we go." I used my right hand to find the button in my left palm. I pinched it and held it above my open hand. Not too high. We were carried by, and part of, the wind, but that didn't mean there weren't gusts that ruffled my hair and clothes. Gusts capable of snatching away the button. For this to work, I needed to catch it in the open palm of my hand.

I opened my fingers and felt an electric snap. A tiny white plastic button appeared and fell into my open palm. I let it remain visible—and subject to gravity—for a moment, then I closed my palm, repeating the electric snap, causing the button to vanish.

"I feel it," Lillian said. "You altered our path. We're moving toward the earth. I don't think the rate is excessive. Nice work, Stewart."

I sensed it, too, and immediately began to worry that I'd applied too much force. We were a long way from land. Andy and I, stuck in similar circumstances, wound up splashing down in the waters of Little Bay de Noc off Escanaba last winter. We were delighted not to die there because our bodies had volume without weight, making us buoyant. The same would surely apply now, except the bay off Escanaba had been glass smooth. Lake Superior below, churned by a winter storm, was anything but smooth. I had no idea what that would mean if the four of us dropped onto its heaving surface with the buoyancy of party balloons.

Landfall was better, but not without risk. If we cleared the rugged, sometimes rocky coast, then dense forest dominated. Tangling up in a tree sixty feet up didn't appeal to me. Or hitting power lines. Or coming down on a highway in front of an eighteen-wheeler.

I had no idea how far over the lake the C-23 had flown before we blew out the back door. Minutes? Miles? And what path did Danzig take? Straight to Point X or did he swing around to line up a "bomb run." In short, I had no idea where we were or how far from land we were.

We drifted and settled without speaking until Lillian broke the silence.

"Wally, what's your aunt's name?"

"Stephanie Cullen."

Lillian nodded beside me. "A lovely woman. I met her. You didn't find her at the ranch?"

"Didn't... *(huff)* ...find anyone... *(huff)* ...all gone."

"Let me, kid." I added getting Wally to a hospital to my list of worries. I explained to Lillian how her inquiry with Earl launched me in the direction of Tammy Day and her ranch in Ekalaka. "You meant that to happen, right?"

Lillian chuckled. "Actually, it never occurred to me."

"Well, happily I ran into Wally the night I got there for a look around. Danzig and his pals tried to throw him off a cliff. He got lucky. He landed on me."

"And you zapped him like this? I'm impressed."

"Am I correct that you two just met? Weren't you two locked up together somewhere?"

"No. Never saw him before today. Carl Danzig caught up to me several weeks ago. They had me locked up. God knows where and God knows why. They could have killed me at any time."

"I thought his name was Scott. Danzig, I mean."

"Don't know where you got that. His friends called him Carl. Anyway, Boyd and I were in Sioux Falls. I was afraid someone was coming for me. A friend of mine warned me that I was asking too many questions."

"Lemme guess. Martian Mike?"

"You know him?"

"I met him. Once. Couple days ago. I—uh, I don't like to have to tell you this—he's dead. Danzig."

"Shit."

"That's not a nice word," Boyd chimed in.

"No, darling, it's not. I'm sorry."

"I'm sorry about your friend," I said.

"He was a dumbass. He got mixed up with the people Danzig works—er, worked for. And no shit, I asked too many questions."

"That's not a nice word."

"Who did Danzig work for?" I asked.

"That's the billion-dollar question. I only got as far as ParaTransit and the name Peter Giles. I found out about him after I visited the ranch and met some of the people there. Most of them were tight-lipped about their affairs, but a few—your aunt was one of them, Wally—shared some of the details. Names of lawyers they used. That little weasel in the plane, his name was Baker. He was one of them."

"I met him. Told him I was with the FBI."

Lillian laughed. "That's probably what killed him. He must have panicked and called management. They decided they didn't need him anymore. I saw it in his eyes when they put me on that plane. Deer in the headlights."

"You know what? I want all the details. Maybe you should start a few chapters back. But right now, I don't think we have time for stories," I said. "Take a look."

The wind carried the clouds at the same pace it carried us. A ragged low cloud dropping sheets of snow had been running ahead of us. From within the hanging curtain of snow, something new emerged. Broken lines of white stretched across our course where the storm-driven waves smashed against rocks on the Upper Michigan shoreline.

I estimated our altitude at two hundred feet and dropping. Thousands of aircraft landings have given me a well-honed instinct for speed, angle of descent, and the point at which my wheels would contact the runway.

We were not going to make it past those rocks.

62

"Okay, listen. We're going to be short."

"You mean in the water? I don't think we will—"

"No," I cut Lillian off, "you're right. We won't sink. But those waves are at least eight feet. We're going to get slapped around before we make it to shore. Worse, I think we're going ashore at those rocks."

A rough wall of boulders rose fifteen or twenty feet from the waterline. Wave after wave assaulted the stone, shattering into high plumes of spray that iced the rocks and the trees above. The rock wall wore a glistening layer, draped in shapes and channels that imitated melted glass.

We descended to less than one hundred feet above the waves. The shore lay more than three hundred feet ahead. I estimated our point of touchdown at roughly fifty to a hundred feet short.

"This is your rodeo, Stewart. What do we do?"

How the hell should I know? It wasn't like I came out to the icy shores of Lake Superior on weekends to body surf.

"We hang on tight. No matter what happens."

It was a lousy answer, but the only one I had.

Compounding the issue, the wind at low altitude lost some of its speed and power. We sailed over the crests of waves at what felt like twenty knots. Hitting the rock wall at that speed would hurt. Worse, it might break us apart. I didn't want to think about what would happen if I lost my hold on Wally or Lillian. If Lillian went down, she would take the child with her.

The deep swells leveled out, but the waves seemed amplified. The tops curled and broke more than fifty feet from the rocks. The strongest of the waves crashed into the ice-covered rocks and exploded upward. Thunder accompanied each break.

Our speed exceeded that of the waves. We overtook them. When we made contact, we might sink a foot or two before the buoyancy would thrust us back up. The question was whether we hit the water on a downslope or upslope. One wrong combination could shoot us skyward. Another wrong combination could propel us into the ice face. Sheer dumb luck would let us rebound with just enough angle to clear the top of the rocks where, if I timed it right, I could make us reappear and drop on solid ground.

Snow fell around us. Visibility sank.

"Tightened up." Lillian and Wally squeezed my arms. I clasped my hands across my chest.

Ten feet to the wave tops. Twenty to the trough bottoms. Worse than I thought. We descended above a breaking wave. Wind lifted foam and spray from the crest. It hung in the air with us. Spray saturated the legs of my jeans, but the temperature of the cool sensation wrapped around us remained unchanged. Small favors.

Ice-coated rocks battled the waves less than fifty feet away, coming on fast. A huge wave hit the wall and threw itself to the sky, obscuring the entire shore in white foam and mist. I felt the impact resonate in my chest.

"Get ready!" I shouted, competing with the relentless crashing. "We'll sink a foot or so, then rebound. If I start running, run with me!"

We crossed a wave racing toward the shore. We cleared the crest by inches. The trough behind of it sank away beneath us, at least fifteen feet down, then rose again. Lillian's muscles hardened around Boyd; she pressed him against her chest.

The wave hit the stone wall. Noise became deafening. Mist from the wave crash joined the snow falling. The mix blinded us.

The water below began to rise. The next wave set itself on a suicide path for the rocks. We rode the wind chasing it. I prayed for that wind to stay strong. If it failed, we would sink into the trough.

Rocks and ice loomed ahead. My feet hit the back shoulder of the wave.
"RUN!"

I pounded the surface. Next to no resistance from the water made running feel impossible, like scrambling on glaze ice, yet the effort generated surprising propulsion. We splashed up the back slope toward the now-cresting wave. Foam and spray leaped from the wave curl. The rocks and ice bore down on us. I felt Wally faltering, losing his breath. I felt Lillian working her legs, impeded by the child in her arms.

Buoyancy held us above the surface. The core muscle kept us upright. Sprinting accelerated us up the back side of the wave.

The ice wall rose above us.

Twenty feet. Fifteen. Ten.

We launched off the top of the wave. The rocks and ice swept toward us, but we had a shot. Our angle was good. The crest of the rocks swept toward us. I blessed our luck and timing. We sailed upward.

Just as we reached the top of what looked like the wall of an ice castle, the wave hit the wall. Thunder filled the air around us, along with blinding foam. We were engulfed.

Our feet collided with the rocks. I feared we would not clear, but the force of the wave striking beneath us vectored our bodies upward—a shot of power from below that sent us skyward.

FWOOOMP! I yanked the imaginary levers back as hard as my mind would allow. Cold replaced the cool sensation. Icy water soaked my skin. Gravity grabbed and pulled us down. Blinded, I slammed into a smooth wet surface. The jolt tore the breath out of my lungs.

I lost my grip on Wally and Lillian.

The surface beneath my body was solid, wet ice. I clawed for a hold.

Lillian screamed.

I twisted and looked for her. The foam and spray cleared away. I found her beside me, alone.

"BOYD!" she screamed, reaching for empty air. She scrambled back toward the edge of the thundering, wave-smashed wall. I reached out and grabbed her shirt and yanked. She tumbled backward. "Let me go! I lost him! I lost him!"

Shit.

I didn't bother to explain. I pulled her away from the edge, which on the slick ice had the opposite effect of pulling me toward it. There was no stopping.

I went over the edge. It wasn't a dive or a jump. It was a flailing, awkward, cascading controlled crash down the ice toward the roiling water below. Gray. White. Foam. Bubbles. The surface gave no hint of what lay below it.

I plunged into ice water for the second time in my life and felt my entire body attacked by a giant, all-engulfing ice cream headache. I sank into black, twisted and spun by mad currents.

I frantically searched the darkness.

Red.

I joined the Hell-bound current, abetting its determination to take me deeper. I reached out. Hit canvas. Felt cloth. Found a strap. Boyd's red backpack.

I grabbed and pulled. His small body collided with mine. He kicked and fought. Pressure stabbed my ears.

I jerked him against my chest.

Fwooomp!

The reversal was instantaneous. We raced toward light above us. We rocketed from the surface. I gasped for air that had been lost when the icy water drove my last breath from my body. A fresh monster wave reared up to smash us against the wall. If it didn't smash us on the rocks, it would shoot us into the sky.

Crack!

Something hit the top of the head. I instinctively reached up to bat it away. My hand hit something sharp. Seconds later, I realized we were among snapping, dry dead branches. I grabbed.

My fingers found a thin tree bough. I grabbed it and pulled to escape the collision between wave and wall. Spray filled the air around us, consuming my vision in a field of relentless white. As I expected, pressure from below tried to throw us into the air, but the branch in my grasp held. I must have come up beneath a shoreline tree.

The branch came alive and jerked us upward and forward.

I blinked to clear my eyes and saw Lillian and Wally wielding a huge dead tree limb like two fishermen with a pole. I tugged twice to transmit confirmation that we were hooked. They pulled and backed away from the edge, slipping and nearly falling. They swung us onto the snowy surface of the land above the rock wall.

Over safe, solid ground—

Fwooomp!

—we reappeared.

Boyd and I tumbled into a bed of snow, a thin cushion over hard ground. I flopped on my back heaving for air. Boyd landed on my chest, gasping and coughing.

Lillian crashed into both of us, sweeping the child up, tugging him against her chest. She was soaked and dripping, but there was no mistaking the tears streaming from her eyes.

I found enough air to speak.

"Fuck!"

"That's not a nice word."

63

As if afraid that the raging lake might reach out and drag us back in, we all moved away from the icy rocks, into the forest.

Wally clutched his ribs and huffed desperately for air. I feared hyperventilation on top of whatever else he had going on. Lillian picked up Boyd and carried him against her chest. He seemed complacent with the affection she gave.

The best I could do was scramble backward on my ass, soaked to the bone and freezing. My hands lost sensation. Shivers attacked me. All of us lost body heat rapidly.

"We have to get to shelter," Lillian announced. "Get up. We have to go or we're all going to succumb to hypothermia."

"I'm already halfway there." I struggled to my feet. "We can't just march off into the forest. We'll get lost. This forest could be miles deep."

"There has to be a highway. There's always a highway or a road," Lillian insisted. "How else can rich people build their McMansions on the beautiful shoreline? C'mon. Let's go!"

We stumbled less than fifteen feet.

"Stop," I said. My teeth rattled. "My jeans are starting to freeze. We can't do this." Boyd had resumed his slightly off-center gaze into the next county. He and Lillian shivered. No wonder. She wore nothing but a single layer blouse plastered against her skin and already starting to freeze solid. Wally looked just as bad in his own way; he stood bent and clutching his ribs. "If we do it this way, we're going to die."

"What do you suggest?" Lillian asked through chattering teeth.

"We gotta warm up." I turned and walked back to the abandoned dead branch that had fished Boyd and me out of the waves. I grabbed part of the branch, planted my foot on it and heaved. A section the length of my leg snapped off. I broke off two more, then carried all three back to my troops and handed one to each.

"Firewood?" Lillian asked.

"Walking sticks." I moved into position facing the fat trunk of a tree. I poked my elbows out. "Okay, line up. Wizard of Oz style."

"Stewart, for God's sake, I'm too cold for—"

"Side by side. Like before. Line up."

Lillian and Wally stepped in beside me. I leaned my stick against the tree. They followed suit.

"Hook up."

We hooked elbows.

FWOOOMP!

Boyd laughed. Lillian cursed. Boyd admonished her about her vocabulary. We instantly lost contact with the snow-covered ground, but more importantly, the cool sensation enveloping us felt like someone lit a warm fire in the room.

"God... *(huff)* ...that's better..."

"Now pick up your sticks." I lifted mine from against the tree. The other two floated into the air.

The sticks remained visible. We settled again, driven down by the weight of the sticks.

"Damn, Stewart. For a dumbass..."

"I did this once with crutches. It won't be easy. I suggest you both lift your feet and let me do the walking."

I felt Lillian comply on my left. On my right, Wally cried out in pain.

"Don't clench, kid. Bend your knees. Let me have your stick. You float." I took his branch with my free hand.

I turned slowly and carefully shuffled forward. Each step threatened to launch us. Walking was like sliding flat-footed on ice. I gained confidence. I tested a few longer strides. I developed a rhythm and soon I gently bounded forward like an astronaut on a low-gravity planet.

64

We found a trail that followed the shore. In a few spots, the trail ran dangerously close to the water. A hiker could easily be knocked off his or her feet and pulled in by a wave. To be safe, we cut inland through the trees, then regained the trail. The trail eventually curved within sight of a narrow road. We joined the road and picked up the pace with longer strides which brought new giggles from Boyd. The road curved back toward the shore. The trees thinned out and we spotted a house, a sprawling wooden structure with a four-car garage and more gables than I could count. It stood alone at the end of a quarter-mile asphalt driveway. I traversed the driveway in twenty-five-foot leaps that entertained Boyd to no end. The land fronting the building was open meadow. At the back of the building, the shoreline dominated. Waves threw up spray less than a hundred yards from the building.

I slowed us to a manageable shuffle when we reached a driveway circle in front of the house. We reappeared on a cobblestone walk near the front door. The instant we emerged from *the other thing* bone-chilling cold cut through my wet clothing. I resumed shivering in seconds.

"If nobody's home, we're breaking in," I said through chattering teeth. I pounded the doorbell and heard it dinging urgently inside. A dog barked. Moments later, a gray-haired woman peered through a narrow window at the side of the door. She looked hesitant, and I couldn't blame her. We were shabby at best.

"Ma'am, we need help!" I called to her through the door.

"Who are you?" she responded.

"Our plane crashed in the lake." I pointed. "Can you please let us in? If you don't, we'll freeze to death."

I heard a deadbolt snap. A middle-aged woman with a cap of short, gray hair and a ruddy complexion swung the door open.

"Good Lord! Come in! Come in!" She waved us into the broad foyer of a home dominated by rustic wood. I gave Lillian the lead with Boyd, then helped Wally across the threshold.

The warmth of the house struggled to penetrate my chilled skin.

"Did you say your plane crashed? Are you alright?"

"This young man is hurt. He needs an ambulance." Wally tried to protest, but I ignored him. "The rest of us are okay but darn near frozen. We went down just off-shore and had to swim for it."

"DAVID! DAVID!" she aimed a shout up a broad wooden staircase. "COME QUICK! We need to get you folks out of those wet things and warmed up. DAVID, BRING BLANKETS! Come. This way." She ushered us forward.

Twenty minutes later I sat on a plush leather sofa wrapped in a quilt and wearing someone else's underwear.

65

Andy didn't recognize the number, so she didn't pick up until I sent a text message that it was me.

"Will? *Are you okay? Where are you? Is Boyd with you?*"

"I'm fine. The boy is here."

"Where's 'here'?"

"According to Alice and David Horton, we're about six miles west of Marquette, Michigan."

"Michigan! What in God's name happened? I've been out of my mind. I've been calling county deputies all over the state."

Alice Horton appeared bearing a tray with mugs of coffee. She set mine on a coaster on a coffee table in front of me. I gave her a smile of thanks for the mug and the phone. She beamed, handed Wally a mug, then hurried back to the adjacent kitchen where she had set Boyd up with a bowl of Cheerios. He ate them dry, O by O. David Horton appeared a few minutes later and pantomimed an offer to top off the coffee from a bottle of single malt scotch he held. I gave him a firm thumbs-up.

"Dee, there's a ton to explain, but first, are you okay? Did you and Leslie catch up to those assholes?"

"Yes. No. Maybe. I can explain it all later. Tell me what happened!"

"I have a better idea. Why don't you call Earl and tell him you need Pidge and an airplane and come up here and get me? If he argues with you, tell him it's his fault I'm here." I could not picture Earl refusing a request from Andy.

"Where again?"

I explained.

"Are you sure you're okay? You scared the hell out of me. You should have taken my phone."

"Wouldn't have done any good. Listen, Dee, I love you. I'm fine. We're safe. I'll explain everything when you get here. Call this number when you land. A woman named Alice will answer."

"I love you, too. Thank God you're okay! It's still snowing here, but it's letting up. I'll be there as fast as I can."

"There's no rush. Don't let Pidge do anything stupid. Love you, too. Crazy day."

66

After she had gained her bearings at the front door, Alice shifted into nurse/mother mode. Her husband David responded to her initial call with an armload of blankets and towels. She ordered me and Wally into a side laundry room to strip down to the skin. David hurried off and returned moments later with two pairs of boxers that he insisted were clean.

Wally struggled to get out of his clothes. I helped him but drew the line at his underwear. He managed, but not without pain.

"Dude, I don't... *(huff)* ...need an ambu—"

"Yes, *dude*, you do." Purple and yellow contusions painted the left side of his chest. "You need to be looked at. Your breathing is bad. For all we know, you're bleeding internally and it's putting pressure on your lungs. Don't argue with me."

"And what the hell... *(huff)* ...am I supposed to say hap—?"

"Stop talking. And the answer to your question is *don't talk to anyone*. If someone presses you, tell them you're involved in a confidential FBI investigation. Tell them to talk to Special Agent Leslie Carson-Pelham. Repeat that to me."

He repeated it.

"Good.

While David Horton, a genial retiree who stood half a head taller than me and three heads taller than his wife, ushered Wally and me into his living room, Alice shoved our clothing into her dryer. She excluded my leather boots and leather flight jacket, which were probably toast for having been soaked. I figured my wallet and gunshot phone went down with Danzig, so there was nothing to save from any pockets.

Flitting back and forth between us and Lillian, who had been ushered to an upstairs bathroom and whom I suspected of enjoying a hot shower, Alice Horton loaned me her phone for the call to Andy. Wally found a wingback leather chair and sat stiffly upright holding a quilt up to his chin and managing his breathing. Boyd ended up in a blanket at a breakfast nook in the kitchen. Earlier, I saw Alice Horton shove Boyd's blinding Seahawks t-shirt into the dryer with my clothes and wondered how she managed to peel it off him.

After my call with Andy, I worked on getting the hot coffee into my core to bring the temperature up. The scotch added heat of its own. No matter how I wrapped that quilt around my body, I could not get warm.

Lillian appeared in a baggy sweatshirt paired with loose sweatpants, each bearing an Ohio State University logo. She was roughly the same height as our host, but Alice carried substantially more weight than Lillian, who has the thin body of a toned high-school track star. She carried her own coffee mug and sat down beside me on the leather sofa.

She leaned in to talk privately, but David Horton joined us.

"What happened?" he asked.

I'd been crafting a lie, but Lillian beat me to the punch. "That's classified, Mr. Horton. Don't get me wrong, you saved our lives, and we are deeply grateful. But if we start answering questions about who we are and what happened, you and your wife will be pulled into a very uncomfortable set of circumstances by my employer, the United States Department of Homeland Security—I'd be happy to show you ID, but it went down with the ship. I know you have questions, but for your own good, it's best that you don't ask. Someone will be in touch with you to verify all of this. But make no mistake, your service to me and my team has earned you the gratitude of DHS and the President of the United States."

His jaw hung slack. I tried hard not to look too impressed. He stammered an apology and excused himself to watch for the ambulance that had been called for Wally.

"Damn," I said. "And I thought I was a decent bullshitter."

"You're just full of shit," she said. She gazed out the bank of windows that added fifty percent to the value of the home. Lake Superior raged all the way to the horizon. "I can't believe we were out there."

"I can't believe those assholes were going to drop us into that."

We each took a moment to think the same thoughts. About depth and darkness. About eternity in black.

I brought us back to the surface and light. "Andy's coming. She said it was still snowing in Essex, but the storm is moving out and then she'll fly up. I just realized; I don't have a clue what time it is." My watch face had water in it and had stopped.

"Two-thirty."

"Wow." It took me a few seconds to link those words to my sense of time. I had a few missing hours to account for. "Okay, Dr. Farris. It's time. What the hell?"

I pulled the quilt tighter and took another sip.

Lillian didn't answer right away. She cast a long look at the child eating Cheerios in the kitchen.

"I love that boy," she said at length. She laughed. "Boyd is a Cray Super-computer. He's a math machine, a language savant."

"We couldn't get him to talk."

"He didn't think you were worth talking to. He's pragmatic. Science has no proof that photographic or eidetic memory is actually a thing, but if it is, Boyd comes close. He remembers everything. Every image he sees. I showed him that map *once*. One time. As a precaution. We were in a hotel in Sioux City, and I was scared. I laid it out for him and showed him the route to take if anything happened to me. The next morning, I woke up and found him shuffling little squares of paper. I wanted to scream, but then I realized —*that's his way of seeing the world*. He has autism spectrum disorder. And he is the love of my life, my heartbeat, my friend, my nemesis at chess and the subject of endless fascination for both me and, of course, Doug, who never misses a chance to take pictures of his head."

Another fascinating subject for Dr. Stephenson.

"Andy said he came from California."

"A polite way of asking if he is mine. No. He is not mine, biologically."

"I know. Andy showed me the news stories. Tragic."

"But he is mine now. I am not a violent person, Stewart, but the human scum that had him understand in no uncertain terms that they are never to come near him or me again. *Ever*." She leveled a look that had steel in it.

"Understood."

"Boyd is living evidence of everything wrong with the foster care system in this country."

"You were in New Mexico?"

"For a while. That's where I found him. We move around. He likes to travel. He likes to drive my car."

"I get that. By the way, you owe me for a mailbox."

"I'm sorry?"

"Never mind. I want to know why you sent him to me, but first, two questions. Does he know sign language?"

"One of his many talents."

"Then it was you. He was carrying on a conversation with you in the plane."

"Of course."

"What was he saying?"

"He told me about you, that he found you and you were there. I couldn't see. He asked if it would be okay to spray stinging powder in the man's face. Something I taught him."

"I wondered why a boy would carry around a Malibu Barbie knockoff."

"No, that's his doll. I added the wasabi powder and taught him what to do with it if he ever got in a tight spot."

I shook my head, astonished.

"What was your other question?"

"Oh, how did you end up in a photo next to a crop circle on Tammy Day's ranch?"

"You saw that photo? Oh—of course. Wally." We both checked on Wally who sat with his eyes closed. I doubted that he had fallen asleep, but Lillian lowered her voice regardless. "You know, some of this is your fault."

"Mine? How is any of this my fault?"

"After we went to see Lewko. After you wrecked his little artifact, and then we leveraged him into helping take down that pond scum in New York, I ghosted Spiro Lewko. He came at me hard. He thought he could leverage me to get to you. I worked just as hard to avoid him. Make no mistake, Stewart, if I want to get off the grid, I'm gone."

"Yeah, Lewko came up to see me and bitched abou—"

"That's not a nice word," Boyd called out from the kitchen.

Lillian smiled.

"I'll put a quarter in the swear jar. How is any of this my fault?"

"After all that business with Lewko, I kept an eye out for you. The government isn't done with you yet. Why do you think they keep your NTSB report on the 'Pending' pile? And my God, Will! What were you thinking, getting involved with the FBI, for heaven's sake! Shame on you!"

"My wife's dream," I said. "That did not go well."

"It's the effing FBI, dumbass."

"So, go on. You were stalking me."

She gave me the facial equivalent of the finger. "I keep my ear to certain channels. And, no, I have not shared anything I know about you or the artifact or Lewko with any of those channels. Some people in the community I associate with would run with it in a way that would do no one any good."

"I appreciate that."

"I picked up on some things that suggested a site in Wisconsin that might tie in with you. Boyd and I needed some fresh air and a road trip. Certain things I did to gain custody of him in New Mexico had a chance of blowing back on me. It was a good idea to get away. I planned on driving to Wisconsin, but then I started hearing about the gathering at Tammy Day's ranch. It had nothing to do with what happened to you, although it turns out she knows your old boss."

"Right."

"I know you think of me as a UFO nut, but I am first and foremost a scientist. I believe in empirical data, analysis, scientific method. The people up there, they were just honest believers. That was apparent from day one. But I also knew that they had been subject to a lot of outside influence, specifically Mike Dodd. Martian Mike."

"You said he was a friend."

"I've known him a long time. We met at JPL years ago. He was a mathematician, you know."

"He went a little off the deep end, wouldn't you say?"

Lillian shrugged. "He was harmless. He enjoyed the limelight. A little like deGrasse Tyson, but less reputable. Mike's name came up *a lot* with the people at that ranch. In fact, when the time came, I had him vouch for me. Tammy didn't want to let me in, but Mike spoke to her on my behalf. I let Tammy think I was there for the same reason as all of them."

"Which was?"

"A seat on the mothership. I know—I know, but this wasn't Heaven's Gate. This wasn't a cult. These were smart, well-educated, well-to-do people. They were just a little misguided."

"A little?"

"Will, I spent several weeks up there. They welcomed me. I had more than enough time to get to know them. If there had been any of that cult bullshit, I would have been long gone. Nobody spouted any weird paranormal crap or sex practices or any of that Applewhite and Nettles craziness. Nobody played the Jim Jones role. Nobody demanded renouncing worldly goods. The opposite. In fact, it was when I learned about their finances that something tripped a red flag for me."

"How so?"

"It was clear they were all well off, savvy investors, good financial planners. But it's not easy to walk up to someone—especially rich people—and ask, 'Hey, what do you plan to do with all your money when you're headed for the next galaxy?' A few people shared with me that they had all their ducks in a row for when the big day came. They were prepared. Like with financial planning and trusts set up. That's how I heard Baker's name. I found out he set up a trust for Tammy and for several of the others."

I realized that my muscles had stopped quivering. The coffee and scotch ignited a warm glow inside. They also put a little weight on my eyelids. I blinked it away.

"A trust?"

"Right. Again, they were up there on fifty percent belief and fifty percent lark. Nobody was sure of anything, so nobody was giving up the Mercedes or the stock portfolio just yet. But if the mothership did show up, they took steps to be prepared. And one name kept coming up."

"ParaTransit."

Lillian nodded. "About a week before I left, those circles showed up. It would have been easy for me to debunk. I mean, my God, that's the oldest hoax in the world. Those guys in England who started it used sticks and string. These were burned in."

"I know how."

"Well, it lit a fire—pun intended—among the folks at that ranch. I didn't see any point in shaking their tree, but I really got to wondering who had done it and why. I went to see Mike."

"He told me."

"You saw him?"

I explained my visit to Colorado and how I witnessed Martian Mike's involuntary suicide. I left out the part about pretending to be an alien. Lillian shook her head sadly.

"He never should have gotten in bed with those people. Mike told me about being bought out, by—guess who?"

"ParaTransit."

She tapped her nose. "Mike tried to defend it. He acknowledged that some of it was pure carnival, but he said it gave him a platform to get the truth out, to reach influential people. He was fooling himself. I knew it was a pure sellout."

"Did you ask him who this outfit is?"

"He wouldn't say."

"He said you asked him about The Gash."

"I told you, Stewart, I still want to know what happened to you. I was on my way to Wisconsin to check it out. Look, I've been doing this dance for a long time, but you're the first genuinely unworldly thing I've seen. So, yeah,

I asked him about an event in Wisconsin that, guess what, happened around the same time as your crash. He knew about it. He had a map and some files. He had your NTSB report. He told me to leave it alone. He wouldn't say why, but I think it was because his partners were looking at expanding beyond Montana. Maybe making the Wisconsin site a thing—their next project."

"That's why Danzig took everything. He didn't want anyone poking around in the deceased's collection."

"Bastard."

"That's not a nice word," Boyd said from the other room.

Both of us looked in his direction. He munched his Cheerios without making eye contact.

"Sorry, honey!" Lillian smiled. The smile faded quickly. "Mike warned me that I was asking too many questions. I tried to get him to tell me about Baker, but he lied and said he never heard of the guy. I know that wasn't true. Mike directly advised most of the people who gathered at that ranch. He was—he was like a celebrity travel agent organizing a destination wedding. And the people at the ranch who mentioned Baker to me said that it was Mike who recommended him. After Mike lied about it, I went to Sioux City to talk to Baker. I shouldn't have. I'm pretty sure Baker called Danzig down on me. Danzig found me outside our hotel. The first time, he just wanted to chat. He treated me like an expert. Made it sound like he had technical questions. I told him to pound sand. I knew he wouldn't let it go. That's why I warned Boyd about him."

"Danzig didn't know Boyd was with you."

"I made Boyd hide. When Danzig and the two others came back later, they claimed that Baker wanted to meet with me and answer any questions I had. I knew they were lying, but there was no way I could run or fight. I had to go with them to steer them away from Boyd."

"What did they want with you?"

"At first, I thought they wanted to get rid of me for poking into their business. But then they treated me like a colleague of Mike. They asked me all sorts of science questions. They asked me what I knew about the site in Montana. And the site in Wisconsin."

"They didn't take you to see Baker?"

"No. We wound up in that van. When I wanted to leave, they showed their hand and locked me up, but it wasn't like they hurt me, or it was some basement dungeon thing. They kept me in a house for a while. They pretended to want to recruit me, to team me up with Mike—then I suspected they wanted to replace him. I knew it was all bull—" She glanced at Boyd.

"—crap. I was scared to death for Boyd…but I also knew he would be okay. I knew he would go to you. What really worried me was that they were interested in Wisconsin, and in you."

"That's why Boyd said 'Danzig is coming.' What about Baker? What was the little weasel's role in all this?"

"The trusts. He set up Tammy's trust. Wally's aunt's trust. And some of the others. I told you, these were not trailer trash UFO nuts. These were believers who had means. That kid's aunt, Stephanie, that woman alone is worth a fortune. To the people at the ranch, the trusts were just another insurance policy. They weren't a cult. They knew the big event might never happen and they were all planning on going back to their place in Palm Beach or Santa Barbara if it all fizzled out. For some of them, it was like a role-play vacation. A jaunt with a group of like-minded spacefarers. Harmless if nothing came of it. And if it did, they had things covered. Or apparently ParaTransit had it covered."

I looked at the steel gray water and ragged waves.

"Jesus," I said. I felt the blood leave my face.

"What?" Lillian asked. "What's wrong?"

I stood up. I walked to the windows and stared out.

Depth and darkness. An eternity in black.

"Stewart, what is it?"

I pointed. "They're out there. Tammy and the others. All nine of them. *They're out there.*"

67

A ndy dropped lightly down the Navajo's airstair and closed her coat against a cold wind skimming the Sawyer International Airport ramp. Her hair leaped and flagged in the breeze. My chest tightened and my breath hitched. She has that effect on me. I hurried out the Boreal Aviation ramp access door and met her halfway in a controlled collision. Her hands found my cheeks, her lips found my lips. She felt warm and firm. My pain and exhaustion melted at her touch.

"Oh, for fuck's sake, get a room," Pidge muttered, hurrying past us. "Fucking cold out here."

Andy backed away and studied me. "Are you okay?"

"I am now." The gold flecks in her green eyes sparkled as a smile chased worry from her face. "Are you? People shot at you."

"People shot at us. We'll deal with that later. What happened? Why are you here? Did Boyd drive all the way up here in that storm? Whose shoes are those?" The oversized Merrell hiking shoes David Horton had loaned me looked clownish. It took three pairs of his socks to keep them on my feet.

"Long story. And then I need to talk to you about a little trip."

"How little?"

"California."

She stopped. "California?"

"Let's get some coffee. This is a bit of a story."

I expected resistance. Instead, I got a hug. "Okay. And then I've got one for you."

68

Lillian accepted Alice Horton's offer of hospitality for a few days on condition that neither she nor her husband disclose her presence or ask any hard questions. Boyd had taken a liking to the sprawling house on the lake. He seemed endlessly fascinated by the battalions of waves marching to the shore. I looked at the water and saw fury and death. Watching him stare out the windows was like watching a calculator at work. He moved his head in tiny, jerky increments, and scratched the air with his index finger, writing equations in unseen code only he understood. Lillian promised to find her way down to Essex, and Andy promised to help recover the Prius. Alice promised to help Lillian get some clothes beyond the single outfit that came out of Alice's dryer. Boyd, of course, was pleased to blind everyone with his Russell Wilson jersey.

Wally abandoned his resistance to medical treatment and agreed to board the Marquette Fire and Rescue ambulance that showed up. Before the ambulance arrived, I explained to Wally my estimate of his aunt's fate. He didn't deny it or argue, having firsthand experience with Danzig and his methods. I reminded him to invoke Leslie's name if anyone asked too many questions. He was free to describe how he'd been injured in Montana in a roadside ambush, which would cover everything the medical professionals needed to know, but after that, nothing. I told him I would have Leslie call and introduce herself. He left my sight without speaking, I think because of the news of his aunt rather than the pain in his ribs.

Tom Ceeves refused to let us back in our house. He made Andy give him a list of necessities, then dispatched officers to collect what wasn't damaged and deliver it to Sandy Stone's home on Leander Lake. Someone gathered up my other pair of boots and my summer flight jacket and spare Ray Bans.

Sandy insisted on putting us up. The home that once belonged to her state senator father had more than enough room. I protested the idea, thinking Senator Keller was there, but Sandy said no, the Senator had returned to Madison. I asked what was happening at the farmhouse, but she claimed not to know. All Tom would tell Andy was that it was a crime scene and under the protection of the Essex PD. He informed her that the road had been blocked at both ends, and she was to say nothing and stay out of the public eye.

After horrifying my wife with the full story that ended on the shores of Lake Superior, I asked her for an update on the troop of brave dress-up soldiers who heroically shot up our windows and gutters. Tom arrived shortly after I took off in the snowstorm with Boyd at the wheel of the Prius. Andy, Leslie and Tom decided to say nothing to anyone except Andy's fellow officers and Leslie's colleagues at the FBI. Leslie wanted time to deploy FBI resources to try and track down the members of Company W, while Tom and Andy investigated their local contact among the *recallistas.* It was that aspect of the case that met us on our return to Essex County.

Leslie met us at the airport when Pidge landed the Foundation's Navajo just before dusk. I couldn't help myself. I fell asleep on the flight. Andy had to shake me awake after Pidge rolled the Navajo to a stop in front of the Foundation hangar. Leslie waited for us on the freshly plowed ramp. I offered to help put the airplane to bed, but my wife and the stern FBI Special Agent almost dragged me to Leslie's car. Then to Sandy's. Then to bed after a meal that acted on me like Ambien.

I slept until almost noon the next day. Sandy was at school. Andy left a note saying she went to the office. Business as usual. There was food in the 'fridge, the note promised. She would be home with dinner, but Sandy had parent conferences at school until 8. I found eggs and bacon and cooked up a huge breakfast after a hot shower of environmentally insensitive duration. A heap of my clothes had been left in the guest bedroom.

I lounged around most of the afternoon but found myself feeling antsy as the sun set on the other side of the lake. Sandy had no land line, and I had no phone. There was no car in the garage, and I still had no power units. After most of a week of non-stop movement, the absence of action unnerved me.

Relief arrived when I heard the front door open. Andy's voice called out to me.

"In here!" I clicked off the HBO movie I'd been half-watching in what had once been Sandy's father's den. I hurried to meet Andy who handed me a bag of food from the Mexican restaurant at the other bowling alley in Essex. The food smelled incredible. I kissed my wife.

"Once again, I declare my undying love for you, darling."

"For me, or my choice in takeout."

"Yes."

"I see. Well, eat hardy. Rest up. We have work to do tonight." She reached in her bag and produced my two remaining power units.

"Indeed?"

69

A little after two a.m. I cruised over the snow-covered landscape on the west side of Essex. The cold sky above me carried whisps of high cirrus ice crystals that gave the stars fuzzy edges. Like most winter storms, the cold air mass that propelled the front brought high pressure and frigid cold air in the storm's wake. Winter had come over a month early, a rare snow event ahead of Thanksgiving. The landscape below me looked like a store window snow scene. Warmly lit homes sent trapezoids of light out across snowy lawns. The white blanket on the land glowed in the starlight. The temperature had dropped into the teens, giving the local climate-change deniers pretend evidence against global warming. Despite the early snowfall, I fully expected it all to be gone before the turkeys hit the ovens in a week, slushy and wet before disappearing entirely.

Andy had driven me to the station well after midnight. Except for Ashley holding down dispatch and Tom at his desk, the offices were empty. I took that as intentional, given the off-book plan at hand. Leslie showed up half an hour later with the paperwork Andy and Tom expected. By that time, I'd been decked out.

"Thinking of overthrowing the government?" she asked, strolling into Tom's office.

"Locked and loaded. I've got my stupid pouches, my stupid flashlight, my stupid vest, my stupid hat and this stupid racist patch." I pointed at the Company W patch sewn into the heavy ballistic vest I wore over camo pants and a camo shirt that Tom had acquired at Fleet and Farm. "I'm a regular militia moron."

"Yeah, well, don't underestimate the extremist types. They may be dumb, but in whatever world they've constructed for themselves, they're not stupid. If that makes any sense."

"It does," Andy said. "And I agree. We're reasonably sure that the Company W players left town after the shooting, but we can't be certain. If any of them are there tonight, abort the mission and we will regroup."

"I love it when you use technical jargon, dear."

She threw me a perturbed look.

I was surprised by the plan Andy, Tom and Leslie hatched. Especially Andy. This veered well off the accepted and confined path of law enforcement, a straight and narrow line that my wife religiously followed. We had yet to talk in depth about the attack on our home, and her feelings. I wore mine on my sleeve. She buried hers in a kind of grim investigative determination. I didn't need to be asked twice to participate in this mission.

Andy opened the flap on the holster at my side and pulled out her Berretta M.92. She dropped the magazine and handed it to me.

"Empty," she said. She pulled back the slide on the weapon. "Empty. Okay?"

"If you insist." I handed back the empty magazine.

"I insist." She slapped the magazine back into the weapon, tucked the weapon into the holster and closed the flap. "Only for show."

"Affirmative."

"Put the gloves on and keep them on," Andy ordered me. I tugged on a set of blue latex gloves. "Are we ready?"

Andy looked at Leslie, then Tom who heaved himself up out of his office chair and loomed over all of us.

"As we'll ever be," he rumbled in his deep baritone.

We loaded up in Tom's big SUV and drove to an empty court in a subdivision where construction had been on hold for several years. We reviewed the plan. I tucked a Bluetooth receiver in my ear.

"Give me about half an hour before you call. I'll probably open the line without speaking," I said.

"Right."

"Remember," Tom said, "no violence."

"I'm a pacifist to the core. And this isn't the first time I've done this," I replied.

"Really?" Tom asked. I'd forgotten that he wasn't acquainted with some of my previous adventures.

"Buy me a beer sometime and I'll tell you."

"No," Andy said, "all due respect sir, no he won't."

"The boss has spoken."

"Final check, Will," Leslie said, "the key word is...?"

"Revolution. I'm off to start one." I hopped out of the SUV, pulled a BLASTER from one of the zillion pockets on this quasi-military uniform, tested it and—

Fwooomp!

—launched straight up into the winter sky.

THE TARGET HOUSE half a mile from where Tom parked was bigger than I expected. One of four at cardinal points of the compass around a circular subdivision court, it featured a three-car garage, a big sunroom at the back and a swimming pool set in a broad tiled patio. Tom said the children were college-aged and not yet home for Thanksgiving. I wondered how he gained that intel, but a lot of people in Essex know a lot of other people's business. Tom asserted that the owner and his wife were likely to be the only occupants, but I was also instructed to abort if that proved untrue.

Andy checked police sources and assured me that the house was not listed as having an alarm system or alarm service. The police department does its best to keep those records up to date because private alarms go off night after night, rarely due to any genuine criminal activity. Andy has often said that the only criminal activity associated with these alarm systems is the monthly fee stolen by the companies selling the systems.

Not showing up on the books as having an alarm didn't mean that the house wasn't equipped, I was told. If I got in and found a keypad or set off an alarm, abort.

I disagreed but didn't say so. The plan called for a home intrusion. Having an alarm go off to wake the homeowner served that part of the plan, in my opinion. I decided to play it by ear.

I circled the house and chose the garage for entry. A door at the back featured a deadbolt and a locked knob, but it also had a multi-pane window, which meant the deadbolt probably required a key from both sides. I eased to a landing in front of the door and grabbed the knob, testing it to see if it was locked. It was. I wrapped my gloved hand around the doorknob to anchor myself and drew the handgun. One tap on the glass broke out the pane closest to the deadbolt.

I returned the weapon to the holster and reached in to unlock the knob, which turned in my other hand. Then I cupped my free hand over the deadbolt lock and *pushed* the levers in my head. The effort had the effect of spreading *the other thing* outward from my hand, over the deadbolt and the wooden door in which it was mounted. The inside of the garage became visible through the hole. I watched the edge of the hole reach the seam between the door and the jamb, then jerked.

Brief resistance preceded a soft snap. The door came open. The deadbolt had sheared as if cut by a laser, leaving a stub in the strike plate.

Fwooomp! I reappeared and settled on my feet. I opened the door, stepped into the dark garage, and closed the door behind me. Two steps in, a light blazed on.

I froze. My heart hammered.

"Crap!" I said under my breath. The garage around me was empty and still, with three cars nudged into their slots. The light that came on had been mounted over the door to the house, a motion-sensitive light, probably meant more for someone taking a bag of garbage out to the can sitting on the far side of the garage than for security. "Huh. I should get one of those."

I moved to the door that accessed the house and tested the knob. It turned in my hand. I pulled. The door opened.

"Idiots." The door had a deadbolt, but neither the knob nor deadbolt was locked. Not a great idea, given what I had just done.

I entered the house and examined a short utility hall. No keypad. I listened for an alarm. Nothing so far.

Fwooomp!

I vanished again and lifted off my feet. A tug on an open doorway took me across a span of tile floor toward the front door of the house. From there, I pulled myself up a stairway to the second floor. A landing at the top of the stairs went in both directions and around the stairs. I counted four open doors that belonged to bedrooms, one closed door that was probably a linen closet, and an open door to an upstairs bathroom.

I pegged the master bedroom as the one hosting all the snoring.

The room was huge. Enough light showed through window shades to define a king-size bed, a chest of drawers and a dresser. A widescreen TV hung on the wall opposite the head of the bed. A tall cabinet filled with DVDs stood in one corner. A dressing table with multiple mirrors occupied a spot near a door to what I guessed accessed both the master bathroom and a garage-sized closet.

Two long lumps occupied the bed. One of them snored loudly. From around my neck, I pulled up a tight black face mask that covered my nose. A set of yellow-lens plastic sunglasses topped the costume, although they made things a bit dark.

Showtime.

Fwooomp!

I pulled the chair away from the dressing table and positioned it beside the bed where the snorer slept. I dropped into the chair and sat back, crossing one leg casually.

I took a minute to rehearse in my mind, then unhooked the flashlight from the utility belt. Next, I unsnapped the holster and extracted the empty Beretta. A flick of the flashlight switch threw bright LED light into the face of Lester Connelly, founder of The Committee Organizing Police Support.

He instantly snorted loudly, squinted, then threw his hand to his face to shield himself from the blinding light.

"What the—?" He scrambled awake rapidly, squinted past his hand at the intruder in his house, then reached for his nightstand.

"Uh-uh." I pulled the flashlight back to near my chest and stretched my gun hand out so that the weapon aimed at his face was clearly visible.

Connelly froze.

"Back it up," I ordered. He retracted his hand and slid away from the edge of the bed. His movement stirred his wife, who faced away from us. She rolled and moaned in her sleep, then brought her hand up against the light. Her eyes came open. She shrieked and scrambled upright, then ducked as much as she could behind her husband. The shrieking continued until Connelly snapped at her.

"Be quiet, Sheryl!" The woman's mouth snapped shut, but not for long.

"Who are you?" she cried. *"What do you want?"*

"Relax. Everybody, relax." I leaned forward and pulled open the top drawer of the nightstand. The flashlight illuminated the drawer contents. A silver revolver lay at the ready. "That doesn't do you a lot of good in a drawer like that. Better to keep it in a holster on the side of the nightstand. Easier access. Of course, if you have kids running around, that's not a great idea either." I slid the drawer shut without removing the weapon.

"What do you want?"

"Just be cool, Lester. Be cool." I leaned back and shifted the flashlight until it lit up the Company W patch on my vest. "We're all friends here. Right?"

"My God!" Sheryl Connelly cried in relief. She made a weird cough-sob-laugh sound. "You scared us!"

"What are you doing here? This is *not* a good idea," Connelly said. He sat farther upright. "You were all supposed to leave after...you know. You can't be here now."

"The C.O. feels that there are some...let's just say, loose ends."

Sheryl Connelly visibly stiffened. Lester put a hand on her thigh.

"Now, take it easy here. Hold on. Just hold on one goddamned minute!" Panic crept into his voice. "We brought you in on this, remember? We did everything just the way we were told, the way you wanted."

The Bluetooth device rang in my ear.

"Wait just one sec, okay?" I put the flashlight in my lap, aimed roughly at the Connellys, then tapped the earpiece. "Dragon here." I made that name up on the spot, figuring Andy would love it. "Are you in position?"

"Dragon? Really?" She spoke softly in my ear.

"Roger that," I said. I turned my attention back to the couple on the bed. "That's my team outside. They established a perimeter. Can't be too careful."

Connelly's panic welled up. His voice rose an octave as he spoke. "Listen! We did everything according to your instructions. No direct contact or communications. We used the encrypted app. There's nothing to connect us to you, okay? There are no loose ends here!" He gripped his wife's thigh.

"Oh," I said, "I'm sorry. I gave the wrong impression. Did you think I was here to blow your brains all over those expensive sheets?" I laughed.

Connelly blanched. He opened his mouth to speak, but nothing came out.

"Seriously, relax. That's too messy. No, the loose end I'm talking about is your computer. Your laptop."

"But everything was encrypted," Connelly protested.

"Doesn't matter. If the feds get their hands on that or your phone, well, they can be resourceful. The C.O. just wants me to pick up those devices. Nah, man. I didn't come here to shoot you or your wife."

Sheryl Connelly gasped-sobbed-laughed again. She grabbed her husband's arm. "Ohmigod omigod *omigod*, you scared the shit out of me! Oh, God!"

"Apologies."

"Me, too! Jesus!" Connelly said. "Listen, I did what we agreed. I didn't use any of my personal devices."

This wasn't what I was expecting.

"No," Sheryl said vigorously, "he didn't. We were super careful."

I felt the mission falling apart.

"We did everything exactly according to protocol." Sheryl Connelly let nervous energy propel her speech. She blurted her words. "Tell the C.O. that. Exactly. Lester only used the extra laptop we bought and the burner phone. There's nothing on any of our personal devices. Nobody knows about the others. Right, honey?"

"Absolutely! One hundred percent! Man, I gotta say, you really put a scare into us, coming here like this. I mean, c'mon! It's the middle of the night. How did you get in here?"

"Broke in through the garage. By the way, you should lock your garage door."

Sheryl slapped her husband on the shoulder. "Dammit, Les! I asked you if you locked up!"

"I thought I did." He lifted the sheets and blankets and swung his legs off the bed. "Do you want me to get them?"

"Please." I picked up the flashlight and waved with the gun.

"Do you really need that?" He pointed at the Beretta.

"Well, yeah. I might still decide to kill your asses." They both froze. I stared. Nobody moved. "Just kidding. Let's keep this friendly, why don't we?"

Sheryl tried to show relief. Lester tried to chuckle. Neither could be sure. Exactly the way I wanted it.

"Have you heard anything?" Sheryl tried sounding casual. "Because we haven't."

"Heard what?" I asked.

"If you got the bitch."

This is why Andy gave me an empty gun.

A cold stone dropped in my gut. My hand tightened on the grip of the Beretta. I stared at the woman who sat on her bed asking if my wife was dead as if inquiring about a bake sale.

"Excuse me?"

"That bitch cop. Did you get her?"

"Sher and I haven't heard a word about it," Lester said. "We've been keeping an eye on the news and on social. *There's been nothing.* I think they're trying to cover it up."

"Tactical maneuver. A lie of omission by the fake news media. Makes sense," I said. "But I can tell you for a fact, ain't nobody got out of that house alive."

"Nice!" Connelly pumped his fist.

"That's really good news!" Sheryl Connelly bobbed her head happily.

Andy could hear every word of this. I imagined the sound of her breathing in my ear, even though she wasn't. She more than likely had her phone on speaker so that Leslie and Tom could monitor as well. I wondered how high Tom's blood pressure would peg right about now.

"That's going to be good news to the party chair. They'll want to get some spin on it right away. I can call them tomorrow. I'm sure it will break by then. They're in touch with the top, you know. The very top," Connelly said. Sheryl slid off her side of the bed and picked up a robe. She put it on and tied the front, but then stopped.

"Oh. Did you want me to come, too?"

"I can get it, Sher. Just stay here."

"I'd feel better if you came, too, Sher. It's a tactical thing." I waved at her to proceed.

"Right." She poked her feet into a pair of slippers.

Connelly didn't bother with slippers or a robe. He wore a t-shirt over boxer shorts and padded out of the bedroom barefoot. He flicked on the upstairs hall light. I gestured for the wife to follow her husband. We descended the stairs and moved into a kitchen. Connelly turned on a ring of recessed lighting around the ceiling.

"You're gonna like this. Nobody would ever find this," Lester grinned.

"He made it himself," Sheryl added proudly.

Connelly stepped to a counter-height divider between the kitchen and an adjoining great room—a set of cabinets beneath a quartz countertop. He dropped to a knee and opened the cabinet near the end of the divider. With one hand, he reached up and moved something. The sound of a block of wood knocking against the cabinet came from within.

Connelly stood up and moved to the end. He gripped the heavy quartz top, roughly six feet long and a foot-and-a-half wide. He lifted. The quartz top had been hinged on the opposite end. A typical installation would have used silicone glue to secure the top to the cabinets.

In the space between the quartz and the top of the cabinet, a depth of a little over an inch, lay a small, thin laptop and generic phone. Farther in, the hidey hole contained an AR-15 rifle and several magazines. Connelly held the top up. Sheryl Connelly lifted both devices free.

"Glory to the revolution," I said. "That's clever as shit."

"Thanks." Connelly grinned. "Listen, can I offer you something? I know the recall didn't work out, but hey, plan B, am I right? A toast?"

"I appreciate that, but I have a long drive ahead tonight. The rest of the squad already moved out. I'm tail-end Charlie. We're just here to tie up loose ends—shit, I'm sorry, I didn't mean it like that. Let's call it mopping up."

Once again, my choice of words stiffened them.

Sudden rapping on the front door jolted both Connellys.

"Who's that?" Sheryl Connelly whispered.

"Oh," I said. "Relax. That's just my guys. If you don't mind, I'd like to slip out the front." I gestured with the gun.

Trust evaporated rapidly. Neither moved.

"Do you really need that?" Sheryl Connelly asked. "It's not safe to be pointing that."

"Sher, please, let's get these guys on their way." Connelly tried to hand me the devices. I waved him off.

"Give 'em to my guys. Got my hands full. Ready for anything." I gestured at the front door. "Ladies first," I added when Sheryl Connelly tried to hang back.

The hesitant couple reluctantly led me to the front door. Sheryl Connelly glanced back nervously. Connelly produced a key from a dish on a sconce and unlocked the deadbolt. He pulled open the door.

Andy stood framed in the doorway holding up her badge and a folded sheet of paper while Tom held open the storm door. Leslie peered around Tom's bulk.

"Good evening, Mr. and Mrs. Connelly, I'm Detective Bitch from the Essex Police Department. I have in my hand a warrant to search these premises for devices instrumental in a recent act of domestic terrorism." Andy glanced at Connelly's hands. "And I see we don't have far to search."

Tom stared bullets at the pair. Leslie grinned.

Both Connellys froze where they stood, then turned around with mouths hanging open under terrified eyes, but not before—

Fwooomp!

—I vanished.

70

A part of me could not shake the sensation of plunging into the icy surf below the rocks on the shore of Lake Superior. I wondered if I would ever feel warm again or if merely touching that memory would always cast a chill through my bones. Two things offered relief.

First, the high California sunshine cut through a cloudless blue sky and bathed my skin with sweet heat. Second, Andy carefully stepped down the Navajo's airstair wearing white sandals, a modestly short red skirt and a sleeveless white blouse that let the sun kiss her light caramel skin. The sight of her warmed me from the inside. She wore her hair bound up in a high pony and added a pair of oversized sunglasses she had picked up on a recent adventure in Washington, D.C. She embodied summer sunshine. I stared for a moment, then watched the reaction of several other people on the busy ramp at Bob Hope Field in Burbank. Celebrities come and go with regularity here. Andy had the look. I enjoyed watching them wonder who she was because surely someone looking like her *had* to be somebody.

I let this play out by reaching for and extracting our bags from the cabin, adopting the role of the attending crewman.

"Are you doing this on purpose?" she asked when I fell in step behind her.

"Kinda fun," I said. "They're trying to figure out who you are."

"Ugh," she protested. "Ridiculous." The dimples peeking from a suppressed smile said she felt otherwise.

"Yes, ma'am."

"Stop it!"

"Whatever you say, ma'am."

She marched on in silence.

"We should get you one of those little purse dogs."

Andy hit the Million Air restroom while I arranged for fuel and a tiedown.

I BORROWED the Foundation Navajo for the trip to Los Angeles. The trip started with a hop to Marquette, Michigan where we picked up Wally. He looked better than the last time I'd seen him. Andy insisted that he ride up front with me. He winced getting in and out of the copilot's seat, but he settled in with a headset on and seemed to enjoy the ride and my pilot talk.

"I haven't had a chance to say it, but...thanks. A couple times over," he said after I leveled us off at ten thousand feet on a heading for Iowa. "Still the freakiest thing I've ever seen or probably ever will. And seriously, dude, you can have the whole collection if you tell me how you do it."

"I'd give up my whole Abba collection for someone to tell me how I do it. I have no freaking idea."

"Are you kidding me? You have an Abba collection?"

I laughed. "No. Just paying you back for calling me dude again. But I'm not kidding. I have no idea."

"Bullshit," he said.

"That's not a nice word."

He laughed. "Fine. I'm in no position to argue."

We rode through the sky exchanging casual conversation until it ran out. After thirty or forty wordless miles, I broke the silence.

"Hey, um, I'm sorry about your aunt."

"Do you think they really did it? Flew them out over that lake and..."

"I do."

"Fucking cold-hearted. I feel like somebody needs to know, but I don't know how or where to report something like this. And I don't know how to prove any of it."

"That was the whole point. I don't think the bodies will ever surface. It's the perfect crime. They create doubt with all that craziness up in Montana. A share of the population will firmly believe they boarded the mothership. People are already flocking to that little town. They're calling it another Roswell."

"I hope it's good for their tourist trade." Wally gave up a light laugh. "I

really wish I could picture Aunt Stephanie on some ship up in the galaxy
rather than…you know."

"Yeah."

"Fuckers paid for it. There's that."

"Yeah. There's that."

"I'm going to tell my mother to fight the trust Aunt Stephanie set up."

"Good idea." I didn't tell Wally what Andy and I had decided. That
Danzig and Shotgun and Big Gun and even that weasel Baker may have paid
the bill, but they weren't the people responsible, which was the reason we
now flew west. We both had hopes that this trip would give Wally some
ammunition.

From Marquette we flew to Sioux City. Andy wanted to search Baker's
office. Wally asked to tag along. I feared he had his hopes up that something
might be found to bring closure to his Aunt Stephanie's disappearance. I
thought it was a long shot and sadly proved myself right. We took a crew car
to the shabby little law office in the shabby little building and found the door
locked. The paper sign on the door was gone. I did my trick with the lock
and snapped the bolt barring entrance. We found the office stripped. Even
the over-ambitious phone was gone. Nothing remained, not even the cheap
plastic chairs in the reception area.

"I guess they sent in the cleaners," Wally mused, wandering back and
forth past the half-wall divider.

"Not really surprising," Andy said.

"You think this was Danzig?" Wally asked.

"Probably. He did scoop up the toad that lived under this rock."

Wally didn't comment.

FROM SIOUX CITY we flew to Colorado. We dropped Wally off at Sterling
Municipal Airport, a field with one hard-surface runway and one grass
runway. The people at the FBO were friendly and gassed up the Navajo
while we said our good-byes.

I shook his hand. "Don't play any rugby."

"So long, dude."

Andy threw him a hug that made him wince, despite her best attempt to
be gentle.

"I hope that hurt," I said. "For calling me dude."

"If you find anything else, will you let me know?" Wally asked Andy.
"Because I get the strong feeling you two are not done looking."

"Yeah, if I come across your Saab, I'll give you a call," I said, sparing her a lie.

"Right. Thanks."

He went to wait for his ride in front of the building while we supervised refueling the airplane for the last leg of the trip, a full four-hour run from Sterling to Burbank. I offered to break it up, or to make a stop where we might rest overnight, but Andy pledged to endure the long ride. I insisted on last-minute bathroom stops, then we launched, leaving Sterling and Wally Vandenlock behind, and feeling the loss for it.

71

I had a car lined up by the time Andy emerged from the restroom at Million Air Flight Services at the Burbank airport. We loaded our bags in the trunk. I extracted the iPad from my flight bag because I find it easier to use for navigation than trying to program the system in a rental car.

We were both tired. It had been a long day. We made the decision to check into a hotel and start fresh in the morning. Andy used her phone and found a Quality Inn for cheap. I vetoed her choice and used the iPad to steer us to the Hilton Garden Inn near downtown. She protested the high cost, but I pointed out that Earl Jackson had handed me the Essex County Air Service credit card before departing. I had stopped at his office to let him know what we hoped to find by traveling to L.A. He reached in his desk for the card and flipped it to me without a word. I knew what he was thinking. Andy argued that it didn't mean we couldn't be frugal. I countered with a proposal to let the rental car decide. It steered us to the Hilton.

THE HOTEL WAS comfortable and every bit as expensive as I expected. Andy and I ate a light dinner and stopped at the bar for an after-dinner Corona to go with the during-dinner Corona we had both enjoyed.

"Leslie texted. She said that the Connellys are being delightfully cooperative. She's been able to flesh out the Company W roll call. She said she's finding a rather messy trail of contacts between state party officials and the militia. She's turning that over to DOJ but warned us not to get our hopes up." Andy lifted her glass. "To the FBI."

We clicked. We drank.

"I wouldn't mind joining her on the hunt for a few of those assholes. Maybe see if they can fly," I said.

"That's not how this works, dear."

"Actually, there's a major league ass at the top of that food chain I'd like a few words with."

"Don't say it," she warned.

"He Who Shall Not Be Named? Why not?"

"Because threatening a person in that office results in federal charges."

"He's still doing it, Dee. He's still lying about what happened. Never in so many words. It's always this wink-wink bullshit where he suggests that something bad is going on and he's got the goods, and the people behind it are going to be revealed and punished. Stay tuned for our next episode. It's a classic move. Invent a conspiracy that doesn't exist, and every time your enemy accuses you of lying, it just makes it sound like they're the ones hiding something. Naturally, he never offers any evidence. Half the time he's incoherent. The other half he's pandering to his rabid followers who desperately want to believe the lie. Look where it took the Connellys, for God's sake. Cheering the murder of a police officer while they plant 'Back The Blue' signs on their lawns? It's dangerous. That's how our house got shot up."

I realized I'd grown loud and a little breathless. Andy fought a smile.

"What?"

"No, go on. Tell me how you really feel, love. Don't hide your emotions." She laughed,

"I'm serious."

"You don't think I know that? Darling, I was the target. But you can't grab everybody and haul them off to the top of a water tower."

"I don't want everybody. I just want anybody who messes with my girlfriend."

Andy lowered her lashes. "Aww. She must be a very special girl."

"She is. And I feel very protective of her."

I liked the combination of blush and glow triggered in her cheeks, and the look that fueled my soul when she lifted those lashes.

"Listen," I said, "speaking of getting serious for a moment."

"Oh? Someone shooting at us wasn't serious?"

"That? All in a day's work. No, I just want to tell you that I know it's been crazy the last few weeks since we got back from D.C. With the recall.

With Boyd showing up. With Earl chasing me off to Tammy Day's ranch. There hasn't been a lot of 'us' time. And there are a few things we need to talk about." She opened her mouth to speak, but I hurried to finish. "And this is not the time, nor is it meant to put any pressure on you—on either of us—to express anything. Just—you know—I need to tell you that I'm open to it, whenever you are."

She gazed at me, seeing something I could never fathom. When she looks at me like that, I wonder if she's looking at someone else, because I can't imagine living up to who she sees in that deeply loving expression.

"You are kinda hard to get rid of."

"Very. It's been tried."

"Really?"

"I got thrown out of an airplane."

"So did I, if you recall."

"Twice for me. No, three times."

We fell into each other's gaze. She held hers for a long time, then kissed me.

"We will talk about everything," she said. "Soon."

72

"This is it. 1900 Avenue of the Stars." The building felt oddly out of place in the sprawl of Los Angeles, even though it was tucked in a cluster of similar skyscrapers. I don't think of L.A. or any part of Southern California as having high-rise office buildings. Obviously, it has its share, and after navigating heavy traffic with a few missed turns, we found the Century City address.

Finding parking was a bigger challenge. Eventually, we locked and left the car and walked to the office building's lobby. Andy carried her satchel. In it, she carried her badge and gun, although I knew she disliked doing so without establishing contact with local law enforcement. I carried a plastic bag with a colorful logo that said *Halloween Headquarters*. It had been a last-second purchase brought about when I suddenly swerved across three lanes of traffic into a parking space beside storefront windows plastered with giant SALE and 80% OFF EVERYTHING signs.

"My God, Will!" Andy had cried out, startled by the maneuver.

"Wait here!" I was gone before she could protest. Less than ten minutes later I returned to the car with treasure.

"What did you do?" Not, *What did you buy?* but rather a question that implied mischief—which, of course, was spot on.

"You'll see." I dropped the bag behind my seat and pulled back into traffic.

Twenty minutes later Andy found the listing for ParaTransit on the directory board in the building lobby. The address and floor matched information she found on a bare-bones web page. They didn't hide, but they didn't explain anything on the web page, either. Except to say that *Your Journey Begins with Trust.*

"No double meaning there," I commented.

The doors opened and Andy pressed the button to the correct floor. We rode up with a static charge between us.

"Are you going to show me?" she asked halfway up. She pointed at the bag in my hand.

"I think I'd rather surprise you. See if you can keep it together."

"Challenge accepted."

We arrived on the correct floor and were instantly greeted by a broad frosted glass wall.

ParaTransit
Your Journey Begins with Trust

The lettering spanned the entire thirty-foot wall. A set of curved strokes etched in the frosted glass suggested the shape of a planet with rings. Saturn?

"Well," I said, "it's not like they're trying to be discrete."

"This is not cheap office space," Andy said.

"There's probably an expression coined by con artists about having to flash cash to make cash."

"I think it's that you have to flash cash to make cash."

"Nah. That's not it." I spotted a restroom down the hall. "Wait here for me, okay? I'll just be a sec."

I hurried away again evading any protest.

Two minutes later, after vanishing in the restroom, I floated up behind Andy.

"Dee, it's me. Don't turn around." I landed a hand on the small of her back and closed a grip on the waist of her skirt.

"Are you ready? You remember how this goes?"

We had rehearsed after dinner last night. "Ready when you are."

"Don't overdo it, okay?"

"Me? Never."

"Right."

She towed me forward to the segment of the glass wall that doubled as a nearly hidden door. Carefully swinging the glass panel wide enough to ensure I would clear without bumping it, we entered the reception area of ParaTransit.

Expensive carpeting stretched to the walls. Fine leather furniture clustered around a small but functioning fountain. A dish of Dove chocolates rested beside an empty white marble wine chiller on the rim of a reception counter. The counter had a marble façade and spanned the same width as the glass wall. At each end, hallways led to offices behind more frosted glass.

Andy wasn't wrong about flashing cash.

No one greeted us. The single chair behind the reception counter lacked an occupant.

Andy walked to the end of the counter and searched the hallway, then did the same on the other end.

"Hello! Anyone here?"

No one answered.

"Maybe everybody is telecommuting," I whispered.

"Hello!" she called a second time.

"Just a minute!" The voice came from the other hallway. We repositioned.

A young man wearing expensive-looking workout clothing jogged toward us between the twin rows of glass. A gold chain at his neck matched the gaudy watch on his wrist.

"Can I help you?"

"This is ParaTransit, is it not?" Andy asked. "I'm looking for Peter Giles."

The man slowed his jog and settled into an appraising examination of Andy that went at least two degrees beyond appropriate.

"I'm Peter. And you are?"

"Andrea Taylor." Andy extended a hand. He took it and shook.

"I'm sorry. Forgive my appearance. I didn't think we had any appointments today."

"I'm sorry. Forgive mine, too. I stopped for a visit on a whim. You come highly recommended by an acquaintance of mine. We share seats on the Denver Arts Council. Stephanie Cullen? She's a dear friend. She said if I was ever in L.A. I should look you up. Stephanie and I share certain… beliefs. I'm told that ParaTransit respects those beliefs."

Giles' assessment took on a more serious tone. He nodded thoughtfully.

"Ms. Cullen is a wonderful woman. And she's not wrong. Our mission is grounded in trust. How can I help you?"

"Stephanie spoke highly of her experience with you, the care she was given, the advice she received. The detailed consideration she obtained for her rather substantial assets. I'm in a similar situation and I'm interested in discussing those services. Perhaps we could talk in your office?"

"Please," Giles stepped to one side and gestured.

"Oh, no. After you." Andy returned the gesture. A good move, keeping Giles in front of us, since I remained attached to Andy's skirt.

Giles led us down the hall and into a huge corner office that overlooked much of Century City, including the big sound stages at Fox. He had a stand-up desk with no chair, an exercise cycle, and a wall of widescreen televisions all tuned to either cable news or financial channels. Scattered modern furniture constructed of chrome and leather decorated one half of the office. The furniture felt dated to me.

"Please have a seat. May I offer you something cold? We have still and sparkling water, and if it's not too early for you, I keep a few choice examples from my cellar on hand. Napa select, of course."

"Nothing for me." Andy chose a seat facing the windows. I let her go. I hung back at the center of the room. Giles dropped into the chair facing her.

"Taylor. Do I know that name?"

"I suppose there's Elizabeth. No relation."

"Yet you share her sublime looks, Miss—or is it Mrs.—Taylor."

"You're kind, Mr. Giles."

"Peter."

"You're kind, Peter. It's Miss Taylor."

Giles dropped his eye to Andy's hand, a move I imagined him making often in L.A.'s finest pickup bars. He noted the modest diamond on Andy's finger and his smile faltered, yet he plunged ahead. "Nice to meet you, Miss Taylor. May I call you Andrea?"

"I don't think so."

He blinked, surprised by the rebuke.

"You see, I lied to you, Peter. I wasn't referred to you by Stephanie Cullen. I was referred to you by Carl Danzig. Or maybe it was Ezra Baker. I forget which." Andy gave him a moment. Some of the color left his face. When he didn't speak, she said, "Can I take from your silence that you disavow your relationship with Mr. Danzig and Mr. Baker?"

"I don't know those names."

Andy laughed. "Well, that's a lie. But I supposed it's to be expected. Mr. Danzig described you as a middle management dweeb. Are you 'middle management,' Peter?"

"I think it's time for you to leave, whoever you are." Giles shifted to rise, but Andy stopped him by reaching into her satchel.

"I have something you really should see, Peter." She extracted her Glock 26 and brought it to rest on her knee, aimed at Giles' center mass. If he had ever seen a gun this close, it was certainly not from that angle. He gulped.

"I don't know what you want, and I don't know this Danzig fellow. If you're here to rob us, take whatever you want. There's nothing of value here."

"You think I'm a common thief?"

"I don't know what you are. I think you should leave. You were misled, whatever you were told about me. Please, just go and I won't report this to the police."

"Oh, I'm sorry, did I forget to mention..." Andy used her free hand to pull her badge from the bag. "I am the police."

"Then I'll be reporting you for threatening me with a deadly weapon," Giles said, finding a bit of backbone. Despite his bravado, he could not take his eyes off the barrel of her gun.

"No. I don't think you will. Tell me about Stephanie Cullen, about the trust you had Baker establish for her. And for Tammy Day. And for a number of other people recently residing at the Day Ranch in Montana."

"I cannot confirm anything you just described, and even if I could, those matters are protected by attorney-client privilege." Giles jumped to his feet. "And in about thirty seconds I will be calling our attorneys to bring hell down on you and your supervisors for—"

"Sit. Your ass. Down." Andy closed a two-handed grip on the weapon and lifted it. "Or I will shoot you in the face."

Her cold tone convinced Giles. He lowered himself to the chair. He crafted an angry pout on a mouth that looked a little too wide for his face. His tan and his tone said he fancied himself as attractive. His initial approach to Andy told me he overestimated himself. Now his smooth affect shifted to sullen, sour, and resentful.

"If you had any kind of career, you can kiss it good-bye."

"Trite." Andy smiled. "I'd like to get you talking, Peter, so let me prime the pump. You and whatever this company pretends to be helped stage what is supposed to look like an alien abduction. Not a simple hoax, mind you. A long con." She relaxed her pistol stance and waved her hand in the air. "All this. Very sophisticated. But I noticed that the offices we passed were incredibly tidy. Picture frames on each desk—probably with stock photos. Note pads and pens. A few trinkets to personalize the offices, but staged, nevertheless. Like the crop circles in Montana. Weeks, maybe months of preparation, am I correct? Were you the one tasked with finding the right candidates? Sincere believers. Not just UFO nuts who show up in Roswell or try to crash Area 51, but well-heeled people, gently nudged along by so-called experts. Martian Mike? Does that name ring a bell?"

"We do nothing illegal. ParaTransit offers people who are broad-minded about the universe a means of pursuing their beliefs with the security of putting their affairs in order should those beliefs come to fruition."

"There it is, the first trickle in the floodgate, Peter. I knew you would realize that it's better if you share everything with me."

"Go to hell. I'm not saying another word."

"Okay." Andy nodded. "Let's try and look at this from another perspective. What you do here breaks human laws against things like fraud, grand larceny, and murder. Setting up a group of individuals with fabricated evidence of aliens, arranging trusts that I'm sure benefit you or some entity you have established, and then murdering them in a way that is intended to support the fantasy that they were lifted into the sky by one of Steven Spielberg's special effects. How am I doing so far?"

"I told you. I'm not saying another word."

"Yes, you did tell me. Here's your problem. We don't care about any of that."

She stopped and stared at Giles. He stared back but could not sustain it.

"What? What's that supposed to mean?"

"It means, Peter, that we don't give a shit what you people do to steal from one another, but we don't like the attention you're bringing to us. To the fact that we are here. Among you."

Andy delivered the line with chilling calm. I could not have been prouder.

Giles screwed his face up to express bewilderment. "We, who? What the hell are you talking about?"

This was my cue.

I hovered on a spot roughly twenty feet from Giles. Distance felt more dramatic.

Fwooomp!

I appeared and settled on the carpet, then held a rigid pose. Behind the tinted plastic orbs of the alien-head mask I purchased, I watched Giles and tried harder than I've ever tried in my life not to laugh. The mask, a glossy green and blue creation that gave me giant black eyes, a massive mouth, and tiny spiked teeth under a veined hairless dome of head, smelled bad on the inside but looked great on the outside. It also looked like a stupid Halloween mask and would never have worked with Giles if not for *the other thing.* Giles could not dispute his own eyes. The creature this mask purported to represent appeared out of thin air in the middle of his office.

He shrieked and grabbed the cushions of his chair.

Fwooomp! I vanished again.

"WHAT THE FUCK!" He frantically searched for what his brain denied that he had just seen. "WHAT THE FUCKING SHIT WAS THAT?" He scrambled to his feet.

"Sit down, Peter," Andy said, raising the weapon again. "Sit!"

Giles dropped to the cushion.

"I told you. We don't like the attention. Living among you serves our long-range purposes. Those purposes would be disrupted if we became something more than nerd fantasies on fringe websites, do you understand?"

"Bullshit! This is bullshit! You're messing with me!"

I tapped the floor and shot up to the ceiling where I used my palms to push myself to where Giles' exercise cycle had a nice view out the floor-to-ceiling windows. I grabbed the handlebar and positioned myself facing Giles, once again a fraction of an inch above the carpet.

Fwooomp!

He caught sight of me and screamed. He scrambled off his chair and backed up against the windows.

Fwooomp! I vanished again.

He pointed at the empty air I left behind and worked his mouth, unable to force out the words. I fought a full-bellied laugh inside the mask.

"Peter Giles, sit your ass down!" Andy commanded. He dropped back in his chair for a third time, clutching the leather as if he might fly out of it against his will.

"*Are you fucking shitting me?*" he squeaked.

"I am not," Andy said calmly. "Now listen to me very carefully. Peter. Peter, are you listening to me?"

His eyes bulged and watered. He frantically searched the room, looking for the next intrusion by the creature he'd seen but could not believe he'd seen.

"Peter!"

"What? Yes! I'm listening! *What the fuck was that?*"

"*That*...is who we are. We are here. We've been here for a long time. We don't like attention. And what you're doing is bringing us attention."

"*It was just a fucking con!* That's all. It was never meant to be real. People want to fucking believe this insane crap, fine. We just found a way to let them think it was all real." He shot his eyes around the room. "You gotta tell me! *What was that? Is it here? Is it in the room with us?*"

"Focus, Peter. The trusts? The lawyer?"

"What—? Shit, these were people with money. Idiots with money. We never imagined it would—I don't know! Interfere with you? *Who are you?*"

"That's not something you want to know, Peter. The people you conned.

The people at the ranch. I'm going to give you a chance to tell me what you did to make them disappear. Peter, are you listening to me?"

He looked ready to go over an edge from which he would not return. His hands shook. His jaw quivered. His breathing came and went in choppy bursts.

"Peter, are you listening to me?"

"*Yes! I told you—I'm listening!*"

"What did you do with the people you led to believe would be lifted off the planet by one of our ships? The people at that ranch?"

"I don't know," he whined. "That was Danzig. He did—"

"Peter, you're lying to me."

"You're holding a fucking gun on me with some kind of goddamned alien in the room, what do you expect?"

"The truth, Peter. Because this gun is the least of your worries. Lie to me again and my associate will take you. And you will be disassembled."

Yes! She used it! I didn't think she would. I pushed that part of the script hard. It sounded great coming from her.

"Disa-what?" Giles gasped.

"Disassembled, Peter. You will remain alive during the process. From what we've seen in the humans we have studied it is highly unpleasant."

This was too much for him. He bolted from the chair and made a dash for the door. I saw it coming an instant before it happened.

Fwooomp!

I lunged to intercept him. He saw me and screamed. He threw his hands up to ward me off. I didn't intend to fight him or grapple with him. The last thing I needed was for this plastic mask to be torn off.

I grabbed one flailing hand and locked a grip.

FWOOOMP!

We both disappeared. I lifted him. I knew what to expect. He didn't. Counterforce pressed my feet against the carpet. He flailed and pinwheeled. I reached for and grabbed a fistful of sleek fabric from his workout t-shirt. I heaved him upward and backward. At the limit of my reach, I released.

Fwooomp!

My hands absorbed an electric snap as he flashed out of *the other thing* in mid-flight. He sailed a few feet, then crashed to the floor. I rotated and prepared myself in case he made another dash for the door.

He didn't. He scrambled backward until his head and shoulders collided with the window. He lifted his hands in my general direction.

"Peter, there is no escape."

"*Please! No! I'll tell you everything!*"

Andy scooted forward on her chair and cradled the gun in both hands, letting the barrel aim safely at the carpet. He broke into a mix of mewling sound and harsh sobs.

"Say it, Peter." Andy coached him softly. "Say it."

"*We killed them! Alright? We killed them all!*"

"Danzig."

"*Yes! It was Danzig!*"

"In Lake Superior. So they'd never be found."

"*YES!*"

"Why?"

"FOR THE FUCKING MONEY!" he cried, snarled, screamed, sobbed at her. "FOR THE FUCKING MONEY!"

She waited. He covered his face. He sniffled and made high-pitched noises.

"*Puh-puh-please! Don't take me! We didn't know! WE DIDN'T KNOW YOU WERE REAL!*"

Andy gave him time. He gained a degree of calm, wiped the snot and the tears off his face and gathered great gulps of air.

After a few minutes she edged a little closer and said softly.

"You really are just a middle management dweeb, aren't you?"

He nodded. "*I am. I swear. That's all I am.*"

"Well, Peter, you're going to tell me who isn't. You're going to tell me who writes your paycheck. You're going to tell me everything."

Fwooomp!

I reappeared behind Andy, folded my arms, and aimed my big black alien eyes at him.

73

"Do you really think he will do it?" I asked after I started the car and rolled back onto one of L.A.'s fat boulevards.

Andy gazed ahead, thinking to herself. I know she heard the question because she offered a light shrug. What I didn't know was what she was feeling. For the second time in a few days, she had stepped far outside her professional and moral code.

"Or do you think he'll tip him off?"

"I don't think he'll tip him off. The other part, not so sure."

Before leaving Giles' office, I stepped around Andy's chair and walked to where Giles remained on the floor. The mask was a good one, but not perfect. I didn't want him to look at it for too long. I grabbed one of the hands he put up to ward me off.

Fwooomp!

I made us both vanish again. This time I didn't lift him. I reached for his head, found it, and shoved my hand down the back of his neck. I used my thumb and forefinger to pinch his skin between my nails—nails which make Andy deeply jealous because they are incredibly hard and rigid. I twisted. He shrieked. Later I found blood under the nail.

We had begun to float. I released him again. He reappeared and dropped to the floor with a hard thump. I let myself drift up and out of his reach.

This was my part of the script. I rotated and lowered my head toward him. I spoke evenly. In rehearsal I tried using the same voice I used on Martian Mike, but Andy could not stop laughing.

"I placed a chip in your spine" I said. "Remove it and your body will shut down. You will automatically disassemble. Do you understand?"

He ducked away from the disembodied voice and tried to reach behind his back. "Why? Why did you do this to me?"

"To track you, to hear you, to know your thoughts. My associate will give you instructions. You will obey the instructions, or you will be disassembled. Indicate to me that you understand."

"I understand! Yes! I do!"

Andy said, "Peter, listen to me very carefully. The moment we leave here, you will gather your wits and go to the airport. You will buy a ticket to Billings, Montana, and you will fly there on the first available flight. You will take a cab to the Division of Criminal Investigation at the Montana Department of Justice. There, you will tell them everything. Everything. Repeat it to me."

"Why?" A hint resistance brewed behind his eyes. "Why do you want that?"

"Repeat it to me or my associate will give you a hint of what you will feel if we decide to disassemble you."

He blurted the instructions back at Andy.

I jumped in again. "Remember. We don't want the attention. We don't want people believing we are real. You will explain that what you did was a hoax and how the people from the ranch were taken and disposed of."

"Are you shitting me? They'll charge me with murder! And if that doesn't stick, the people I work for will have me killed!"

"Not our concern, Peter," Andy said. "But you're a smart guy, right? An operator? You set all this up. You'll think of a way to protect yourself. Make a deal."

"And if I don't."

"The chip will tell us," I said. "And you will be disassembled. Simple."

Andy punctuated the point with a smile.

"THANK you for doing the bit about Montana. I'll let Richardson know. And if Giles doesn't show, who to look for," Andy said.

She gazed out the windshield. I didn't expect celebration, even though I thought what we had done deserved one. The gambit seemed like a huge success to me. I wasn't sure she saw it the same way. Her subdued affect had me worried.

"Look, Dee, I know that this isn't your methodology. First, the Connellys. Now the dweeb. All this theater—I know it runs against your grain. But sometimes it's the only way. These guys were smart. That thing with Lake Superior, Jesus, that's going to be nearly impossible to prove."

She didn't answer.

"But I did like hoaxing the hoaxers."

Still no answer. I decided to just drive. Half a block later, her hand slid across the center console and found mine on the shifter.

"You want to know what the problem is?" She closed a warm grip on my hand. "The problem is that this *is* the only way. I deal with people who lie quicker than their next breath, people who abandoned accountability when they were in the crib. People who have so much money that they can spend more on lawyers filing a single motion than someone like me will make in a lifetime. Buying justice. Delaying—no, *decaying* cases that were marginal to start with until we can't get a jury past the word 'doubt.' I'm not endorsing vigilante justice, but *I am one hundred percent clear that there is zero chance of bringing this whole mess before a prosecutor.* The problem is that what I believe in doesn't work."

"That's not true." I looked over at her. She did not meet my eyes. "Seriously, Dee, that is *not true.*"

She sighed. "I know. I know it's not true. But here's the other problem." Now she did meet my eyes. "And I don't know what to do about this one."

"What?"

"I liked what we just did."

I knew better than to cheer, but I felt a weight lifted. She would never change the core principles that guided her. She would never forsake the profession she loved. But for the first time since the accident, I felt that she saw in me and *the other thing* a weapon that had a place in her arsenal.

She squeezed my hand again.

"Let's go back to the hotel. I'd like to do a little research on what the dweeb just told us."

74

This had a familiar feel to it. A high wall. A gate. A guardhouse with an armed guard inside. My reconnaissance of Bargo Litton's estate in the desert had been entirely via *the other thing*. This time the approach vehicle was a rented Nissan with Andy at the wheel and me clutching the seatbelt beside her so that I wouldn't float off the seat. To the guard peering out of his air-conditioned hut the woman who pulled up to his station was alone.

"Morning, ma'am. Can I help you?" I pegged him for a retired officer, but not just a beyond-the-prime rent-a-cop. He wore his shirt tight so that the product of his gym membership could be displayed. The sidearm at his hip used a standard law enforcement issue holster that balanced security with quick access. His eyes were keen. He swept the inside of the car, including the back seat, before he allowed himself to check out the attractive woman behind the wheel.

Andy lifted her badge.

"Detective Andrea Stewart, Essex Police Department. It's in Wisconsin, since you're about to ask."

He smiled. "In addition to being out of your jurisdiction, I can tell you without looking that you're not on the roster for today."

"And you would be correct, officer. Or was it sergeant?"

"It was Lieutenant. Nevada Highway Patrol, Detective." The smile remained and looked sincere. "You have a good eye, but it doesn't get you in the gate. Sorry."

"You wouldn't be doing your job if you let just anyone through. Please

303

ring the administrative assistant inside and tell them that someone is here to speak to Mr. Dodge about how he will not be using the ParaTransit trusts to evade a critical shortfall in his short bias strategy, and that if he is not interested in discussing it, I will be leaving here and driving directly to the regulatory office of someone who will be very interested."

"Well, well. Sounds like Essex is not to be mistaken for Mayberry."

"That would be correct."

He ducked back into his hut and picked up a phone.

Ten minutes later the electric gate parted.

WE WERE MET at the front door of the massive Malibu beach home by a pair of similarly uniformed security officers and a woman in a business suit that included a man's shirt and tie. Her silky hair hung long, straight, and jet black. Her eyes suggested Asian genealogy. The suit suppressed feminine curves. She had a severe, unsmiling face which made guessing her age a challenge.

We knew that entry to the house would be the most difficult part, so I prepared for it on the way up the driveway by crawling out the open sunroof of the car. I gripped the frame until Andy rolled to a stop. She took her time releasing her seatbelt—time I used to shove off on a shot toward the house. The architecture was modern. White walls. Curves. Lots of glass. Not conducive to handholds, but a light fixture beside the door provided a nice grip. Andy crossed the front grille of the car and walked as far as the two uniformed guards would allow.

"Keys, please." One of the two security guards held out a hand.

"Your car will be moved back down to the gatehouse. It will be returned to you when you leave," the woman in the business suit said.

"A reasonable precaution," Andy said. She handed over the keys. The security guard hustled for the driver's door like a pro parking valet.

"Detective Stewart, my name is Lin. I am Mr. Dodge's executive assistant. How do you do?" The woman looked and sounded polite, but I sensed resentment for the interruption to her day.

"Very well, thank you."

"And what is your business with Mr. Dodge?" she asked.

"None of yours, Ms. Lin."

Standoff. The Nissan was already rolling. I wondered if they would call the driver back or if they would make Andy walk back to the car. If the latter, I would have to deploy a BLASTER to catch up.

"I handle Mr. Dodge's affairs, Detective. Any business you have with him, you first have with me."

"I see. Then can I assume you're willing to be prosecuted along with your boss?"

"I think your business here is finished. Your car will be returned shortly."

"ParaTransit, Ms. Lin. If you're familiar with the word, you will know that what I have to say to Mr. Dodge is worth his time. If you are not familiar with the word, then you will learn that Mr. Dodge does not make you privy to all his interests, and when you send us away without his consent, the consequences will fall on you."

"Us?"

"Excuse me?"

"You said, 'us.' Who are you referring to?"

Shit. Andy had slipped up.

"Mr. Dodge will know."

Lin stared at Andy. Andy didn't move.

"I'll speak to Mr. Dodge. Wait here."

Lin went inside, which helped because I gained a sense of how far and fast the front door moved. I needed to position myself to the left of the door and be ready to pull myself in at the top. The door reached a height of eight feet, which provided clearance above anyone entering.

We waited. Andy didn't move. The remaining security guard didn't move. After two or three minutes I sensed that it had become a contest between them, like a tourist facing one of the Queen's Guards. I suspected Lin of playing a game, making Andy wait, but the door popped back open in relatively short order. Lin did not appear. Another security guard appeared, this one a woman. She also didn't open the door wide enough for me. She called for Andy to follow her.

Andy stayed still for one more breath, then winked at the security guard who smiled back, calling it a draw.

The woman at the door pushed the big door slightly wider, but still not enough. I hung on the light fixture.

Andy grabbed the door handle and pulled it wide open. A little excessive on its face but the move let me grab the jamb and swing myself inside.

The interior of this beach property looked more like a modern art museum than a home. Marble stretched in every direction under curving white walls and banks of glass that showcased a view of Malibu Beach and the Pacific Ocean. Artwork decorated the walls, along with tastefully placed sculptures. The front door opened on a huge room that blended into other huge spaces with no defining borders. A dome overhead provided frosted sunlight. To my right, in a side space, I saw the front bumper of a classic red sports car. The chrome and paint looked factory new. If a fingerprint was to be found on the finish, I suspected someone would lose their job.

"Ma'am, stop here please." The female security guard held up a stop sign hand and stepped in front of her. Andy had anticipated this part and left her bag with the Glock 26 in the trunk of the car. "May I have your sunglasses, please?"

Andy handed them over. The guard slid them into her pocket.

"I will be conducting a very close, personal search of your person. If this is not acceptable, your business here will be concluded. Is that understood?"

"Affirmative."

"Do you have any electronic devices on your person?"

"No."

"Do you wear hearing aids?"

"No."

"Please remove your wrist watch."

Andy complied.

"Please remove your shoes."

Andy complied.

"Please open your blouse."

Andy complied. The search began and it was thorough. I can't say I was pleased, but I would have been furious if it had been conducted by some leering male rent-a-cop. The woman conducting the search was quick and efficient and missed nothing. Andy stood at attention. At the end, Andy re-buttoned her blouse and repositioned her skirt. She brushed down her hair, which had been carefully probed.

"I will return your shoes, watch, and glasses to you outside."

During the search process, I handled a small piece of business of my own. I had a BLASTER in hand from the time I left the car. I used it to cruise slowly, quietly to a high ledge that concealed recessed lighting. I pulled Andy's phone from my pocket and laid it on the ledge, then carefully released my fingers. It snapped into view. I swiped the screen and opened the camera app, then touched the video button and ensured that it began recording. Orienting it properly with the lens facing outward, I covered the phone with my hands, careful not to touch the screen or any of the side buttons. The device disappeared.

I rotated and maneuvered down to Andy's level. The female security guard left Andy where she stood. A moment later, Lin appeared from the direction of the adjoining room that overlooked the ocean.

"This way, please."

I used near silent BLASTER power to follow Andy. She crossed the floor and walked into a room roughly the size of a small gymnasium. The space contained only four pieces of furniture—four antique dining room chairs, utterly out of place within the white walls, marble floors and glass vista.

A man sat in one of the chairs with one leg crossed, watching Andy. He wore blue jeans, a black t-shirt, and sandals. His black hair looked like it had been slicked back with tractor grease. He wore round wire-rimmed glasses, the kind once favored by John Lennon. I found no jewelry, not on his hands or around his neck. He did not wear a watch. He wasn't heavy, but he had a gut that a steady regimen of walking would probably eliminate.

He matched any of a dozen photos Andy had shown me on her laptop in our hotel room last night. He dressed the same in every photo. Apparently, this was his favored look for the media.

"Are you a hooker?" he asked Andy. "You look like a hooker."

Okay. Plan B. I lift you up and throw you in the ocean.

"Then you must spend a fortune on hookers, Mr. Dodge."

I glided in behind Andy. Lin peeled off and left the room through what looked like the curved entrance to a maze.

"What do you want with me? I don't have time for bullshit."

"Or pleasantries, apparently." Andy approached the back of one of the four chairs, which sat in a square facing each other. She remained standing. I could not imagine what this arrangement was about. Maybe there had been a table here. Maybe rich people are just off their nut. Dodge did not rise.

"If this is fucking blackmail, you're barking up the wrong tree. Are you really a cop?"

"You haven't confirmed it by now?"

"Fine. Yeah. I know who you are. You're in some shit with the President's loyal minions." He laughed. "Just when I think they're as dumb as a box of rocks, they do something that lowers my opinion."

"I didn't come here to discuss me."

"No. You said something about ParaTransit. Never heard of it."

"Then how did mentioning it get me past your gatekeeper?"

"Call it curiosity. Whaddya got? Because I'm busy."

"Myron Dodge. Hedge fund manager. A George Sorros wannabe. I think that's what *Forbes* called you. Not quite the raging success of a Sorros or Dalio."

"If you came to insult me, you're going to have to do better than quote *Forbes*."

HOWARD SEABORNE

"I didn't come to insult you."

"Then get to the point."

"You created an entity called ParaTransit, a blend of new wave boutique cult and UFO lore packaged for wealthy believers who want a seat on the mothership but who don't want to leave their assets to chance if the ship doesn't arrive as promised. You hired a quasi-scientific clown named Martian Mike to steer the marks to ParaTransit. You conned a woman in Montana with phony crop circles, using Martian Mike to grease the wheels, and then you steered the wealthy UFO believers down a path to the ultimate communal experience in the Montana wilds, all the time assuring them that if nothing happens, they'll be back in time for The Masters at Augusta, *but if something does happen* their assets will be protected by a series of trusts that you helped them establish. I don't purport to be a financial expert, but I'm willing to guess that when all these people mysteriously disappear, those trusts wind up getting lost in a financial fog that eventually puts the money in your hands."

He laughed.

"Wow. Fucking unbelievable. Do you have any idea how much money I have? How much money I control? It starts with a B. Ripping off some seniors who have a few bucks in a mutual fund is not worth my time. Get lost."

"Stephanie Cullen. Tammy Day. Alan Westman. You're up over three hundred million with those three alone. Shall I go on? Because I bet you've already seen the spreadsheet."

Dodge's face reddened slightly. "Still doesn't trip my trigger. That wouldn't cause a ripple."

"That's a lie. The analysts looking at your fund have been putting the squeeze on your numbers for some time. You've got a few problems that a cash infusion might not solve, but it would certainly help keep the dogs at bay."

"Who made you an expert?"

"Google. A few hours of surfing the web last night. And if a lowly cop like me can put the pieces together, what's *Bloomberg* going to say? Or *The Wall Street Journal*? You're in some deep shit, Mr. Dodge. It wasn't that hard to find."

"The markets go up and down by the minute."

"But stink doesn't go away quickly. There's been a stink on you for a while, hasn't there. It's getting harder for you to play the wunderkind and draw investors. I read the *Kiplinger's* story—when was it published? Six months ago? Not good."

308

"Whatever. This bullshit you brought in here is pure fantasy."

"Not according to Peter Giles."

"Giles? He's—"

"A middle management dweeb. We know. Carl Danzig describes him that way. You know Carl, don't you Mr. Dodge?"

"Never heard of him."

"Well, he knows you."

Andy's bold lie caused the red in Dodge's face to deepen. I admired her bluff, but I didn't think he would fall for it.

Dodge stopped speaking for a moment. He took a deep breath and leaned back in his chair. His jaw shifted back and forth a couple times, as if warming it up. He snorted.

"It...gets...tiresome...people like you."

Andy said nothing.

"It's like... I don't know. Imagine a physicist trying to explain a bouncing ball to a preschooler. You can't grasp wealth at my level. What it's like trying to get it through the heads of people like you. People try all the absurd analogies, like how many million dollars you would have to make each day for how many thousands of years or some such bullshit. Pathetic attempts to define wealth. Do you want to know the only way to put it in perspective? To truly describe *wealth*?"

He stood up. I guessed him to be about Andy's height, which made him smaller than me. I didn't think he would be stupid enough to get physical, but I wasn't prepared to take the risk. If he came anywhere near her, I'd go with Plan B.

"Tell me."

He strolled away from her to the window. He stared out at the hundred-million-dollar view the way Boyd stared through the windshield of the Prius. Seeing without seeing what the rest of the world saw.

"Those nine people with their real estate investments and portfolios and piddly little crap—yeah it added up to almost seven hundred million—those nine people, I fucking wiped them off the face of the earth and no one can do a damned thing about it. You can't. I'm standing here telling you, sure, it's all true, congratulations, you figured it out, and do you know why? Because who are you gonna tell? They're at the bottom of goddamned Lake Superior." He laughed. "Who would have guessed that a stupid pop song describes the perfect murder? And the rest of it? Try to get a jury to figure it out. People are fucking idiots. Residual Trust Management? Equity Allocation Clauses? The paperwork alone would bury a grand jury for years. And think about it—a jury of my peers? Where're you gonna find that? The pool you have to select from is the same fucking pool that believes you were part of a plot by a major political party to assassinate the President. Jesus! Massive stupidity is the only thing less comprehensible than my wealth."

He turned to face Andy.

"And this? My confession to a police officer? Don't get your hopes up, Detective. You can't record this. Think you can testify to this conversation? You were never here. My security logs show no visitors for today. I can produce a dozen reputable witnesses who will confirm that I was in Singapore at this very hour. Or Dubai. Or wherever I choose. If you're expecting me to play the villain and threaten to erase you from the planet the way I erased those nine fools, don't flatter yourself. You don't matter. If you take this anywhere, you'll just be made to look like the crazy that the White House has been suggesting you are. I don't have to lift a finger. You'll do it to yourself. That's got to be eating you up. You need an answer, or you wouldn't have come here. Would you like the *real, true, absolute answer* to your impotent accusation?"

Andy said nothing.

"It's...*so what? So...fucking...what?*"

The red in his face reached full bloom.

"SO FUCKING WHAT? What are you gonna do about it? You can't touch me. You can't get an indictment. I never heard of ParaTransit, or Peter Giles, or Carl Danzig or fucking Tammy Day or any of them. Their money didn't go in my pocket, it went into financial instruments so complicated that half of Wharton's faculty couldn't unravel it. You were never here. I never heard of you. What're you gonna do? Get some minimum wage county prosecutor to devote his career to putting together a case that will just get thrown out after seven years by the fourth appeal that I—or I should say my army of lawyers—files? Shit, I'll probably never even hear about it."

He took two steps toward Andy. I tensed.

"You'd have to get me to stand up in front of a stadium full of judges and confess with my hand on a Bible before you'd have a chance of winning. That's never gonna fucking happen. And this? Here? Now? You and me? Fuck. You're just another stalker. A nutjob. So, like I said before...get lost."

He turned and walked to the chair he'd been sitting on. He planted one hand on the chair and shoved it across the marble. It hit the glass wall but failed to shatter glass or even tip and fall if that was his intent.

"LIN!" he shouted as he marched out.

A minute later, Lin appeared and ushered Andy out.

· · ·

ANDY PULLED OVER HALF a mile down the road. She held out her hand. I dropped her phone into her palm.

Fwooomp!

I reappeared and settled into the seat. She let the Nissan idle by the roadside while she played the video. I leaned over and watched.

"Pretty damned good for not being able to see what I was doing. Check out that framing. Nice."

"I don't think Tarantino needs to worry."

"I was scared to death I'd push the wrong button."

"You get a gold star, love." The video ended with me fumbling with the phone after Dodge's chair tantrum.

Andy opened a new app and busily thumbed the screen.

"What are you doing?"

She lifted her face and issued a sweet yet deadly smile.

EPILOGUE I

I told Andy I needed to return to The Gash. Myron Dodge, who found himself on the front pages of nearly every newspaper in the country after his confessional video reached the editorial offices of *The Wall Street Journal* and half a dozen other news outlets, may have planned on pushing a false narrative about The Gash in his next hoax-based scheme, but I could not deny what happened to me when Boyd and I walked that channel in the woods. The notion of returning did not please my wife, nor did she jump for joy when I told her I wanted Lillian to go with me. Andy interpreted the proposal as me leaning toward some of Lillian's unearthly ideas. I told Andy I made no assumptions about what lay hidden in that deadfall, nor could I leave the question unanswered. I suggested she come as well. She told me she would think about it. The question was answered for her when Tom Ceeves ordered his Detective to stay away from the office, citing the furor that erupted around arresting Sheryl and Lester Connelly.

Andy tracked down Lillian's Prius, which had been towed by the Oconto County Sheriff's Office. She arranged for the towing fee and abandoned vehicle fine to be paid, and had the vehicle released for pickup, a roundabout process that began with Pidge flying Andy and me back to Marquette, Michigan where we picked up Lillian and her ward.

I let Pidge do the flying. Andy and I occupied the club seats in the cabin. We talked all the way to Upper Michigan. About Lillian. About what I thought we might find on the second leg of this trip. About the equipment I

ost*

brought along. And about the way I intended to handle Lillian if, as Andy put it, she went off the deep end.

Lillian and Boyd met us at the Marquette airport. When Andy fetched them from the FBO office, Boyd scooped up her hand and walked beside her as they crossed the airport ramp.

I waited beside the airplane. "Look at you! Are you ready for an airplane ride, Boyd Wonder?"

"My name is Boyd Farris." I caught Lillian smiling.

"Indeed, it is. But you will always be a wonder to me."

I could not tell if Boyd enjoyed the flight or not. He strapped in and plastered his nose to the window and did not move until the airplane came to a stop in Oconto and Lillian released his seatbelt. During the flight, I saw the same sky he studied, yet I wondered how amazing and different it must be seen through his eyes and processed by his mind.

Andy accompanied Lillian and Boyd off the Oconto ramp and into the FBO office to line up a ride into town. I circled around to the nose baggage compartment and popped the hatch.

"You want me to come along? Lend a hand?" Pidge asked. I lifted the big plastic case from the compartment and handed it to her, then untied the straps that secured a one-gallon plastic gas container and a canvas bag.

"Nah, I got this."

"Right. Seriously? You're not going to tell me what you're doing? Or why you're pretending to be Paul Fucking Bunyan?"

I closed the hatch and double-checked the latches.

"If this works, I'll let you buy me a beer and pry it outta me."

I took the case from her and told her not to prang my airplane on the flight home.

UBER DELIVERED us from the airport to the Oconto County Sheriff's Office. Andy handled the paperwork. A deputy escorted her to the lot behind the county jail building. A few minutes later she parked the Prius on Washington Street adjacent the Sheriff's Department entrance. She met Lillian on the sidewalk and handed her the key that had been on Andy's desk since Boyd arrived in Essex. Lillian popped the trunk. I loaded my gear. Boyd called shotgun without a word by claiming the front passenger seat. His map squares littered the floor, but he showed no interest in them. Andy and I slid onto the back seat.

Half an hour later, after stopping to fill the near empty gas tank, we pulled over at a familiar spot on an empty country road. The pavement was clean and dry compared to the night Boyd navigated the Prius through a snowstorm. Since then, another snowfall brought an additional four inches, more than enough to eliminate any chance of finding the BLASTERs or the Ray Bans I had been forced to abandon. I carried two spare power units in my pockets, but still wasted a few minutes searching.

"Forget about them," Andy said. "It's getting dark."

Lillian agreed. "I want to see this while we can still see."

Boyd offered no comment. He stood patiently beside the Prius.

"Is it okay to leave the car like this?" Lillian asked. "It got towed last time."

"After sitting here for days." Andy scanned the landscape around us. "Somebody owns the property, but I'm not seeing a candidate."

"Are we trespassing?" Lillian asked.

"We are. But I'm afraid this is a 'forgiveness before permission' operation."

Lillian popped the trunk. I extracted my equipment. Andy volunteered to take the gas can. I carried the plastic case and canvas shoulder bag.

I turned to Boyd. "Okay, Kiddo. Lead the way."

The boy corrected me again, slow learner that I am, and stepped off.

WE DESCENDED into the woods as light drained from the overcast skies above us. Our footsteps crunched the snow and the dry sticks and leaves beneath the snow. Boyd took point, accurately retracing the path we had taken before. When we entered the channel in the woods, Lillian stopped. She looked both ways.

"My God," she whispered. "I never imagined..." Even Andy seemed impressed, though she offered no comment.

I pulled my iPad from the canvas bag. I launched the ForeFlight app and selected the map page. A touch of the screen planted a waypoint at our present position. Next, I selected a user waypoint I had previously entered. The program scribed a magenta course line between the two points. I held up the device for Andy and Lillian to see.

"Look. Dead center."

The line connected the ground we stood on to the spot in Essex where the fire department found me strapped to my pilot's seat with a broken pelvis —the point of impact where Earl Jackson's Piper Navajo had been torn out of the sky.

The course on the screen matched the channel cut through the forest.

This forest was the other end of the crash scene.

Boyd resumed his advance down the center of the channel, skirting the stumps we had avoided the last time. The rest of us followed in his tracks.

The *need* began to stir halfway to the terminus.

Andy sensed my change of pace. "You okay?"

"It's starting."

"Should we stop?"

"No."

We marched another thirty yards.

"This is as far as I can go."

Lillian drew up beside me. She pointed at the deadfall terminus.

"Are you seeing this?"

At the end of the channel less than fifty yards away, beneath tumbled dead trees, I made out a faint outline—a hidden circular image within an image—the kind you cannot unsee once you've seen it.

Ahead, I saw the airport beacon, but the itch I couldn't scratch loomed to one side, dark and empty. A black hole, into which memories were sucked as if by irresistible gravitational force.

I took a step forward. The *need* grew exponentially stronger. I dropped the plastic case. Andy lowered the gas can to the snow and touched my arm.

The levers in my head crept forward, propelled by an overwhelming impulse to vanish.

"Get ready."

Boyd abruptly turned. He ran to me and threw his arms around my waist.

FWOOOMP!

We vanished together.

"Boyd!" Lillian called out.

Boyd laughed. He wiggled into position at my side. I hooked my arm with his, just to be sure.

"It's alright," I told her. "He's fine. I've got him. Keep going."

The *need* vanished with me. Winter chill ceased to seep through my clothes. My skin felt both cool and warm in the same instant. I tapped my toes. Boyd and I broke away from the snow-covered ground. I pulled a BLASTER from my pocket and fixed the prop in place. The device hummed and harmonized with the laughter sparkling in the air. We surged forward.

I felt light. Unburdened. Maybe it was Boyd's giggling. Maybe it was relief from the all-consuming *need* that flooded me. Whatever it was, I felt—

Joy.

We climbed, quickly topping the trees. I added power.

"What do you say we have a look at this thing?"

Boyd didn't answer. Above the treetops we swung left in a wide circle.

The gentle turn took us over the pasture, over the winding creek, and halfway across the winter wheat field. We climbed to nearly two hundred feet. As we came back around, the scar in the forest stretched out like a runway.

The Gash.

Snow on the forest floor revealed the feature in stark relief.

I lined up as if for landing. Andy and Lillian stood in the channel searching for the sound of the BLASTER. Boyd and I swooped down and raced through the air. My eyes watered from the speed. We caught up to the two women and shot over their heads. Their upturned faces followed the ghostly laughter of a child.

I threw the BLASTER into reverse and applied full power. The prop screamed. We drew up short of the stacked black trunks and limbs and stopped. I cut the power before reverse thrust sent us back the way we had come.

Boyd's crystalline voice broke the fresh silence of the forest around us.

"The force of gravity cannot be felt. It is not a contact force. It is an at-a-distance force."

We hung in the air near enough to the tilted trunks to touch the naked branches.

"Matter in an altered state."

He spoke like a child repeating something heard on television; atonal words delivered without emphasis or understanding. Except I had the feeling Boyd's understanding extended well beyond anything I could imagine.

"Matter in an altered state. The force of gravity cannot be felt."

"You might be right, Kiddo."

"My name is not Kiddo. My name is Boyd Farris."

"Amen, brother."

"Your name is Will Stewart."

"That's me."

I felt a curious urge to hug the kid, despite knowing that a physical expression of affection may mean nothing to him.

"Your altered state is interesting," he said.

"Finally. I meet your high standards."

"It's a life support system."

"What?"

He didn't answer.

"What did you say?"

Nothing. I felt movement. I tucked the BLASTER in my pocket and traced my hand down his arm to where his forearm made short, jerky movements. I found his hands, then his busy fingers. He ignored my touch. His fingers danced and spoke a language I could not understand.

What's sign language if you can't see it? What else? The boy was talking to himself.

Andy and Lillian approached. I turned us to face them and descended until our feet sank into the snow. I released my hold on Boyd.

Fwooomp!

Boyd reappeared without missing a syllable of his busy messaging. Lillian watched his fingers fly, then smiled and joined the sign language conversation with rapid strokes of her own.

I tried pulling the levers back to reappear, but they resisted. I could make them move, but with movement came increased resistance to a point where they wouldn't budge.

A note of panic tightened my chest.

What if you can't get back out?

I took a breath and shoved the thought aside.

I rotated and faced the deadfall. Toppled trees angled upward and extended well above my head. Half a dozen trunks lay on top of each other. The pile appeared to rest on nothing. The image within an image.

A hole. A void.

At the base of the void, a circle of dry leaves four feet in diameter formed a dry carpet. Not a single snowflake had reached those leaves.

I moved forward and almost didn't notice that for the first time, after trying for months, I made *the other thing* move me in a direction I wanted to go. Without a power unit. Without pushing off from a fixed object. Without thinking.

I stretched out my hand.

I touched it.

I tried breaking hard right to steer around it. The yoke turned but the airplane remained on course. My hands slid on the controls, wet, shaking. The emptiness, the thing I couldn't remember hit the left wing. Sudden. Explosive. The left wing vanished along with the side of the cockpit. I flew on with the wind ripping at my clothes. Pieces of the airplane dropped off, cast down into the countryside like discarded litter. The wind wrapped itself around me now, penetrating my clothes, my skin. It became a living sheath, cool and fresh-feeling, and it lifted me against the seat belt. And now I knew that the seat belt would tear me in half because the airplane was falling away around me.

I pressed my hand flat against the unseen object. The surface felt smooth with a fine sandpaper finish. I pressed, expecting to be pushed away, but was surprised that the core muscle running down my center, the one that now answered to my wishes, held me in place. The object's skin beneath my fingers gave way like Styrofoam.

Spiro Lewko, standing in my driveway with his ridiculous Harley jacket and Harley bike, had described it.

"Nothing special." He shrugged. "Seriously. Nothing out of the ordinary. We thought, maybe this is it. Maybe this establishes proof of an advanced civilization. We thought we might find an element that could not be sourced here on Earth. But no. It's nothing special. A variation on the same stuff that made the tiles for the space shuttle. Any half-assed lab with a dozen MIT grads could create it."

I once read that the tiles that protected the space shuttle from burning up in the atmosphere could be dented by the touch of a finger.

Precisely what I felt under my hand. Light. Insubstantial. Easily damaged. Then how did this thing tear a path through tree trunks up to ten inches in diameter?

"Lillian, come here. I'm right beside it."

She stepped forward and bumped into me. The core muscle held me in place. I didn't move. She patted her hands over my back, my shoulders, and my arms to determine my position.

"Here." I took her hand and pressed it forward. "Feel it?"

"Holy Mother of God!" She probed with both hands.

"Andy, come here! Touch this!"

Andy moved as if traversing a mine field. She hesitantly held out her arm. Lillian reached back and guided her hand to the surface of the object.

Fear or wonder—it was hard to tell which—enveloped my wife's face.

"Will...what is it?"

"I think this is it, Dee. This is what I hit."

"What's it doing here?"

"Best guess—the collision knocked it here from the point of impact. Straight as an arrow. It came down here and cut a path through the trees."

I ran my hand over surface bumps, protrusions, vanes. I now understood the piece that Lewko had in his possession. The angles and shapes under my fingers matched the shape his team of researchers had mapped in three dimensions.

"I don't understand," I said. "It's as soft as Styrofoam. I can dent it with my finger. How did it survive the impact? How did something this soft tear apart the airplane? The prop alone should have shredded it."

"Poke it," Lillian said. She jabbed a finger forward.

I followed suit.

"Ouch!" I did it a second time. Where my finger made contact, the surface hardened. I pulled back and made a fist and pounded. My fist slammed into solid steel. A second later, I touched the same spot and felt it give.

"What the hell?"

Lillian said, "This material has properties that translate kinetic energy into tensile strength. The harder you hit it, the harder it becomes. When this thing hit your airplane, it might have reached a material strength exceeding compressed carbon."

"Compressed what?"

"Harder than diamonds."

"No wonder it flattened the left wing and engine."

Andy pulled back her hand. "I don't think we should be touching it."

"Nonsense," Lillian replied.

"Lillian, this thing could belong to the U.S. Air Force or the Russians or the Chinese."

"Oh, I completely disagree. No, this is more like the couple hundred million dollars-worth of junk that we've dropped on the moon, or Mars, or crashed into Venus."

"Are you saying this is a NASA probe?"

"I very much doubt this belongs to NASA. But yes, same idea."

Andy watched Lillian poke and stroke the object. A grin bloomed on the woman's face, the inverse of Andy's worried expression.

"What are you saying?"

"The obvious. This isn't from around here."

Andy shook her head.

Here we go...

"How is that an outrageous idea, Andrea? Change your perspective. You're out tilling your red dirt field on Mars one day when a parachute blooms overhead and a crazy little mechanical thing lands in your yard. A door opens and a goofy wheeled device with a NASA decal pops out and starts poking around. How is this any different? We've been doing this very thing for decades."

"Hardly the same."

"Exactly the same. Just better technology deployed over greater distances."

"Then I repeat," Andy said, "we should not be touching it. This has properties we can't begin to understand."

"So does your husband. And I would argue that the properties of this thing transferred to your husband for the purpose of saving his life."

I looked at the autistic child who had ceased his messaging and had wandered away from what might be the most significant object on the surface of the earth.

"Boyd said something to me. When we were flying just now," I said.

"I know," Lillian acknowledged. "He told me, too. He said, 'It's a life support system.'"

"I thought he meant *this*." I patted the surface of the object none of us could see. "But I think he meant *the other thing*."

"He did. He had quite a bit to say about flying with you—about the thermal properties, the abeyance of gravity, inertia. An altered state of matter, he called it. I think he's right. He'd like a look at your subatomic structure when you disappear."

"Can it be that simple? Did this thing throw me a life preserver when we collided?"

"How is that possible?" Andy asked. "Why would it do that to you?"

"Beats the alternative," Lillian said. "Maybe this object or something inside it did the math and could not accept an outcome that involved killing you."

"What...*you're saying this thing acted consciously to save Will?*"

"Consciously, or automatically. Programmed to protect an organic being..." Lillian mused. "Programmed to do no harm..."

"That's a big assumption, Lillian," Andy said.

"You got a better answer?"

Andy ignored Lillian's challenge. "Will, could you please just...reappear?"

"I tried. I can't. It's the proximity. I can't get out of it."

"The failsafe is still armed. You're still connected," Lillian said. "I bet if you go back a hundred yards, you'll be fine."

"Why isn't it affecting us?" Andy asked.

"It didn't hit us at high speed," Lillian replied. "We're not falling out of the sky. Genius. It's pure genius."

"I don't like this." Andy took a step back.

Lillian paid no attention. "We need to take some measurements. And get a sample. I wonder why a piece of it broke off and ended up in your airplane? I bet that was a low impact event within the high impact collision. If we can take—"

"Lillian," I interrupted, "we're not doing any of that. We're not taking samples. We're not calling the Air Force or SETI or Martian Mike Enterprises. We're not tying it to the top of the Prius and driving back to Essex. Dee, would you go back and get the equipment?"

"Wait!" Lillian did not move. "What are you doing?"

"We're cutting this thing loose."

"And then what?"

"And then," I pressed my hand flat against the surface, thinking I might feel something that would back my play, "and then we're letting it leave."

"Say that again?"

"You heard me. We're cutting it loose."

"Stewart, you—!" She froze. I recognized the rigid posture I'd seen the first and second times I met her, when she tried to order me and Andy to upend our lives and go off the grid.

Andy squared herself to Lillian, prepared for the fight we both antici-pated. The Lillian Farris full-court press. Arguments about the scientific evidence, the technology, the advancement this might mean to humankind's store of knowledge. I expected to be called a dumbass. Worse.

Lillian drew a sharp breath, setting the fuse for her barrage. I braced. Andy tensed. The forest held its breath in silence around us.

Lillian did not speak or move. Her gaze drifted to an empty middle distance.

After a moment of imitating a statue, she turned and walked back to the nearest severed stump. She sat down and loosened a scarf around her neck. She released a long and thought-filled sigh.

"You're right."

I reached for and dropped a grip on Andy's shoulder. Her hand rose to cover mine.

"I'm right?"

"Yes. You're right." Lillian nodded. "We need to cut it loose."

"That's it? No argument? No protest?" I scarcely dared to ask. "Not that I want a fight, but…why?"

"What's the catch?" Andy asked guardedly.

"Maybe later. Maybe over shots I'll give you both an earful. But no. You're right."

Lillian couldn't see me, but she read the distrust on Andy's face.

"What? You think I'm not thrilled to find something like this? This is everything I've argued, everything I've believed in nearly all my adult life. And here it is. And you know what?" She shrugged. "I don't need to prove anything to anyone."

"I can't believe I'm asking this, but…are you sure?" Andy asked. "You're not going to change your mind and go all 'scientific find of the century' on us behind our backs, are you?"

"Trust me, I fully comprehend the significance of this." Lillian chuckled.

"It's funny, but in the academic sense, this isn't a scientific revelation. The tech might be, but its presence isn't. Anyone with half a brain knows that this dumb little orb we're on can't be the only host of life in the universe. That's like a blind blade of grass thinking it's the only life in the lawn."

"And you're okay with not getting your picture on the cover of *Scientific American*?" I asked.

"Please. I don't need to prove the obvious. I've proven it to myself. It's here. I was right. That's enough. That's why you brought me here, isn't it?"

"Maybe..." I conceded.

"Do you think there's someone inside?" Andy asked.

"I doubt it," Lillian replied. "More likely it's just tech like our research probes. Voyager. Viking. Pathfinder. The Sojourner rover. You know, the Russians have sent almost a dozen probes to Mars. Look at everything we've sent. And that's to a dead planet. Earth is far more interesting. Why wouldn't someone send something here? Someone is reaching out to understand the universe with the science and technology they have at hand. Whatever this tech is, I bet it can go fast. Might even break Albert's speed limit."

"I can only get up to about sixty," I said, instantly aware of how dumb that sounded.

"I'm talking about in a vacuum, Stewart. *Sheesh.*"

"I really, *really* hate to be the grownup here," Andy said, "but are you sure we shouldn't report this to someone?"

"Who?" Lillian asked. "The Air Force? The government? So they can hide it and lock us up while they figure out how to weaponize it? Can you imagine what they would do to your husband, Andrea? Should we give it to Lewko, so he can add to his billions? Or how about someone like Josiah James, so he can rile up the pitchfork and torch crowd? Talk about illegal aliens! How about Fox News? I'm sure they'd love to give their audience a new fear that sells dick pills during the commercial break. Fuck, no. We have to cut it loose."

"What if it doesn't go anywhere?" Andy asked. "What if we cut it free and it just sits here?"

"Stewart, you said it yourself. When you're in this state you have no inertia. This thing has been caught under these dead trees for over a year. It's trapped. Whatever drives it obviously can't overpower the weight of the trees."

"Why not? It knocked them all down," Andy said. "Why didn't it just push them off?"

"Impact energy knocked the trees down," Lillian said. "I think whatever drives it doesn't have that kind of power. Or it wouldn't still be here. Look, the probes we send all over the solar system barely have the power of a household blender. Less. I think this thing needs help. We need to clear the obstructions and let it go."

"When I got within a few hundred feet of this, I *needed* to vanish. The feeling was overwhelming. Maybe that's not the only *need* I was feeling. Maybe I'm feeling its need to break loose."

"Don't go all hippy on me, Stewart." Lillian said. "Come on, Andrea. Let's get that equipment."

I DID NOT WANT to make a running chainsaw vanish with me. From the fact that gunpowder igniting within *the other thing* caused me damage, I inferred that internal combustion from a two-stroke engine would be equally devastating. I started the unvanished chainsaw on the ground, then lifted it. The weight drove me down. Despite the way proximity to the object gave me new control and movement using the core muscle, I could not ascend with the chainsaw's weight in hand. In that sense, Lillian's hypothesis about the object being unable to lift itself from under the trees seemed proven.

The problem was that I could not do the job from the ground. Limbs and trunks had to be cut away above the object, as much as ten feet up. I didn't think to bring a ladder. I considered climbing the deadfall with the running chainsaw in one hand and ruled that out as a great way to cut off one of my own limbs.

The solution required Andy to hold up the buzzing saw after I floated above the object and anchored myself to one of the tree limbs. I reached down and took it from her. Handing a running chainsaw to me might be the bravest thing I've ever seen my wife do. She backed away quickly after I lifted it from her hands.

I maintained a grip on the deadfall and went to work on weak, thin ends and branches. Most of the tree trunks were already nothing more than long poles. Impact forces had broken away many of the branches. I sliced away the rest. Andy and Lillian pulled the severed limbs off the pile. I cut the heavier trunks just above the object. The top ends fell away; lower pieces had to be pushed aside. Litter and sawdust formed a circle around the void.

Boyd ignored the noise and activity. He found fascination in a stump twenty yards from where we worked. He showed no interest in an object that challenged rational thought or the magic chainsaw that floated and moved about the top of the pile, working its way down.

Little by little the pile diminished.

Eventually, only one large tree trunk remained. I dropped to the ground and cut off the top close above the object, taking care not to hit the surface. The saw labored through the dead wood until the extended end of the trunk snapped. A second later, the remaining portion, still leaning against the object, shifted.

I killed the motor and laid the chainsaw in the snow.

"Did you see that?"

Andy and Lillian, working together to wrestle away the cut portion, stopped. Lillian ventured closer. She reached out and pressed one hand against the void.

"It moved," I said.

"I think you're right," Lillian said.

"Might be a good idea to stand back." I shoved off on a line that took me to the remaining tree trunk. I fixed a grip and anchored my feet in the snow.

Andy hurried to Boyd and took him by the hand. He relinquished his interest in the stump and fell in step with Andy. They moved about thirty feet away.

"What's the plan?" Lillian asked.

"If I can push this big piece off, it might go. And I think it wants to go."

Lillian pressed her hands on the unseen surface of the object and cocked her head to one side. "See if you can move it."

I placed my shoulder under the dry, dead tree trunk. I shoved.

"Whoa!" Lillian cried out. "It shifted!"

"Step back."

She didn't argue. She trotted to the stump Boyd had examined so thoroughly. Then thought wiser of it and moved to where Andy stood with the boy.

"Be careful!" Andy called out.

"No worries. I checked the calendar," I tucked in against the trunk and heaved. "Today's a 'be careful' da—"

The tree trunk rolled and dropped.

I heard a loud crack, then the snapping of branches.

FWOOOMP!

Utterly unprepared, I reappeared and awkwardly stumbled backward, which probably saved me a pair of broken legs because the big trunk I had shoved away fell to the ground where the void had been, then rolled across where I'd been standing. I scrambled, tripped, and landed on my butt firmly in the grasp of gravity. The log stopped at my feet.

Branches from above rained down. I heard what sounded like a rogue gust of wind, the kind that comes out of nowhere ahead of a thunderstorm. The air filled with snapped twigs from trees just beyond the deadfall, which itself collapsed into a smaller, lower pile. The space that had been filled with nothing, where the void had prevented snow from reaching the leaves, now filled with debris that had been piled around the trapped object.

I looked to the sky. A hole appeared in the bottom of the gray clouds. Mist chased itself into that hole, sucked upward. The hole didn't last. In seconds, it was gone.

Gone.

Like the object that had been trapped.

Like the void I had detected an instant before the collision.

Like the hole in my memory.

The forest returned to silence.

"Are you okay?" Andy rushed to me and kneeled on the snow beside me.

"Yeah. Fine." She helped me up. I brushed snow off my butt.

Lillian gazed at the sky. I tried to pick out the place where the object tore a hole in the cloud. I could not.

"Okay, Stewart," Lillian said, "if that thing saved your life, I guess you just returned the favor."

WE GATHERED UP THE CHAINSAW, the tools and the gas can and retraced our snow tracks back to the Prius. No one said a word until we reached the middle of the wheat field.

"This would have blown Mike's mind," Lillian mused.

"Blows my mind," I said.

"You know what blows my mind?" Andy asked. "Dodge and Danzig wanted to make this their next hoax—and unwittingly chose the one site that isn't."

"Oh, my celestial gods!" Lillian cried. "Detective Andrea Stewart, did you just admit that UFOs are real?"

Lillian laughed. Andy frowned. "I don't have any idea what you're talking about, Dr. Farris."

"Of course, you don't. But you make a good point. Can you imagine if those pirates had found this?"

I didn't want to try.

Lillian and Boyd marched ahead of Andy and me. Andy wrapped her gloved hand around mine. I leaned close and spoke softly.

"Lewko and Lillian like to say how arrogant it is for us to think we're the be all and end all of creation in the universe. I guess this is their 'I told you so' moment."

"Does it scare you? Letting it get away?"

I contemplated the flood of feelings. The changes I felt near the object. The *need* over which I had no control.

Boyd's comment rang in my head like an earworm.

It's a life support system.

"No," I replied. "You know what I never felt back there? Near it? Fear. I never felt fear. Did you?"

I expected a Yes. Andy's avowed skepticism might easily have turned to distrust and fear. She didn't answer quickly, but after a moment, she looked me in the eye and shook her head.

"Not if you didn't."

I wanted to tell her more. Because I remembered. It was like finding a photo album in an attic. Grainy dream images transformed into tangible memories. I remembered the impact. The blast. The crush of the plane's aluminum skin. The pieces dropping to earth. I remembered the fall. The searing pain in my torso.

I remembered the cool sensation.

And I remembered, as I fell, the strangest and worst moment of all.

I could not see myself.

I remembered thinking of Andy in that moment, consumed by deep and irrevocable loss.

I'll never see her again.

I wanted to tell Andy that the void had been filled. That the nightmare that taunted me for the last year and a half had become memory, but before I found the right words, the walk back to the Prius ended.

I loaded the gear into the trunk. No one spoke. I felt an absurd impulse to pull us all back to Earth.

"Hey, Lillian," I said, "we just proved the existence of intelligent life in the universe. Wanna get a beer?"

My attempt at levity landed like a dead ash tree with Lillian. No matter. Andy suppressed the smile I had been seeking.

Lillian installed Boyd in the right front seat and closed his door. She used the remote fob to start the car, then turned and caught my arm and pulled me to the back bumper where we stood in a red glow cast by the tail-lights. Andy joined us. I thought Lillian intended to hold a quick conference to get our story straight or establish what we had or hadn't seen out there—what we would say or not say.

She faced me.

"Do it."

"What?"

"Do it. That thing. Do it."

Andy's eyes met mine. We speak at times without words. This was one of those times.

I steadied myself and focused. I envisioned the aircraft cockpit I had constructed in my mind after the accident. The instruments. The control levers. I pictured my hand closing on that phantom set of levers.

I closed my eyes. I took and released a solemn breath.

After a moment, I opened my eyes to find Lillian fixing cold assessment on me, arms folded.

"I can't. It's gone."

EPILOGUE II

Tom Ceeves picked us up at Sandy Stone's house the day before November surrendered to December. It had been a couple of quiet days since we said our good-byes to Lillian and Boyd and the mailbox-maiming Prius. A part of me hoped never to have to deal with that woman again. Another part looked forward to dropping in on her in New Mexico and having her see me as something other than a science experiment. I promised myself I would learn some American Sign Language first.

Tom didn't say where we were going. He alluded to police business—something to do with the Connelly arrest. Because Andy had been the intended victim, Tom locked her out of the investigation. It drove her to distraction. I felt grateful that he had relented, and that I was included. I sensed that Tom understood my need to see justice land like a ton of bricks on two people who tried to have Andy and me killed in the name of a political lie.

It didn't hit me that we weren't going to the cop shop until we approached the road to our shot-up farmhouse. Since the attack, Tom had refused to let either of us return to our home. He barricaded the road at both ends. Now, as a brilliant red-orange sunset promised 'sailor's delight' another type of light and color spread across the landscape. Most of the snow had melted. What patches remained among the corn stubble glowed like Christmas candy in yellow, blue, white, and red flashing lights.

Vehicles lined the length of the road. Police cars. Fire trucks. Ambulances. Snowplows. City utility pickup trucks. Every one of them illuminated their emergency lights, flashers, and spotlights. My first thought was a fire, but that didn't explain the trucks from the public works department running their orange warning lights and emergency flashers.

Tom turned and maneuvered past police barricades. He drove slowly down the open lane. We passed vehicle after vehicle. People we knew— friends, neighbors, Andy's co-workers—and people we didn't know stood grinning and waving.

"Jesus, Tom, what is this?"

The big man at the wheel said nothing. Beside him, in the front passenger seat, Andy gasped and put her hand to her mouth. I heard her sob.

"*Oh my God, Chief,*" she whispered.

Tom turned in the driveway. We passed the mailbox, which stood upright on a fine and sturdy post. Competing with the extravagant show on our road, every light inside and outside the house had been turned on. The interior lights glowed through windows without shattered glass, mounted in walls that had no holes. The gutters had been repaired. Siding had been replaced. The porch had a new storm door. Strands of colorful Christmas lights draped the eaves.

Rows of people lined both sides of the driveway. I lost sight of the faces when my eyes flooded. Andy reached for and squeezed my hand so hard, I feared losing fingers.

How they had done it would take me weeks to unravel. It would take longer to stop noticing where wood trim had been replaced, or walls had new wallpaper, or shades worked that hadn't worked before. Even the dishes and appliances were new. But no matter how hard I searched, I never found a bullet hole.

Andy cried off and on for the next hour.

EPILOGUE III

The party lasted well into the night. I worried about a crime wave in Essex what with all the cops and cop cars at our house, including Leslie and two visiting FBI agents. Or that the city might burn while the fire department pumped beer from kegs on our front porch. Earl and Rosemary II and Lane joined us, sipping soft drinks. Dave Peterson rolled in with his new girlfriend and several other pilots from Essex County Air Service, dragging Doc from his maintenance shop. Most of the Saturday morning Silver Spoon Diner Congress appeared, including the owner of the house, our landlord, James Rankin. Sandy Stone hurried about the kitchen, managing the catering and snapping orders to hapless helpers. She hugged Andy, bringing a fresh flood of tears to my wife. Pidge dragged Arun to the center of our living room to dance when someone fired up the music. He looked like a hostage. There wasn't enough room for everyone in the house. Someone built a bonfire in the back yard using debris from the repair work. A crowd gathered around it, talking, laughing, and drawing warmth from the fire and from each other.

I drank a lot and endlessly thanked people. Most of them told me to shut the fuck up and pressed another drink in my hand.

Well before the festivities showed signs of letting up, I slipped away to the garage for a dose of solitude. Under a single bare bulb, I looked over the history of my flight experiments—the parts and pieces of my SCUZ and ZIPPY and SCRAM and DOLT and FLOP and BLASTER units. I picked up one of the originals—one of the old units with the fixed propeller. It still worked. Taking the heavy old device in hand, I wandered up the barn hill to the hay loft where I'd learned to fly. The alfalfa-scented space had served me well. This night, it was too dark to see inside, so I stood in the open door gazing at the sea of corn stubble that stretched to a dark line of trees in the distance. Many of the trees were dead ash trees, yet soaring above them never lost its thrill, a thrill that tugged at me now.

The black sky brimmed with stars. Not Montana stars. They have more. But Essex has enough.

A nice night. A perfect night, in fact.

A perfect night to fly.

DIVISIBLE MAN: NINE LIVES LOST
October 21, 2021 to January 23, 2022

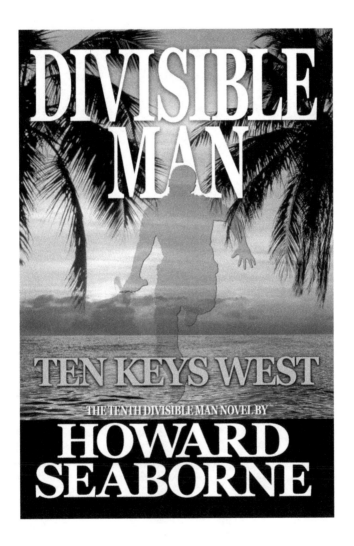

DIVISIBLE MAN

TEN KEYS WEST

THE TENTH DIVISIBLE MAN NOVEL BY

HOWARD SEABORNE

"So…what you're saying is…it's not all beach sex and umbrella drinks?"
— *Will Stewart*

ABOUT THE AUTHOR

HOWARD SEABORNE is the author of the DIVISIBLE MAN™ series of novels as well as a collection of short stories featuring the same cast of characters. He began writing novels in spiral notebooks at age ten. He began flying airplanes at age sixteen. He is a former flight instructor and commercial charter pilot licensed in single- and multi-engine airplanes as we as helicopters. Today he flies a twin-engine Beechcraft Baron, a single-engine Beechcraft Bonanza, and a Rotorway A-600 Talon experimental helicopter he built from a kit in his garage. He lives with his wife and writes and flies during all four seasons in Wisconsin, never far from Essex County Airport.

Visit www.HowardSeaborne.com to join the Email List
and get a FREE DOWNLOAD.

DIVISIBLE MAN

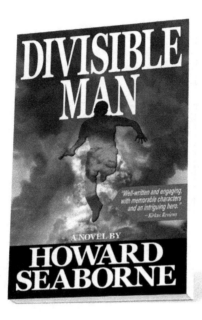

The media calls it a "miracle" when air charter pilot Will Stewart survives an aircraft in-flight breakup, but Will's miracle pales beside the stunning after-effect of the crash. Barely on his feet again, Will and his police sergeant wife Andy race to rescue an innocent child from a heinous abduction—*if Will's new ability doesn't kill him first.*

Available in print, digital and audio.

Learn more at **HowardSeaborne.com**

DIVISIBLE MAN: THE SIXTH PAWN

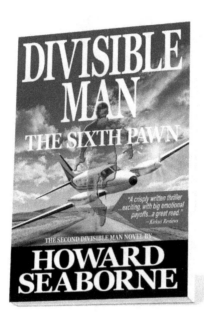

When the Essex County "Wedding of the Century" erupts in gunfire, Will and Andy Stewart confront a criminal element no one could have foreseen. Will tests the extraordinary after-effect of surviving a devastating airplane crash while Andy works a case obstructed by powerful people wielding the sinister influence of unlimited money in politics.

Available in print, digital and audio.

Learn more at **HowardSeaborne.com**

DIVISIBLE MAN: THE SECOND GHOST

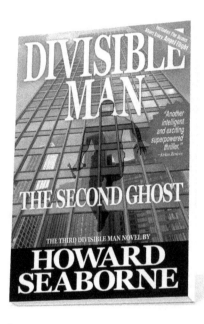

Tormented by a cyber stalker, Lane Franklin's best friend turns to suicide. Lane's frantic call to Will and Andy Stewart launches them on a desperate rescue. When it all goes bad, Will must adapt his extraordinary ability to survive the dangerous high steel and glass of Chicago as Andy and Pidge encounter the edge of disaster. **Includes the short story, "Angel Flight,"a bridge to the fourth DIVISIBLE MAN novel that follows.**

Available in print, digital and audio.

Learn more at **HowardSeaborne.com**

DIVISIBLE MAN: THE SEVENTH STAR

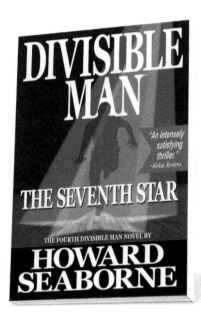

A horrifying message turns a holiday gathering tragic. An unsolved murder hangs a death threat over Detective Andy Stewart's head. And internet-fueled hatred targets Will and Andy's friend Lane. Will and Andy struggle to keep the ones they love safe, while hunting a dead murderer before he can kill again. As the tension tightens, Will confronts a troubling revelation about the extraordinary after-effect of his midair collision.

Available in print, digital and audio.

Learn more at **HowardSeaborne.com**

DIVISIBLE MAN: TEN MAN CREW

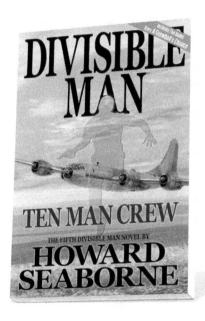

An unexpected visit from the FBI threatens Will Stewart's secret and sends Detective Andy Stewart on a collision course with her darkest impulses. A twisted road reveals how a long-buried Cold War secret has been weaponized. And Pidge shows a daring side of herself that could cost her dearly.

Available in print, digital and audio.

Learn more at **HowardSeaborne.com**

DIVISIBLE MAN: THE THIRD LIE

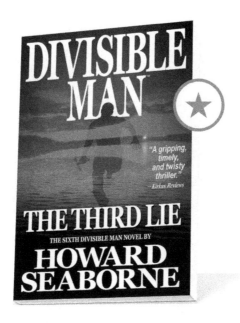

Caught up in a series of hideous crimes that generate national headlines, Will faces the critical question of whether to reveal himself or allow innocent lives to be lost. The stakes go higher than ever when Andy uncovers the real reason behind a celebrity athlete's assault on an underaged girl. And Will discovers that the limits of his ability can lead to disaster.

A Kirkus Starred Review.

A Kirkus Star is awarded to "books of exceptional merit."

Available in print, digital and audio.

Learn more at **HowardSeaborne.com**

DIVISIBLE MAN: THREE NINES FINE

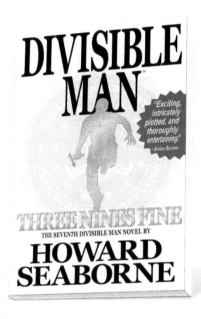

A mysterious mission request from Earl Jackson sends Will into the sphere of a troubled celebrity. A meeting with the Deputy Director of the FBI that goes terribly wrong. Will and Andy find themselves on the run from Federal authorities, infiltrating a notorious cartel, and racing to prevent what might prove to be the crime of the century.

Available in print, digital and audio.

Learn more at **HowardSeaborne.com**

DIVISIBLE MAN: EIGHT BALL

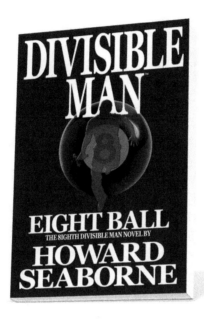

Will's encounter with a deadly sniper on a serial killing rampage sends him deeper into the FBI's hands with costly consequences for Andy. And when billionaire Spiro Lewko makes an appearance, Will and Andy's future takes a dark turn. The stakes could not be higher when the sniper's ultimate target is revealed.

Available in print, digital and audio.

Learn more at **HowardSeaborne.com**

ENGINE OUT AND OTHER SHORT FLIGHTS

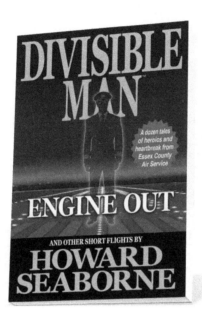

AVAILABLE: JUNE 2022

Things just have a way of happening around Will and Andy Stewart. In this collection of twelve tales from Essex County, boy meets girl, a mercy flight goes badly wrong, and Will crashes and burns when he tries dating again. Engines fail. Shots are fired. A rash of the unexpected breaks loose—from bank jobs to zombies.

Available in print, digital and audio.

Learn more at **HowardSeaborne.com**

DIVISIBLE MAN: NINE LIVES LOST

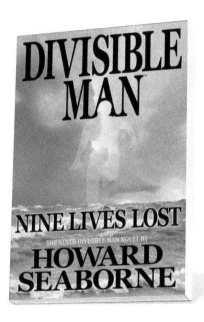

AVAILABLE: JUNE 2022

A simple request from Earl Jackson sends Will on a desperate cross-country chase ultimately looking for answers to a mystery that literally landed at Will and Andy's mailbox. At the same time, a threat to Andy's career takes a deadly turn. Before it all ends, Will confronts answers in a deep, dark place he never imagined.

Available in print, digital and audio.

Learn more at **HowardSeaborne.com**

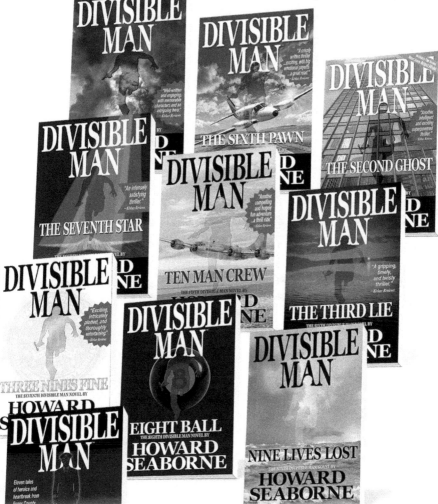

Printed in the USA
CPSIA information can be obtained
at www.ICGtesting.com
LVHW010209090823
754738LV00012B/514